FACTOR-7

To: Becky
I hope you enjoy!
Best regards,
J. L. May
(Marnie)
what my friends
call me!

FACTOR-7

BY J. D. MAY

Palmetto Publishing Group
Charleston, SC

Factor-7
Copyright © 2020 by J.D. May
All rights reserved

First Edition

Printed in the United States

Paperback: 978-1-64111-865-1
Hardcover: 978-1-64990-599-4
eBook: 978-1-64111-205-5

For Annlyn, my precious daughter, who nudged me back into my joy for writing and encouraged me the entire journey.

For Buster who patiently and quietly watched me as I sat the many hours at the computer leaving him to meals and household duties— including the daily feedings of all the feral cats.

For my girlfriends, Kay, Barbara Sue, Deborah, Pam and Kat who were always there to read a line or the early drafts.

And for my wonderful parents. If not for the insidious Alzheimer's disease, they would be jumping for joy, knowing I had fulfilled my passion.

With sincere love to all.

Special thanks to Jack, Jessica and their team at Palmetto Publishing Group. Thank you to the editors that did a fantastic job. And thank you to everyone at MindBuck Media. Ya'll are all great!

PROLOGUE

The screams came from seemingly everywhere. The sounds were deafening. I could hear rapid gunfire and loud shouts from angry men in the street below. Mother grabbed me and pushed me into a space beneath the kitchen sink. A blue-and-yellow curtain sealed the opening, and I was a prisoner in the dark, wet cabinet. I could only see outlines of figures as the horror continued. Frightened and confused, I curled into a ball under the sink and pulled a big dish towel over my head. My tiny hands covered my ears. But the loud noises and the screams of terror could not be silenced. The vibration of heavy boots rattled my senses. Doors were slamming, and glass was breaking around me. But I stayed quiet as instructed, despite the trembling of my small body. I heard my mother scream and then a brief cry followed by a hideous gurgling sound. It burned an imprint into my ears that I shall never forget. Suddenly the sound of gunshots tore through the room.

I heard Zena, my sister, begging for her life, but she had no answers for the men who shouted questions. They kept chanting, "Jew girl." They would cut her throat if she did not tell them what they wanted to hear. But Zena was innocent of any crime, just a young girl caught up in a battle and part of a Jewish family who resisted the new order. Hitler's Final Solution was happening around me. I heard her beg for mercy and then another gurgling sound and a large thump. There were stomping sounds from their boots, and a rumbling, rolling tremor engulfed the apartment. The men laughed and shouted something about Jews as they played out their kickball game with my sister's head.

It must have been hours as I waited. When all quieted, I crawled from my secret place. My mother lay dead on the kitchen floor. Her neck was cut, and her head lay in an unnatural position, almost detached from her body. My sister's body lay next to her, but her head was on the other side of the room. The floor was flooded with human blood. The stench was unbearable, and I needed to vomit. I couldn't scream from terror, and I couldn't feel my legs because of the bitter cold. I somehow got to the corner of the kitchen where there was no blood and again crawled into a ball. It was dark now, and I was alone with my mother and sister in a blood-bathed room. My father was nowhere around. All I heard were distant voices and dogs barking. Rain came through the broken window and washed over me. It was cold, yet I was numb.

My father was fighting the enemy. He had been unable to save his wife and daughter as he fought for others. He was a member of a group that now devoted their lives to preserving our freedom. Hell had broken loose in our homeland. The Nazis were in control, and their vicious hegemony seeds were generating death and torture to anyone they deemed inferior or who questioned them.

My father was smart and cunning. He somehow got to me that night. As he carried me down the two flights of stairs, I hid my eyes from the stacks of bodies that had yet to be removed. But before he laid me on the back floorboard of an old car, I saw the wooden panel trucks with bodies piled on top of one another. I saw women, men, and children, all together and going to what I now know was a mass grave outside Bialystok. We drove for some time, and he said nothing but that he loved me. Then I felt the car slow and heard the breaks squeak to a stop. The engine rattled and then finally became silent. He said we had arrived where he would find help for me. We entered an old building. A rabbi was there with many other men. Each man touched me and swore to my care. My father cried as he hugged me. I didn't understand what was happening. He then led me to an opening in the concrete floor. It was dark, and cold, stale air wafted from it. He held me in his arms and whispered that I would be cared for by this group of men. I remember him saying to me, "Remember this, my son: freedom and liberty are goals of righteous men. Learn from this group, and become a keeper of peace." Suddenly the echo of automatic machine gun bullets penetrated the empty room where we all stood. "They are coming," he said to the others. I begged him not to leave me. Then a bullet hit him. My father's blood splattered my face. Another man fell on top of me and pushed me into the hole. I moaned as my body hit the damp ground. Then there was darkness as the man closed the hole with something heavy. Sounds were muffled, but I knew the familiar shouts of the men who wore brown shirts. I hated that sound. I hated them. That night would go down in history as Kristallnacht—the "Night of Broken Glass."

I was in hell, and I swore that if I ever got free of the terror, I would be strong like my father.

The remaining men did keep me safe, and they nurtured me. As I grew, they educated me. The time came for the men to tell me the secrets of their mission. I took a lifetime oath. I would never break the codes that had saved my life that awful night.

I taught the codes to my sons, and they will to theirs, and on through perpetuity. We are patriots of every nationality. We are not protecting any one country, religion, or political ideology, but the basic freedoms of mankind. We are the Keepers.

CHAPTER ONE

"Emergency Department...Trauma Level Two...Dr. Samuel Hawkins to Emergency Department...Trauma Level Two...Emergency Department Trauma Level Two...Calling Dr. Samuel Hawkins to Trauma Two-B...Dr. Hawkins to Emergency Two-B."

The speaker echoed its three-code level-two emergency calls. The halls were now empty at St. Peter's Memorial Medical Center, the area's only level-one trauma center.

It had been quite different only a few hours earlier, when every party-going celebrant or indigent drunk had shown for medical care. The law was to never turn away an emergency patient. St. Peter's and Dr. Sam Hawkins also would never deny medical care, so that Independence Day holiday had been particularly busy and difficult. The Shock and Trauma Department saw injuries all that day and night. Sam had six gunshot victims and three horrific drunk-driving victims in the Trauma Unit at one time. There had been drug overdoses and one suicide. The Emergency Department had seen everything from

1

Roman candle burns to near drownings. It had been a gruesome eighteen hours, and it wasn't over yet.

Dr. Hawkins slid his fingers down the pale-green panels of his office door. His break from the Trauma Unit had been only fifteen minutes and was far too short. His nails made a scraping sound that matched his irritated mood.

"Not again. Fuck this shit. Why can't some trauma resident handle the rest of this night…anyone but me? Geez, enough already!" he angrily mumbled. But he knew it was his job, and when all was said and done, he would rather handle the cases himself than pass them off to someone less qualified. It was because of Dr. Sam Hawkins that St. Peter's had such a high survival rate in the Shock and Trauma Unit.

The nurses and the exhausted residents who had shuffled through the corridors earlier in the night had been gone for hours. Sam should also be home in bed with his wife, Lauren. But he wouldn't be, not that morning of July 5. As head of the department, he was the first to arrive and the last to leave. So he answered his own question. Such it was that early morning.

Sam bent over to tie the laces on his Sketcher sneakers. He slipped covers over his shoes, as he had done so many times. The speakers monotonously repeated their calls. His ears were tired of the sound, tired of the voice on the speaker. Nonetheless, he increased his speed as he turned the corner to the final few steps toward the Trauma/Emergency West Wing. Sam punched in the code to enter the Emergency Department. The metal doors parted just as he felt a firm hand grip his right shoulder.

Startled from his exhaustion-induced trance, Sam turned to see Dr. John Albright. John was a good three inches taller than the almost-six-foot Sam Hawkins. His jet-black hair glistened in the brightly lit corridor. His slender body matched the long, thin fingers that still held firmly to Sam's shoulder. It was no wonder that he could have any girl he wanted when the two were back in medical school.

Sam glided through the open doors, Albright in tow. Gathering himself, Sam jerked away from his would-be hindrance with one swift pull and half-body spin.

"What the fuck do you think you're doing, Albright? Let me go."

"Hey, man, sorry. Didn't mean to startle you."

"Startle me...fuck, you nearly gave me a coronary! I hate when people sneak up behind me."

"Couldn't be in a better place for that heart attack! I heard there was a great trauma surgeon who works here," Albright said.

Sam frowned. "Yeah anyway, what the fuck are you doing here at four a.m.?"

Dr. Albright smiled and simply said, "Sitting with a sick friend."

His perfectly aligned, too-white-to-be-real teeth reminded Sam of some cartoon character, but he couldn't remember who. He had a smile that was something between sincere and menacing. Sam didn't want to chat, especially to him. He didn't care the least bit why John Albright was at the hospital.

"Can't talk...got a warm body in there...gotta get to it." Sam held up his squawking cell phone. "I have an emergency in there." He walked away but glanced at Albright one last time. From the corner of Sam's eye, he saw that Dr. Albright's smile had turned into an unsettling frown. His blue contact-enhanced eyes narrowed a piercing last gaze at Sam.

John Albright had an uncanny way of making Sam Hawkins feel unusually uncomfortable. He grimaced at the thought of their past. It had been problematic, to say the least. Sam had never thought of Albright as a friend, and lately he hadn't thought about him at all. Sam had always considered him a fake and a user, out for himself at any cost. He had to admit that Albright had been a great student at University of Texas Medical School and then a superior resident at St Luke's Medical Center in Houston. He could have picked any hospital to make his career had it not been for his incessant narcissism. He had skipped around for a while, according to the proverbial hospital grapevine. John Albright was beyond the conventional term of handsome and was always the charming ladies' man. Sam's spare time was spent on the golf course, at a fishing spot, or on the back of a cutting horse. Albright's was on the tennis court, on a yacht, on the back of a polo pony, or on top of the wife of one of his best friends. They were as different as night and day.

Humming the Carly Simon tune to himself, Sam comically mumbled, "Vain son of bitch!" He glanced at his own reflection in the glass panes of the door. Sam wasn't bad looking. In fact, some people would definitely call him handsome. He laughed out loud that he felt the slightest bit jealous. But Sam was tired, and his forehead was accordingly furrowed. He had slumped shoulders from the weight of his personal and professional life and struggles. His jaws ached from gritting his teeth to get through the days and nights. And his temperament had become terse at best. Even so, his sandy-blond hair set off his tanned skin, and he felt somewhat pleased that he had not aged too badly.

St. Peter's Memorial Medical Center had been a not-for-profit hospital before being purchased by a large health care corporation and joining with the other part of the medical center. Catholic nuns and an occasional priest still frequented the Trauma Unit on long holidays when there were multiple causalities. That was the case that early morning of July 5. They were huddled around the patient as the trauma team prepared for Dr. Hawkins to arrive. The nuns had been around the head of the Trauma Department long enough to know when to make an exit, and so, upon seeing Sam, each made the sign of the cross and began to depart the area. One elderly nun laid her frail hand on the patient's forehead and whispered something. Sam knew it was a prayer, and by the look on the faces of everyone, it must be a particularly critical case, so they were going to need it.

Sam saw more nurses and technicians than the usual shock-trauma response team. A man wearing a black yarmulke and a long, dark coat stood at the side of the gurney. The EMS guys who had apparently brought the patient to the hospital were talking to Sandra, Sam's lead trauma nurse. Others from the team were prepping the largest of the trauma rooms, which was usually reserved for the most critical of patients. A small-framed woman leaned down and whispered into the patient's ear. Sam recognized her immediately. It was Ana Roberts, the wife of the hospital's chief of staff, Dr. William Roberts. He felt as though his heart had fallen into his gut. Bill was the patient.

"Ah fuck..." Sam mumbled under his breath. He didn't try to apologize. "Everybody please move, please let me in. Ana, what happened?"

Ana Roberts raised her head from her unconscious husband. Her voice was weak but definite. "He felt poorly at dinner and took a couple of aspirins, then went to bed. I heard him a few hours later go into the bathroom. I didn't know..." She paused as the tears filled her eyes and the fear tightened in her chest. "He was on the floor. I found him on the floor! Maybe an hour...maybe more." She held her head in her hands and started sobbing. "I didn't know he was sick. Oh God, help him, Sam."

Sam raised his hand and showed the familiar two-finger gesture. His nurses knew from experience to clear the room of all nonmedical personnel. Seconds passed. He moved to the EMS team that was still standing near. Awe and fear were apparent on each face. "Why was Dr. Roberts brought here? Wasn't he at his house? It's closer to Methodist or the Medical Center. This is trauma, not"—he paused and glanced at his unconscious friend— "whatever this is."

One of the emergency response team spoke in a low voice. "Yes, we picked him up at their residence. Mrs. Roberts insisted we come to you."

Sam nodded but didn't answer. "Ana, let me take care of Bill." Sam took a step from her. He squeezed her hand as he passed. The man in the yarmulke took Ana by the elbow and moved her from the narrow hallway. Her sobs were still audible when Sam started to examine his old friend.

"OK, let's do our stuff, people. BP?"

"Seventy over forty, Doctor. Respiration shallow, eight; heartbeat thirty-five. Temperature one hundred and five degrees Fahrenheit, Doctor."

Sam quickly looked at the nurse with a questioning gaze. "One hundred five?" He shook his head and mumbled, "Let's concentrate on the pyrexia—let's get this fever down, now!" Cooling blankets appeared almost simultaneously as the orders left his lips. Sandra, the head nurse and an old friend of both Sam's and the patient's, nodded and held firmly to his stare.

"He's cyanotic and appears to be in shock, Doctor."

Sam frowned. "OK, one milligram atropine, stat. Sandra, let's give him a milligram of epinephrine IV immediately. OK, team, I don't have any idea what we're dealing with. We've got to get this man's core temp down! Start cold IV infusion, and I want fresh cooling blankets every ten minutes. Start a drip of vancomycin, and let's get some fluids running. Get quinolones IV going stat. We don't know what this is. Get blood off to the lab, and tell them to push it through immediately. We need answers!"

Seconds seemed like hours in the organized chaos. Dr. Roberts presented with high fever, facial and neck edema, swollen tongue, extended abdomen, seizures, and internal hemorrhage. Whatever strange illness afflicted him; it was progressing quickly. Sam knew that nothing could be ruled out at that point.

The emergency team had seen the recent epidemics of influenza and novel viruses, and it had even been through the Ebola scare and coronavirus pandemic, but this seemed different. The drill was always the same in that department when someone presented with unidentifiable symptoms, but Dr. Roberts was the exception. Everyone knew the renowned physician and everyone knew something horrid was happening to him. His appearance changed from moment to moment as the team struggled to stabilize him. That was Sam's job. He was supposed to stabilize the patient and then turn the ill person over to another specialist. But what specialist would that be? He was lost except to treat each individual symptom.

Sam ordered everyone to get into their level A personal protective ensemble and equipment. "Full face gear, folks; there might be particle contamination." He also slid into a Bio 4 biohazard suit and bio boots. He threw the protective gloves to the side and slipped on another pair of nitrile gloves.

"Heavier bioprotective gloves and full-face covers are protocol and should be worn, even by you, Doctor," said the older surgical nurse.

Sam ignored her. "Ana said he had been apparently fine until early evening, when he simply took aspirins. What do you make of this, Sandra?"

Sandra moved close to Sam's ear. "Too strange to call."

Whatever it was, Sam knew it was progressing far faster than he had answers.

Suddenly, Dr. Roberts's eyes opened wide and rolled in the sockets. His body arched with the seizure. He convulsed violently and nearly fell from the bed. Sam pushed the side rails up and forced his full body weight onto his friend. Holding him down, Sam shouted, "Constraints!

I need constraints!" The IVs were running wide open with the largest gauge needles available for the fluids. He convulsed violently again, and this time the needles were ripped from his arms. Sam was thrown almost to the floor. The team had been splattered with both the medicine and the blood. But fortunately, they were all in personal protective suits by then.

Sam looked around to check his team. They seemed to all be fine. He glanced at his glove. "A hole." His voice became a low-pitched whisper. "Damn it, a hole!" Sam pulled back from the patient. "Draw more blood, and send to lab for HIV and protocol tests. My glove was compromised," he stated calmly. It was not the first time Sam had been nicked while attending patients. Accidents like that came with the territory and happened all the time. But the combination of symptoms that Dr. Roberts was experiencing was completely foreign, and Sam was aware of the danger. Sandra was already ahead of him. She tied a large rubber tourniquet around the upper part of Dr. Roberts's right arm and hunted for a vein that was still intact. "Got it," she said. She handed the vial of blood to one of the attending technicians. "Rush this to the lab. Please keep this sample separate from Dr. Roberts's other specimens." She paused. "Dr. Hawkins, I can't stop the bleeding. Bleeding profusely from IV too."

"Put more pressure and wrap it." Sam looked at the amount of bleeding when Sandra removed the needle, but it was the least of his concerns at that moment. Sam knew the drills when there had been a compromised glove and when the patient presented with unknown symptoms. And Dr. Roberts certainly had unknown symptoms. But Sam Hawkins had a reputation of being something of a rebel in the ER, and Sandra knew from experience that he would do as he wanted. Coercing him into following rules to the finest degree was just a waste of her time.

There were beeping monitors in every corner of the small room. From every angle, techs and nurses announced the patient's vitals. Sam separated and processed each voice and each word the way a hunting dog deciphers the scent of a raccoon from a squirrel.

"Pressure dropping, Doctor," announced one male nurse. Sam kept his eyes on Dr. Roberts. Nothing they had done was helping the old man. He and Sandra had a special connection. Her angry eyes burned though Sam, but she would say nothing yet about his infraction and subsequent possible contamination. He glanced at her and bit his lip as a scolded child might do. She pulled the bio-antiseptic from a cart and quickly began to swab Sam's hand and fingers.

"It doesn't appear to have broken the skin, Doctor," Sandra whispered. "You stupid ass." Only Sandra could get away with such insubordination. She was almost old enough to be his grandmother. "When will you ever learn? Biohazard gear is for a reason." She frowned. "Sam, he's not clotting at the injection site at all."

"Got it. I'll try to follow the rules." Sam forced a half smile and a wink. He knew she was the most competent trauma nurse in the hospital. She could probably do his job. He then glanced at Bill arm. "Try again to get that bleeding stopped. Stay at it."

A nurse took over for Sandra and began to wrap gauze around Dr. Roberts's arms. Blood dripped onto the floor. Sandra prepared to take a baseline blood sample from Sam.

"You're next," Sandra ordered. Sam held out his left arm while he listened to the older doctor's heart. One of the male nurses tied another rubber tube to Sam's extended arm. He drew a vial of blood. Sandra wasted no time. She assisted Sam into another set of heavy nitrile gloves. She knew, even then, he would not accept the bioprotective hand guards. They were too cumbersome, and he had always refused to wear them. Today was certainly not going to be the exception.

Despite the commotion, half the team had continued to replace the IVs. The others sterilized the immediate area, which had been splattered with potentially highly biohazardous substances. The team worked together like a well-rehearsed ballet.

Something was terribly wrong, and Sam knew that none of their efforts were changing any of Dr. Roberts's vitals or chances of recovery. "Call for barricade tape," he ordered. "We've gotta seal off this area. And George…" He glanced at the tall nurse closest to the door that led to the outside hallway. "Call it in—code four-five-one-zero, and code orange. We need to be sure the proper staffing is in place. People, I want you to be very careful now. I don't know what this is. Watch yourself."

"The electrocardiogram is looking worse, Doctor." Sandra paused for a moment. "Dr…ah…Sam, he's going into ventricular fibrillation!"

"OK…Sandra, let's give him one hundred milligrams of lidocaine and have the defibrillator set at three hundred joules." Sam grasped Dr. Roberts's hand. "Hold on, Bill. Stay with me now."

Sam studied the peculiar rash and extensive bruises. Blood pooled in the tissues. Large volcanic-looking sores were popping up all over his frail body. Dr. Roberts was hemorrhaging inside and out. Anxiety was evident on all the faces of Sam and the team. Most of the ED team had seen terrible, horrific things. Trauma teams saw that regularly, but Sam sensed a special trepidation. This was, perhaps, a disease they knew nothing about or how to treat. In addition to all the obvious, each person of the team had potentially been exposed.

Sam shook his head in confusion. He needed something that looked remotely familiar—anything that would give him a clue how to combat this thing, perhaps an unknown pathogen that was killing his friend.

A voice came from behind the head of the bed. "Dr. Hawkins, his heart has stopped. We have no pressure here." Another nurse chimed in, "And we still have not stopped the bleeding. He simply won't clot."

He glanced at the multitude of monitors. Then Sam jabbed a long needle into Dr. Roberts's chest and exhaled sharply through his clenched teeth. "Epinephrine first, then we'll try CPR. He's so frail. Hold off." Sam threw back his head and sighed loudly. "Do we have a pulse with the Adrenalin?"

"Nothing, Doctor. Does he have a DNR, or is he full code?" whispered Sandra.

"I don't know and don't care." Sam stared into Sandra's eyes. "I've got to try everything. For God's sake, it's Bill." He took a very deep breath. "All right, let's prepare for full CPR and be ready to intubate the patient. Get the respiratory therapist here, stat. Paddles! Three hundred joules…clear!" Sam shouted. Dr. Roberts convulsed, and his body arched from the electrical shock.

"Doctor, we have a pulse…at thirty-five. We have a rhythm back. It's weak, but he does have a rhythm and a blood pressure of sixty over forty again." Sandra gazed sympathetically into Sam's eyes. She knew the slight improvement could only be temporary.

Suddenly, Ana threw open the curtains. She gasped at the sight of her husband and the blood-splattered area. Dr. Roberts was gray with large bluish-red splotches over his face. He had tubes running from both arms; his chest was covered with electrodes, wires, and blood. His nose oozed bloody mucus that stained the oxygen tubes and rendered them almost useless. Blood-soaked gauze, cotton, and sheets littered the entire room. She stood deathly still; the color drained from her face. Shock and grief blanketed her demeanor.

"He's dying. Bill's dying, Sam. What are you doing for him?" she cried.

"Get her out of here. Now!" Sam tempered his tone. "Ana, I'm sorry, honey, you cannot be here. We don't know what we're dealing with, but I…we…are doing all we can. Please! Somebody get her out of here, now!" He glanced around. His eyes glazed over with anger. "Who allowed that?" he said. "Clear the entire area! Seal off this end of the ER with security personnel. Obviously, the damned barrier tape isn't working! Come on, people, this isn't your first rodeo with biohazards—or at the very least, you've been trained for this! Get your shit together." Sam bowed his head and gathered his thoughts and tempered his anger. He raised his eyes and scanned his team. "I'm sorry, guys. I lost my temper. I am sorry. You guys are the best."

The trauma team had, in fact, been trained for almost anything. They had seen virtually decapitated car accident victims, gunshot patients, people who barely had limbs still attached to their bodies, and every hideous type of injury known to man, but none of them had ever witnessed anything like what lay in front of them.

The old man's entire body had begun to swell. His gut was so extended that Sam had to lie on top of him to get close enough to hear his heart and lungs. His hands were bluish black and clinched into hard fists that had turned under, almost touching the underside of his wrists. They had begun to resemble some grotesque, monstrous, wild animal's hoof. His body had been peculiarly rigid but now had visually begun to curl. His back arched, while his feet and toes were curled under, giving them also a radically disfigured appearance. His neck was arched backward, and it had swelled to twice its normal size.

Sam felt the joints around his feet, neck, and hands. "Looks like hemarthrosis, but he's bleeding more profusely into his joints than I have ever seen." He felt the congealed blood around Dr. Roberts's ribs. "Hematomas," he mumbled." He shook his head and grimaced at the hideous sight and his lack of an answer.

His eyelids and cheeks were now dark purple. His lips were swollen and almost black. Nothing the team did reversed the horrors that Dr. Roberts was experiencing. It only became worse as the moments ticked by.

Sam was a trained surgeon, and his main discipline had been trauma care for the last twenty years. He had a good knowledge of transmittable diseases, but he was not an infectious-disease specialist. He had seen one case of hemorrhagic fever while in Africa and cases of Middle East respiratory syndrome while in the Philippines and South Korea during his stint on a navy medical ship. He had studied strange diseases such as Morgellons and Ebola. But although Dr. Roberts had all the indicators of those deadly diseases, there were so many symptoms that didn't fit any single illness. He seemed to be riddled with infections, and his entire body was hemorrhaging. Sam knew that his friend and patient had something that was much different and deadlier than anything he had even read about, and it was hideous. As skilled a physician as was Dr. Sam Hawkins, he could only stand by and watch his friend morph into some repulsive creature. Dr. Roberts's disease was progressing too rapidly. There was no time to call or consult a specialist. And anyway, who would he call? He was on his own, and he was scrambling for answers.

Sandra had escorted Dr. Roberts's objecting wife out of the trauma suites and into a private waiting room. "I'll be back soon, Mrs. Roberts."

"Is he dying?"

"We're doing what we can. He's in the best hands with Dr. Hawkins."

Ana Roberts reluctantly nodded. "Yes, I know."

"What's the pressure now? What's Dr. Roberts's pressure?" Sam repeated loudly, his endurance wearing thinner as the hours passed.

"Doctor! BP holding at sixty. Heart at forty-five."

"Blood results are in." Sandra read the computer screen aloud. "Shows a viral infection, unidentified, but says a massive bacterial infection, unidentified, too. Liver enzymes, blood proteins are way off the chart, and kidneys going fast, Sam." She paused. "Septicemia," she whispered.

Sam held his hand up, indicating she should wait for further instructions. He shook his head. "No! Damn it…that answers little for me. Unidentified? Damn. How do we treat unidentified?"

Suddenly, the elderly Dr. Roberts gasped. He reached out his swollen, disfigured hand. Two fingers grabbed the neck of Sam's protective gear. The Adrenalin straight into his heart, or perhaps the CPR, had worked its magic. His heart was beating, and he had regained consciousness. He forcefully pulled Sam down to his face. His strength was anything but that of a dying man. His dark copper-colored eyes could barely open and were cloaked in blood. He stared hard into Sam's eyes. His breath gurgled in his throat, but he opened his mouth in an attempt to speak. Sam took Dr. Roberts's hand from his collar and gently held it in his own. The older doctor began to shake his head as if saying no.

"Bill"—Sam's words were staccato—"you're a wonderful…scientist and…my friend. Your research has saved many lives. You're a good husband." He paused. His breath was as disjointed and quick as his speech. "Hey, buddy, I'm not done with you. We're gonna get you through this. We still have courses to play and fish to catch."

Dr. Roberts shook his head. "Closer," he murmured in desperation. "Brother…seven." He strained out the garbled words.

Sam bent down and put his ear almost on the elderly doctor's mouth. "I don't understand. Do you want your brother, Steven?" Sam moved from his patient and whispered to Sandra, "Rambling. His brother died years ago. Keep him out of pain." Sam frowned and looked away momentarily. Seeing his friend in such distress hurt Sam to his core.

Dr. Roberts groaned. He shook his head again, indicating another negative response. "Safe…safe…seven." He took a shallow, belabored breath; his chest rose only slightly with the effort. He tried to take another breath. His chest heaved. Muffled, gurgled noises emanated from his mouth when he whispered what sounded like "Custos Collegium."

Sam recalled from his limited nonmedical Latin classes that the first word meant something like *to keep* or *keeper*. The second was vaguely familiar, but he couldn't recall precisely its meaning—but then again, had he even heard it correctly? If he had heard what Dr. Roberts said, he thought it might mean something like *club* or *society*, but he was just guessing. None of it mattered anyway. It made no sense. He quickly dismissed it. Dr. Roberts was much too ill to think lucidly, much less speak anything clearly. The older doctor had simply demonstrated a dying man's ramblings. Sam had witnessed the terminally ill attempt to say things that no one could understand. The lack of oxygen to the brain and the imminence of death often made for horrific exhibitions, and Sam was confident that was the case with Bill Roberts.

Dr. Roberts tried to enunciate more words again, but he didn't have adequate breath to expel the sound.

Sam surveyed the monitors. He looked at Sandra. She frowned and turned away.

The respiratory therapist had arrived. The shock of seeing Dr. Roberts's condition caused the young woman to physically shake. She grabbed George's arm to steady herself.

"No intubation," Sam whispered as he leaned again toward his friend.

The therapist quietly gasped in horror while she moved closer and obtained a clear view of the patient. Clearly rattled, she tried to regain her professional composure. "But Dr. Hawkins," argued the therapist, "he's having extreme difficulty breathing. Are you sure of this?"

"Yes. He wants to talk." Sam shook his head resolutely. "We're certainly not going to injure him with tubes down his throat at this point."

Sam glanced at the floor. A puddle of opaque pink liquid was dripping from the side of the bed and puddling at his feet. He paused and whispered, "It won't do any good now, anyway." Blood and fluids flowed from every orifice. Dr. William Roberts was on the brink of death.

"Safe…" The older doctor barely produced breath to form the word, and red bubbles of blood drooled from the corners of his mouth.

Sam was not sure what he heard, but he repeated back, "You *are* safe, Bill." Dr. Roberts moved his head in opposition. Outwardly agitated, the old doctor attempted to speak again. As the word "seven" left the older doctor's lips, he again wheezed out, "This…seven." Sam was confused and moved closer as the older doctor struggled harder to tell Sam something. Dr. Roberts coughed. Thick red clots and black mucus hurled from his mouth. Red blood flowed from his nose. He gasped for oxygen. Then he mumbled a last indistinguishable word. It sounded as if he said, "All right," but Sam could not be sure. He could not be sure of anything at that point. Dr. Roberts's body jerked and trembled, then fell still. His dark eyes were ominously fixed and glazed in a death stare, directly at Sam.

Sam tried to shake it off. Death was a normal occurrence in that part of the hospital, and Sam saw it almost daily. But there was something almost paranormal in Dr. Roberts's gaze. It beckoned Sam, even in death. "OK, let's get him back. Shock him—three hundred joules. Clear!" Sam shouted. "Again, clear. Do we have a pulse?"

"No, Doctor. Nothing."

"Again. Clear!" Sam paused.

"Dr. Hawkins, he's gone," whispered Sandra. "Please, Sam, let him go."

Sam shouted again, "Give me three hundred joules. Clear!"

"Sam…Dr. Hawkins." Sandra didn't need to say more.

Sam lifted his head from the patient and looked resolutely into Sandra's eyes. He knew she was right. He stood back from the bed.

The monitors beeped a sorrowful flat-line monotony. The team waited quietly. A familiar death stench filled the room. The body was wrapped tightly in blood-saturated sheets and cooling blankets. Sandra touched Sam's arm. "Call it, Sam. You have to call it."

Sam bowed his head and gently pounded his fist against his own forehead. He was outwardly shaken and deeply saddened. Then he seemed to gather his emotions and recover some strength. He stood erect and took such a deep breath that his shoulders rose in the effort. He ran his hand softly over Dr. Roberts's eyes and closed the swollen eyelids. Sam stared at his friend's hideously ravaged and lifeless body, as if he were speaking to him without words. He pulled a sheet from under the bed and gently laid it over the dead man's body and face. Then Sam took a step back. The team had never seen their boss do anything like that. His voice was soft yet resigned. "Time of death... six oh seven a.m."

There was an eerie silence in the entire Trauma Department. No one spoke, and there were no sounds of monitors anywhere. It was as if time stood still, in mourning. Sam held on to the moment longer than seemed in character. He stood over the body of his friend. His hand lay on the dead man's chest. He took a long cleansing breath before he spoke. "Together, we did what we could. Thank you, Sandra and team. George, get hazmat. You people get out of here. Follow all decontamination procedures. You know the drill. Do what you have been trained to do. This is level-two code orange."

CHAPTER TWO

Dr. Hawkins was left alone with the body of this friend. A tear welled in his eyes. He angrily kicked the pile of clothes, gauze, towels, and biohazard gear that the stripper/bagger team had not yet retrieved. "Damn it…fuck!" He pounded his fist into the end of the bed. "Damn it." Moments passed. The Trauma Unit's overhead speakers were humming with code yellow and code-orange announcements. The agony of his loss was tremendous. But his grief was much less than would be Ana's. It would be his responsibility to tell her that Bill was gone. He couldn't talk to her until he was cleaned up and emotionally under control. He had to get himself together, if for no other reason than for Bill's wife. But how? He was devastated to his core, and he was appalled by the appearance of his friend. Nothing Sam knew from years of medical training and practice could have done such terrible things to a human body, and so quickly. What insidious disease took Dr. Bill Roberts? He couldn't allow Ana to see her husband that last time—not the way Bill looked. No one could handle that. Sam was having trouble erasing from his mind the horrific image of his friend. She, his wife, would be permanently scarred and devastated. She had already lost her only child, their son, James, several years earlier in Afghanistan. He had been in a secret special-operations troop fighting alongside the insurgence. The story told to Sam was that the team was not supposed to have even been in that part of Afghanistan. It had been a suicide terror attack, and all of them, including Lt. James Roberts, were unmercifully slaughtered. How was she to cope with losing both her son and her husband? And both had died in the most revolting of manners.

Sam carefully removed his gloves, conscious of the extreme risk of his contamination. He pulled on another pair of gloves and removed his own blood-splattered hazard gear and shoe covers. He placed each in a plastic bag and sprayed bio disinfectant into the bags. He then sealed the zippered tops. Sam knew the risks, and he dreadfully feared the mysterious disease that had taken his friend's life. But he was intact, and his skin and scrubs were clean. So he proceeded with his plan and piled everything in the corner of the room. He then sprayed the disinfectant head to toe on himself. The shower in the doctor's lounge wasn't far, and he keenly knew the potential seriousness of being exposed to bodily fluids and blood, not to mention leaving the Trauma Unit with an active code orange. He should go to decontamination showers and perhaps be quarantined until a diagnosis of what killed Dr. Roberts could be made. It was a serious infraction, but he was not going to do that, not then. The last thing he needed or wanted was unwarranted quarantine. Sam knew well what to do and would adequately take care of himself, thus taking major precautions to not contaminate others. His team would definitely follow the rules. It wasn't his first rodeo with biohazard exposure, but he admitted to himself that this time was the worst and he *was* extremely shaken. Sam convinced himself that the situation was under control. If he had to answer later to his breach of protocol, he would be prepared.

The hazmat crew would clean up. The Centers for Disease Control would be called, and investigations would certainly ensue. There would be bedlam for a while as all the various safety divisions did their work. An autopsy would be performed, and more precautions would be put in place. And then the media…exactly what he did not want.

Sam decided he would have none of it. He cleaned up and tried to purge his senses of the stench in his nostrils and the horrors embedded in his brain. He had been on the floor for twenty-three hours straight. The holiday was gruesome enough in the Trauma and Emergency Care Unit, but the last few hours trying to save his dear friend's life had taken its toll and maybe his reasoning. Sam slowly shuffled down the same hospital halls where he had walked only a few hours earlier. The darkness had turned to light, and the morning shifts were going about their normal routines, all without a thought of what Dr. Sam Hawkins had just been through. He felt alone and abandoned, even in the hustle. His head told him he couldn't have done anything to save Bill Roberts, but his heart was nonetheless heavy. Had he made the wrong call on the meds, or had he acted too slowly or pushed the meds too fast? Had he done too much? Had he artificially prolonged Dr. Roberts's life for his own selfishness or ego? Questions and grief consumed him.

Ana knew the outcome before Sam arrived at the family grief room, but that did not make the task any easier. A man—she called him Simon—was with her. He seemed to be able to comfort her even more than Sam. It was disconcerting. Sam didn't know Simon at all, and the Robertses, Bill and Ana, were like family. How had they kept Simon's name from him? And more puzzling…why? Sam kissed Ana's cheek and told her that he would call later. She nodded and again buried her face in Simon's chest. Simon motioned for Sam to leave. It was not a gesture to rid himself of Sam, but, rather, sympathetic permission for him to leave. He apparently understood the depth of Sam's grief, as well as his fatigue.

Ana's reactions played over and over in Sam's head. It was odd and uncharacteristic of her. She had leaned on Sam for many things for quite some time. But that dreadful morning, Ana was distant and drawn to Simon. Confusion, frustration, and grief clouded Sam's thoughts. He was too tired, too drained, to drive the 45 minutes home. The couch in his office would do fine for a few hours of rest. He called Lauren, but again, as so often, he only got her voice mail. It was tennis day, and she would be taking her lesson and then having lunch with the girls at the club. He pulled the drapes tightly closed, blocking out the light. He reclined on the cold leather sofa. Exhaustion overcame Sam, and he fell into a deep sleep.

Suddenly he woke in a panic. He jerked into an upright position. The room was spinning, and his ears were ringing. He steadied himself. It had been a nightmare, yet in this case a daymare, if such exists. Sam had dreamed he was with John Albright back in medical school. John was standing over him with a hypodermic needle filled with red liquid in one hand and dropping Sam's notes for the biology final into the fireplace with the other. Smoke was filling the room, and a year's worth of work was going up in flames. That same sinister smile, the one that was written on Dr. John Albright's face during that early-morning chance meeting, was in his dream.

Sam walked over to the sink and splashed cold water on his face. It was a dream, he thought, just a dream. He stared at himself in the mirror while water dripped from his chin. John Albright dropping Sam's notes in the fraternity house fireplace had not been an accident, as he had claimed in 1991. Sam had put that incident to rest, he thought. However, the day's experiences had heightened his subconscious and rekindled his disdain for Albright. Had it really been *chance* to run into his old college roommate? Why would Albright be at St Peter's Memorial Hospital at that early-morning hour? Sam dismissed the thought of Albright with one swipe to his face of the clean towel. Albright was not worth what energy Sam had left.

Sam's thoughts returned to Dr. Roberts. Those garbled, incoherent words—what had they meant? Had Sam heard the words correctly? Dr. Roberts had a high fever and was in shock, which certainly could have been the reason for the ramblings. As gravely ill as Bill was, it was hard for Sam to conceive that he was able to even speak, much less make sense of what he said. But the words haunted him. What was *seven*? Why did he keep saying *safe*? Sam was sure Bill had said "all right" with his last breath. Perhaps he had known he was dying, and he was all right with that. Sam shuddered. *No,* he thought. Bill had never been lucid enough to make any sense, and it was purely the ramblings of his deathly ill friend. It would be illogical to think otherwise.

Sam sat down at his computer and typed out a brief report highlighting what had transpired in the ER earlier that day. He felt sick as he relived the moments that led to Bill Roberts's death. He had determined that anything said by Dr. Roberts was not relevant to the report, so he did not mention it. After typing a couple of pages, Sam realized that he really had little to tell. The disease was mysterious and had caused the most horrific death he had ever encountered. He could not make a judgment of what killed Bill Roberts, and he refused to call it unidentified. So he simply left out any diagnosis from the report. He signed the report and emailed it to the proper hospital department.

By 4:00 p.m. he realized he had not eaten for some time and was hungry. A burger and a cold beer sounded incredibly good. It was rush hour, and it would surely take over an hour to get off the causeway and onto the mainland. Then it would be another hour to get home. But sadly, Lauren would already be wasted. Sam knew her routine, which was to play tennis with the young pro for an hour, then sit with the girls until midafternoon, gossiping and drinking margaritas. The driver he hired for club days would take her home around four-thirty, and she would start on her Gray Goose martinis, until she passed out. That would be about seven p.m. "So why hurry home?" he mumbled.

Sam walked across the catwalk that connected the hospitals systems and down the elevator, which opened into the parking garage. The daylight, which Sam had not seen for too many hours, cut a path through the garage. It nearly blinded him. Even so, he got a glimpse of the Doctor's Residence, a local watering hole that was frequented mostly by the medical students, nurses, and residents. It would do just fine for a burger and that beer.

The room was dark and had the familiar odor of a bar, yet he could still smell the hospital. He didn't know if the scent was permanently embedded in his nostrils or if the bar itself had picked up the scent of the people who came to unwind. He looked around the room. There were a few tables with young men, but his eye caught a couple in the corner booth. They were very much in love, or—he chuckled to himself—in lust. His mind ran to Lauren. Things between them hadn't always been so bad. He and Lauren met in Galveston his third year in med school. She was stunning. Her long strawberry-blond hair set off her porcelain skin and aqua-green eyes. She had taken time away from her studies and lived in Galveston. She worked for an art gallery. He innocently stalked her. He even bought more paintings than he could afford or hang in his tiny apartment. She finally agreed to go out with him. After the first date, they became inseparable. They married two years later. She had been a good wife during his many years of residency, fellowships, and boards. She had waited patiently while he did his duty as a navy surgeon and those long nine months in the Middle East and Southeast Africa. They had been happy in the lean years, but the more successful Sam became, the greater the chasm between them grew. Sam knew it was because of his prolonged absences, and Lauren had been alone far too much. He realized his profession consumed him, but then again, Lauren should have known what to expect, he thought. He was, after all, a physician in a level-one trauma unit, and he had hardened himself to believe he had done his best. About a year earlier, Lauren told Sam that she was bored and needed a change. He urged her to go on a two-month world cruise with some friends. When she returned, Lauren had changed. She had become worldlier, more frivolous with money and with her health. She disappeared for hours during the day and returned with bags of expensive clothes. She always reeked of liquor and tobacco after her outings. She abandoned her old friends for the new "lunch-club" as Sam, none too affectionately, referred to them. The house was no longer big enough for her. So Sam bought her a new home in Clearlake, on the water, complete with an infinity pool, a pool house large enough for massive parties, an aviary, exquisite grounds, and a full-time gardener and housekeeper. He groaned. "Who has time for parties?" He knew that all he had done was not enough, because he was an absent husband. So Lauren remained dissatisfied. The more time he spent at the hospital, the farther they grew apart, and each action perpetuated the other. The effects of Sam's dedication, one major factor that had initially brought them together, was the cause of their marital suffering. Sam knew that giving her monetary things had always been his answer. But in the back of his mind, the old Sam knew it had been his scapegoat for the real difficulties. He was an enabler. He gave her things instead of the attention and help Lauren needed. Sam thought of his dad's adage: "If money can fix it, then it's not a problem." Money hadn't fixed it, and it continued to be a big problem. He had left her lonely and bored, and he knew he had not done much to make it right. So her desolation became his misery.

A hot blast of air steeped with the fragrance of leather enveloped Sam as he slid into the driver's seat. The Texas July heat had not relented while the sun had moved westward. The traffic slowed, and the drive north would take only 35 minutes. It was good therapy. Sam loved his Carrera, and he rarely minded the traffic when he drove it. It was when he sat still that Sam became bored. But most things had begun to bore him. In fact, he even bored himself, he thought. Satellite radio blasted out Deep Purple's song "Smoke on the Water." Sam immersed himself in the early rock and roll music and the exhilaration of the Porsche's speed.

Just as he had thought, Lauren was passed out in the pool house, the stereo blaring. He carried her to their bed. Tomorrow would be another day. He needed to discuss his horrific day, but that would not happen. Discussions were not something that happened anymore between them. Virtually every conversation deteriorated into an argument.

The moon shone on Lauren's face as it broke through the thunderstorm clouds. She was still magnificent. Her slender yet shapely body was perfectly formed under the sheet. Sam wanted to make love. He wanted to be held and desired. He put his hand on her waist and slowly stroked it. He did still love her, and at that moment, she looked like the innocent girl he had married. But the reality of his failing marriage soon crept into his mind. He and Lauren had very little, if anything, left. But neither of them could call it quits.

JULY 6

Dawn came too quickly. Lauren had not moved all night, and Sam took her pulse to be sure she was alive.

She just groaned.

Suddenly the phone rang. Sam glanced at the clock. It was 6:15 a.m.

"Sorry to have to phone this early, Dr. Hawkins. I know you've been on duty too long, but there's been a pileup on 45 North near Friendswood. Twenty-two people were on a church bus, with kids. We have half coming here. Methodist gets the others. We need every available surgeon on hand."

"On my way. Get the rooms ready."

"Sure thing, Doctor," said the faceless voice on the other end of the phone.

It was a mess when Sam arrived at the emergency rooms. Trauma was what they did best at that level-one center. Sam had been an excellent naval surgeon, and he had only honed his skills since. He had seen and dealt with just about every kind of horrific injury. However, when he worked on children and babies, the task was particularly difficult and always an emotional drain. People wheeled injured patients from every direction. Doctors shouted orders, and nurses ran with liquid-filled bags and tubes. It was a familiar scene for Sam, but it was never easy.

Hours passed, and the critical were either pronounced dead or taken to the intensive care units. The less-than-critical were sent to rooms, and the lucky few went home.

Sam rested in the corner of the Trauma and Emergency Departments and wiped the perspiration from his face.

"It's been a hard few days, huh, Doc?" one of the male nurses asked, interrupting Sam's feeble attempt to escape for a moment.

Sam stood slowly while he gripped the sides of the chair, which assisted him to his feet. "Yep, but this is what we bought into, buddy. It's just what we bought into."

———

Ana Roberts would be home, and Sam felt an urgent need to see her. They needed to talk and perhaps make arrangements for the funeral.

By the time Sam arrived at the Roberts's' home, cars lined the drive, and people were everywhere. As he got closer to the house, he noticed a young woman walking from her car with an armload of flowers and food. He offered to assist her into the house. After setting the food down, he noticed that she was staring at him peculiarly. He brushed it off and left the room without getting her name or introducing himself.

Ana was smothered by all the well-meant attention. He pulled her aside and led her to the backyard. Bill's favorite place had been the rose garden, and being next to what he had loved made both feel closer to him. The air was perfumed with the smell of roses, Carolina jasmine, and freshly cut grass. The fragrance of cut grass took Sam back to his youth, when the carefree summers were filled with fun and laughter. For a moment, he saw his mom with a plate of hamburger buns and another of hand-formed patties. The pungent fragrance of the grass drew his mind to his own father and those days when the family gathered in the yard after he had cut the lawn and carried the bags to the field in the back of the house. Those long-ago days were filled with happiness and so much family love. He missed them terribly, especially on this day. There was no happiness or laughter. There had been little of either for Sam for quite some time.

"May I help you with the arrangements?" Sam asked.

"Thank you, Sam." She pointed to the garden. "Did you see all the new rose bushes? If only my James were here." Ana cuddled a red rose in the palm of her hand. "Bill planted these when James died, you know." Her mind seemed to wander to a faraway place, and then she whispered, "Simon and John are at the funeral home now."

Ana had a tendency to extend any conversation beyond Sam's attention's limit. He had not listened carefully to everything she had said.

In fact, he had momentarily zoned out trying to find reason for the tragedy and reminiscing about better times. Sam pulled her closer to him. "I know, Ana, I know." Then he suddenly replayed her full statement. He stopped in his tracks. "What did you say? John...John who? Albright?"

"Yes, Sam...I knew you were busy. I heard about the bad accident, and I knew you were at the hospital. Anyway, I want you here with me."

Sam faked a smile and tried to calm himself. "Ana, I don't know Simon, and I don't like John. I don't trust him. He's a royal ass. Excuse me, but please...please watch yourself."

Ana took Sam's hand and put it up to her cheek. "Yes, Sam, I know your past with John. Do you still hold that grudge after all the years? I can't believe John would have stolen your anatomy notes. Anyway, you passed all your medical exams, and look at you now. So, not to worry."

"It was biology, and he stole them and burned them. He said he thought it was trash papers from the printer. That was bullshit," Sam said. "I couldn't ever prove it, but he's a liar now and was a liar then. I barely scraped by with a C on that exam. I had never made a C in my life! I know he took the notes. Anyway, Ana, I never knew you were close to Albright."

"John came around the house about six months ago. He and Bill had a lot of meetings. I think they were working on something together. You know John has been in Atlanta at the Institute for Disease for some time. Oh, Sam...you know I don't get into those things with Bill." She paused. "I didn't get into those things." She began to slowly walk, still talking. "I got to know John fairly well. He was always a gentleman, and I liked him. He showed real concern about Bill after his..." She paused again. Her voice cracked. "After Bill was gone."

Sam handed her his handkerchief. He tried to process what Ana had told him, but it simply would not compute. Dr. John Albright had not been a friend of Dr. Bill Roberts, and he certainly was no longer a friend of Dr. Sam Hawkins.

Ana continued her story. "John came back a couple of weeks ago. He and Bill went to Washington for a few days. Then they came back here together. They worked several nights here at the house. I know you think John is arrogant and maybe a few other things, but I think he's a changed man. I mean, that tiff you had was years ago. You should give him a chance."

Sam shrugged. "Arrogant, self-centered, and a thief! Changed? Maybe." But he thought not.

"Where's Lauren?" Ana asked.

"I left her sleeping this morning before I went to the emergency." Sam grimaced.

"No better, Sam?"

He shook his head sadly but said nothing. There was no need for words. Ana knew how things were.

"Come in and have a bite to eat," Ana said. A tear ran down her cheek. "At least I won't fret over Bill's pathetic hairless lab rats anymore," she mumbled as she took a small step forward.

Sam forced a smile. The two walked back to the house. He stopped and took a deep breath. "Ana, can we talk about what Bill...oh, never mind. We'll talk, ah...later."

"You're fumbling words. What are you talking about, Sam? Tell me," Ana said.

"It's just that Bill said some things."

"Said what? When?" Ana's stern eyes glared at Sam. "Tell me what he said."

Sam stopped and plucked a gardenia, smelled its sweetness, and then handed it to Ana. It was Sam's way of gathering control of his thoughts. "In the hospital, he just said some peculiar things. I'm sure it was the fever."

Ana cocked her head, and her eyes narrowed.

Sam couldn't identify her expression. It was anger or intense interest. "OK, Bill said the word 'seven' several times and something about a 'safe,' or he was 'safe'…I don't know. Then he said a strange Latin word. 'Collegium.' It means something like 'club' or 'society.' My Latin has never been very good." Sam waited for her response.

"Seven?" Ana shrugged and shook her head. "I have no idea what that would mean. But he does have a safe in his office. How could he think he was safe when he was in so much trouble medically?" Ana paused. "Strange words. He was so ill." She whispered, "Strange."

"What? What's strange?"

"John asked if Bill's last will and testament was in his safe. He wanted me to open it so he could see if he had made any requests for his funeral or last wishes. Maybe Bill wanted you or John to know the will or something was in his safe. I mean, since John asked, and Bill mentioned it to you. Why else would he say that?"

"Albright asked to open Bill's safe? Geez, Ana. You didn't? That's insane. Did you open it for Albright?" Sam knew his voice went up an octave with each word.

"No. I told him that Bill and I had discussed our final wishes, and he had wanted to be cremated. I wasn't ready to review the will. I like John, mind you, but I did think that asking to go into the safe was very odd…but probably innocent."

Sam bit the side of his lip. "Odd, to say the least," he mumbled. "Innocent? Never."

Ana gave him a harsh look, the kind of look one might get from a disappointed but loving mother.

The two strolled slowly back toward the house.

"Bill told me a while back that he wanted to be cremated, and I joked with him. I asked him if tomorrow was too soon." Ana forced a smile and a small giggle, but a tear ran down her cheek. "I never thought that my silly joke...I just never thought."

"That's pretty funny. I'm sure you and Bill had a laugh or two over that," Sam politely said.

"The cremation is taking place today." She began to cry.

Sam held her in his arms. "I'm so sorry, Ana. My heart aches for you. But we don't know about this very strange illness that took Bill from us. We need a full autopsy. So we need to postpone everything a few days."

She pulled away. "Sam, they did an autopsy last night. The medical examiner's office will have the results in a day or two. John and Simon got the body transferred to the funeral home this morning. Cremation was to be at three o'clock."

"Three o'clock? Today? Ana!" Sam said louder than intended. He looked at his watch. It was 3:20. "It's already done! My God, Ana, that's so quick...so very quick! Forensics could not have been adequately done. Didn't anybody try to stop them? They can't...they can't do that. I think that's illegal. No! I know it is. Geez, Ana..." Sam's thoughts were disjointed, and he stammered his words.

"Well, I can't answer that. Surely, they know the law. After all, John's a physician, and Simon was with the Israeli government. I signed the paperwork. It's no underhanded deal, Sam. It's OK. I can't tolerate dragging this out. Every moment is hell, and I need closure. I wanted to see him. I thought that would be my closure, but John and Simon both said that was not possible. They said that he looked very bad." She began to weep. "I need this awful thing over. I need to remember him as he was...healthy and..."

Sam took her in his arms again and hugged her firmly. He whispered, "Ana, Bill went through a lot before he died. I'm sure your memory of him laughing and picking roses is much better than...well, it would just be better. Let's stop talking and go inside." Sam knew things were anything but right and certainly not kosher. He was amused at his own thought—*kosher*. He thought about Simon. It troubled him that Simon was suddenly Ana's new best friend. He seemed a nice enough guy. *But who the hell was he?* How had Bill and Ana Roberts come to be so close to someone from the Israeli government? Sam knew that whatever had happened over the past twenty-four hours had been highly irregular and, frankly, bordered on criminal. His thoughts raced. *Who released the body to Albright and Simon? How did they get the body released?* He would find answers in the morning. Interrogating Ana was not the way to get any information.

The rest of the evening, Sam sat with some of the Robertses' friends. Even in the crowd, Sam found himself consumed in his own messed-up personal life. He pondered how quickly life was over and his own mortality. He was a fine doctor and a pretty nice guy, but he had been an absent husband. His marriage was awful. What was important in life? He had fought hard to get to his position at the hospital and community. He had respect from all his colleagues, but he lacked so much. Sam wondered, if he and Lauren had had children, would that have saved their marriage? Would it have made him a better husband? Would he have felt more fulfilled in life? He put his head in his hands. The fact was that Sam didn't really have a life. Every day was the same drill, and as worthy a drill as it was, at that moment, Sam wished for so much more. He didn't want it all to end with a houseful of people who stood around feeling sorry for whomever he left behind. He then chuckled regretfully to himself. *What if I leave no one behind?* He had to try to make things right between him and Lauren. Sam resigned himself at that moment to do whatever it took to make his marriage work. After Bill's funeral, he would take Lauren to the little bed-and-breakfast in the Texas Hill Country, the one they once loved, the one where they had made love all day and into the night until they both were so spent that they couldn't get out of bed for the entire next day. Sam sincerely smiled for the first time in weeks.

Suddenly he was jarred from his long-ago memories and future hopes by Julia, the housekeeper.

"Dr. Hawkins. Mrs. Roberts is asking for you, sir."

"Be right there," Sam said. He glanced at his watch. It was 7:15 p.m. He should call Lauren too.

Ana was in the kitchen. She leaned feebly against the counter. She seemed to have been in deep thought, and whatever she had been thinking had distressed her. She wiped her brow with the back of her hand when she saw Sam. The gesture appeared to be her way of wiping away an unwanted expression or perhaps a façade.

"You needed me, Ana?" he asked.

"Sam, I was thinking about what you asked in the garden...what Bill said yesterday. I remember him talking to John Albright one evening at a dinner party, here at the house." She paused, thinking a moment. "Did you say Collegium? Is that what Bill said to you? Well, I was coming back into the room...I think I was getting the desserts... or maybe it was coffee...oh well...I don't recall." She paused again, reminiscing about that evening. Again, Ana exhibited her knack for making the shortest of sentences the longest in history.

Sam smiled lovingly. Her stories were often destroyed by the details. He patiently waited for the conclusion of her point. He widened his eyes and cocked his head as if he was trying to hear her and then politely asked, "And what?"

"I heard Bill speaking very firmly to John. He said something to the effect of, 'You tell the Collegium for me...seven will not.'" She cleared her throat. "Uh, he might have said Steven, not seven. You said 'seven' outside, didn't you? Yes, maybe Bill said Steven. Well, I don't recall the exact words, but that's the gist of it." Ana was rambling. "I'm almost sure he said something in Latin, and it might have been the word you told me. Collegium—is that what you said?" Ana's voice was notes higher than normal, and her body language was confusing.

"Did I say I also thought he might have said Steven, not seven?" Sam didn't remember telling her that, but perhaps he had, or maybe she was just confused by the word, the same as Sam had been.

Ana apparently ignored Sam's question and continued her long-winded story. "Bill saw me, and he stopped in midsentence. Does that mean anything to you? Does that help you with your questions? John didn't reply, as I recall. The room got quiet. I didn't think anything of it then, but now, after what you said, well…maybe I'll remember more. Maybe I misunderstood. Oh well." Her eyelids fluttered, and a frown came to her face. She seemed to drift off, as if she had to discover the rest of the story somewhere buried in her mind.

Sam watched her strange expression and the odd way Ana presented her recollections. She sounded almost demented for a moment. Her voice changed tones, and she strung out some words and held on to others. He couldn't make sense of it, but she had just lost her husband, and that could account for almost anything. He tried to answer her questions, but she no longer seemed very interested in the conversation. He shook his head anyway. "No, it makes no sense to me either. Perhaps I'll talk to Albright. But thanks for letting me know what you remember." Sam recalled that she had been hospitalized after James died. The government was unable to present her with his body. They had claimed it was too decimated to open the casket. He had been a few feet away from the suicide terrorists when the bombs were detonated. Bill had told Sam that Ana suffered what he called a mental breakdown and was admitted to a place to rest. But she returned home in a few weeks and seemed to be her old self.

It didn't make any sense to Sam, but what it did was confirm that whatever *seven* and *Collegium* meant, it was important to Roberts. And it was something so important that he took it to his grave.

Sam pulled into his driveway and parked the Porsche under the porte cochere. He glanced at the clock on the glowing dashboard. It was 10:48 p.m.

"Lauren, I'm home," Sam announced quietly while noting that the house alarm had not been set.

There were no sounds in the dark house. He went upstairs, but Lauren was not around.

"Ah, hell, where is she now?" Sam was tired and frustrated, and he had to deal with his "missing in action" wife. But he had a good idea that she was in the pool house, most likely passed out, with Led Zeppelin's "Stairway to Heaven" blasting on repeat. He fell crossways on the bed. He wanted to yell at something or push his fist through a wall. It had been that kind of day, but either would be out of character for Dr. Sam Hawkins. At the same time, he wanted to talk. He wanted someone to listen to what he had been through. He wanted to be stroked and made to feel like a man. He wanted to make long, easy love; fall asleep with Lauren in his arms; and hold her all night. He wanted what they used to have. He wanted the one thing that he knew was not coming back, and for a moment, he felt physically ill with the thought. There was nothing to do but to retrieve her, carry her to their room, and put her to bed. Sam knew the routine.

But Lauren was nowhere on the property. He dialed her cell phone. She answered with slurred words.

"Where are you?" he shouted.

"I'm on my way home. I drove to Austin this morning."

"Austin? Why?"

"I saw Roger and Samantha. I needed to get some papers signed on the property in Corpus. We're selling it."

"Why didn't you tell me you were going to see your brother?" Sam shouted in an attempt to be sure she heard him over her loud radio. "Damn it, put me on Bluetooth. I can't hear you!"

"I did call you. Didn't you see my message?"

"No." Sam paused and looked at his phone. There were no missed calls or voice mails from Lauren.

"Well, no matter," Lauren replied. "I'll be home in about twenty minutes."

"Are you drunk?" Sam asked. Sadness and disappointment were clearly in his voice.

"Nope." Lauren disconnected the phone call.

Sam slammed his cell phone against the granite countertop, shattering the glass front. "Damn it," he screamed. "Damn it!"

He poured himself a glass of Merlot and sat down at the kitchen table to wait for Lauren.

As promised, he heard her Mercedes enter the porte cochere and then the slamming of the car door. Lauren staggered through the kitchen door.

Sam watched but didn't rise from his chair. "I will not allow you to drive in this condition," he snapped.

"You...you will not allow? Who died and made you my king?" Lauren snapped back.

"Lauren, you could have killed yourself or someone. Hell, woman, you can't even walk." He paused and stared at her. Confronting her activities would get him nowhere. "And by the way, since I have not seen or talked to you in three days..." He stopped in midsentence, realizing his continuing raw grief. "Anyway, Bill Roberts died yesterday."

"Oh, that's bad. Oh well, he was a stuffy old man anyway. He and Ana never liked me."

"You arrogant, cold-hearted bitch!" Sam paused and took a deep, cleansing breath. "Lauren, I'm sorry, I didn't mean that. It's been a tough last few days. But that's no excuse. I really am sorry." He reined in his anger. "They liked you well enough. But if they didn't like you, it was because of what you have become."

"Loosen up, Sam. You're tighter than a drum and just about as exciting." She blinked rapidly, trying to focus on Sam.

"Lauren, what's happening to you? I just told you that my best friend died, and this is all you can say?"

"I'll send flowers tomorrow! How's that?" she replied snidely.

"You're sick, Lauren. You need help. I want the woman back that I married."

"I want the man back that I married, but he lives at the hospital. And me? I live in a bottle."

Sam heard the bedroom door slam. He would sleep, or at least try to sleep, in another bedroom. It would not be the first time. And unless something changed, he thought, not the last.

JULY 7

It was a restless night, and Sam wasn't sure how much sleep he got. At least he had the day off from the hospital. When he arrived at the kitchen, Lauren was sitting at the table with a cup of coffee, rubbing the sides, as if to warm her hands.

"Good morning," he said as he poured a cup, but he did not make eye contact with his obviously hungover wife.

"Is it?" she replied.

"That's your call, Lauren. Only you can make it good."

"Sam, I'm sick of your sanctimonious self-righteousness. I'm sick of it. Got it?"

Sam said nothing as he stepped onto the outside deck and felt the hot July sun hit his face.

Lauren raised her voice. "Did you hear me? I am sick to death of your attitude!"

Sam wheeled on his heels, replying to her from the open door. "Lauren, I'm sorry about that, but you're a lush—a drunk—and frankly, I'm getting sick to death with *that.* You are pathetic, and you need professional help. I'm either worried about you or angry with you. This behavior is beneath you!"

"Beneath me? Is that right? What's beneath you, Sam? Certainly not me. I've not been beneath you in a very long time." She smirked.

"You think you're so damned clever, don't you?" Sam shook his head. "You're not."

"Doesn't matter. You're so boring. You've become so clinical, so textbook, even when we made love. B-O-R-I-N-G," she shouted.

Sam said, "Well, our bed has felt like a bag of ice for a very long time. Kinda hard to warm up to an ice cube. I'm not calling you a bag, Lauren. So don't cut those eyes at me. You used to not complain." He pointed to the large hall mirror. "Look at yourself, Lauren. Answer your own question. I never know who or what I'll find when I get home. You need help."

"Oh, big doctor thinks I need help, does he? Where were you when I needed love, or help, or company? Where are you now, Sam? You're in that damned hospital. You're married to that damn trauma unit and that fucking hospital. So, if you don't know what you'll find, then don't come home."

"Lauren, please. Get a hold of yourself. This bickering is getting us nowhere." Sam paused. Finally, there was silence. He inhaled sharply and stared at her. "Go with me tomorrow afternoon to the memorial service for Bill, and then, please, let's drive to Galveston and have dinner, or let's go to the Hill Country and spend the night. I want to help you, and I want to help our marriage."

"Too late, Sammy boy. Just too damned late for that." Lauren rose from her chair as she strung together the last words. She held Sam's eyes in an angry stare. "Yep, too late." Lauren walked slowly to the stairs. She held on to the banister and bowed her head. "Oh...damn it! OK, I'll go to the damned service," she huffed. Taking one step up the stairs, she cut her eyes one last time at Sam. "Guess that's the least I can do for Ana." She then mumbled, "As if she really cares...but I'm not doing this for you, Sam...I'm not going for you. Let me sleep a few more hours."

Sam shook his head. He didn't know if he was angry, bewildered, or amazed. He only knew that Lauren was right about one thing. It was indeed too late.

CHAPTER THREE

JULY 8. THREE DAYS AFTER
DR. BILL ROBERTS'S DEATH

They buried Dr. Bill Roberts's ashes in a Talavera printed urn next to James, their son. It was on a slightly higher mound than the rest of the cemetery and shaded by a line of wild olive and pecan trees. Wisteria vines grew on a trellis that Ana had planted next to James's grave. By the trellis was a cantera stone bench. The seat was engraved with "Padre Dios, sostén a mi más querido en tus brazos amorosos." Ana insisted they do it that way so she would have a place to come and talk to her beloved husband and son.

Sam whispered to Lauren that they had the bench made in San Miguel de Allende, after James died. "It says something like 'Father, hold my dear one in your embrace.'" He expected a response from her, but she only cut her eyes at him and then smiled at Dr. John Albright. Sam ignored her obvious attempt to make him jealous or hurt him. Whatever her reasoning, Albright seemed to like it.

Lauren wore a black silk sheath dress with a large-brimmed black-and-silver straw hat. Her oversized Gucci sunglasses concealed her swollen and bloodshot eyes. Although nothing was right with them and her attendance was a sham at best, Sam couldn't help but feel a sense of pride to have her next to him. She received more than a few compliments after the memorial service. Dr. John Albright delivered the most lavish praises. Lauren seemed to eat up every word and even offered a few more flirtatious responses. Sam was disgusted, but still he wondered if it was Albright's charm, or had she deliberately delivered another jab at him? He held his tongue from lashing out at Lauren and his fist from flattening Albright.

"It was a very nice service, Ana," Sam whispered as he gave Bill Roberts's widow a loving hug. "Bill was a great man. I miss him. May we help you get home?"

Ana straightened the brim on her straw hat. The hot summer wind had wreaked havoc on her hat and hair. Her one hand secured the hat to her very blond bobbed hair, and the other clung to Sam's arm. "No, Simon has already planned to take me home in the limousine."

Sam walked Ana to the waiting limo. He caught a glimpse of John Albright getting into another limo on the far side of the grassy drive. Sam pulled away from Ana so he might better see Albright. Their eyes met even at the distance. He turned back to Ana. "Be careful of John. He's trouble." Ana did not respond. Sam held on to her hand until the last tip of her fingers slipped from his. "Love you, Ana," Sam whispered.

Ana quizzically tilted her head. "We will talk soon, Sam. I love you." Ana slid into the long black vehicle.

Sam gave her a kiss on the cheek, and the door closed.

Simon walked quickly toward Sam. "Wait." He shook Sam's hand and uttered a quiet "Thank you."

Sam detected a slight Israeli accent for the first time. Bewildered with it all, he slowly walked back to Lauren and the Porsche.

She was by the passenger side, smoking a cigarette.

"Put that damned thing out before you get in my car," Sam growled.

Lauren looked straight at him. She took a long draw off the cigarette and blew the smoke into the Porsche.

Sam glared at her. He realized she had not worn her wedding ring to the service, but he said nothing. His rage had built to a crescendo and was almost out of control. He rolled down the driver's-side window and took several very deep breaths. It was an effort to clear the air in the car and to free his head of his desire to explode on her. But there was no need to say anything at all. She was just putting the last nails into their marriage coffin.

JULY 9

The next day, Sam was consumed with questions. Bill's ravaged body had been cremated too quickly. There should have been many more tests performed. The coroner was performing a toxicology test, and the laboratory at the medical center was running tests on the blood taken in the ER. But even so, what had killed Bill, and why so quick to cremate? Why did the medical examiner release his body with only a standard and rushed autopsy? Or was there even an autopsy, at all? No one seemed to address that Bill had presented in the level-one Trauma Emergency Department with a very serious and mysterious illness. No one even asked Sam what he thought killed Dr. Roberts. That alone was inexplicable. The symptoms were so remarkable and bizarre that any other time, the hospital would have been under some form of lockdown and his team quarantined—or at the least in a full code-orange mode until answers were obtained.

Sam shook off the thought. He had patients being wheeled in from every door, and all the trauma rooms were full. It was a typical summer's day on the Texas Gulf Coast. He didn't have time to think about Bill or Ana or Lauren or John Albright or anything that had occupied so much of his mind and time.

As the typical day in the Shock and Trauma Unit of St. Peter's wore on, Sam found himself unable to keep up with the caseload. He was tired and felt weak. His head ached, his throat was sore, and he was feverish. He felt worse as the hours passed. Had he contracted whatever had killed Bill Roberts? His mind reviewed those early-morning hours when he attended his old friend. He shuddered at the thought. After all, his glove had been compromised, and he had virtually had his face in Bill Roberts's face on multiple occasions. He very well could be exposed, and his heart sank. Sandra had warned him. If he had contracted what killed Dr. Roberts, then Sam was a dead man.

Suddenly he felt nauseous. One of the technicians recognized that he was ill and assisted him to the nurse's station. Sam called his associate, Kelton Thomas. Dr. Thomas saw him in his office that same hour.

Dr. Thomas ran the normal blood tests and did a thorough examination of Sam. Sam would not tell him his suspicions—or, rather, his intense fear—until the blood and other test results came back. He didn't want to even think the worst, and he didn't want to alarm Kelton Thomas or color his unbiased diagnosis. Sam and Dr. Thomas were friends, so his nurse encouraged Sam to stay in Dr. Kelton's office until the test results were completed. She turned off the light and gave Sam a blanket. As the minutes passed, Sam tried desperately to ward off thoughts of having the deadly disease that took his old friend's life on July 5. But the fear kept creeping in as Sam's temperature rose. He felt awful, and his mind games only made things worse.

An hour passed. Where was Kelton? Had he found something and didn't know what it was or how to treat Sam? As the chills became worse, he pulled the blanket up around his neck and curled up into almost a fetal position to get warm. It didn't take long for the fever to put him to sleep.

Sam didn't know how long he had slept, but he heard a brief knock on the door and saw Dr. Thomas come into the room. He had a large hypodermic needle in his hand.

"Feeling punk, I see. No doubt. Roll over. Let me see that cute butt of yours." Dr. Thomas laughed.

"What'd find?" Sam coughed out the words.

"Strep throat. You have a fine, upstanding case of strep. This shot will get you feeling better real soon. I've got some antibiotic samples in a bag up front for you."

Sam began to laugh. "Strep? Oh, thank God. I've got strep throat!"

Dr. Thomas smiled playfully. "Well, I've never heard someone thank God for strep throat, but whatever floats your boat, Sam."

Sam sat up on the examining table. "I thought it was something worse. Why'd ya take so long?"

"Pulling corn out of a two-year-old toddler's ears takes time. Like wresting an alligator with the lungs of a Banshee."

"Yep, been there, done that."

"Sam, go home, sleep, take the antibiotics, and you should feel better in a day or two. Call me if you want." He smiled. "Maybe next time I can tell you that you have the clap, and you can get excited and do a happy dance. I'd like to see that!"

JULY 11

Dr. Thomas was on the money when he said that Sam would be better in a couple of days. He woke up feeling great after being laid up in bed for less than two full days. He had things to investigate, and what plagued his mind could not be put off any longer.

Sam unlocked his office door. He had not been there since the day Bill Roberts died, but he had made some dictation on the Roberts case and emailed it to his laptop. He opened his Mac and finished his notes on Dr. Roberts's death. He knew he had not covered the morning adequately in his short initial report. Doing it right had been a chore that he had put aside, but it was time he finished it and sent his remarks to the proper department. Otherwise, his hospital privileges could be in jeopardy. He knew that wasn't really going to happen to him, but even so, he would follow the rules, at least this one time. It saddened him recalling moment to moment the early hours of July 5, but he muddled through it all, including the indistinguishable ramblings. He listed each muffled word that he recalled and his responses to Dr. Roberts. He wasn't sure why he wrote so much detail, but it helped clarify and identify the issues that haunted him.

But there were so many more matters and questions about Bill Roberts's death that were unresolved, confusing, and downright outrageous.

That afternoon, Sam was waiting outside Mr. Don Huitt's office. The new hospital administrator must have an answer to Sam's questions, or he would surely have to answer to the board or perhaps the law. Sam hadn't had time to meet the new hospital boss, but he would surely be welcomed, based upon his stature at the hospital.

Huitt arrived about 1:15, flanked by two men in suits. Each man carried a briefcase, and one had several file folders under his left arm.

"Mr. Huitt...uh, Don...I'd like a word with you," Sam said, not sure how to address the man.

"It's Don, please. I don't have much time, as you see. We're in an audit, and it's my first week here. Guess you can imagine the workload.

I'll be tied up for several days. But come in." He motioned with his hand for Sam to enter the office and then signaled to the two men to wait. Before he sat down, he leaned over and pushed a button on the side of his desk. "Do you mind if I record our conversation? I keep better track of things when I replay a conversation. Your reputation as a fine doctor and trauma surgeon precedes you," Huitt said.

"Thank you, but this visit isn't about me…and fine…record away. I have nothing to hide. But I can say that I've never been recorded in the administration office." Sam smirked sarcastically. "Just another weird thing happening here at St. Pete's, I guess." He shook his head in disgust. "I want to know what you know about Dr. William Roberts's body being rushed out of the coroner's office and cremated so quickly. This hospital should have been involved, mainly because he died here, and frankly, his death is very alarming. And apparently, you hushed this from all media, because nothing has been mentioned about his death." Sam leaned closer to the administrator and noticed that the other man's jaw had begun to twitch. "In fact, there should have been a complete inquiry, as his symptoms…I'm sure you know…were very disturbing and puzzling. I've seen a lot of very ill people with all sorts of exotic and rare diseases, and none presented like Bill Roberts. And he was chief of staff! You'd think there would be more concern over all this."

Huitt stretched his neck and twisted it from side to side, as if to release tension. "I suppose you're saying that this hospital was amiss in the handling of this. Am I correct?"

"You tell me. I know I've not been asked anything about Bill's death, and I was the attending physician. I don't think Sandra, my head nurse, or George Santos and the rest of the team that morning, were asked anything. I know his body was taken out of this hospital and to the county coroner's for autopsy and that the next day his body was cremated. I know the biohazard codes were lifted. I know that no tissue samples are in the path lab upstairs, and—"

Huitt interrupted Sam. "Well, to begin with, Dr. Hawkins, your team was briefed in a meeting that you failed to attend. An email was sent to you and you failed to even answer that. Because of the hospital's high regard for you, I chose to not take disciplinary action and attributed your lack of response to your personal grief."

"I did not receive any email from you. Nor have I seen or heard from anyone on my team."

"They were given an option to take a leave of absence. They all were shaken, and Dr. Roberts was a loved man. The corporation suggested allowing them a paid leave."

"Paid leave? I have never..." Sam paused. "This is nuts."

Huitt didn't react to Sam's statement. "Regarding your other concerns, everything has been addressed and the results are as reported. I can tell you that tissue samples were sent to the medical school lab and elsewhere for further analysis. The hospital is out of this case entirely. It was one of the first things that I did when I came on board. I looked into it. Nothing there. Sam...may I call you Sam?"

Sam nodded. His face was strained and stern, which exactly reflected his sentiments.

Don Huitt continued. "The right people came in and took over. I think you're overreacting. Dr. Bill Roberts died from cancer. I read the autopsy. You're just too close to the family, and for some reason you're thinking it was more than that. I assure you that it's a cut-and-dried case of advanced cancer and sepsis as a result of the cancer in the bile ducts...pancreatic cancer. You must see that."

"I know you're not a physician, and this is the business office, but come on, Huitt! Dr. Roberts did not directly die from cancer. That dog won't hunt, and you know it! *You* must see *that*!" Sam's words were direct and empathic. "Roberts said cryptic things. 'Seven' or 'Steven' and 'safe.' He said something that sounded like Latin. Maybe you should follow up on that. He was too ill to speak, yet he did, and I think you need to see what this entire mess means. Perhaps it means nothing to his ailment, but I assure you that Dr. Bill Roberts did not die from complications of cancer or sepsis or anything that you or the county people say. Did you search his lab for a pathogen or something? Maybe there are notes about something he was working on, and it killed him."

Huitt's eyes widened, and his face turned almost as red as his wiry hair. "Everything has been investigated. Nothing is there, and nothing was ever there."

Sam took a step back and glared at the administrator. "The new complacency of this hospital appalls me! And that falls squarely upon your shoulders." Sam took a deep breath and thought about what Don Huitt had told him. "The right people came in?" Sam nearly shouted. "What do you mean, the right people? Can you tell me with a straight face that you have ever encountered anything like Bill Roberts's death, and can you say that you have seen a hospital that literally did nothing but pass it all on to"—Sam shook his head in disgust and astonishment—"the right people?"

"I'm beginning to take offense to your innuendos." Don Huitt stood up and leaned against the large desk, almost getting into Sam's face. "I have other pressing hospital business now; I must ask you to leave."

"Oh yeah, it's getting too fuckin' hot in here anyway. I don't know where you came from, but I do know that this hospital is not being run properly." Sam walked from the office into the reception area. "Maybe the board will give me answers. I'm certainly not getting anything from you."

"I advise you to drop this matter, Dr. Hawkins. I strongly suggest you forget this and get on with your own business. Perhaps, Dr. Hawkins, *you* need a leave of absence." Huitt said firmly.

Sam glanced at the two men who were waiting to go into Don Huitt's office. Both stared directly at Sam, and for some reason, he sensed that they were no more hospital auditors than he was.

Huitt's answers, as cryptic as they were, and the anger he portrayed just didn't pass the smell test. Huitt was nervous, and Sam noticed the color burned into his cheeks when he was challenged.

Sam was now even more convinced that something was very wrong, and he was right in the big middle of whatever it was. "Has everyone lost their minds?" Sam uttered angrily as he left the office. He was immersed in his thoughts and steaming mad.

Suddenly, there came a small voice from behind him. He turned to see a young woman walking quickly down the hallway toward him.

"Dr. Hawkins, please, may I have a word with you?" whispered the young dark-eyed receptionist. "I might lose my job for telling you this, but Mr. Huitt didn't have a meeting with auditors today. He had no meetings at all on his calendar. I have heard very nice things about you as the hospital's head of trauma, and I just don't know why Mr. Huitt would lie to you. He's been here less than a week, and I've had some very difficult dealings with him already. He doesn't know much about running a hospital. If I might say so, he's a strange man and nothing like Mr. Williamson. I wish Mr. Williamson was back as head of this administration office."

"Thank you for telling me this. Don't I know you? What's your name?" Sam strained to find a smile.

"You carried the hospital's condolence gifts into the Roberts's house for me the other day. It's Brenda, Dr. Hawkins. Brenda Newman."

Sam vaguely remembered her but acknowledged that he recalled helping the young woman. He thanked her and started to the elevator. Just before the elevator door opened, he saw Huitt and the two men going to the exit that led to the stairwell. Why would they not take the back elevator down four flights, unless they didn't want to go through the main hospital lobby? Sam huffed. "It's not for the cardio."

When Sam got to the lobby, he rushed to the west parking lot. Neither Huitt nor his two friends were to be found. If they had gone to the ground floor, they would have had to exit the door to that parking lot. The floors under Huitt's office were patient rooms, and the floor above was the laboratory. A light bulb went on in Sam's head. Huitt had gone to the lab.

Sam rushed to the fifth floor. He waited outside the door to the main lab. Several technicians filed out. One of the male techs held the door open for several females. For a brief moment, Sam had clear view of the inside of the large white room. He saw Huitt put something into a bag. He then handed the bag to one of the men, who put it inside his briefcase. Sam shuddered. His thoughts ran rampant. Insanity! No hospital administrator would handle biohazardous specimens. Who was this man?

CHAPTER FOUR

JULY 12

The old man, whom the med students called Dr. Rick R. Morris, was a pathologist and part of the coroner's office team. He or his staff had autopsied Dr. Roberts. Sam had known him for some time. His real name was R. A. Morris, and his friends called him R. A. Sam had never known what the initials stood for, and he was among the ones who commonly called him by his nickname. The old doctor never seemed to care and even appeared to find humor in the joke. He was a peculiar but kind man. When Sam was younger and in medical school, he always wondered how Dr. Morris could do his job day in and day out. But after the years at a level-one trauma center, Sam also wondered about himself. He felt certain that he could get the truth from Dr. Morris, so he made a visit to the pathologist.

———————

"We found nothing to indicate anything other than his cancer had advanced, and he had contracted a severe bacterial infection resulting in sepsis and ultimately hemorrhagic septicemia."

"That's insane," Sam shouted. "Did you see the body? Nothing I have ever seen remotely resembled the remains of Dr. Roberts. It was gruesome and hideous."

Dr. Morris simply gazed into the distance over Sam's head. He displayed a calculated nonchalance mixed with some kind of fear. The old man was too brief, too abbreviated for Sam. His organs had simply shut down and the sepsis killed him? Sam would have none of that nonsense, even from this respected forensic MD.

Sam moved closer to the desk and leaned toward the coroner. "I ask you again: have you or your team ever seen anything identical or remotely like Dr. Roberts's symptoms? Did you see the body? And where are the pictures of Dr. Roberts's body?"

Dr. Morris nodded, but he didn't directly answer either question. Instead, he opened a small black notebook on the top of his desk. He ran his hand over the open page. He stared into Sam's eyes for longer than was comfortable, as if he wanted Sam to read his mind. Then mysteriously, he placed the book in a drawer and locked it away. "Dr. Hawkins, I don't know about where the pictures are, and it is just what I said. Nothing more."

Sam was mystified and infuriated at the same time. "Dr. Morris, please. Blood poisoning, internal bleeding, system and organ shutdown. Yes! But that was not even half of what I saw happening in that room on July fifth. Something caused that, and no one at the hospital or the county even thought to run tests, and now Bill Roberts's body is reduced to ashes in an urn. Any evidence is now gone," Sam shouted as he moved to the other side of the room.

Dr. Morris gazed strangely at Sam. His voice was calm but insincere. "Perhaps you're just too close to this patient. You can't take every case you lose so personally. *It will kill you.* I have…ah…to go now. You must leave, Sam."

His old tired eyes again stared straight into Sam's with such intensity that Sam felt his skin begin to crawl.

The pathologist's last words had trailed off with a singsong tempo, but his eyes spoke volumes. He appeared to want to tell Sam something but couldn't. It was almost a warning. It will kill you. Sam repeated the words to himself. Strange choice of words, he mused. Dr. Morris had responded to Sam's questions but hadn't answered any of them. He had added nothing to the conversation or to Sam's knowledge. As hard as Sam pushed, the old pathologist had pulled back. It was as though Sam had been talking to a brick wall. He sensed something—maybe fear—in Dr. Morris's eyes and body language. There was something that he was not willing to say. There was something he was hiding, especially when Sam asked him if he thought there had been or was an intentional cover-up.

The old man had not moved from behind his well-worn desk but again motioned for Sam to leave. If it was not fear, then it was something that truly puzzled Sam. Perhaps it was anger, or maybe he felt insulted that the question sounded similar to an accusation.

Whatever it had been, Sam would never know. The cleaning crew found Dr. Morris that night. He had been shot dead, and his office had been ransacked. It was being called a robbery that had gone terribly wrong.

JULY 14

Dr. Morris's death was sad and equally perplexing. Who would want to rob an old pathologist in his crummy office? It didn't make sense. Sam was certain he was hiding something and was afraid of whatever it was.

So the days following Dr. Bill Roberts's death had been harder than Sam had ever anticipated. Not only was Bill gone; he was gone without explanation. Sam was battling demons from all angles. He had a constant nagging feeling that something big was being concealed. His short but hostile visit with Huitt and Huitt's odd behavior in the laboratory were bewildering. Why would Don Huitt try to hide details and lie to Sam if there was nothing there? And why would the two men in Huitt's office go along with the lie? Sam's phone call to the chairman of the board had only perplexed him further. He had parroted exactly what Huitt had said. What was it that everyone he had talked to knew but was hiding? *Maybe they didn't know and were morons, ignorant and burying their heads in the sand.* Or was Sam just exhausted, impatient, and paranoid?

The pathology lab and the medical examiner's office had signed off on Bill's autopsy report, and Sam knew Ana had a copy of the results. Sam wanted to see the official papers, but he also knew that Ana Roberts was feeling as alone as he. He called her cell phone.

The soft southern accent on the other end replied. "Hi, Sam. I saw the caller ID. Julia has lunch in the works. Please come on by when you can and eat a stuffed avocado with her famous chicken salad with me. Sam, I'm looking forward to your company." Her voice cracked. Sadness sprinkled her words as she apparently held back tears.

Sam knew that Bill's death was becoming a reality for her. The first few days are always a blur, but the truth and the anguish of death evidentially becomes very real, and generally far too soon. "I'm also looking forward to seeing you. I'll be there shortly."

Sam thought back to what little he had gotten from the old forensic doctor two days earlier and his subsequent strange murder. Maybe with Ana he could find answers.

Ana handed him the large white envelope. "I got this by courier day before yesterday. I didn't open it until last night with Simon."

Sam glanced up at her but had no response. He pulled out the official papers. "They really finished this report in a hurry. Just a week to get it all to you? Hmm...must not have much of a workload at the county," he said snidely. "I don't think I've ever heard of an autopsy and the written report being completed and in another's hands this soon after..." Sam caught his words. *You stupid jerk*, he thought of himself. Ana didn't need Sam's paranoid suspicions added to her grief. But it was nearly impossible for him to contain his doubts. Sam quietly perused the multiple pages of the typed copy. "They say here..." Sam read the first two pages to himself. "Ana, ah, the report says..." he huffed. "It says, in layman's terms, that it was a vast bacterial infection, and vital organs started to shut down because of his compromised immune system from his cancer. They're saying that Bill died from complications from cancer. I'm hearing this from everyone I've talked to. Huitt said that at the hospital, the coroner said it, and now the written copy. Well, they might believe it, but I simply cannot." Sam's tone was purely sarcastic. "Hell, Ana, I didn't even know Bill had cancer before he died. This doesn't make sense to me." Sam felt ashamed for his harshness and sarcasm, but if there was something erroneous and the truth was not being told, then Ana also needed to know.

"Nor did I. I fear he didn't know about his cancer either, Sam. But why are you so sure that you're right and all the others are wrong? Sounds pretty arrogant of you. I know you're a fine doctor, but these are pathologists, and they're trained to diagnose almost anything. We have to live with what they say. That's the end of it."

Sam shook his head. He'd been scolded, but he didn't care. Above all things, Bill not knowing that he was ill seemed ridiculous. "Ana, he was a physician and one of the best infectious-disease and cancer researchers in the nation. How would he not know he had cancer? Makes no sense. Anyway, what I got from…" Sam paused. Suddenly his gut told him that he should not mention any more names, bring up that he had visited with Dr. Morris the day of his murder, or tell her what he had or had not learned from the man before someone silenced him forever. The whole picture was getting vaguer, but something clicked inside Sam. Lies and cover-ups were clearly coming into focus. Someone or some group was deliberately hiding facts. But why?

Ana continued talking. "John Albright said that he thought Bill might have known and just didn't say anything for fear of worrying me, or maybe he was afraid what would happen to his research at the hospital. You know he thought of that lab as his own."

Sam hung his head, trying to conceal his frustration. John Albright; John Albright; John Albright. Seemed a day couldn't go by without hearing that revolting name. Sam composed himself. He looked hard into Ana's sad eyes. "Albright said that? Well…" He bit his tongue, but his brain would not be silent. He stopped and laid the folder on the coffee table. Thoughts were flying through his head. "By the way, where's your friend Simon? I haven't seen him around since Bill's service."

"New York," Ana replied. "Simon went to see his daughter in New York. It's the anniversary of his wife's death, and they're having some special memorial."

"Where's Albright been?"

Ana cut her eyes at him. "Now, Sam, I don't want to sound rude, but how the hell do I know, and why are you asking me?"

"Well, he and Simon seem to have shadowed you, and I just thought…"

"Thought what? Sam, you must get over this hate you possess for John Albright. It's eating you alive."

"No hate, Ana. I'm just in a quandary as to what really happened to Bill. And Albright and Simon, ah…whatever his last name is…just add to my questions."

Ana frowned. "Well, there's nothing going on, darlin', with either of those gentlemen. Not with me anyway." She patted Sam's knee, as if to console a small child.

"Hum mm," replied Sam with more lingering questions than he cared to consider. He knew John had been out of the area for almost a decade. Now he was back and right in everyone's face. He didn't work at any local hospital or in the university research departments, and he didn't appear to have any real reason to be back in Texas, other than his flimsy explanation of being around for work with Bill. And Bill was mysteriously dead. *And that suspicious Simon.* Sam shook his head… *yes…suspicious Simon.* Who the hell was he?

Julia served lunch in the gazebo. She had prepared a vase of red roses, which sat in the middle of the table.

Sam touched the petals. "Why did Bill plant these? They're hard to grow in the heat of Texas, aren't they?"

Ana turned on the outside fans, and although the July heat was sweltering, the shade and southeast breeze felt comfortable and calming. "He planted the Freedom Rose bushes after James died in Afghanistan, and he planted the American Beauties and Peace Roses after Steven died in Washington. He seemed to forget about the other roses in his garden after that, but José kept the entire garden going."

"Seems fitting." Sam knew the continual grief Bill had felt when the Afghanistan civil war rebels or terrorists had killed his only son. It was evident in all things Bill did or said. Then the loss of his only brother in a car accident soon afterward had been devastating. Both men were involved with the pursuit of freedom and their love of America. Bill seemed strangely changed after the two deaths, but Sam never thought much about it other than his friend being in a constant state of mourning. "Yes, Ana, these flowers are a true memorial to them. I never realized Bill did this for them. Beautiful sentiment."

Ana smiled, but her eyes showed heartache. "Yes, but also a bit obsessive. Bill was fixated on these roses. The past few months, he did little around the house but sit in his office with the door closed or out here among the roses. He was troubled much of the time, and I saw sadness always on his face. Oh, don't get me wrong. Bill was the love of my life, and we had a perfect marriage…right to the end." She took a sip of her iced tea. "I see the same look in your eyes right now. You're obsessed or troubled, aren't you? Bill's gone. He died, and we're alive. We must move on."

Sam took her hand. "There are just questions, Ana. There are just a lot of questions." Sam was reconciled that no matter what it took, he would find out who Simon was and why Albright was hanging around. "Ana," Sam blurted loudly without thinking, "I need to see in Bill's office."

Ana glanced briefly at Sam. A puzzled look came to her, but then she looked away into the distance. "Oh, Sam, what do you expect to find? We have the autopsy report, and we're not going to bring him back."

"Ana, I just told you. I have too many questions, and maybe I can find something that will settle my mind or help you."

"Help me? You can't help me. I'm alone. I've lost my son and my husband. All I have is this big house and memories." She took a deep cleansing breath. Then, as if she were no longer with Sam in the garden but in some faraway place, she whispered, "We must move on. Yes, move on." She once again stared into the distance, and then she turned her eyes directly to Sam's. "Of course, anything you want."

Ana's behavior was unsettling. She flipped from one emotion to the next. Her voice was strong one moment and a weak whisper the next.

Sam was beginning to wonder if Bill's death had truly been too much for her.

He took her hand. "There might be something in his desk. Maybe something from a lab or an oncologist. I'm not sure what I'm looking for. Honestly, Ana, I'm really conflicted. I don't like the autopsy results, and I don't like John Albright! There are simply too many irregularities." He caught himself again. He was too transparent and too blunt. He could no longer talk to Ana with the sincerity he had always been able to exhibit to her. She was too fragile.

"John Albright is not your problem, and you've indicated your disdain for him more than once." Ana seemed irritated with Sam, but then, just as quickly, she softened her tone. "You are a scientist. I see that you're searching for a tangible answer. But sometimes there are no clear answers. Sometimes you just must accept. You need to stop being so suspicious or angry with Dr. Albright. He really has been a great help to me. You're obsessing."

"I'm sure he has, and yes…maybe I'm consumed with this. I don't know, but I need to follow through with my search for any answer." Sam's words pleaded his case.

———————

Ana unlocked Dr. Bill Roberts's home office door. She told Sam that Dr. Roberts had, abnormally, locked his office the night before he died. Her husband did not live to see the next morning. She had just recently found the key in his bathroom. She said she thought little of it at the time but agreed that Sam might find something that her husband had locked away.

Sam thought, *and…maybe took to his grave.*

She added that she assumed it was to keep Julia, the housekeeper, from rearranging his papers that were piled at least a foot high on both sides of his desk.

Sam was stunned by how the office was in disarray, but tried desperately to not show it. "Ana," Sam said, "go about your business. I'm fine in here. I just want to see if Bill left anything that would give me a clue that he knew he was ill. You don't mind if I go through his papers, do you?"

"No, no, bless your heart…not at all. You're like a son. You can do whatever you want. In fact, I guess I really appreciate it. I was harsh with you outside. Anyway, sorting through these papers is going to be a daunting task, and I didn't want to throw away anything important. Take care of that for me, please, Sam. But tell me if you find anything of interest."

Sam acknowledged her concerns and sat down in the oversized leather chair. He ran his hand over the arms of the desk chair as if stroking his old friend. Inhaling a very deep breath, Sam thought he could smell Bill Roberts in the office. He took a stack of papers and began to explore their mysteries.

Hours passed, and Sam's eyes were tired of the small print without any consequential information, or at least without anything that he felt was pertinent to Dr. Bill Roberts's death. Then he opened a file folder that had been stapled closed across the top. There were yellow legal pad sheets inside. Some were folded, and others seemed ripped from the pad rather than carefully torn out. There were notes written in the margins in what Sam recognized as Bill Roberts's own handwriting. There were printed copies of a Wikipedia search. It was a list of terror attacks across the globe dating back to 1995.

Sean Smith was the first thing Sam noticed. Sam recognized the name as the US Foreign Service information officer killed in the 2012

Benghazi, Libya, attack. Under that, Dr. Roberts had written "F7TR3B, strategic defense initiative," and finally, in red ink, "Factor-7." He had written "James" in several places on the paper. The word "Justice" was handwritten in multiple places. Sam opened the second file folder and flipped through the pages. It was more of the printed internet search, but this time Bill had used a yellow highlighter. Sam saw "Paris massacre, 128 die in attacks, April 23, 2016; Boko Haram kill 33 Chad, kill 13 in Niger; Taliban suicide attack Kabul 2015; ISIL claim deadly attack on West Bank." Then he had written "Simon Reznick." Sam read: "November, 2001, Terrorist threat remains high." Dr. Roberts had underlined and highlighted the date. Sam knew it was the month and year that James was killed. The record of terrorist or Jihadist strikes went on and on, listing terrorists attacks through 2019, 2020, and to the present year. Sam became more confused as to the reason for so much research on terrorist attacks. Of course, if James had been killed in one of the strikes he had highlighted, then that made sense. But forty-five pages of listing attacks seemed excessive, even for a grieving father.

Another handwritten line popped out at Sam. It simply said, "Shadow government/Black Ops." The handwritten content in the margin was coded in what seemed to be a mathematical formula, perhaps a physics formula. Whatever it was, it was foreign to anything Sam Hawkins had ever seen. Suddenly, one line in the typewritten copy made sense to him. He read aloud to himself. "36.7995 N. 42.090E." It was clearly some sort of map coordinates, but he didn't know the location. Sam's mind went back to his navy days. It could be the start of a flight plan or just a destination plan. The faded pencil scribbles covered the front and the back of several pieces of paper. He could only make out a few of the numbers. He pulled out his cell phone and searched the coordinates: 34.482842N, 40472E and 30.1345N,

62.262663E. The first showed a location on the Syria-Iraq border, and the other was near the border of Iran and Afghanistan. Perhaps he was trying to pinpoint exactly where James had died. Why the interest in so many Islamic terrorist-ridden regions? He leaned back in the leather chair, trying to make sense of it all. Suddenly he heard loud voices and shouting coming from the other side of the house. He rushed out to find Ana sobbing in the foyer.

"Ana, what's wrong?" Sam asked.

"President Winger is dead!"

"What?"

"Fox News just had an emergency interruption, and they announced he was dead. Vice President Housier is about to speak." Ana turned up the volume.

"My fellow Americans, I come to you now with an extremely heavy heart. President Miles Nelson Winger was found dead in his residence of the White House at eleven thirty-four a.m. eastern time today. The initial suspected cause of death is an insulin overdose. Mrs. Winger is with their children, and we ask for prayers for her and the family. With a saddened heart, I wish to assure the American people that our government is doing everything possible to confirm the cause of his death. We do not suspect foul play. We are in complete control, with nothing for the American people or our allies to fear from domestic or foreign adversaries. I will be taking the oath of office and assuming the position of president of these United States this afternoon, but in the meantime, please do not fear. Our government is stable, and every possible precaution and appropriate action is being taken now to transition me from your vice president into the office of the president. As we learn more of the untimely and tragic death of our commander in chief, you will be informed. Excuse me now, but I have official duties to tend to. God bless President Winger and his family, and God bless America." Reporters shouted questions, but Vice President Housier walked from the podium and disappeared from the cameras. No more questions would be answered by anyone in the government at that time. The stunned and clueless news commentators and anchors repeated the same things that Sam had heard from the vice president. Nothing new was being told.

"What? Insulin overdose?" Sam wailed. "How is that possible? Doesn't the president have a physician or someone to administer his insulin, or at least prepare it? There must be safeguards in place to ensure safety with an injection. He's the president of the United States, for Pete's sake."

Ana sat weeping. "How much more can I take? James, Bill... Steven, and now our new president? We've had two presidents die back to back. How? How's that even possible in this country? Everything is taken from us!"

Steven was Bill Roberts's only brother. He was a few years younger than Bill. He had been killed in a multiple-car accident outside Arlington, Virginia, just six months earlier. Steven had been career military and at the time of his death was working at the Pentagon. Sam never knew exactly what he did or his official title. Bill had never gone into detail, and Sam had never asked. Why were all the Robertses dead in such a short time? The thought haunted him. And how did Ana cope? Sam put his arms around her. "We will be fine. The country will be fine." But Sam was beginning to doubt everything he heard from the news and all he had been told.

Major networks ran commentaries and reports throughout the day. But over the next few hours, nothing new was presented, and what the media had reported sounded incredible to Sam. Supposedly, the president had left a meeting in the Oval Office and had gone into the family residence of the White House. Per the sketchy reports, President Winger administered his midmorning insulin injection and was simply found dead twenty minutes later.

Sam leaned back on the couch. His thoughts were reeling. The previous president had suddenly died from a heart attack, but he was only fifty-five years old and supposedly in excellent health. Sam knew those things happened, and at that time, he thought little of it. But that day, Sam was sure that something was not right. Something was happening. It was as if someone was cleaning house. "All of this is pure crap," he whispered. "Somebody's keeping info from us." He turned to Ana. "I don't trust most of those Washington sons of bitches." He shook his head in disbelief. "Fucking liars. May God help us," he whispered.

CHAPTER FIVE

It was quite late when Sam finally got Ana settled down and in good hands with Julia. She would help Mrs. Roberts to bed and tend to her during the night. But Sam's situation was much different. He had to go home. He had called multiple times and always got Lauren's voice mail. He had given up about midnight. She hadn't called him, so it was clear that she wasn't concerned about him. The drive from Ana's Houston estate was easy at 12:45 in the morning. He made it to Clear Lake in less than thirty minutes.

The house was dark. The side door was unlocked, and the alarm, again, was not set. Sam ambled to the kitchen for a glass of ice water, mostly to cool his anger. *She's going to drive me crazy.* Then he huffed a laugh. "Short drive these days."

Lauren must be upstairs, Sam thought. *Surely, she's asleep at this hour.* He searched the upstairs bedrooms. It was a very large home, and she could have passed out almost anywhere. Sam felt certain she was home because her car keys were on the bedside table of the master bedroom. He hadn't pulled his Porsche into the garage. He was so tired that he avoided the long walk to the house and parked instead under the porte cochere. Therefore, he had not gone through the pool house. *That's where she must be*, he thought. Sam was rather indifferent about the thought of her there. Lauren spent many nights there, so she should spend another.

He had been lonely for too long. He pulled off his boxer shorts and slipped into the crisp, cold sheets. Sam felt isolated in his own bed even when Lauren was there. Frustrated from the mounting number of questionable events, Sam needed a bit of relief. He straightened out his penis and cupped his hand over his balls, holding firmly to both. He began to massage himself gently, getting the beginning of a self-generated erection. It felt good. He pumped gently at his penis. It wasn't a woman, it wasn't Lauren, but it would have to do for the night. Sam couldn't help but fantasize it was Lauren. They once had great sex. However, it had been a very long time. Sam was still a young man with normal needs, and neither his emotional nor his sexual needs had been met for a very long time. He fantasized on when Lauren would kiss him with open mouth, her tongue circling inside his mouth. She would kiss him down his neck and chest until she reached his hardened penis. She would suck hard, then quiver her tongue on the underside and move back to the head of his penis. Sam would be sent into near unconsciousness with pleasure. Lauren knew precisely when to slip his penis inside her lubricated body, and they would rotate back and forth, up and down, until they climaxed together. Sam released himself hard in his own hand and fell into a relaxed state of sexual euphoria thinking of the past. It was relief, but not satisfaction. As Sam drifted off to sleep, he heard the low rumble of thunder in the distance.

———————

He didn't know how many hours had passed when he was suddenly awakened by the crash of loud thunder. The bedroom was illuminated brightly with the lightning that preceded each clap. Startled at first, he sat up in bed. Lauren still was not there. He glanced at the clock. It was 4:19 a.m. Feeling the urge to urinate, Sam wearily found his way to his side of the bathroom. The crashes of the thunderstorm continued. He walked into Lauren's side of the bathroom and peered through the window that overlooked the pool and backyard. Strangely, there was little rain. The storm had begun to move south. Sam looked upward to see only a few streaks of light cross the distant sky, but as he looked back down toward the pool, he thought he saw something move. He wasn't sure what he saw in the incredibly dark yard. He dismissed it momentarily, picking up a towel that was on the floor. When he lifted himself back up, he saw a hand mirror on the counter. A white substance was assembled in neatly lined rows. A razor blade lay beside the rows of what he knew to be cocaine. He went into a rage. Lauren not only was drinking herself into a grave, she was doing coke! He knocked the mirror off the counter with one angry swipe of his forearm. "Fuck! Damn shit…" Sam shouted. "I'll be damned if she does cocaine in my house." He had to tiptoe out and around the broken mirror but couldn't avoid stepping into the white substance that sprinkled the entire bathroom floor.

Sam slipped on his boxer shorts and flip-flops and returned to the window, cringing at the broken mirror and white powder that littered the tile floor. "She can have the fucking seven years of bad luck. It's her fucking mirror!" Sam fumed with anger. What did he see outside the window? There were no lights and no music, but he heard faint muffled sounds. Not knowing exactly what he heard, he cautiously opened the window.

The voices became clearer yet were indistinguishable. Then he heard Lauren and a male voice. Sam began to shake and perspire. He was unable to see clearly from the window, but he could not grasp what little he could see. Lauren was in the pool with Bruce, the pool boy. Their naked bodies were now clearly visible in the moonlight that escaped between the broken storm clouds. Bruce had Lauren pulled closely to his bare chest. Lauren's body rested on the pool steps. Her neck arched back while Bruce caressed her face and throat. He ran his hands and head down to her breasts. Pulling her from the water and reclining her on the deck, he slid his face down her wet body until his head rested between her legs. Lauren secured him to her with one leg over his shoulder. She slithered into the water again. They writhed like two snakes; bodies entangled in rippling water that glistened in the dim light.

Sam froze, horrified at the sight, and then he vomited. His heart raced, and he was soaked in perspiration. His ears rang as he tried to breathe. Still sick, he slowly tried to gather his senses and shattered emotions.

Lauren and her young lover were amid their act, both unaware of their surroundings. Water splashed around them while their bodies moved in slow methodical motions. Lauren reclined on the top step, and Bruce knelt on the step below her. He then moved to the top step while he lifted her to sit on his lap. She moaned as he slipped his penis into her and rocked her body in motion with his own.

It was all clear now, and Sam saw every disgusting moment and action below. He could hear their heavy breathing and the erotic sighs of their ecstasy. His mind reeled, and his thoughts scattered in a million directions while he was left frozen in the dark bathroom.

———————

Sam rushed down the stairs, flipping on every light as he passed. Stopping momentarily at the kitchen door to breathe a strong breath for strength, he saw Lauren's breasts heave out of the water and her back arch as Bruce drew her closer to him.

The kitchen door was locked from the inside. There was no key in the lock. Sam jerked open the drawer by the sink and began to fumble frantically for the extra key chain. He was so angry that he considered killing both on the spot. He pulled a butcher knife from the block and squeezed the handle in the palm of his hand. His upper lip quivered, and his body shook. His breathing was rapid, and his heart pounded in his chest. Sam angrily slammed the knife blade into a cutting board that sat near him. He looked out the window above the sink as he searched the drawer. He again became nauseous as he had a perfect view of his wife and her young lover.

Bruce had pulled Lauren up as he stood to his feet, waist deep in water. Lauren's arms flew over her head; her hands grasped the stairs' handrail, securing her position, her legs wrapped around his waist while her pelvis tilted higher. Bruce held her buttocks with both hands as he obviously penetrated her deeply and forcefully again. His thrusts banged into Lauren's pelvis with such force that the water splashed outside the pool. She screamed with unbridled pleasure with each thrust.

Sam pushed the key into the lock and turned it. He could still see them as he cracked the kitchen door that led to the patio and pool. He gathered his strength and again took several deep breaths.

The two bodies clearly exhibited Lauren's execution of her adultery. Bruce let out a loud moan like some wounded animal. Lauren screamed and moaned from deep in her throat.

Sam froze for a split second. He had just witnessed his wife fuck another man in his own pool, and he had been too stunned, too confused, too everything, to stop it. The whole disgusting act had taken moments, but it felt like a lifetime had flashed before him. It was a hellish eternity, and Sam had been condemned to watch it.

Sam swung open the kitchen door to the patio. Lauren and Bruce heard it at the same time. Sam reached into the pool and grabbed Lauren by her long, wet hair and pulled her to the edge. Bruce scrambled to get out of the water but slipped on the sides, unable to get a firm hold. Sam grabbed him and with superhuman power pulled the man half his age and twice his strength out of the water and onto the pool deck.

"Stand up, you son of a bitch," Sam ordered. "Get your fucking ass up." Sam glared at Lauren. She was crouched on the edge of the pool, covering her naked body as well as possible with her folded arms. "And you…get up. Get your things and be out of this house by morning. I don't want to see your fucking face again. Ever! You fucking bitch!"

As the last words directed at Lauren spewed from Sam's mouth, Bruce had managed to get to his feet. Sam grabbed his arm with his left hand and threw a right punch in the middle of Bruce's face. Blood streamed from his nose and mouth, but he made no sound.

Sam bent over, grabbing his own bloody right hand. "Damn it. I've broken my fucking hand. Get out of here before I kill you, you stupid motherfucker." Bruce ran naked across the backyard like a scared rabbit. Lauren slowly got up and staggered into the house.

Sam stopped in the kitchen and wrapped his injured hand in a towel filled with ice. "I'm going to a hotel. I want you and your things out of here within twenty-four hours. You will hear from my attorney." His voice softened, and the sadness and disappointment filled his every word. "I knew we were having trouble, but this? This is even beyond you, Lauren." He grabbed his yesterday's jeans and a shirt from the laundry-room basket and tucked them under his arm. He shook his head and slowly walked to his car. Tears filled his eyes. It was too much to handle. Life was over as he knew it. Sam couldn't take any more. So much had happened in too few hours. So much for a lifetime had invaded Sam's mundane life. Suddenly he wished for that mundane experience. It was too much for one man to handle, even Sam.

He sat in the driveway for at least an hour. His hand was not broken, but his heart was. He had lost his best friend, unable to save his life. He had lost his wife. Where would he go? How would he do it? How would he move on with life? He wondered if he had a life to move from or to move to. How would he do anything? Sam was shattered, replaying each horrid scene of Lauren's infidelity in his head, over and over again. All he could think was how his life had been reduced to shambles and how few hours it had taken to happen.

At daybreak, Sam called the realtor. He would put the mansion on the market, and he would split the proceeds with Lauren. It was the only decent thing to do, he thought. They had had good years. Since they had no children, there would be no further need for payments to her. Texas didn't have alimony, so a settlement of property was fair and would be the finale to his marriage and that chapter of this life. He would split up the funds and be done with it all. Lauren had no source of income on her own, but she would be well set after the divorce. Sam could see it no other way. Anyway, he had no need for such a place, and he had loved her once—maybe he still did. But if Sam had learned anything in his forty-five years on this earth, it was that you can't go back. He would do what he had to do, and he would move on. Lauren was his past.

CHAPTER SIX

JULY 28

Two weeks had passed since Sam and Lauren's split. It had been less than a month since Bill Roberts's death. Sam had not recovered completely from Lauren's infidelity, but each day got a bit easier. Nor had he dismissed the unusual circumstances surrounding Dr. Bill Roberts's death, and he certainly had not forgotten the older doctor's deathbed ramblings. But immersion into hospital work had seemed to numb the pain and the nagging questions of each. The weeks had been filled with the same routine of treating trauma patients, many of whom could have avoided treatment except for their participation in illicit drugs and other unlawful activities. He had to treat the legal and the unlawful the same, but it was never easy. There was often a victim and a perpetrator in the same trauma unit. There were police, and there were loving families. Sometimes he found it hard to differentiate between the good and the criminal. But that wasn't his job. The blood ran red and the pain was equal, no matter the person's color, moral or immoral intentions, or economic position. The opposites were becoming a blur, and his dedication to trauma was waning.

Lauren was not contesting anything. Sam's lawyer said that both attorneys were close to finalizing the divorce, and it would be history within a couple of weeks. The summer had been a blur, a horrible, pathetic blur. Sam had secured a smaller house on a tiny island located on the mainland side of the Galveston Causeway. Tiki Island would now be his home and his new start. He had not even seen Ana Roberts in over a week. He decided that enough was enough and that it was time for a few days off. Sam would do a bit of investigative work and maybe take in a few rounds of golf or fish all night, if he wanted.

He called Ana.

"Hi, Sam. So happy to hear from you, darlin'. I need your help. Bill had a new will drawn. I need your help to decipher a few things and help me sort through his desk…and some more papers in his study that I found this morning. I want you to review things before I see our attorney. Do you have time to come over this weekend?"

"Of course. How about ten a.m. on Saturday."

"That's perfect. See you then. We'll have some brunch. Huh?"

"Yeah, that's great. Saturday then…see you, Ana."

Since the Robertses' son and Bill's brother had died, there were not many people left for Ana. She never spoke of her side of the family, and Sam had never asked. Sam began to realize that there were a lot of things he had never asked the Robertses, and even more questions had recently surfaced. Sam had been like a son to Dr. Roberts for over fifteen years, and the older doctor had been Sam's mentor and buddy. He blew off the questions that haunted him. It was only natural that he would assume the responsibility of helping Ana with the estate.

Julia promptly answered the door and directed Sam to Dr. Bill Roberts's study, where Ana was waiting.

"Coffee, Dr. Hawkins?"

Sam smiled and nodded agreeably. "Love some."

Sam entered Bill Roberts's office, where he had been two weeks or so earlier and at least a hundred times before that. It was different. Ana had cleaned off Bill's desk. It was starkly empty from his last visit. There were no more piles of papers, books, and journals.

"Hi, Sam, darlin'." Her Texas drawl was profoundly apparent. "I got rid of so much wastepaper. John was a neat freak. I came in here, and it was like a bomb had gone off. Don't have a clue what that was about...so unlike him. Papers on the floor, piles on the desk..." Tears flooded her eyes. "Bill never left things so messed up. His will had codicils and handwritten notes. His desk was full of papers with nothing but crazy words and numbers written on them. He must have just sat in here doodling. I didn't want to go to the attorney before you saw all of this. And that word and number seven...geez, Sam...it was everywhere." She bowed her head, so Sam couldn't see her expression, or perhaps her confusion.

Sam had not intended to involve Ana in any of his uncertainties. He figured he had said too much before, and it seemed that all it did was upset the widow. But she was directing him to find answers in Bill Roberts's paperwork. Sam already had his questions. Ana had a newfound interest in the cache of documents and files. He tried to brush off her new interest for what Bill's scribbles meant, but something about her tone and the questions she asked seemed odd. "Ana, I was in here a couple of weeks ago. It was messy, and there were piles of stuff, but not like you're describing. I did see something, 'Factor-7,' on a sheet but thought nothing of it. Sounds like a new perfume, like Chanel No. 5." Sam tried to laugh, but his little joke did not even warrant a smile. He continued. "I found one file that I have and will look over the rest of its contents this week." Sam paused and thought back to the handwritten papers. *What were the purposes of the latitude and longitude coordinates that Bill wrote?* "Who else has been in here?" he asked.

"I think Simon was in here the other day using the computer to call his daughter. He was Skyping or something. You know I have no idea about anything except simple email, and then I seem like a moron."

Sam glared at her. "You sure do trust that guy. I'm a bit amazed, Ana, how he has weaseled himself into your life, and you even let him into Bill's private things."

"First off, Sam, I didn't let him into Bill's private things, and secondly, I don't consider him weaseling in on me. Don't scold me, darlin'. He's a widower, and I am…" She paused. "We have had a few evenings together lately. It's lonely in this big house, and Simon has been a nice diversion. But that's the extent of it."

The afternoon was fading into dusk. Sam had spent half of the day going over things that made no sense but instead added more questions to his already lengthy list. Then he saw a computer-generated map. It was a map of the world, each continent and region on the continents colored in various shades of orange to yellow. "This is odd. What do you think of this?" Sam asked.

Ana shook her head. "I found something like that but threw it in the trash."

"Where's that trash?" Sam asked.

"There in the can by the desk."

Sam poured the trash onto the floor. He waded through the papers on the floor and proceeded to sit crossed legged, going through each sheet. There was another map with the same colors on it and handwritten notes. He began to read out loud. "Southeast Asia—third most active region in the world in terms of terrorist attacks. Philippines and Syria,

Iraq, Mosul, Lebanon." Sam looked up at Ana. "Was he planning on traveling? Just kidding, Ana. Of course, he wouldn't go to these places. I wonder what his interest was in these regions of the Middle East."

"Bill would most certainly not go to a terrorist hot spot," she said.

Sam turned over the map and continued to read. "Al-Murabitan-Southern Algeria/Southwestern Libya/Tunisia/Yemen. North Africa—AQIM—Segal, Mali, Algeria, Niger, Chad, Sudan, and Eritrea. Sounds like a geography lesson." Sam shook his head in bewilderment.

"Wait..." Ana unfolded another paper and handed it to Sam. "Look at this. What do you think of this?"

Sam read it out loud. "Bangsamoro Islamic Freedom Movement; Moro Islamic Liberation Front; the Movement for Unity and Jihad in West Africa, MUJAO; Boko Haram; Islamic Movement of Uzbekistan; Al-Qaeda; the Islamic Jihad Union; Eastern Turkistan Islamic Movement: Abu Sayyaf Group; al-Murabitan; Islamic State of Iraq and the Levant; ISL, al-Nusrah; ISIL; Al Qaida in the Islamic Maghreb; Hizballah; Taliban; ISIS...now this looks like a laundry list of terrorist organizations to me. Bill should have no need for this stuff either." Sam put down the sheets of rumpled papers. "I think I'll take more coffee now. Looks like a long read," he said, rubbing his forehead and eyes.

As Ana went to call Julia, the doorbell rang. Julia met Mrs. Roberts in the foyer, and both answered the door.

Sam heard a familiar male voice. It was Simon.

"Well, good evening, Ana, Julia. How are my pretty ladies today? I'm sorry that I didn't call first, but I saw these potted geraniums, and I had to get one for you. And, well, I bought one too. It will brighten my hotel room."

Julia took the plant from his hands, and Ana stroked one of the soft velvety leaves. "They are so pretty. Thank you for this, Simon. Won't you come in? Sam is here. I think you know him, right?"

Simon walked into the large office. Sam had now come to his feet and was stretching out the kinks from the sit on the floor. Sam held out his hand. "Nice to see you again, Simon. Forgive me, but I don't recall ever hearing your last name."

"It's Reznik. But I insist you always call me Simon."

Sam smiled graciously and nodded in agreement. Sam analyzed the man standing in front of him with intense scrutiny. He had been spending a lot of time with Ana, and he just showed up at her house unannounced. It seemed to Sam that Simon was taking a lot of liberties. That puzzled him. Perhaps Sam was just being overly protective of her, but then again, there was something about Simon that just made the hair on the back of his neck bristle.

Ana offered coffee to Simon, but he declined, stating that it was too late in the afternoon, and it would keep him awake.

"I know what we can do! I have two bottles left of that Bordeaux that you brought over after the service for Bill. I'll get Julia to open one now for us and another to breathe." Ana excitedly called for Julia. It was as if she was in desperate need of fun and diversion. Or maybe she wanted to leave Bill's office. Maybe she was also hoping the wine would bring Sam and Simon out as well.

"So, Simon, how do you know the Robertses?" Sam asked, almost blurting out the words.

"I met William…Bill, a few months back in New York, and we just instantly became friends. He invited me to Houston, and I spent time at their beach home in Galveston."

"Are you a US citizen or live here? I hear an accent," Sam said, wondering if he had phrased his question offensively.

"Yes. But I am from Israel. I was born in New York, but my parents moved to Israel in the fifties when I was three. So I am more Israeli than American."

Sam looked hard at the tall, slender man. He was not wearing his usual kippah. "And you still live in Israel?"

"That's correct. Seems you want to know more about me. You are leery of me with Mrs. Roberts, right? It's written all over your face." Simon smiled. "I assure you that I have no designs on Mrs. Roberts. Ana and I are just friends, and I felt she needed help after Bill passed away. I know how that feels. You see, my wife and only daughter were shopping near the West Bank two years ago. A suicide bomber grabbed Rachael, my wife, in the marketplace. The terrorist was a woman actually, from Iran, and she exploded herself, taking my wife with her. My daughter was seriously injured, losing both legs and…she is disabled for life…both physically and emotionally."

Sam's mind flashed to where Bill Roberts had written "Simon Reznick" next to a terrorist attack. "Simon, I can't tell you how sorry I am to hear that." Sam was suddenly ashamed of his suspicions. Obviously, Bill Roberts had been looking into Simon's wife's death. That could answer all the words and scribbles. Sam felt better about Simon and the massive internet searches in Bill's office. Mostly, things seemed to make sense for the first time.

Ana returned with a tray and three long-stemmed glasses. Julia followed behind with a bottle of red wine and a small tray of various cheeses and crackers.

"Allow me to pour," said Simon.

Ana handed him the open bottle. He poured the three glasses half full and began to swirl his in his left hand.

"Do you like my Israeli wine, Sam?"

"Yes, very much. Thank you."

"What are those papers you're studying?" Simon asked.

Sam had begun to warm to the stranger with a mix of curiosity and sympathy. He handed the sheets of paper to Simon. "Take a look. We found these in Bill's office. There are some strange things written, and for the life of me, I can't think of why he would have written them or even have had an interest in the subject matter."

Simon looked at the sheets of paper rather quickly and laid them on the coffee table. "There is a lot of news about terrorism and other trouble internationally, and I'm guessing that Bill was simply trying to get a handle on where it was. I would not think too much of it."

"Yes, you're probably right." Sam nodded his head in agreement, but he wasn't completely convinced.

They chatted leisurely for about an hour, and then Simon announced that he had a meeting and needed to leave. Sam took the opportunity to leave with him, so the two walked with Ana to the door. She handed the manila envelope that contained Dr. Roberts's last will and testament to Sam.

"Thank you, Sam, for looking at my Bill's final wishes. I will be going to the attorney on Monday, if you find nothing out of the ordinary."

Sam grinned and hugged Ana. "I'm sure Bill took care of things. I'm no lawyer, but I'm happy to look it over."

"And...Simon..." Ana started. "It's always good to see you. Please...both of you come around often. It's lonely now in this big, empty house."

Sam kissed her cheek, and Simon held both of her hands in his. The two men walked side by side to their cars.

Sam reached the Porsche before Simon got to his black Volvo. He beckoned Simon. "Simon, you never told me what you do for a living."

Simon lifted his head from opening the car door, and in a resigned but quiet reply, he said, "Mossad."

CHAPTER SEVEN

JULY 29

First thing the next morning, Sam googled the Israeli Mossad. If Simon worked for that intelligence agency, why had he hung around the Houston area for so long, and why did he loiter around the Robertses'? Simon, the odd scribbles on Bill's office papers, and the horrific manner that Bill had presented in the Emergency Department nagged at him. Dr. Roberts's obscure ramblings and what now seemed inevitably a cover-up by the hospital and coroner obsessed Sam.

He found Simon's name only in one place during his online search. Simon had been in the Israeli military and then became an agent with the elite Mossad. It said active duty in military and the agency from 1973 to 2002. There were a few honors mentioned and a short story about the death of his wife. If that was correct, Sam knew he was either retired or had resigned. That was not how Simon had sounded in Ana's front yard. Simon's response had a ring of intimidation, and Sam couldn't figure out why.

Everywhere he turned, he hit a wall of either inept or crooked people, and the thought of either repulsed the physician side of Sam. The hospital issue was unconscionable, but the forensics had been appallingly neglectful or delinquent of duties. He knew that the county was required to take skin and organ samples of any unusual death for study at the medical school. The Federal Laboratory housed curious death specimens as well as highly contagious bacteria and viruses. The research facility's sophisticated high containment of research specimens served as a critical resource in the global fight against infectious diseases. Certainly, someone would have considered Dr. Bill Roberts's death of critical importance.

JULY 30

Monday morning Sam hurriedly dressed and rushed to the Federal Laboratory, which should have been holding the last specimens of Dr. Bill Roberts. He had hit a dead end everywhere else, but he hoped the med school and Global Reference Center for Emerging Viruses and Arboviruses had the specimens. If so, he might just get his answer. He lied to the lab tech who was armed to the max with protective gear. He told her he needed to enter the cold pathology laboratory. Sam dropped a few names and added that he had graduated from UT Galveston Medical School. He told her he was in the research department of the Institute for Infectious Diseases and Immunity. He handed her his physician's license for the State of Texas along with other forms of ID. There were several long forms to complete, and she made a call to the central office, who ran a check on Sam. He passed the initial screening. After he signed all the forms and a register, a photo was taken, and he was fingerprinted by a touch-screen computer. She led him to the area, where he was to put on a full hazard bio suit. He precisely followed her instructions, knowing full well he could be denied entry if he made a single mistake.

"So this is where the cytology slides are stored?" Sam asked.

"Some of them, yes, sir. Each box is labeled and kept at a certain temperature behind the glass doors of the freezer boxes."

The specimens were arranged by year, then categorized by alphabetical order and finally by month. They walked down aisles of boxes in the frigid room. Sam saw where smallpox, Ebola, Marburg, and MERS viruses were stored. The lab was always to be prepared to study dangerous pathogens that could be weaponized, the young woman told him as they passed the highly restricted areas. The laboratory was a dangerous place if ever the wrong person were to be admitted or if an accidental spill or exposure were to occur.

Sam and the lab tech located the proper shelf. She opened the sealed freezer, and a blast of cold steam billowed out. There were clear boxes with sealed vials, petri dishes, glass slides in sterile cases, clear bags with what would have held tissues samples, and a small label that read "William Walker Roberts, MD, DOB 12/4/50. It then showed the date of his death.

Sam pulled one of the boxes from the shelf. He could see clear bags, each with a white label. But there was nothing in them. Then he pulled out one of the clear sealed petri dishes. It was empty as well. The glass sides appeared to be completely sterilized and replaced on the shelf completely void of specimens or tissue of any kind.

Sam looked at the lab tech. He held out his hands and shrugged silently, as if to ask her why all the specimens were gone.

"Perhaps someone has checked these out for a project of study. But it is odd that every specimen is gone, and the boxes and bags were left empty." She began to replace the empty specimen cases.

Sam's eyes grew angry. "Yes, I'd say it is more than odd. So all this for empty bags? Where would I get info that it was checked out and by whom?"

"Anyone in or out is on the video security system, and they have to sign in and sign out, just like you."

"Isn't it true that there are more stored viruses and bacteria samples here than perhaps any other place, short of Atlanta and maybe DC? Seems there would be some procedure in place that when something is removed, something saying what is taken and by whom would be put in its place. Kinda like we do with medical files."

"Dr. Hawkins, of course there's protocol! I don't control the security, but I don't know of any time that there's been a breach."

Sam gathered himself and brushed off the anger. "Yes, of course you aren't responsible. But I assure you, *someone* is."

The main office of the chairman of Elevated Risk Containment Laboratory Operations was a short walk away, and Sam made it in record time.

"I want to see Whitten," he announced.

The older, stout woman at the front desk immediately detected an angry man, and her fear was evident. "What can I do for you, sir?" she asked timidly.

"I'm Dr. Samuel P. Hawkins from St. Peters Surgical/Shock and Trauma Unit. I need to see Dr. Whitten immediately."

"Dr. Whitten is on a leave of absence," replied the secretary.

Sam took a couple of steps toward the closed door to the chairman's office. "Well, who then is running this show?"

"Dr. Andres Rodriguez is in charge while Dr. Whitten is away."

"Then I will see him. He knows who I am," Sam said.

"Yes, sir. Allow me to see if he is available."

"I beg your pardon, ma'am. I didn't ask if he was available. I said I have to see him right now."

She froze in her tracks. Then she backed away from Sam and moved to the closed door that led to the chairman's office. "Yes, sir!" She cracked the door, pushing it open just far enough to allow her head to poke through. "Dr. Rodriguez, there is a Dr. Hawkins from St. Peter's here to see you."

"Why, show him in." His Mexican accent was clearly distinguishable even through the office door. "Well, Dr. Hawkins, so very nice to see you. It's been quite a while. What has it been…the medical conference in San Diego five years ago, right? What may I do for you today?" The bushy gray-haired man held out his large hand to greet Sam.

"Rodriguez, this isn't a social call. I know you heard that Bill Roberts died July fifth. I was the attending physician, and he presented with some very ominous symptoms…symptoms that your department should know about. My understanding was that some specimens and blood samples came here to the med school and Federal Lab for study. I know I might not have had the right, but I got one of your lab techs to get me into the laboratory, and to me, it seems pretty important that I did. Actually, it was incredibly easy for me to gain access, and that equally alarms me, but that's for another day. I wanted to see the samples. I wanted to see whatever results the school's research had come up with. Well, nothing's there. All the samples—the specimens—are all gone. There are the bags and the trays and his name, but nothing else. How do you explain that?"

The older doctor leaned on his desk, rubbing his forehead. He mumbled something derogatory in Spanish. "I can't."

"What do you mean, you can't?"

"Just what I said. They must have been checked out by some group. Maybe studying them. I don't know every time someone starts a study."

Sam glared at his colleague. "You mean to tell me that with the terror threats and the viral pandemic that…thank God…we barely survived…ravaging our country in every way…that someone has been able to get in and out of the labs without you, the head honcho, knowing?"

"It's not that simple, Sam. Please sit down." Dr. Rodriguez pulled out the chair and motioned for Sam to be seated. "There is a chain of custody, but I don't see each and every one." His accent became more evident with each word.

The story just didn't hold water, Sam thought. Dr. Roberts had died of some bizarre illness, but no one at the hospital or county or CDC had made an effort to talk to Sam. But someone had thought to take Dr. Roberts's specimens for study? There would have been no reason for anyone to want to study something that no one thought important. No one seemed to care when it happened, and no one had cared during the days that followed.

"If I find it is a breach, then the proper people will be notified."

Sam shuddered. Huitt had used the same phrase when challenged about how the hospital had handled Dr. Roberts's death.

"I mean, if there was a breach—and I'm not saying there was—we would need to keep it under wraps so it didn't turn into mass hysterical behavior with the public. The media would make it out to be another cover-up like in China. Do you have any idea what this could do to the medical school or the vital research we do here at the Federal Lab if it got in the hands of some radical journalist?" He paused. "But that is not going to happen, because I am quite certain that it is not a breach in security. Some group is studying them. You'll see."

"Sir, with due respect, do you know what would happen if a virus got into the hands of some radical wannabe terrorist?" Sam paused, calculating his words. "Do you have any idea what it could do to the population if a virus or something from those labs was allowed into the general population? We certainly would then be talking about a real pandemic where millions die."

"Let's not go that far, Dr. Hawkins. I'm looking out for the university. Your university, as I recall. You don't have a dog in this fight. Go back to your business, and I'll take care of mine."

"You are an inept, foolish man, Dr. Rodriguez. Either you're hiding the truth from me or something is very wrong. And as much as I hate being lied to, I find the thought of your lack of concern with such a serious matter even more troubling. I'm taking this to the top."

The director glared at Sam. "And if you do, Doctor, you will not be happy with the outcome."

"Is that a threat?"

"Not at all. It's just a fact. There's nothing here of interest. Go home and tend to your own business."

With that, Sam stormed out of the chairman's office. He was so infuriated that his eyes began to tear and blur. He had to stop and gather himself. "Impossible," he whispered. "Utterly preposterous and impossible." *Go home and tend to my own business? What the hell?* He focused on the doors to the outside without speaking or acknowledging anyone on his way to the parking lot. Getting into his car, he was oblivious of his surroundings, too stunned and confused to see the dark-haired woman standing beside the Porsche. He heard a knock on the passenger-side window.

"Dr. Hawkins?"

Sam looked up to see her standing at the window, gesturing for him to open it and talk. She had a worried furrowed line above her brow, yet she was stunningly beautiful. Sam rolled down the window and unlocked the door. The lady, dressed in hospital scrubs with white pelicans printed all over them, opened the door.

"May I talk to you?" she asked.

"Sure, get in," Sam said.

"I'm Dr. Rainee Arienzo."

Sam detected an Italian accent.

"Dr. Hawkins. I need to speak with you soon, but not here and not now. I know about Dr. Bill Roberts. He was an acquaintance from several years back, when he visited me at St. Paul's Hospital in Naples. He came to see my research on a new virus that I accidentally uncovered in a patient from the Congo. It was like nothing anyone had seen. I think I have some information that would be interesting to you. But I may be watched. I think you might be as well."

"What? Why would we be watched?" Sam asked.

"Dr. Hawkins, I can't be sure. I really can't be sure of anything. But I know there's something going on, and Dr. Roberts knew what it was. He called me two weeks before he died. He asked me to come see him. I met with him July third, and the next thing I knew, he had died. Bill told me something that I need to discuss with you. I followed you here so I could introduce myself. I will be in touch. Don't say anything to anyone, and don't make yourself a target."

"What are you saying? This is crazy," Sam stammered.

"Dr. Hawkins, you will have to trust me on this. I will be in touch before the end of this week. I'm waiting on some information to arrive that we must review together." She quickly exited the Porsche and got in a light-blue older-model sedan. She backed out of the parking lot, leaving Sam stunned and perplexed.

CHAPTER EIGHT

AUGUST 1, 6:45 A.M.

Sam's cell phone rang. He fumbled in the bed to find it lying next to his head.

"I'm not calling too early, am I, Sam?" Ana asked.

"No, I'm up. Well, am now." He laughed. "Had to get up to answer the phone. Glad you aren't the hospital." He laughed again. "What's happening? Are you all right?"

Ana giggled. "You're in a good mood."

"Gotta be. No alternative," Sam said. "What's up?"

"You never called me. I postponed my attorney appointment. I called you several times, but it went straight to voice mail. I was worried about you. Anyway, it's been almost a month since Bill passed, and I really do need to finalize his affairs and probate his estate. I guess that's the steps, as I'm not the only heir. I think he's leaving some funds to the research lab at UT Med."

"Ahhh, man…Ana, I'm sorry. I'm fine. It's been a tough few days. It's been a tough month, for that matter. But no excuses. I'm so sorry. I got tied up with urgent matters, and I haven't even looked at the will. Honestly, with all I'm doing, I just plain forgot."

"Sam, I'm so sorry to bother you with this," Ana said sadly.

"No, Ana, I'm the sorry one. I promised you that I'd do that. Give me a couple of hours, and I'll call you back."

"I'm glad you're keeping busy. You've been unhappy for some time. I think you need a woman," Ana said.

Sam huffed. "Can't even think of that." He shook his head, but no one was there to see his frustration.

"Well, this old woman thinks you should. I know some very nice ladies. Just go out and have a few laughs. It would be good for you. Call me."

Sam slowly got out of bed and poured a cup of already-brewed coffee from the machine in his bathroom. He stepped into the shower, took a quick one, and dressed in record time. He still had one more day off and reluctantly knew that half of that time would be consumed with the lengthy last will and testament of Dr. Roberts. His conversation with the new chairman at the lab plagued him. What did he mean when he said that Sam would not be happy with the outcome? Sam knew there were multiple infractions happening, starting at St. Peter's and leading to the Federal Laboratory. But he had nowhere to turn and not enough information to tell anyone without causing new panic issues. He tried to file it away in the back of his brain for the time being.

The will, for the most part, showed nothing unusual or anything that Ana should question. Bill had multiple properties, bank accounts, bonds, stocks, and personal loans out to various people. Each loan had a specific repayment date and interest percentage listed beside the original loan amount. Sam figured they were medical students. Suddenly one name came up that Sam recognized: Rainee Arienzo, MD. Bill had loaned her $50,000.00 at... what...no interest and without any repayment specifications? Why would Bill even list the debt as income to Ana if there was no income to be had?

Sam read the will three times, and the only thing he questioned was the loan to the Italian doctor. He thought long about the $50,000.00. It was probably totally innocent, but it was listed so differently from the other loans. So Ana would not become alarmed or think Bill was having an affair or that there was something nefarious going on, Sam told her of the loan. But he lied, and it took all his strength to tell her that he knew Dr. Arienzo and that Bill was funding research for her. Anyway, Sam thought, what other reason could it be? And if it was anything else, it should be buried with Bill!

AUGUST 3

Thursday morning at the hospital cafeteria, as Sam was getting coffee, a young woman moved closer to him in line.

"Hey, Dr. Hawkins," she said coyly.

"Hi, Brenda. Please, its Sam."

"Sa…mmm, OK." She drew out the name. "I like that. I was thinking…ahmm…I'm a pretty good cook, and…well, I was thinking… maybe I'd do some shrimp fettuccini tomorrow night. Nothing fancy. Want to come over for a casual dinner?"

Sam stood bewildered for a moment, unable to remove his eyes from the brown pools that held on to his gaze. "Well, Brenda, it's been a long time for me. I'm not even divorced yet."

"Sam, it's dinner."

He had not been out, nor had he eaten anything but takeout for a while. Hesitantly, he responded. "OK. Sounds good." As soon as the words left his lips, he began to regret accepting the invitation. He was unaccustomed to being with anyone but Lauren, and for some reason it just felt wrong.

"It's a date, then."

Sam smiled a childish grin as he took his coffee and muffin. "Uh…OK… it's a date?" He smiled. It had been over fifteen years since he had "a date."

Oddly, Sam found himself looking forward to the evening with Brenda.

Saturday came. He put on a starched white button-down shirt and freshly laundered jeans. He slipped on his light-brown ostrich boots and rinsed one last time with mouthwash. Things that were all so new for him suddenly became peculiarly refreshing.

———

"Hi, Sam," Brenda said as she opened the door to her small but attractive condo. "Dinner will be ready in a few. Wine or a cocktail?"

"Wine, please."

Brenda went to the kitchen to pour his wine, and Sam stood astonished at her beauty. He had never noticed how attractive she was before. She was always dressed in rather dowdy polyester skirts and a blazer. She generally had her hair pulled up in clips, and she came to work without much makeup. Now she was quite a different vision. Dressed in a dark-pink low-cut and sleeveless sundress tightly cinched at the waist, her shapely body was on full display. Her legs, tanned from the Galveston sun, glistened in the dimly lit room. She was barefoot.

He took a breath. "Nice table." He hated that statement. Nice table? Geez, he could do better. "I mean, this looks wonderful."

Brenda smiled. She said nothing, seemingly to control the whole situation.

The table was set with two plates with folded linen napkins on top. Two candles flickered, and Sinatra was singing a romantic song quietly in the background.

"You like Sinatra?" she asked, tossing the salad.

Sam paused. What had he gotten into? *Before my time...of course.* Sam laughed at himself. "Ah, yeah. Who doesn't?"

She turned and stared into Sam's eyes. She made a low sigh. "He's the sexiest man I can think of, and he was dead when I first heard him."

"Hum…well, you're younger than I, my dear." Sam chuckled.

"Only in years."

Sam's mouth rose on one side, and he huffed out a questionable laugh. *So, what did that mean?*

Throughout the dinner, Brenda would sip her red wine and allow it to sit on her lips. Then she would slowly and sensually lick it off the bottom lip, then the top lip.

Sam wanted to think she was being coquettish, but it came out extremely sexy. No, he thought. This is erotic. He then understood the "only in years" statement.

"The shrimp fettuccini was really great. How did you learn to do that? It rivals any fine restaurant." Sam wiped his lips and set his napkin to the side of his plate. "Yeah, that was great."

"Dessert?" she asked.

"Oh…I'm just stuffed. Thinking not, but…Brenda, do you have something special? I wouldn't want to spoil your plans."

"A little cheesecake…that's all. And honestly, I bought it."

"In that case, save it. You eat it tomorrow."

Brenda stood from her chair and walked behind Sam's chair. She touched his shoulder and then bent down and blew lightly on the back of his neck. "Dance with me," she whispered.

Sam stood and reached out for her. "I warn you, I'm no Fred Astaire."

"Who?" she whispered in his ear.

"I mean I'm not a great dancer. Astaire was a dancer long before I was born, but great," Sam said in a less generational-gap manner.

"Don't worry; I know how to lead." She motioned for them to move to the sofa. Brenda moved closer to Sam, pressing her breasts to his chest. She put her lips on his neck and whispered, "Maybe we can make our own dessert." Without another word, Brenda loosened the tie around her waist and slipped the straps off her shoulders. The dress appeared to fall in slow motion down her naked body. She started to unbutton Sam's shirt and reveal his bare chest in the candlelight.

He took a deep breath. "Brenda." He cleared his throat. "What are you doing?"

She moaned but said nothing and then began to kiss his neck and face, running her tongue up and down in a circular motion. She ran her wet tongue down his neck and chest two or three times. Each time the moisture got heavier and warmer. Brenda took Sam's right hand and held it to her breasts, helping him knead them. She threw back her head and moaned erotically. Using her left hand to unbuckle Sam's jeans and with her right hand holding his hand to her breast, she started a descent down his body. She pulled his pants down, and they crumbled at his knees. She crouched on the floor; Sam's manhood was fully exposed.

"Brenda, I'm not sure this is what we should be doing. Really, Brenda, I'm…ah, shit…" Sam's body became tense with excitement.

She ran her tongue down his bare chest and into his groin. She touched his penis with her left hand.

Sam flinched and let out a low moan of pleasure. He was not about to stop her now.

She secured his now-firm balls in her right hand. With one small move, Brenda inserted Sam's penis into her mouth and began to move her tongue up and down, around and around, concentrating on the tip of his penis. As Sam's penis got harder, Brenda sucked harder. She moved up and down, rotating her tongue on the head of his manhood and then its underside. She put the entire penis in her mouth and gave it several very strong pulls with her mouth, always tickling the head with her tongue.

"Oh, baby…get on me. I'm gonna cum in your mouth," Sam whispered.

"No, I want to taste you. Cum, baby. Feel the pleasure. Cum in my mouth."

Sam pulled her closer, caught up in the moment. His back arched, bringing her body next to his. With a much-needed release, Sam groaned and filled Brenda with what she had asked.

"Ahhhh, baby," Sam moaned.

"Yum…" Brenda moaned deep within her throat. She then licked her lips and moaned again.

Sam leaned his head on the back of the sofa. He took several deep breaths. "Wow. Shit, baby! You blew my mind!" He then looked down to see her sitting on the floor in front of him. She had her legs bent at the knees and spread as far as humanly possible. She stabilized herself by leaning back on her left elbow and a throw pillow. She had three fingers inserted into her vagina and was rapidly massaging her clitoris. Her hips rose and fell as her fingers vibrated around inside of her.

Whatever turns her on, Sam thought. He watched her with a mixed sensation.

As she moaned and climaxed herself, she leaned forward and held on to Sam's penis and started to try to sit on top of him.

Sam gently pushed her to the side. He had been sent into ecstasy, but something about her had suddenly sickened him. The sight of her masturbating in front of him was more than he expected and honestly something he had never experienced except in frat house triple-X porno films. On the one hand, it turned him on, and on the other, it disgusted him. His senses were rattled. He felt like a prude, but what she had done to herself and for his viewing did not make him want to make love to her. Something about the display on the floor just didn't sit well with him. Nonetheless, he was the usual gentleman. "Ah,

Brenda. I prefer to satisfy a woman. I'm sorry, but I can't get it up right now. It takes an old man like me a few minutes to go again. You're just too good at that. You got me too excited, and it's been too long. Sorry I couldn't last."

"Well, spend the night, and we'll see how it goes."

Sam caught his breath. She had taken him to the heights of sexual pleasure. But he did not want to spend the night. Truthfully, although she had been incredibly good, she was now pushy and someone he had no desire to be around. "Brenda," Sam said, "this is all so new for me, and it's so fast. I'm no prude, but this is a bit much tonight. I mean," he stuttered, "not that it's not wonderful, and you're a beautiful lady… but I'm not ready for this. I'm not ready to spend the night with you or anyone. Geez, I didn't think I was ready for what just happened." He took a deep breath, stumbling over his words and not sure what to say. "Damn, you're good."

"Damn, I'm good?" she shouted. "Is that all you can say? Well, damn right, I'm good. And you'd do well to find another like me… Doctor!"

Sam raised an eyebrow to her verbal lashing. "No offense, Brenda. It's not you. It's me. I've just separated, and I'm not even divorced yet. I'll call you," Sam said, hurrying to put on his pants and button his shirt. But he knew he would never call.

"This is not what I expected from you," Brenda snapped. "I had plans for us."

Sam looked at her, pausing to gather his words. "I thank you for everything. This is not what I need now, and Brenda, I'm certainly not what you need."

Brenda slammed the door hard behind Sam. He stood in the hallway for a moment contemplating what he had just done. Damn, she was definitely good.

The next day at the hospital, Brenda didn't look Sam in the eye. He felt like a dog. She had given him the ultimate sexual experience, and he had shunned her. But he couldn't help it. It just was not what he wanted. But he had to admit that it was a boost to his otherwise deflated ego. It also was a great diversion from the issues that haunted him night and day. And if he ever just wanted a damn good blow job… he scolded himself for such a chauvinistic thought. He heard later that morning that she had asked for a transfer from Huitt's office to the Admittance Office on the other side of the medical center.

CHAPTER NINE

AUGUST 4

Sam was reviewing charts at the nurse's station when he was told there was a call on line five for him.

"This is Dr. Sam Hawkins," he said.

"Dr. Hawkins, this is Dr. Arienzo. I would like to see you today if possible."

"Well, yes, I think that's possible. I'll be free about seven o'clock tonight. Does that work for you?"

"Yes, that's fine. I want to meet in a very public place."

"I know a little oyster bar near the Strand. It's generally packed. Seven forty-five OK? I'll text you the address—or shall I pick you up?"

"No, thank you. I have a car. Please text me. I will be there at seven forty-five sharp."

Sam arrived a few minutes before the female doctor. He located a table with only two chairs near the window and as far as possible from the front door.

"Hello, Doctor," Sam said happily.

"Hello, Doctor." She slightly smiled, but her face remained serious. "Thank you for meeting me. I don't think you will feel quite as jovial when I tell you what I need to say. This is not a social meeting," she said intensely.

Sam recognized her nervous demeanor and tried to relieve the apparent first-meeting tension.

"May I call you Rainee?" Sam asked. "I wish you'd call me Sam. You can't have a bottle of wine without calling someone by their first name."

She smiled a belabored grin. "Of course, Sam."

"Wine? Let me pour. I have a dozen oysters Rockefeller coming," Sam said.

"Thank you, Sam, but I need to get to the subject of this meeting."

"OK. Shoot."

Dr. Arienzo took a deep breath and a sip of her wine. She began to speak rapidly, and each word came out faster than the one before. "I think Bill Roberts died from a manufactured infection. I think he did that because he knew there was no other way to get the information out about what was happening, and I think, perhaps, he sacrificed himself for the good of many."

Sam put his glass on the table and narrowed his eyes. "What did you say? That's insane. What the hell are you saying?"

"Sam, I told you the other day that Bill had called me in Naples. I'm good at what I do. That isn't a boast; it's a fact. Bill knew that. He knew I had studied the disfigured corpse of a man from the Republic of the Congo several years ago. He died while in Naples, and I was assigned to review his death. I found a virus that was like nothing I had ever seen or could find in any journal or textbook. Years ago, Bill was just interested in what I had found, but just before his death, his interest in the virus had changed. He knew what it was. Bill told me of a plan…a clandestine, horrific plan. I was going to do some research and follow up with him. But he died at your hospital before that happened. I think he knew you would help."

"Help what? Help how?"

"He apparently trusted you and knew that you were an honest man who would follow through on what needs to be done."

"Oh. Man…what is this crap?" He was about to call her some whacko name but held his tongue.

"I waited for a dear friend to retrieve some documents from my home and send them to me. Now that I have my father's files and my own on the African man—my proof—I can tell you what I know. Bill knew of a sinister plan. I don't know from whom or how, but he knew a lot. Apparently, from what Bill said, these men, and maybe women, among others now crisscrossing the globe, are all ex-something. Maybe CIA, FBI, MI6, Mossad, KGB—that sort of thing. But all have gone rogue. He said not to trust anyone. There are people outside their governments, from five to seven allied nations. They are highly trained people who will be deployed to infiltrate into the deadliest terrorist organizations. This cadre will carry or release, in some manner, new bioweapons on terrorist organizations. Apparently, this bio-germ kills quickly. I'm sure that Bill was infected with this secret pathogen, and I think he very possibly did this to himself so you would become a part of my search for the answer. Even in death, he needed an ally."

Sam leaned forward in his chair and stared straight into Dr. Arienzo's brown eyes. "I'm sorry; I don't know you, and I'm just as skeptical of what you're saying as I would be of any stranger on the street. No offense, Doctor, but you're talking doomsday conspiracy craziness." Sam shuddered, trying to dismiss her claims. But there was a ring of possible truth to her tale.

"You must trust me," she insisted. "I've been involved in this… or at least knowing there was indeed a huge conspiracy…if you wish to call it that…for over seventeen years. Your September 11 was not the start date of this plan, but my father alerted me of it shortly after that horrible event. I was still in medical school. I just didn't know the details, and honestly, until I heard from Bill, I wondered if what I had been told years ago was real or even valid any longer. It was all too fantastic to be true. So I know how you must feel. When Bill contacted me, I knew it was real and the plan was going into fast motion. It was getting ready to be launched."

"Launched? What?" Sam asked, fearing the answer.

"It is my understanding from Bill that this is a plan to eliminate terrorism and entire groups or ethnicities. From what I have been told, it's ethnic cleansing on the largest scale ever known to mankind."

"If what you're telling me is true, my whole trauma team was exposed to Bill's blood. Geez, everyone at St Peter's and everyone they have been around have been exposed. Is that what you're telling me?"

"You followed protocol for hazardous substances, I trust."

"Yes, we did," Sam said empathically. "But my glove was nicked."

Rainee raised an eyebrow. "Bill said that a cocktail of several morphed elements can stop the bacteria/virus from infecting people and that a doctor by the name of Albright, among a few others, has that cocktail…the countermeasure, if you will. He called it a bacteria/virus."

"Who? Albright?" Sam shouted.

"Don't yell, Sam, please!"

"Sorry. Who did you say had what cocktail?"

"Yes, a doctor by the name of Albright." She opened her eyes wide. "May I please continue?"

"Yes, please do. I know the bastard."

"You know Albright?" She leaned toward Sam.

"Sure do, and he's a piece of work—no, he's a piece of shit. Excuse my vernacular, but little else describes him."

Rainee remained silent for a moment, analyzing Sam's expression. "Well, that might put a new spin on everything. Anyway, for some reason, I don't think any of your team or you are at risk. I don't think Bill would have intentionally put you at risk. And there was something else he told me. Something to do with persons with specific DNA, but Bill never was able to tell me more about that." She paused and stared at Sam, who was giving her a disingenuous smile.

"This is not funny," she snapped.

"This would be the kind of sick practical joke that John Albright would do. He set you up to do this to me, right?" Sam sneered.

Rainee took a deep breath and then slowly exhaled. Her face turned rosy, and her nostrils flared. "no! I said this is no joke. And I do not even know John Albright. You had better listen to me, Dr. Hawkins!"

Sam focused on her anger and reined in his skepticism. "All right. Tell me more."

She took another breath and quickly exhaled. "The pathogen, whatever breed of germ it is, might only be effective to those with a certain DNA genome. It's supposedly a resistant bacterial variant that has been exposed to a manufactured virus—the mutagen, if you will. All I know about the bacterium is that it is the house that holds the virus. That is the uniqueness of this pathogen. If it is like other viruses, once it has a host, it replicates or clones its own DNA. Bill said it's a virus, but he did not know the gene sequence. The virus replicates using a DNA-dependent DNA polymerase in sets of seven. Also, it has something to do with gene mutations. Bill knew all this and couldn't keep silent and allow such madness. He said his time was limited."

Sam shook his head. "If this has even a smidgen of truth, then whatever happened to 'Do no harm'? These are physicians, medical doctors." He found himself repeating *seven* in his head.

Rainee nodded and continued. The incubation period is six to twelve hours, according to a letter I got from Bill. So that also tells me that you and your staff are not in any danger. Bill said he would get back to me, but he died first. He mentioned something about a safe and then mentioned Mexico. He said I needed the documents inside."

"This is an insane amount of knowledge or nonsense. Why in hell would he tell you this and not me or someone in government? How do I know you're telling the truth?" Sam's anger was obvious. But he didn't know if he was angry because she was telling him such incredible things or if he partially believed it.

"You don't have a choice. Bill Roberts reached out to you when he could, even if on his deathbed. I am reaching out to you now. He told me that I was to not trust anyone but you, and together we should not trust anyone else."

Sam held her gaze. "How was his time limited? Did he say?"

"No, but that statement has stuck in my mind. Two days after he said that, he was dead."

Sam shook his head. "This is incredible stuff." He took a sip from his glass.

Rainee waited for Sam's reply or reaction. He said nothing, but she could see him carefully processing what she had told him. "Maybe he died so you would know."

Sam slapped his hand on the table. "This is insane. He died so I... so I would know? This is utter insanity! You believe in Bigfoot and Nessie too, right?"

Rainee frowned and looked around the room. "I'll ask you again. Do not make a scene. I don't know who might be watching us." She shook her head in frustration. "I realize it sounds like insanity, but I assure you this is real. This is so real that I'm personally terrified of the consequences. I don't know a timeline or the people in this sick biowarfare plan. But I know one thing: Bill wanted you to know."

"Then why didn't he tell me? He didn't have to die to get my attention," Sam said angrily.

Rainee shook her head and shrugged. "I don't know. Perhaps he was going to tell you."

Sam placed both hands on his forehead and rubbed them past each temple into his hair. "Well, I'm very skeptical."

Rainee ignored his statement. "I know this must have taken years to develop, and the stockpile of vaccine or whatever it is even longer. This didn't just happen yesterday. This has been in the works for many, many years."

Sam stared at her with something between anger and perplexity. "I still think this is incredibly crazy, and I don't know whether to call the authorities and have you arrested or committed."

"Dr. Hawkins..." She stood up. Fire flashed in her dark-brown eyes. "I have tried to be as honest as I can with you. I have told you everything I know. You saw Bill Roberts die. Can you tell me what killed him? Do you know someone who can figure out what killed him? Can you answer any of these questions? I'm begging you. Listen to me! You fell into this on purpose, I feel sure. Bill knew you would follow up. Perhaps you were not to become involved at first, but now you are, and for some strange reason, I think Bill thought he could entrust this to me and apparently to you. But it seems that Bill's choice in *you* was wrong. Good night, Doctor!"

Sam's eyes glazed over. "Please sit down."

"Only if you will think about what I'm telling you. This is real, and time is wasting while I argue with you about its validity." She pulled the chair out slowly and sat down.

Sam sighed, almost resigned to her story. "Bill died over a month ago. I'll grant you that it was definitely a bizarre case. A lot of other innocent people could be at risk if what he had was contagious. Bill would not have been so reckless. I knew Bill very well."

Rainee remained calm. She leaned closer to Sam and lowered her voice to just louder than a whisper. "It's possible that innocents can be affected now, but again, I don't think so. He said it's targeted."

Sam chugged half a glass of wine. He collected his thoughts as Dr. Arienzo stared at him for an answer. "So who or what is pulling the strings in this operation?"

"I don't know that answer," she said resolutely.

"Then if you don't know who's in charge, who is involved, and who to trust, then what the hell can we do to stop it? We don't even know what we're dealing with…a bacterium…a virus…that attacks DNA? Whose DNA? And it mutates genes? It's absurd to think that you and I can stop something that…what? Multiple governments are planning?" Sam was raising his voice with each word.

She slowly spoke the next sentence. "Not governments, but crazy people within governments…rogues. Madmen from governments. Scientists in labs with reckless disregard for human life. You…need to know something…else."

Sam leaned back in his chair. "For God's sake, what else?"

"The reason I wanted my father's files. My father, Frederic Arienzo, was also researching infectious diseases. He was far ahead of most scientists in this field. He concentrated on the DNA or RNA of bacteria and virions. Bill said something about a virus that devours bacteria. A bacteriophage is a virus that infects and replicates within a bacterium. Phage means to devour and bacteriophage literally eats the bacteria, its host. I feel sure that was what Bill was referring to. Also, my father was one of the first to prove that DNA synthesized in a test tube, by purified enzymes, could produce all the features of a natural virus, ushering in the age of synthetic biology. In 2003, it was reported by a couple of scientific groups that the genome of ΦX174 was the first to be completely assembled in vitro from synthesized oligonucleotides. The ΦX174 virus particle has also been successfully assembled in vitro. Recently, it was shown how its highly overlapping genome could be fully decompressed and remain functional. Man-made viruses." Rainee took a very deep breath. "I'm certain this is the basis for what Bill referred to as Project Factor-7. The virus is named Factor-7. But do you remember your hematology courses? Remember factor XII?"

Sam sat speechless for a moment. "Bill had written that on papers in his office. He hemorrhaged and bled from every orifice, among other horrific issues. The factor XII protein is one of the factor proteins that causes blood to clot. An f7 deficiency is caused by mutations of the gene, but is inherited—hemophilia, right?"

Rainee continued. "Yes, most of the time, but it can develop later in life. However, if a person can manipulate chromosome thirteen and the f7 gene, then it would cause a lack of blood coagulation. In that case, a person could bleed to death pretty quickly. If a virus can do that, then you have a brand-new fatal disease. My father told me, years ago, about a genetically redesigned bacteriophage that had been written about in an obscure medical journal by a young US doctor named John Albright. So I had heard of Albright before Bill told me his name. Apparently what Albright discovered or created then"—she paused and took a breath—"was a highly potent bacteriophage for use against antibiotic-resistant bacteria. But he must have also stumbled upon something else during his research. He must have seen the possibility of creating a super bacteriophage, and perhaps that's his pathogen Factor-7. He apparently named it for what it did. A person bleeds to death in a matter of hours. But apparently the virus's gene sequence does other deadly damage to the body. My father knew or was close to knowing that gene sequence. That alone would have disclosed what these madmen are doing. He knew more about this than he should have, and he was murdered last year."

"Your father was murdered? How?" Sam asked.

She rubbed the back of her neck and took several long, deep breaths, as if talking about it was physically painful. "He was in a laboratory fire. The Polizia di Strato called it an accident, but I know that it was murder. The fire was unquestionably deliberately set. All his work was on the hard drives in the three offices that burned. My father was too trusting of those around him." She bowed her head and a tear dropped onto her leg. "Maybe that was his biggest...no...to me, his only flaw." She lifted her head in resolution of the reality of her father's murder and her conviction of revenge. Anger hardened her normally soft face, and her eyes took on a glazed determination that Sam had not seen before. She continued. "Bastards." She took a long breath, gazing over Sam's head. "And coincidentally, those computers were missing after the rubble had been cleared. I had a few notebooks of his"—she pointed to her briefcase—"because he asked me to take them for safekeeping. At the time, I never thought the research or he was in danger. I was mistaken on both fronts. So this is not going to be easy, and it's not safe. But Sam…I need your help. We may be among the few good guys who know about this, and we can't just sit back and let this plague unfold. My father's files don't prove what I have learned from Bill, but they prove that it is plausible and very possibly already being created. We have to get our hands on Bill's documents."

Sam nodded and cut his eyes at Rainee. "I am sorry about your father. But by the way…it's none of my business, but since we're talking about such a tremendous threat and perhaps a worldwide conspiracy… and the world may come to an end…" Sam said flippantly. "Maybe you can tell me why Bill loaned you fifty thousand dollars…without any interest."

Rainee leaned forward in her chair and took out a napkin from the container in the middle of the table. Sam had become overwhelmingly annoying. But she refused to once again lose her temper. As rude as he was, she knew she needed his help. She wiped her mouth gently. She looked straight at Sam and spoke with a tone of something between disgust and resignation. "Honestly, I don't know why Bill chose you to take this on, but apparently, he did. I don't give rat scat if you care about what I'm telling you, or if you hate or love me. And your last question after I spilled everything to you was so rude and phrased so harshly that I'm about ready to walk out of here. But unfortunately, you are all I have, and I need you."

Sam was outwardly embarrassed and ashamed of how he had approached the loan with her. "I am sorry. Forgive me. I shouldn't speak to you in such a rude manner."

She nodded as if accepting his apology. "It's taken a toll on me and many others like my sweet father. It's going to take an even greater toll if we don't do our best to stop these maniacs. So, about the money Bill loaned to me. Here's your answer, Doctor! I couldn't take out that much cash from my bank account and not be noticed. I couldn't use credit cards without being traced. I am here without any of my colleagues or family in Italy knowing. They think I'm on a pleasure cruise with some handsome hunk. And right now, I wish I were. I'm here secretly and at Bill's request. People have died with this knowledge. I was not going to take that risk and…I felt a duty. I'm here to try to get an answer to what I believe is the most important task I may ever encounter and perhaps the greatest man-made threat in history."

Sam was taken aback by her tenacity and bluntness. He considered what she had said for a few moments. It was all too incredible, yet Bill had mumbled the words "seven" and "safe" and something in Latin. And John Albright had been in the Emergency Department in those early-morning hours without apparent reason. Albright had hung around Ana and now was not to be seen. "Rainee, do you know an Israeli man named Simon Reznick?" Sam blurted out.

Her eyes widened. "Bill once mentioned him, but I only know of him by reputation. He's with the Mossad—or was, right? I know he lost his wife to the hands of a terrorist and has a name in Israel for being a Nazi hunter or something like that."

"How do you know that? Not many Nazis left."

"Sam, there are Nazi sympathizers. And the Middle East has terrorists. This bioweapon is meant to kill terrorists—or so I've been told."

"So Reznik is one of them? He was with Ana Roberts the morning Bill died."

She nodded. "I believe he very well could have something to do with it. He's certainly capable and has the resources."

"Well, he's still in Houston," Sam said, resigning himself to the fact that maybe she did know something. "I have more questions for you. How did Bill get involved in this travesty? Who else knows? What are we to do…if—and I repeat, if—I agree to help you?"

Rainee smiled, mainly to further her alliance with Sam. There was really nothing to smile about. "I don't have the specifics. I can't be seen here, and you cannot be seen associating with me. The wrong person seeing us might begin to put two and two together. Right now, no one knows that you suspect anything. Keep it that way. And I don't think anyone knows I'm here or who I am. You should be safe. I need you to talk to those who might know about Factor-7, especially Albright. But be careful how you approach it."

"Whoops, maybe not. I threw a fit at the medical school and the Federal Laboratory."

"Damn. Well, we'll deal. Watch everything around you constantly. In the meantime, that can be explained. You were most interested in your friend's mysterious death. You would have no reason to suspect anything else. Stop snooping and drawing attention to yourself and your concerns. You have my cell. Call me tomorrow." She stood and nodded without expression.

Sam watched her leave the restaurant. "Bossy," he whispered. He glanced down at the oysters that the waiter delivered, and his belly turned at the thought of introducing anything into his stomach, except perhaps a very strong drink. He touched the arm of a passing waiter. "Bring me your best whiskey, neat, and make it a triple."

CHAPTER TEN

Sam tossed and turned that night. He thought he must have looked at his clock fifty times and gotten up to pee just as many. His mind reviewed the morning hours when Bill died. He thought about John Albright and his history with him. He replayed everything that Rainee Arienzo had told him. It was beginning to come together but was still so unbelievable. It was what science fiction movies were made of and couldn't be real life, but then again, he knew the threat of biological warfare was real. It was considered in the top three threats, right up there with nukes and cyberattacks. The world had seen multiple novel viruses arise in the twentieth and twenty-first centuries. Were these Mother Nature's hand at work or something else? China had lied about the H1N1 and underplayed SARS and MERS, and they claimed to have had a security breach with Covid-19. They were notorious at keeping secrets right up to allowing or causing their medical community to die if they blew the whistle on the new viruses arising in China.

But what could a man-made pandemic achieve, and how would it be played out? How could it be proven that the pathogen was manufactured? And if it could be proven, would the major world governments even report that or do anything about it? Panic would spread, causing world economic and collateral devastation. If intentional like Rainee suggested, innocent collateral damage would be a war crime, but who would prosecute? Sam had no idea how he could help with stopping such an atrocity, especially if it was so secret. Dr. Arienzo had no proof. Bill Roberts's autopsy specimens and blood had all been stolen and most likely destroyed. Where were the pictures taken during the autopsy? Dr. Morris had been killed. *Could he have known too much?* Sam wondered. There were no breadcrumbs to follow on Bill's death. If the pathogen Factor-7 existed and existed for the purpose that Rainee outlined, then the players might be about to engage in the rawest barbarism, and what would Sam Hawkins, MD, do to stop it? So rogue agents or not, there surely was someone in the United States government who had heard about the threat of the Factor-7. No way could something this large not be leaked. So perhaps if Sam did contact someone within the government for help, they might already know. *Would that be a good thing or a bad thing?* he asked himself. But if they knew the scope of Factor-7 and feared the secret getting out, and Sam and Rainee knew about it, then they could be seen as a detriment...a liability. They needed proof to tell someone in the government, or they didn't have a chance in hell of getting anyone's attention. And that proof could also be an insurance policy or a death sentence. Maybe there was no proof. Maybe it was all a big hoax. But he knew that was wishful thinking. If Albright and his cronies were willing to make a bacteriophage to kill people they did not agree with, Sam's life was not worth a flyspeck to them. If those government officials in charge wanted complete silence to avoid panic, then Sam and Rainee would equally be worthless to them. But Sam knew deep in his heart that Rainee was right. They had to take a chance. They were not people made to do nothing in the face of such an atrocity. They must have proof. *Yes*, he convinced himself. *Knowledge could be dangerous, but knowledge could also save our lives.*

Sam rolled over and buried his head in his pillow. It must have been an hour, and then suddenly he sat up in bed. There was a blood sample, and no one would know about it except his emergency team. They took Bill's blood when Sam's glove was punctured. That was protocol when an attending physician, nurse, or technician was nicked or even possibly nicked by a needle or sharp instrument. Sandra had told the technician to keep the blood that was taken after the compromised glove incident separate from the blood taken to the lab for immediate analysis. His strep scare was just that; now he was surely in the clear. The samples could still be in the pathology lab at St. Peter's. Sam glanced at the clock again. It was 4:45 a.m. He showered and rushed to the hospital, arriving at 6:00 a.m., just as the shift was changing from those who worked all night and those who got to see the daylight.

When Sam entered the laboratory, he glanced around and sighed a breath of relief. He recognized the technician who was just arriving and putting on his blue protective overalls.

"Jesse, hi. Remember me? I'm Dr. Sam Hawkins."

"Sure, Dr. Hawkins. I know who you are. How ya been?"

"Oh, saddened by Dr. Roberts's death. I had an incident in the ED the morning he died and had blood taken for a test. An IV needle nicked my glove…don't think it got me, but just the same, we followed protocol. Did you run that test?"

"No, Doc, can't say I recall that I did. I'm a tech, and we run routine tests. But the pathologist had to read the results and make their conclusions. That should have been sent to you by email."

"Yes, of course, that would have been the case." Sam bit his lip. *Two emails that I didn't get.* "But…well…I seem to not have those results. Anyway, can you please look it up?" Sam asked, trying to be patient.

"I can do that, sure," said the young technician. He began to scroll though the many files on his computer. "Here…says, hum…da…da… da…nothing remarkable."

Sam moved closer to the computer screen. "So nothing shows as infection or what might have caused Dr. Roberts's death?"

"Hum, seems the blood was tested for…hum mm, let's see…" He began to read off the lab tests that were run on the blood. "HIV, Hep A, B, C, full panels, VCA antibodies, IgG, Epstein Barr EBV, PCR, qualitative. As you know, these are routine under the circumstances of what happened to your glove in Trauma. So to answer your question, it seems no advanced tests were ordered. That's all we are asked to check."

"I see. So, there could be infections, or the like, but ya'll wouldn't have checked for that. Right?" Sam asked nervously. "Is the sample still here?"

Jesse shrugged. "Wow. Computer says it was a month ago. I don't know. Normally we would keep blood samples for about two days after these tests." He began to read more on the computer. "Dr. Mendoza read the test and sent you the email with his results. The email copy is right here. He has a note here that we weren't to destroy the specimen until you answered the email. I guess you didn't answer, because it shows that it is in the biorepository."

Sam sighed with relief. *Extraordinary luck*, he thought. "So where is the biorepository? Can you get me that specimen? I want to run some independent tests." Sam pursed his lips, hoping the tech would ask no questions. Sam also knew that if anyone else walked in, he would be asked more questions.

"Here's the file number. I need to go into the storage on fourth floor to retrieve it. I need you to go too, 'cause there's papers to sign. You can't take a specimen out without following protocol. You know the chain of custody issue is mandatory at St. Peter's."

"Yeah, sure," Sam said. "As it should be."

The two walked hastily to the elevators and went up to the fourth floor. Sam thought again of Huitt and when he had spied on the administrator. Seeing him and the two men taking out something from that very lab he was leaving still troubled Sam. *Just as long as he doesn't come up here now,* Sam thought.

The biorepository was like a library. It covered most of the floor. Everything was white or silver. The smell of sterilization was mixed with formaldehyde. Sam considered the room. They were no longer alone, but no one seemed to pay any attention to either of them.

Jesse punched in a four-digit code to open a heavy metal door that housed the temperature-controlled biological samples. He handed a gown and mask to Sam.

One side had tissue and blood samples at a certain cold temperature, another held specimens from clinical trials, and another wall housed vaccines. Everything was kept at the perfect maintenance temperature. Sam followed Jesse to the far wall.

"Here's the number." He pulled out a tray from the wall and read the label on the vial. "Date of birth: 12/4/1950, William Roberts, MD. This must be the one."

Sam smiled. "That's it."

Jesse led Sam out of the storage room. The closing of the heavy door sounded more like a prison cell than a laboratory.

"You'll need cold insulation to keep the whole blood specimen at proper temperature. We have insulated containers and ice bags over here," Jesse said authoritatively.

Sam took the white heavy plastic bag and held it open for Jesse to place the specimen inside. He firmly sealed the bag.

"Are you taking it to another lab? I have to record it, and I need your signature." Jesse held out a clipboard.

"Thanks, Jesse. Do I sign here?" Sam held the pen on a line and tapped the paper briefly.

Jesse nodded. "Yes, sir. Just sign and lay the clipboard here when you're done. I need to get back to my floor. Thank you, Dr. Hawkins. It was nice seeing you."

Sam nodded as the tech walked away. He signed "John Albright, MD," and replaced the clipboard to its proper place. He grinned as he left the room.

Upon reaching his car, Sam dialed Rainee on her cell phone. He began to speak as soon as she answered. "I remembered that we took blood in the Emergency Department from Bill. I told you that my glove was nicked, right? I had forgotten about the blood that was taken as standard practice, until last night. This may be the only remaining sample of his blood, and I don't think anyone else knows it exists, or at least no one who has any interest in it."

"That's incredible news. Do you have a safe place with a powerful scope? I need, at least, the power of an electron microscope to see what I hope to find." She paused. "Maybe I hope to not find anything. I don't know." She shook her head in frustration. "I *need* to look at the blood."

Sam thought for a moment. "St. Peter's has a blood chemistry analyzer and electron microscopes, but I think Galveston General only has an electron microscope. I rather think we shouldn't do anything more at Pete's. There are too many probing eyes."

"I just need the electron power to see the viral particles, if there are any. The blood analyzer only looks for about ninety diseases, and this is likely something that's not in its data bank." She paused. "I want to see what's floating around in his blood," she said.

"Meet me in thirty minutes at Galveston General. The lab will be closed for lunch. We'll have about an hour." Sam set the phone in the seat. He leaned his head into the steering wheel, wondering what he had gotten himself into. But then again, he realized he had no choice.

Sam arrived before Rainee. He watched as the employees filed out of the hallway that led to the laboratories. He could see inside the main pathology lab. No one was there, and the lights had been dimmed. He heard steps behind him. He nervously spun around and, fortunately, saw Rainee.

"I know how you feel," she said empathetically.

"I'm not sure how I feel, Rainee. I still don't know if I believe all this, but I'm here. Let's get to it." Sam handed her the vial of blood, and they entered the lab, locking the door behind them. "I have privileges here, so I think we're cool to be in here. But I'd like to, just as well, not be seen by anyone," Sam said resolutely. "Here take these gloves, the mask, and goggles. You might need them."

"Thank you. I can't believe St. Peter's didn't destroy this. Lucky for us," she said, placing one glove on and then the other. "I hope this blood will tell us the story. I'm sure time has compromised its integrity, but we might find something. I don't want to think that Bill died for nothing." She took a sterile dropper and placed four small beads of Bill Roberts's blood onto a glass slide. She turned the slide from side to side until they ran together in a smear. She slid it under the lens of the high magnification microscope and began to focus the view. The computer screen illuminated, and the images began to appear.

Sam watched her every move as intently as he watched the door. He felt like he was watching a tennis match as his head moved from her to the door and then repeated it again.

"Look here, Sam. There they are. There are the bacteriophages, just as I thought. See the top or the capsid?" She moved the specimen around with a small instrument. "Then there's the core and the sheath. These are very well defined. We truly lucked out that the specimen is intact, and that little bugger is still alive. But that's what those things do. They can live in many environments for a *very* long period."

Sam moved closer to the screen. "I see it. Looks like the Lunar Landing Module."

She allowed a small laugh. "Exactly. Phages are used as curatives when antibiotics won't work or are unavailable. They have been used for centuries, although I don't think medical science used them until the early nineteen hundreds. Some think these are present in rivers and can cure all sorts of diseases. They also thrive in salt water. That's probably why it will live in the blood."

Sam stood away from the microscope. "I took my biology courses, Doctor."

"Of course, I know you did." She paused, taking another view of the specimen. "But this phage is different. You can see it here." She moved the phage with a thin probe. "I can see the virion. See the nucleic acid has been compromised with the virus. I can't see it well with this magnification, but it's there. Look."

"I don't see what you're talking about."

"These aren't very well defined. There has been some deterioration of the bacteriophage's integrity. But we truly lucked out that the specimen is intact, and those little buggers—the virus—are there. There are probably others more defined and perhaps still alive eating on any live bacteria that remains. I just can't see them at this magnification.

Can you get a picture printed of what I have on the screen?" Rainee waited until the paper copy slid from the machine and then removed the slide. "I think I want to send the specimen to a friend in Vancouver. He works for Briscoe Biotechnology Company. I won't tell him why or where I got this unless I have to. I know he can find all the elements in this bacterial virus," she said decisively. "I went to school with him. Very brilliant, but he's kind of a geek and not much personality. He won't ask much, if anything. I think I intimidate him."

Sam smiled. "I can see that." He touched her arm and smiled again. "Just playing with you." But to some extent, she intimidated Sam. "But you've been saying that no one can know. Won't this compromise our secrecy and consequently our safety?" he asked.

She was quick to snap back. "We have a sample of blood perhaps with Factor-7. Sam, do you know what this means? If this checks out, we have our proof!"

CHAPTER ELEVEN

AUGUST 7

Simon Reznick mumbled Hebrew as he stared out of his hotel window. He took a sip of red wine from his glass and opened a small black book. He read aloud, highlighting the ancient Biblical verse as he spoke the words of Numbers 24:8.

> God brought them out of Egypt;
> they have the strength of a wild ox.
> They devour hostile nations
> and break their bones in pieces;
> with their arrows they pierce them.
> Like a lion Israel will crouch and lie down,
> like a lioness—who dares to rouse them?
> May those who bless Israel be blessed
> and those who curse Israel be cursed!

He took the book and held it to his chest. Then he read on. "And the Lord God said, 'See, I have given you this land. Go in and take possession of the land the Lord swore he would give to your fathers—to Abraham, Isaac and Jacob—and to their descendants after them. The avenger of blood shall put the murderer to death when they meet. This is to have the force of law for you throughout the generations to come, wherever you live.'"

Simon laid the book gently on the table and picked up the phone. "For you, my beloved wife, and Israel." He dialed a number. "We are ready to proceed."

CHAPTER TWELVE

Two days passed, and Sam had not talked to Rainee. The silence had been unnerving. She said she would call when she had an answer from the Canadian lab. He couldn't take the suspense any longer. Had they found something, or had she been exposed by sending it? He had to know. He dialed her cell.

"Hi, Sam. I was going to call you tonight. I think we have something. I'm waiting on the overnight letter with the written results, but talking to Cameron at Briscoe Labs, I think we have what we were looking for," she said rather calmly.

"You sound pretty cool about it," Sam snapped.

"Not at all. Don't take my tone of voice for nonchalance, Sam. I'm trying to put together the pieces and stay calm. I can't freak out now, nor can you."

Sam took a deep breath. "I have a contact in Washington, but he won't think my suspicions are credible without proof of some kind."

"No longer suspicions. As I said, I feel confident we have the proof," she replied firmly. "We just don't know the scope or the players."

Sam paused, trying to connect his next sentence without sounding enraged by this woman who had told him to take every precaution and now wanted him to go to someone in the US government with…what? Yes, he thought…with what?

"Are you there?" Rainee asked.

"Yes, I'm here," Sam replied snidely. "Where the hell else would I be? You make me wonder about you, Doctor."

Rainee remained calm; her voice was reassuring. "We can't expose this alone. No one will take us seriously, even though the blood tests that Cameron ran showed a new strain of a bacteria virus."

"So, the tests *are* conclusive, and we have the smoking gun…so to speak."

She continued. "We do, but how to stop it is the million-dollar question. If you go now to some senator or someone in the State or Defense Department, even with the conclusions of the virus, we probably won't be taken seriously. And that could mean trouble. They could just say it's a new strain and start the usual pandemic media madness or they could bury the truth. Either way, we're sunk. We really can't prove that it's a plot to use against their enemies."

"Rainee, I agree. We need more. I've worried about what we're getting into. I mean, if we expose this, and we really are the only ones who basically knew, then we are perhaps heroes. But if we go to the authorities…whoever that might be…and they know and wanted to keep it secret, then we're trouble for them. But either way, if you are right or not, we should not be talking on the landline. Meet me at St. Pete's back parking lot in an hour."

Sam then dialed the extension for the IT guys. "Can ya'll check my office computer? I'm not getting emails for some reason."

"Sure Doc. We'll get to it today."

Sam locked his office door and walked down the long hallway to the elevator that would take him downstairs and over to the parking garage. Thoughts frantically ran through his head. Bill was dead, the blood specimen showed a new strain of a bacteria virus, Albright might be involved, and Sam was to trust and partner with a woman whom he barely knew. He opened the door to the Porsche, and the normal heat boiled out. He climbed into the driver's seat, but then suddenly he realized that something was not right. He started to close the door and then glanced to his right. The passenger-side window was shattered. The glass was still in place, but as Sam slammed the driver-side door, fragments fell to the ground. He jumped out of the sports car and ran to the passenger side. The entire door was dented and scratched as if someone had taken a large bat and a knife to the metal. The two right-side tires were slashed and flat. The convertible top was sliced, and the front bumper was knocked off. The right side of the hood was flattened, and oil or something had flooded the ground. Taped to a large dent on the right side of the hood was a folded piece of paper. He ripped it from the car, cursing at the top of his lungs. It was written in red ink and resembled the handwriting of a first-grader.

It simply read, "You will not get away with this."

Sam pulled his cell phone from the pocket of his white coat and called the hospital security. He then called the Galveston police.

Sam's anger and the July heat were unbearable while he waited for the authorities. The hospital security arrived first. They assured Sam that the security cameras would have certainly recorded whoever did the damage.

"Did the Porsche have an alarm?" asked one very overweight security guard.

"Hell yes, it has security alarms," bristled Sam.

"Hum, must not have worked right or alarmed for very long. Battery's not dead," the second guard said as he closed the door and flung the keys to Sam.

Sam was livid. The guards were of no value to him. They must have been away from the monitors. They would have certainly seen the perpetrator on video, or if they had patrolled the lot correctly, they might have seen it happen. And the dealership would definitely hear about the faulty security system. Sam was disgusted with it all.

Within fifteen minutes two uniformed police officers arrived and took pictures of the beaten-up Porsche 911 Carrera and tried to lift fingerprints from the car. But as they were fingerprinting Sam, they advised him that it would be almost impossible to tell what print belonged to the culprit. Their best bet was to consult with the hospital security to see what the video camera might show. They gave Sam little hope of finding the creep unless there was a clear photo on the security recorders.

"Ah, this is just fuckin' great." Sam grunted as he got into the battered $200,000 car. His hand trembled from anger as he texted Rainee. *I have a problem. Will meet you where we agreed, but I'll be walking.*

Sam grabbed his few valuables from the car and stuffed them into his coat pockets. As he stepped out of the Porsche, he heard a familiar voice. Overcome with anger and frustration, Sam bowed his head and rested his forehead on the top of the car. "What now? What the fuck is going on now?"

The voice shouted his name again.

Sam turned to see Dr. John Albright's glistening, smiling teeth. He took a deep palliative breath. "Hey, John. What's going on?" Sam cringed at his attempt at camaraderie. He stepped away from his car to shake Albright's hand, continuing the charade. "What brings you here today, John?" Sam asked.

Albright continued smiling. "Man, someone really did a number on Lizzy here." He patted the dented door as if consoling a child.

"Yeah. Guess you didn't see anything?"

"No, wish I had. You sure have a mess on your hands. I just got out here. I had a little knee pain, and it was affecting my tennis game, so I saw Jim Givens. He's a good guy. Gave me a shot from hell, but the pain's gone." He walked around to the front of the Porsche. "What a shame. This is one hell of a machine."

Sam nodded, again trying to look as normal as possible, knowing that he could be face to face with the person who had destroyed half of his car or with an international killer. And then again, maybe not. He wasn't going to comment on the damage or start up a conversation. He just wanted to get away from John Albright. "Yeah, good guy, that Jim." Sam's head was spinning with thoughts and with seething contempt. And at that moment, his disdain was for anyone or anything in his immediate orbit.

"We should get together soon. Sorry to hear about your divorce." Albright ran his hand across the hood of the Porsche. "And sorry about this."

Sure, Sam thought, *I'm sure he's just torn up about both.* He sharply exhaled and forced his reply. "Thanks. She'll be happier." He paused. "Yeah, sure, John…sure, we should visit soon."

"Dinner at La Playa tomorrow? See you about seven!" Albright shouted as he walked briskly away without giving Sam time to agree or decline the invitation.

Sam watched Albright drive away, all the while scanning the parking lot. What had he become involved in? Someone vandalized his car and left a threatening note, and he just made nice with a man he truly detested. His colleagues at the hospitals were asking why he had taken so many breaks from work. If they were wondering, anyone checking up on him would see the unusual behavior as well. It was too late for regrets or changes. He was involved in something hugely dangerous, and he felt certain someone knew, and they were not happy about it. Sam shuddered as the jumbled thoughts flashed through his mind. He walked from the garage parking lot and made a swift left turn into the patient parking area.

A gray Ford compact pulled into the parking space to the right of him. He saw a woman in large sunglasses and a sun hat sitting in the driver's seat. She rolled down the window.

"What happened?" she shouted.

"Someone beat up the Porsche. Someone doesn't like me very much," Sam said, touching the brim of her sun hat.

"Apparently. Did that just happen?"

Sam nodded. "Sometime today." He handed her the note.

"Not good. Either you really pissed someone off, or you and I had better watch ourselves. Maybe they know that we know."

"And get this…Albright was in the parking garage. He claimed he was there to get a cortisone shot in his knee."

"Do you believe him?" she asked.

"I don't believe anything out of that man's mouth."

"Let's drive. I don't like sitting here." She pulled her hat down to cover the left side of her face. "Get in."

"I didn't recognize you when you pulled up. Good disguise." Sam got into her car, and they drove onto the highway.

"That was the plan, Sam." She laughed at her unintentional rhyme. She pulled off the hat and shook out her long dark hair.

Sam smiled at her, and then his expression went somber. "Albright wrangled me into dinner tomorrow night. I didn't have time to say anything."

"Strange…hum. But you know, that might just be a break. I'd like you to talk to him and see if he slips any information or a hint of the Factor-7 and his involvement. Or if he indicates that he thinks you know something."

"Oh, great. Put me in the lion's den." Sam huffed. "I think maybe—I just won't show up." He saw Rainee's disapproval. "Anyway, do you really think he's that stupid? I mean, he wouldn't just tell me his involvement."

"No, but maybe if he gets liquored up, he might just say something of value."

Sam shook his head. "I don't know. He's a pretty smart guy, and if this plan is so covert, then he won't mention anything."

"Perhaps," she said, "but I heard he's very arrogant and a braggart. He just might like one of his old buddies to know he's involved in such a monumental act of genius."

"Genius?" Sam shouted. "How can you call this demonic plan genius?"

"It's definitely genius. Wicked, yes, but nonetheless genius."

"Turn here. We'll pick up my truck," Sam said.

Rainee took a hard left into the tiny island community. "Is this Tiki Island?"

Sam shook his head, rubbing his eyes and forehead. "Yep. I call it home now." He rubbed his eyes again. "I suppose it would take a brilliant scientist or scientists to develop a new deadly strain, release a pandemic, and prevent World War III by not having it seen as an act of war, and still not be called madmen." Sam's reply was a mix of sarcasm and acknowledgment of her statement. It was a contradiction for sure. But brilliant arrogance or not, Sam wasn't sure he could get Albright liquored up enough to talk.

Sam opened the door of his black GMC pickup and helped Rainee into the high-set front seat.

"Nice truck, I guess," she said snidely. "Not sure I've ever been in the nosebleed section of a pickup."

"The bigger the tires, the bigger the belt buckle." Sam snickered.

"I beg your pardon? I don't understand."

"Never mind. Just a Texas joke." He snickered again.

Rainee shook her head in amazement. "Men and their toys," she mumbled.

Sam was overpowered by this five-foot, four-inch Italian beauty, and he suddenly realized it.

"I must believe that there are others who know about this and are either too afraid to come forward or, like us, don't know what exactly to do. We have to ferret out these people," she said, almost under her breath.

Sam slipped in his last caveat. "It would be nice if that was so, but I'm beginning to think you and I are the only people who are not involved with this thing." But she had made it clear, and she was persuasive, they had no other choice. He thought of his past choices. He had made good ones and bad ones. This choice fit somewhere in between.

The only sound was the heavy-duty engine of Sam's truck. He was deep in thought, and Rainee was calculating their next move. Although she was more informed than he, both knew very little of the challenges that lay ahead, and neither was qualified or prepared for any of it.

Rainee took a deep breath. She had to finish telling Sam what the Canadian lab had discovered. But she knew he was not ready to hear what she had to say. "OK, I had Cameron run quantitative studies on the extracted bacteriophages. He found multiple specimens fully intact. This bacteriophage virus replicates itself just like many viruses do. The nucleic acid is a double-stranded DNA, but like the Poxvirus family, it does not replicate within the nucleus. He exposed the bacteriophage to fifty-one point six seven Celsius or a hundred twenty-five degrees Fahrenheit, and the bacterium survived. He exposed them to subzero temperatures, and they survived. He broke the capsid of the bacteriophage. He has photos of all of this. The virus apparently dies once compromised and it loses its host, the bacteria, unless it has another host—a human. Cameron also said the virus holds a resemblance to the many hemorrhagic fevers, but it lacks some elements and is not a RNA virus, so he couldn't identify. He had never seen anything like these bacteriophages. It's a new mutation. Someone, perhaps John Albright, has taken multiple viruses and created one big daddy. And he created a host for it: the bacteriophage, which withstands heat, cold, drought, or moisture, so it has an indefinite shelf life. If the bacterium is alive, the virus is alive. When the bacterium enters a human body, the body's immune system may fight if off. The bacteria could make a person sick, but if they have any well-working immune system, it would not be deadly. The bacteria will ultimately die or perhaps could be killed by antibiotics, but nonetheless, the big danger...the virus... survives in the victim's body and makes the human sick. And as you know, we really have no therapeutic for many viruses and certainly not this one." Rainee exhaled and then took a long breath. Her rarely detected Italian accent and her anxiety had become more apparent as she told Sam the alarming facts.

"So the bacteriophages were indeed resistant but do not replicate inside the bacterium's nuclei? The virus replicates?" Sam asked, showing he was not totally ignorant of his years of biology. He felt sort of proud of himself. He blew breath through his teeth. He was trying to impress her, but her understanding of the bacteriophage was so far ahead of his that he was sniffing the dog's tail. He smiled at his thought. *Cute puppy at that...and damn cute tail.*

"Precisely. And mutates quickly, according to what Bill told me." She smiled, amused at Sam's efforts at biology, or maybe she read his mind. "And so, Bill had a compromised immune system. His body was attacked first by the bacteria, which his body or your antibiotics could not kill fast enough and he became very ill. But soon the bacteria that caused massive internal damage ultimately died and the virus took over. The virus replicates outside its own nuclei after it has no bacterium host, but that can only happen when it has another host…the human body. Its replication is fast once inside the body. Death within hours."

Sam stared at her. "Indeed, that could be the reason that Bill Roberts suffered such a horrific death. Like we used to say in med school, the virus sheds its overcoat and does that again and again and again. Factor-7 must be a very virulent bug."

Rainee nodded and continued. "If they're going to release this into the atmosphere, perhaps from the air, like an aerosol, it must survive. Some viruses will live on surfaces for several hours, but that's about it. Bacteria can live for much longer. A bacteriophage is the answer—kinda a full meal deal. This new bug might even be able to withstand being released from as high as the stratosphere, and that would mean it would be virtually undetectable. It could even fall as rain. Let's face it, some scientists believe that microorganisms came from deep space, thus the theory of panspermia. This might not be so different. Sam, these mutations are like I have never seen or dreamed possible. This is out of my range of expertise, but I'm not so naïve to think that it's not plausible that a new strain of bacteria viruses has been manufactured with the intent to wipe out races or religious groups. There is so much hate in this world. Remember, my father said this attacks DNA like any biological mutagen, and once the DNA is attacked, the chromosomes become weak, and bingo…his pet project, Factor-7. When the f7 protein is damaged, there is no clotting in the coagulation cascade. Every organ and tissue hemorrhages, and the victim literally will bleed to death."

Sam had a sense of what she was saying. "So, like gamma rays or metals can cause diseases like cancer?"

"Similarly, some bacteria can be inserted into the genome, which disrupts genetic function, causes DNA damage, and reduces efficiency of the DNA repair system. It thereby increases mutation. The virus may induce the cell to forcefully undergo division, which may lead to transformation of the cell and ultimately cancer. But this thing kills before the cancer cells can divide or maybe not. It might divide so quickly once in a person with their targeted DNA so that the cells go erratic and overtake the body. Rous sarcoma virus—Human Papillomaviruses? Literally viruses that cause cancer and may result in DNA strand breaks or adducts? I don't know. This is something new and uncharted for me. So that's just a guess."

"Ah, yeah, sure." Sam was a trauma surgeon, and although he knew about many diseases, his main work was surgery, removal of foreign objects, gunshot wounds, heart attacks, drug overdoses, and the like. His main objective was to keep an emergency patient alive and stable until a specialist could take over.

Rainee smiled coyly, knowing full well that Sam had some idea of what she was talking about, but she was not totally getting through to him. "This isn't your expertise. I know. But you have really incredible skills, so you'll be a big help explaining this to those who have no medical background." She hoped Sam didn't think she was patronizing him, which, in fact, she was. She thought a moment, then spoke. "We saw a resistant bacterial variant that has been exposed to a manufactured virus, and it replicates or clones its own DNA in sets of seven. The virus eats the bacteria, replicates itself, invades the vital organs and tissues, destroys DNA and chromosome

13, and then kills the factor XII proteins. The body is ravaged, and then it bleeds out. Nothing alive could survive something like that. That's their Factor-7 microbe in a nutshell, but how they did it—I'll probably never know." She gazed out the window. "Impressive."

Sam turned away from her and paused. "Bill knew all this?"

Rainee frowned. "Unfortunately, yes. Absolutely. I've been trying to tell you that since the first day we met. We just now have the details of their test tube germ. Cameron did his job well."

"OK, I get it. But this must take billions of dollars, a huge army of Trojan men and women, scientists willing to risk their lives and careers, and tons of people who will close their eyes to such madness. God Almighty, how many people are involved? That sickens me. This is an act of war and an enormous war crime." Sam was speaking too loudly. He took a deep breath. "Rainee, if we can figure this out, why can't a dozen other far-better-equipped scientists do the same?"

"I'm a pretty incredible scientist." She smiled but really had found his statement a little condescending. She gazed at a distance and spoke softly. "It's because...most likely, no other legitimate or honest scientists know anything about this, and honestly, if I had not had the background from my father's research, heard the name John Albright from him, and seen the Congo man's corpse, I would have thought Bill was some crazy old man."

Sam nodded. "Others know. Be sure of it."

"Perhaps, but we don't know who, and we certainly don't know who to trust. So it's you and me, babe." She tried to force a smile but squelched it when she saw the seriousness in Sam's eyes. "Bill chose us."

Sam groaned. "Sorry about what I said. Certainly, you're a talented doctor. You know more about this stuff than I ever will." He pressed the gas pedal, pushing the pickup into high speed. "You mentioned that Bill said that information was in a safe in Mexico?" he asked.

Rainee held on to her seat belt. "All he said was that he had a safe. Another time, he mentioned Mexico. I put that together. So much of what I have told you has simply been piecemealed together. But, yes, he said there were important documents that I must see. You've been in his home safe. Were the answers there?" Her voice vibrated as the large truck hit bumps in the road.

Sam glanced over to her. "I didn't find anything like you're talking about at his house. He also mentioned the word *safe* to me the morning he died. I still can't wrap my head around the idea that Bill Roberts would become involved in something like this."

"Sam, slow down. You're going to kill us or end up in jail." Rainee held tightly to her armrest and her seat belt.

Sam said nothing but rode the brake until the truck had slowed to fifty-five miles per hour.

"Thank you," Rainee said, expelling a sigh of relief. "I know you were close to Bill and his wife. But did you know that Bill's brother was involved with the US National Counterterrorism Center?"

Sam cut his eyes at Rainee. "No, I *didn't* know that. Bill never mentioned anything like that. Geez, you're an encyclopedia of information. I knew Steven Roberts worked at the Pentagon, but never knew his specific position." Sam rubbed his forehead. "That's pretty damn interesting and getting mighty close to scary. It's all getting so weird." He slowed the truck to almost a crawl and looked at Rainee. "That's operated by the FBI or CIA, isn't it?"

Rainee smiled. "Do they even make encyclopedias anymore? I don't think so. Certainly not the box-set of five hundred and fifty books that weighed twenty pounds each." She winked at Sam. "You're funny, you know that? But yes, I feel sure the FBI and CIA are involved. Your CIA is definitely into counterterrorism both inside and outside the United States. I did a little research on them after Bill told me. Easy to get info, but not so easy to get anything on Steven. I'm not exactly sure why Bill told me about Steven."

Sam liked the way she played back with him. He thought a moment of how easy it had become to be with her. "We know John Albright is involved. But where does Bill and now Steven fit into this scenario, and why did he get me involved? *You* should have walked away. This is insane."

Rainee nodded. "How can you say 'walk away'? With all you know now?"

Sam felt scolded, and she was right. No person who had any regard for humanity would just walk away.

Rainee remained calm on the outside, but Sam was like a yo-yo. One moment he was convinced and ready to fight, and the next he was the proverbial doubting Thomas.

Rainee recognized his concern and conflict with each thing she told him, but he had to know what she knew, and quickly. "I have to believe that Bill was in big trouble somehow. I wish we knew more about Simon Reznick."

Sam was stunned by how candid, or perhaps transparent, Simon Reznick had been that day at Ana's when he asked him about his profession. He had nonchalantly exposed himself as Israeli Mossad. The man apparently had no fear. But Sam suddenly became very afraid of him and the entire situation. "Reznik readily told me that he was with the Mossad, after Bill died. He had no hesitation in telling me. The Mossad are known for their art in espionage. They are outside Israel's democratic organizations. Kinda do what they want, I hear. I've even heard them called the finest killing machine. I'm freaked, to say the least," he said.

Rainee had been silent while Sam seemingly processed the new information. "I think we both are frightened, Sam. But we don't know what Bill was doing. I suppose no one knows everything about anyone. We all have our secrets and skeletons in the closets. I don't want to judge Bill until we have more facts."

Sam huffed. "John Albright and Simon Reznick, all at the hospital when Bill died. I should have known then that something wasn't right. I didn't know Reznick, but I knew it was odd that he was with Ana. And I guess now I know why Bill was brought to me that night, even though there were several hospitals closer to his house. EMS said that Ana insisted they take him to St. Peter's. What is that all about if she doesn't know anything? And talking to her, I really don't think she knows a thing. She said she didn't even know Bill had cancer."

"I don't know that answer, and it's definitely odd. Perhaps Bill did tell Mrs. Roberts to take him to you, and she forgot in her grief. She's getting up there in years, after all."

Sam huffed. "Bill was pretty much involved, if he exposed himself to the virus and then died."

"I didn't say that was for sure. Maybe he did, but he might have been murdered. We don't know." Rainee took a deep breath. "Again, let me be clear. I don't know whom to trust with this information. I figure he didn't either, but he knew my father had died having uncovered a portion of the secret plan, and I was the next logical ally. And Bill surely was desperate. He was either murdered with the secret germ or intentionally killed himself with the Factor-7. He showed you Factor-7, either way. His blood showed us the secret that he could not tell himself. He chose to die with you by his side."

Sam pulled off the main highway before reaching Houston. The word *murdered* spun in his head. He had not considered that Bill Roberts could have been murdered.

A few miles down the two-lane country road sat a small wooden building on the water's edge. The sign beckoned him as it flashed

"Fresh Seafood and Cocktails." "Welcome to Charlie's," he said. Sam parked, and they went inside. "Murdered," he mumbled.

Sam ordered two beers. "An Italian gal needs to taste our Texas beer. How about a dark bock? Don't know about you, but I could use a drink," he said.

"Yes, please."

"I'll introduce you to other favorites. Looks like we might be spending some time together. Real Texas fajitas, homemade flour tortillas and huevos rancheros are next. My favorite for lunch and breakfast."

Rainee smiled agreeably. "I don't think I'll be with you for breakfast any time soon, so don't get any funny ideas, Dr. Hawkins. But maybe someday I'll introduce you to our limoncello."

"No, no," he replied. "Been there…done that. Two-day hangover." Sam moved his head from side to side, acting as if wishy-washy on the subject. "Well, maybe, just a little sip."

They both laughed, and it felt good to get the momentary relief. After a brief respite from overthinking everything and the puzzling questions that could not be answered, Rainee spoke quietly. "Sam, Bill mentioned a safe to both of us. He mentioned Mexico."

Sam looked at her as if saying, *honestly…can you just stop?* But although he was sickened by it all, he answered her as calmly as he could muster. "Bill and Ana have a villa in San Miguel de Allende, but Mexico can be so very dangerous with the drug cartels. There are United States travel warnings for much of Mexico. The cartels and gangs there scare me almost as much as the Factor-7. But I know people are going again to San Miguel and to resorts on the Yucatan, so I guess." He wasn't so sure.

"So, we have one more obstacle. Where is the nearest airport to their villa?" she asked.

"You really want to go?" Sam shook his head, already knowing what her reply would be. "I think León is the closest commercial airport, or we could perhaps check into a charter and land at the small San Miguel airport."

"We have to go, Sam. Charter would be safest and perhaps fastest, don't you think? The safe that Bill mentioned must be in Mexico, and I believe all the information that we need to go to the authorities is documented somewhere there. The answers have to be there. And we can do nothing without confirmation and answers. We have no choice."

"Choice? I keep hearing and thinking about choices. Have we had any of those?" Sam shook his head. "Going to authorities…ah…not sure that's a choice anymore. But we'll know better when and if we are better equipped with the truth." Sam motioned to the waitress for two more beers. "OK, again, I get this. I'll need to talk to Ana. I'm sure she wouldn't mind if I used the house, but she might find it suspicious. We just had a long talk about Mexico and the increase in violence. She wants to sell the villa. So we should find what's there and get it out of Mexico before Ana starts the ball rolling on the sale."

"Make your story good then. If she knew what we're doing and it got back to the wrong people, all of us, including Ana, could be in serious danger. If Reznik and Albright have, in fact, been hanging around her, then we must protect her. Perhaps they think she knows something."

"Well, I can tell you from experience, Albright isn't there for a knitting club. If it's not for his own benefit, he wouldn't be there." Sam sat back in his chair and folded his arms. "I'll make up something."

"OK. Mexico, and then Washington. Sam, we must be sure of your Washington man, or maybe we can locate some honest investigative journalist to expose this."

Sam sat quietly. "I'm as sure of Grimes as anyone, which is not saying much. But again…don't hold me to that yet." He laughed sarcastically. "An honest journalist? These days, I think, that's a contradiction of terms."

Rainee tossed her hair to one side, dismissing Sam's remark. "I'm as frustrated as you. Let's hope we get information as to whom we can trust. Or the best scenario would be that Bill left us instructions in Mexico."

"Yeah, assuming the cartel doesn't kill us first." Sam touched her hand without thinking. Perhaps it was the fragrance of her perfume or shampoo that wafted through the air as her hair took flight. "Don't just write off what I'm telling you, please. It's a real threat, my dear. I live in Texas. I know what the cartel guys are capable of pulling off. Recently it was reported that one cartel gang didn't like some guys from probably another cartel. They caught them, made them drink gasoline, and set them on fire. That's who those guys are."

Rainee took a huge, uncharacteristically unladylike swig from her beer bottle, indicating she could hold her own. "But you don't know what the people with the Factor-7 are capable of doing. The cartel might be a minnow in a tank of sharks."

CHAPTER THIRTEEN

Sam considered the day with Dr. Rainee Arienzo. She was more pleasant than any time before, and Sam realized that he had become fond of
her. The mutual concern was part of it, but there was more. He wasn't
sure what he was feeling, but he liked the new emotion.

Morning would come quickly as he set his alarm for 4:30 a.m.
There was much to do before seeing Ana about the villa in Mexico.
There would be the routine work at the hospital, and he could only
hope to have no new surprises. He'd have the Porsche towed away, he
had to get an insurance adjuster, and he would order a new Porsche.
His nerves were ragged. All the newfound information was hard to
process. Sam's last thought before falling asleep was the dread of having
to meet Albright for dinner. He pulled the down pillow over his head.

Sam woke abruptly and glanced at the clock. It was only 2:00 a.m.
He had at least two more hours to sleep, but he had fought the mattress
and pillows all night, unable to scrub the thoughts from his mind. He
reached under the mattress and pulled out his grandfather's snub-nose
.38-caliber revolver. There were six bullets in the chamber. He laid it

on the bedside table and considered what he would do if he had to use it. He had a Texas license to carry, but until then, he had never felt the need to carry a firearm.

He tossed and turned in the hours before the alarm released its awful buzz. But he had obviously slept, and when the alarm jolted him, he moaned out loud at the annoyance. Normally he would awaken on his own, but he didn't generally get up at 4:30. He slammed his hand on the alarm clock, shutting off the gruesome sound. *Just ten minutes more*, he thought. His head ached, and the alarm still rang in his ears. He could feel his heart beating wildly in his chest. The day ahead ran through his mind. Between every regret of what he had to do, he flashed on Rainee's soft face and the smell of her hair in the breeze. It comforted him, and he knew he was feeling something for the Italian doctor. The trip to Mexico would give him time to find out more about her. He realized they had not talked much about either of their personal lives. She could have a boyfriend, or worse, he thought, a husband.

As Sam dressed, he rehearsed what he would tell Ana Roberts. He would avoid any questions of his traveling companion. He would suggest to Ana that he could begin the selling process of the house and bring back their most valuable items. He wasn't quite sure how to say he would empty the safe and bring back the contents, but he would find the words. He would tell her that he needed a few days away, and the cool mountain air of San Miguel de Allende was just that ticket. Kill two birds with one stone, so to speak. Ana wasn't the suspicious kind. She would likely not ask many questions. But Sam couldn't be sure she wouldn't tell his location to Simon Reznick or John Albright or…God knows who else, because to her, there would be no secret in him taking a trip. The story had to be better concocted to assure that Ana would say nothing. But how would he not set off alarms in her head if he specifically asked her to not tell anyone where he was? Sam had to do some very creative thinking on his way to the hospital.

There was little traffic over the bridge to Galveston Island. Sam would be at St. Peter's in record time, but it was 5:30 a.m., after all.

———————

Sam placed the pistol in his right-hand desk drawer and turned the key to lock it safely away. But tucked away in a drawer, it would not protect him. He shrugged off the thought. He had never been afraid of much in his life. He attacked every setback with strength and fortitude. He had been in enough scraps and always came out on top, or at least with nothing more than a bloody nose. But there was one thing Sam feared. It was the unknown, and the more he learned, the darker the hole of uncertainty became. His phone's loud ring startled him back to the present.

"Dr. Hawkins? Leonard Turner from IT here."

"What'd ya find?" Sam asked.

"You've been hacked. Guessing you had files in your documents. Well hum, they're all gone. Yep, pretty sophisticated hack job…deleted everything on the hard drive too. We'll get it fixed up for you. I've told administration of this breach. Hope if files were important, you have exterior back up."

Sam found himself looking closely at each person he passed. He scrutinized their expressions and their eyes, questioning everyone's intent. He had no idea whom to trust or who was part of the conspiracy. And who would want his documents and emails? He had to know why the Houston-Galveston area was apparently the center of the snake's nest. Neither Albright nor Reznick lived there. Bill had, but how involved had Dr. Bill Roberts been? How much did he really known, and why and when had he known it? But even though Sam and Rainee had discussed it, what still haunted Sam as much as any question was why Ana had Bill brought to St. Peter's Memorial in Galveston. There were over ten hospitals near the Roberts's home that would have been more convenient and certainly quicker. And anyone would have recognized that Bill was dying.

Sam finally had made peace with himself. He knew that no medical facility or physician would have been able to save Bill. But the odd behaviors and strange events were mind boggling. The fact that someone had been in his office and hacked his personal computer was alarming. All the clues pointed to something huge. It was not just a series of mistakes, poor judgment, or neglect. Sam was now totally convinced that Rainee had not traveled from Naples to simply sit on the beach. She knew the seriousness and was committed to finding the answers and stopping the Factor-7. Sam totally believed her.

During a brief lunch, he started to reduce his list of chores. He called the insurance agency and arranged for an appointment with an adjuster. He called the Porsche dealership and told them that he needed his Carrera picked up and that the insurance adjuster would look at the damage at their dealership.

Within the hour, they made him an offer to buy it and sent him several photos of the new models. He got a price for a new pearl-white 911 Carrera convertible and ordered it. He continued his day's agenda a bit excited over his new toy.

He would not make any more calls to Rainee from his cell phone. He would buy more ammunition for his gun and perhaps buy another one or two weapons. Sam wanted to arm himself against trouble they might encounter in Mexico, but there would be no transporting of guns over the border. He'd put them away for their return. He would see Ana and somehow get the key to the Mexico house and the combination to the safe. He would see Albright at dinner and subtly grill him for any morsel of information. Perhaps then, he and Rainee would know how to proceed. Sam found himself sweating over the daunting tasks ahead and the imminent dangers. He could walk away and just let it all play out, but that would not be in Sam's character. He had never been a coward—cautious yes, but never had he been a deserter in the face of danger. He was a healer, not a killer, and he couldn't stand by and see potentially thousands of innocents die. He hated the terrorists as much as anyone, but he couldn't wrap his head around setting off a territorial plague to wipe out the Islamic jihadists or any of the murderers' potential targets. The proof must be found to shut them down, and if Rainee was right, it would be in Mexico.

His thoughts went to Rainee. He wondered what she was doing. Sam shook his head. They had just met. He didn't know her. And he actually didn't like her at first. Why was she on his mind so often. He rubbed his eyes. She was getting to him.

He had just finished his dictation to send to the medical transcriptionist when the phone rang. He answered the internal call's annoying ring. The hospital operator spoke softly. "Dr. Hawkins, I have Mrs. Roberts on the phone for you."

"Hi, Ana," Sam said sweetly. "How are you?"

"I'm well, Sam," she replied. "I wanted to call you to let you know that I'm off for few weeks in British Columbia. I'm going to see some friends and take the train across BC into Alberta. I simply can't take this Texas heat."

"I hear that. Well, your trip sounds wonderful. You need the change of geography, and it will definitely be cooler. I had wanted to talk to you about using your villa in San Miguel de Allende for a few days. I need a rest and some cooler air as well. Maybe I can be of help, since you want to sell the house now. I'm chartering a plane for safety. I was leery of the highway between León and San Miguel. You know—that cartel thing."

"Yes, I surely know about that. Bill and I should have sold the place years ago. It's not safe for an American—or even a Mexican national, for that matter—to be on the Mexican back roads."

"Since I have a charter and won't go commercial, I was thinking I could clean the house out a bit and bring back the valuables."

"Would you, Sam?" she replied. "That's so thoughtful of you."

Sam calculated his words. "I'll, ah, need a key, and…" He paused, almost choking on words. "If I clean out the safe, I'll need the combination." There it was. He had said it. Sam held his breath in anticipation of her answer.

"Certainly. You can pick up the key from Julia in an hour, and she'll have the combination to the safe in an envelope."

Sam released an audible sigh of relief. That was easier than he had imagined. "Great. One more thing. May I ask that you not mention this to anyone? I mean no one, Ana. I need my privacy right now." He stumbled on his words again, feeling guilty about his deception.

"Sure Sam. Not an issue. I won't say anything. Have a great trip. My taxi is here. Gotta run. Tootles."

Sam leaned back in his chair. His heart was pounding. Normally he would not have thought twice about asking Ana for anything. They had been that close for many years. But the lies and the deception as well as the safety issues for all concerned had clouded his senses. He had only considered what he would do if Ana had asked questions or if she had wanted to go with him. That had not happened, and for the first time all day, he felt overwhelmingly relieved. Next would be Albright. His temporary solace flew out the window. "Albright, damn it."

Sam got all his errands and phone calls made in record time. He advised the hospital of his upcoming absence and put his weapons and new ammo in a duffel bag. Finally, he opened his bottom desk drawer and retrieved a bottle of 2008 Domaine De Chevalier that had been a birthday gift from Bill. Perhaps he and Rainee would find a moment to toast the old doctor's fine life, but Sam feared that what they might find could leave a bitter taste. So he would take the bottle home but reserve planning the tribute.

As the July sun glistened across Galveston Bay, Sam crossed the causeway and headed for his house on Tiki Island. He had much to do before the early departure for Mexico, yet only a few minutes to head north and meet Dr. John Albright.

Sam intentionally arrived at the La Playa restaurant before Albright. He went directly to the bar and gave his American Express card to the bartender. "I'm meeting a friend. It's his third marriage, but I'm helping him celebrate anyway." Sam forced a laugh.

The bartender smiled snidely as if saying he'd heard that one too many times.

"It's a twosome bachelor party, if you will." Sam continued. "I want you to give him doubles of whatever he orders. Put no alcohol in my drinks. I'm driving."

"I'm not sure I can do that, sir. I can't give him doubles unless he wants it. Comprende?"

Sam's lips pursed, and he bit the side of his cheek. Albright was going to walk in at any time, and he had a too-scrupulous bartender who would not cooperate. He pulled out his wallet and handed the young bartender two crisp one-hundred-dollar bills. "Can you do it now? I want to make my buddy's last night of singlehood great. I'll be sure he doesn't drive. You comprende now? Help me out, will ya? We want a table for drinks and food here in the bar. Make it happen."

The young man nodded, took the money, and winked. "OK, yes sir. But please, be the driver, because I can go to jail, you see."

Sam nodded. "Of course." He walked to the darkest side of the bar. The room was very cold and almost empty of patrons. The aroma of charbroiled beef, grilled onions, and beer permeated the air. He found a table in the far corner. It was a square metal table with retro plastic-and-metal chairs. The Tejano music played a bit too loudly for Sam's tastes, but he would say nothing to his bribed bartender. The last thing Sam wanted was to piss him off, but it surely would be difficult to hear everything that John Albright might say. So he would persuade Albright to tell the barkeep to lower the tunes.

If Sam could get Albright plowed, then just maybe he would say something…anything that would lend credence to what Sam had been told. He sat down and waited for his prey.

Dr. Albright paused at the door. Sam observed him momentarily while Albright stood blinded by the sunlight. He tried to focus in the darkness of the Mexican bar. Sam knew Albright well. He could be as gracious as he was handsome, and Sam almost thought he could like the man. *Almost* was the definitive word. He knew John Albright could charm the skin off a snake.

Sam waved his hand, and Albright, now able to see, started toward him.

"Well, Sam, this is a nice surprise. I really didn't think you'd show up. I don't have any buddies here. I wanted some good ol' Mexican margaritas, and I remember this place had the best. Glad to see ya, guy!" Albright extended his hand.

Sam stood and shook his hand. "It's been a while since we had drinks…what, fifteen or so years?"

The bartender interrupted the pleasantries and took both men's orders. He returned quickly with two margaritas in large global iced mugs.

"Yep, just like I remember. Huge drinks." Sam paused, deliberating his next move. "So, you're here for a short vacation?" he blurted, trying to start the difficult conversation.

Albright took a sip from the mug. "Whew, they make these things with cojones! Nah, I'm here on some personal business, and it so happened Bill Roberts died, so I'm sticking around a few more days."

Sam was taken aback as well as appalled at the nonchalance at his friend's death. *It so happened?* His patience for Albright's familiar attitude was short lived. "That's a strange way to describe his untimely death, John."

Albright looked strangely as Sam. "Well, it *was* untimely. I guess I meant I was glad I was here for Ana."

"Yeah, I was wondering about that, John." Sam chose his words carefully. "I honestly don't recall you being close to either Bill or Ana." Then he tried to make an excuse for Albright's association with the couple. "They are…Bill was…very easy to like and be around, so it's understandable."

Albright took another large gulp from the margarita. "Bill and I had been working on some things together. Ana and her cooking were just an extra bonus." He laughed.

Sam again was stunned, or perhaps disgusted, by Albright's choice of words, but he said nothing.

Albright continued. "Bill and I got reacquainted when he came to Washington after his brother's car wreck. I ran into him there about six months ago."

Sam continued to quiz the other doctor. "Washington's a big place. Coincidence you met up in such a large city."

"I guess you could say that." Albright continued to drink his margarita. "How did that bad deal with your Porsche turn out?"

"Still working on it. Seems there are no suspects." Sam was happy to see how easy it was to get him to talk. But he knew he would have to get more than how Albright and Bill were associated for their meeting to be of value. "Mind if I ask what you and Bill were working on?" Sam cringed at his blatant question. Albright's answer could be, "Yes, I mind the question." That would close the doors to any further information, or he could answer it with the truth or a lie. It was a reckless inquiry for Sam to introduce so early into the evening, but he had blurted it out, and he had to live with the consequences.

Albright took no time to answer. "Not at all. I was a bit displaced."

Sam looked puzzled. "Displaced? What do you mean?" Sam leaned closer toward Albright.

"I didn't really like seeing patients and the day-to-day doctoring thing," Albright said. "I like research, and I'm damn good at it. Yeah, I was in New York working for Lenniles Pharmaceuticals. I had developed a new drug that appeared to be very helpful in slowing the progression of at least three types of malignancies. I had developed mutated polio and herpes viruses that killed cancer cells in lab rats. It worked with a person's DNA and immunity. I was on the way to a cure for three major killers—hell, maybe more. Well, making a very long ordeal short, the suits sitting on the board of directors—idiots—didn't know anything about medicine. They had one interest, which was their bottom line. They didn't want me to go public with my research, and they didn't want to manufacture it either. It wasn't one hundred percent proprietary, you see. I had natural elements in the formula. Pharma's a big business, you know. Cancer is very, very profitable. Ah, hell, *disease* is profitable. I threatened to go to another pharm, but they put a bigger threat on me. They hung a noncompete over me and said anything I had developed belonged to them. I could have gone to prison if I took it. Man, these guys fucking put an end to my work, and I hate them for it. I went to the CDC for a stint, but that also was far too confining for me. Those guys are inept and slow to make any moves. I recognized the coronavirus problem in China long before any case hit the States. Dumb shits…those Chinese. That deal was very interesting. I mean, the virus just slipped out of the lab." He laughed. "Like hell it did." He took a very large drink of his margarita, emptying the mug.

Sam narrowed his eyes. *Did John know something about how the coronavirus pandemic started or was he just being himself and a know-it-all?* Sam motioned to the bartender, who started the blender immediately. "We'll never know how that virus started." He heard Albright huff, but ignored him. "Yeah, I've heard that the government…" Sam held his hands over his ears. "Hey man, ask the bartender to lower the volume. I'm getting a headache." He continued. "…is the last group that should get into the medical biz. I wish they would stay out of our lives, especially medicine. Too much red tape." He paused. "You were in China?"

"Dos más, señor. And quiet the music, kid!" Albright said a bit too loudly. "Nah, I work with some scientists there. I work with scientists all over the world."

Sam's supportive statement and interest in what John did, although muffled by the music, must have been heard. Albright seemed to be pleased that Sam had agreed with him. If Sam was to keep him talking, he knew he had to continue the flow of tequila, and he had to continue to endear himself to Albright by agreeing with his every word.

"You see, Sam, I'm the modern-day Wernher von Braun. Hell, the United States wanted his genius, and they whitewashed the reason to bring a Nazi to America. They called it Operation Paperclip. That was crap. All they paperclipped was a Nazi who had worked directly with the führer to our space program. I'm sure he and I are alike in that neither of us hold, or in his case, held, any interest in the political aspect of our grand ideas and we both possess the intellect to carry them out. Geniuses are valued no matter their political, economic, or religious affiliations. Such as I." He laughed cynically. "Genius is often confused with insanity, you know," Albright stated coldly, losing his jovial attitude.

Sam wasn't sure how to respond. "And vice versa, I suppose."

Albright seemed to be on a roll and somewhat in a world all his own. "I like a challenge, and I want a Nobel Prize someday. I've always wanted that. Fuck it, I have worked too damn hard to be shut out. I even went overseas but basically got the same responses. Then I met a group of scientists at a convention in Geneva, and I found my niche. Someday people will know my name." He angrily hissed in Spanish what he had just said. "Algún día la gente sabrá mi nombre."

Sam leaned closer to Albright. "So you speak Spanish?"

"Sam," Albright said sarcastically, "doesn't everyone in South Texas speak Spanish? Ha…even some of those with Mexicans DNA!" Albright laughed. "¿De qué manera de joder una señorita?"

Sam understood enough of the Spanish. "Only you, Albright, would know pickup phrases in Spanish." Sam forced a laugh but remained not amused. Albright had just all but admitted to what Sam knew was happening. He also now realized that Albright did not have a political interest in what he was doing. It was strictly the need to do something big in medical science and be recognized. *So, he thinks everyone will know his name forever*, Sam thought. *Hopefully on the most wanted list.*

"What do you think of the president's death? It seemed strange to me how he died," Sam said.

"Very unfortunate."

"I agree, but that's not the terminology I would have chosen."

"Winger was an uncompromising weakling, and he also didn't see the big picture. He just didn't have the balls to be president," Dr. Albright said.

"The balls to be president?" Sam asked. "What do you mean?"

"Well, all I can say is that when an opportunity arises for the good of many, then the good of few must be discounted. Winger didn't understand that."

Sam glared at Albright, trying to contain his disdain for everything Albright said. He had well established his role with the Factor-7 bacteriophage without coming right out and saying it. Of course, he wouldn't say it, and apparently, to Sam's benefit, he didn't suspect that Sam knew anything about the plan. So to John Albright, his innuendos were innocuous. As Rainee had surmised, Albright was a braggart, and he couldn't contain his discoveries. After all, his interest was clearly the glory. And apparently, Albright would go to all lengths to gain that notoriety. Dr. John Albright was something between a genius and a monster.

The rest of the evening, Sam just listened to Albright's rants as he got drunker by each margarita. He reiterated multiple times that he had been mistreated and that the powers that be were inept idiots. By 11:00 o'clock, Sam had had his fill of the arrogance and trite conversation. Sam offered to call a cab, but Albright refused. He had his car, and his hotel was only twenty miles away. Sam wouldn't allow him to drive. He didn't give a rat's ass about Albright's safety, but he did care about the innocent person he might kill in his drunken stupor. Sam convinced him that he would take him to his hotel, and he could get his car in the morning. Reluctantly, Albright agreed.

John Albright slept while they drove the thirty minutes to his hotel. Sam pulled into the Four Seasons in downtown Houston. Albright stumbled from the truck, mumbling something as Sam put it in reverse. From the corner of his eye, Sam caught a glimpse of Simon Reznick. Reznick was walking quickly toward Albright. Sam sped from the hotel. Meeting Reznick at almost midnight was not going to happen. But, unfortunately, even if Reznick didn't know Sam was there, he most certainly would know when Albright sobered up.

Everything was done. Sam felt drained from the day. He had been successful with Ana, and he knew more than ever that Albright was involved in something. But seeing Reznick spooked him. Would he put two and two together? Did he know that John Albright was a windbag and a braggart and that he most probably had told Sam about the Factor-7? Sam momentarily pushed the fear of Reznick aside. *Albright will have hell remembering much...and he'll have a time finding his rental car in the morning.* Sam laughed. *He'll have a pisser of a headache.* He huffed, "Poor bastard." But Sam's amusement soon faltered. He couldn't stop thinking of Reznick. Albright would definitely deny to Simon that he had spilled his guts to Sam. But that might not even matter. Just the mere fact that Albright and Sam had met and that Albright had gotten so drunk could create suspicion as to what Sam might now know. Albright was a bigmouth, and that would be dangerous for Simon. That alone could be enough for Sam and Rainee to be in danger right alongside John Albright. If what Rainee suspected about these people was true, they would not take chances that some revelation could be leaked about them or their plan, and they would undoubtedly take all measures to prevent it.

CHAPTER FOURTEEN

The jet would depart at 7:00 a.m. Both Sam and Rainee needed their rest, but he had to call her.

She answered with a sexy, sleepy voice. "Sam, is everything all right?"

"Yes, I guess. It was an experience, and I saw Reznick when I let Albright off at his hotel. Strange how he gets around."

"He's trouble, I think," she replied, seeming to awaken a bit.

"Right. Albright was too drunk to drive and wouldn't take a cab. So I had to drive all the way to downtown Houston. I just got home. I'll tell you everything in the morning. We're ready to go at seven a.m. I'll pick you up at six." Sam gave her a few more details of the trip before they hung up. He sat on the side of his bed imagining her lying in her bed. What side of the bed? Did she like blankets or none? Did she sleep in pajamas or naked? He shook his shoulders as if a chill had come over him. "Stop it. Shake it off," he said out loud. She was an incredible lady, and Sam knew he was more than simply interested in the Italian doctor.

Sam saw the Bombardier jet on the tarmac. They didn't have a smaller plane available, but the luxury of the Bombardier was just fine with Sam. It was being prepped for the trip. He and Rainee sat at a long granite-topped bar and sipped on complimentary coffee as they waited for the crew to arrive. Sam was greeted by a young man. He thought he must have been about twenty-five and hoped he wasn't the captain. The man was dressed in a freshly starched white shirt with Gulf Air Team embroidered on the pocket. His navy-blue pants had a starched crease that would cut paper. Sam mused that they must be terribly restrictive as he glanced at his faded, tired, yet incredibly comfortable jeans. Sam started to lift his and Rainee's bags.

"I'll get that for you, Doctor. We will be ready to leave as soon as you and Dr. Arienzo provide your passports and complete the brief forms. No firearms, meats, or vegetables, I trust."

Sam nodded. "None." He whispered to Rainee, "Wish I could have brought an arsenal."

She ignored him.

The young man looked at Rainee. "And you, ma'am?"

She replied, "None."

"We will be serving breakfast and beverages once we are in the air at cruising altitude. I will see you on board." The young aviator smiled and opened the door that led to the waiting aircraft.

Sam and Rainee walked up the narrow stairs and sat in the first row of seats, she on one side of the aisle and Sam on the other.

Once in the air, a cute woman came to ask what they wished to drink.

Sam asked for a Bloody Mary. Rainee ordered only coffee.

"Kind of early to be drinking, don't you think?" she asked.

"Normally, yes. Today, no," Sam answered, emphatically.

As the plane cruised at thirty-two thousand feet, Sam felt safe, perhaps for the first time in days. He sipped his drink and began to detail his meeting with John Albright. Rainee was enthralled with the conversation. Although Albright did not exactly admit his role in the Factor-7, Sam felt that he had successfully drawn out a lot of information over margaritas. And if nothing else, Albright's attitude was the perfect temperature to be a part of such a dreadful scheme.

"He should have a pretty big aching head this morning, and I bet his tongue feels like it's growing mushrooms," Sam said. "Those margaritas can be mighty deadly. I stopped counting the globals at five. So he had the equivalent of about ten shots." Sam laughed. "I hope his head's killing him."

"What are globals?" Rainee asked, smiling.

"Huge round mugs. Global...globe..."

Rainee smirked. "I get it."

The flight attendant interrupted them. "As you requested, Dr. Hawkins, we have eggs Benedict or huevos rancheros. Both come with fresh fruit."

Rainee stared at Sam and grinned. "I guess I am having that breakfast with you after all."

Sam smiled sheepishly. "If they're good, I'd suggest trying the Mexican fare."

The flight attendant kindly interrupted. "I've had no complaints, sir."

Rainee nodded in agreement.

"Then we'll have the huevos rancheros," Sam said, faking an exaggerated Spanish accent and rolling both *r*'s in "rancheros."

"Yes, sir. It will be a few minutes," she replied, and then she started toward the rear galley.

Sam's drink was making him feel better, and the food would set off the morning perfectly. He couldn't, however, dismiss that some of his newfound contentment was that he was with Rainee. But he also recognized the worry in her face, and there was nothing he could do for her. They were going into unsafe and uncharted territory. Neither of them knew what to expect, but both were confident that whatever answers they were chasing were in the safe at the villa in San Miguel de Allende.

Sam broke the silence. "I know very little about you," he said. "Tell me about yourself."

She glanced at Sam and smiled self-consciously. "What do you want to know?"

Sam shrugged. "Everything?"

"That would take a very long time." She laughed. "Well, I was born in Naples. My mother was Swiss and my father Italian. My father was a scientist and a medical doctor, as was my paternal grandfather. My parents divorced when I was three. I went back and forth between Naples and Geneva until my mother married an American when I was thirteen. We moved to Santa Barbara. I was educated in Italy, England, and the United States. I have a PhD in neurobiology from Stanford and am a doctor of medicine with duel disciplines in infectious diseases and neurology. I guess you could say that I didn't know what I wanted to do when I grew up." She laughed again.

Sam laughed at her joke but was stunned by her accomplishments. He thought she was too young to have done so much. He couldn't, however, bring himself to be so bold or brash to ask her age.

"I'm thirty-eight, if you're wondering," she said, smiling.

How the hell did she read my mind? He knew he was in trouble if she also possessed mind-reading abilities. "I wasn't wondering that," he blurted.

She smiled. "I think you were."

"OK, I was."

"And you want to know if I'm married, right?"

Sam shook his head in awe. *She should work on the psychic hotline!* he thought, or was he that incredibly transparent? Reconciled that she had supernatural abilities, he said, "Yes, yes…I was wondering that."

She giggled almost childishly. "You are so easy to read, Dr. Sam Hawkins. You make me laugh."

Sam didn't know whether to be flattered or insulted. "Well, Dr. Rainee, you are beautiful, and you had not mentioned a family."

"I didn't dodge that bullet. I was married about seven years ago. It lasted about eighteen months. He was a cardiologist in Naples. Very accomplished man…very prestigious doctor…handsome as hell, but very fond of his outside affairs. He couldn't keep his dick in his pants." She smiled, waiting for Sam's response.

Sam coughed, almost choking on his cocktail. He was shocked by her candid answer and the vernacular. He cleared his throat. "Yeah, my wife couldn't either."

"Your wife couldn't keep her dick in her pants?" She laughed heartily.

Again, Sam shook his head. This woman had him by the balls, and she apparently knew it.

"You know what I mean. I caught her in our pool…well…with the twenty-two-year-old pool boy."

"Get them young and train them right. But I insist on them being legal age too." She smirked. "Just kidding, of course. I actually prefer a mature and refined gentleman."

Sam sneered, but then they both laughed. Rainee reached across the aisle and took a drink from Sam's third Bloody Mary.

"I think I'll have one of those," she said seductively.

"What, a pool boy or a drink?" Sam joked.

"Either or both." Rainee took another sip of his drink and instead of placing it back on his tray table, she put it on her own.

"A thief too, I see," Sam teased.

Rainee smiled and touched Sam's hand. "I'm glad we got to laugh." She turned toward the window and stared outside.

The brief break did both good, but it was impossible to avoid the true nature of their business.

"We should be there soon. What's your story?" she said, taking in a deep breath.

Sam touched her arm and gave it a quick squeeze. "Well, I'm divorced, as you know. You can't set buzzard eggs and hatch canaries."

Rainee looked puzzled. "I beg your pardon?" she said and then figured out the Texas colloquialism. She laughed again and shook her head. "You're too funny."

"Well, the marriage failure was mostly my fault. Seems I spent too much time wrapped up in what I do at the hospital, and not enough in my marriage." He sadly smiled. "One learns along the way. I messed up, but maybe it was to be." He expelled his troubled past with one massive breath. "Regarding Mexico, don't worry about being here. It will all be fine."

She turned and forced a smile but didn't mention his divorce. She took a long pause, perhaps thinking about what he had said. Then completely changing the subject, she asked, "Do you speak Spanish?"

"A bit. We call it Tex-Mex."

"Ah, I see." She turned back toward the window.

"You?" Sam asked.

"I speak seven languages. Six would be considered fluent. I have a bit of trouble with Japanese."

Sam sat back in his seat. "Well, la-di-da, I've got a genius for a partner in crime." He laughed and said, "Now, I'm joking, of course."

Rainee smirked and shook her head in amusement. "So, you don't speak anything but English and a bit of Spanish? You arrogant Americans." She genuinely smiled at Sam this time.

"Not so," he replied. "I speak enough Spanish to get me into trouble. I speak dirty French, and I can order a pizza in Rome. So there, smart-ass. Oh yeah, I can also order sushi, so I guess I'm better with Japanese than you." He grinned.

Her eyes sparkled, and she bit her bottom lip. "I'll do the talking in Mexico. You might order us a prostitute for dinner."

Their joviality was interrupted by the overhead speaker.

"Doctors, we are approaching San Miguel de Allende. Be sure your seat belts are fastened and tray tables are in the upright and locked position. We will be on the ground in less than fifteen minutes. The State of Guanajuato customs will meet you at the door of the plane. The temperature in San Miguel is sixty-eight degrees Fahrenheit. There is a light breeze and it is overcast with a chance of afternoon showers. The flight deck appreciates your business, and we hope you will fly Gulf Air Team again very soon."

Sam turned to Rainee. "It rains pretty much every afternoon here in the summer."

"I like rain," she replied softly.

"So, Rainee likes rainy days." Sam was embarrassed at his pun as soon as the words left his mouth.

"Oh, and that would be the first time I ever heard a joke about my name. And no, my siblings aren't Sunny and Stormy."

Sam jokingly cowered. "Sorry. Do you have any brothers and sisters?"

"No, just me."

"How 'bout that? Me too. As a kid, I always said I was a lonely child. I meant only child."

"Sounds Freudian to me."

"Nah, I was a happy kid. I had a lot of cousins and friends."

Rainee only nodded.

Sam wasn't sure she had experienced such a fine childhood, but he would not pry. "What makes you happy?" he asked.

"Good books, great movies, and music, among many other things." She smiled sheepishly.

Sam grinned, hoping she might be flirting a bit. "I like the same, but I love old classic rock and roll, fast cars, and new country-western music...and fast cars. Did I mention I like fast cars?" He laughed.

The flight attendant interrupted, telling them that they had time to finish their drinks and that the car they had reserved would be waiting outside the small terminal. She thanked them and returned to the front jump seat for landing.

Sam smiled at Rainee. "It has begun, my dear."

"What is your reason for visiting Mexico?" asked the older man dressed in the Mexican customs uniform.

Both doctors replied in unison, "Pleasure."

He stamped their passport and motioned that they could proceed.

Pleasure, Sam thought. *If only.*

The car was, in fact, parked outside the small bright-yellow stucco building. A young man handed them the keys and asked, in part Spanish and part English, if they needed directions.

Sam laughingly stated that he could understand about half of what he had said.

Rainee shook her head in pure exasperation at Sam's constant silliness. But she actually was amused at his quick wit, especially considering the stress of their trip. She responded to the young man in perfect Spanish.

"I know the way to the house," Sam said confidently. But it had been over five years, and surely things had changed. He reconsidered. "Maybe ask him how to get to Colonia Guadiana."

The directions were good. Sam recognized the Hospital de Fe, better known to the tourists as the blue hospital on the hill. Soon he knew where to turn, and they parked in the narrow street in front of the Villa de Robertos. He opened the small gate. Rainee walked into the courtyard. The fragrance of flowers perfumed the air.

"I need to open the double doors and get our car inside," Sam said.

Once they were parked inside with all gates closed and locked, Sam pulled the luggage from the trunk. He paused to soak up the atmosphere and to consider everything he had gotten himself into. But mainly he considered Rainee. She was something special, and he knew he was in big trouble.

The house was as he remembered. A twelve-foot-tall and approximately eighteen-inch-thick brick barrier walled the entire property. Vines of red, coral, and pink bougainvillea covered three-quarters of it. There was a large courtyard in both the front and the back, and each was filled with flowering plants and trees. Ana had decorated the outdoor furniture with vividly printed fabrics. Talavera pottery and Dias de los Muertos characters sat on tables and in the garden. There were decorative painted skulls, artisan treasures Ana found in San Miguel. The Mexican skeleton lady, Katrina, was everywhere. She had collected Katrinas dressed as mermaids, brides, pirates, and classic historical figures. The colors were bright and cheerful. The sleeping quarters were downstairs of the main house. The living room and kitchen were on the second floor. Several smaller rooms were on each side upstairs. Sam thought they had been small bedrooms when the house was owned by a highly decorated Mexican general in the mid-1800s. But Ana had made them into a small study and closets. A balcony was suspended off the back wall of the living area, and one could see the large Parroquia, the cathedral, in the center of the quaint town. The wall facing the street consisted of glass, making a solid window from the first floor to the second, which allowed in an abundance of light. That had been changed from the original nineteenth-century architecture sometime before the Roberts bought the villa. There was an enclosed covered patio on one side of the yard with a one-bedroom guesthouse attached. Carefully laid ceiling bricks that looked like a finely knitted quilt held together the arched ceiling. Another equally gorgeous domed boveda attached the house to another larger patio, which was complete with dog paw prints forever "glyphed" into the old Saltillo bricks. An old original building that must have been a slaughterhouse and smokehouse when the house was first built remained on the opposite side of the property. Ana had turned it into a type of combination laundry and tool room.

Sam rushed from the car into the villa, trying to not get soaked by the regularly scheduled afternoon rain shower. He set Rainee's luggage in the largest bedroom, with the king-sized bed. He took his bags to one of the other bedrooms.

Suddenly there was a loud buzz. Rainee looked quizzically at Sam. "Only Ana knows we're here, right?"

"The housekeeper, I imagine," he said. "Ana must have told her we'd be coming."

Delores had worked for Bill and Ana for over twenty years. She only came when the Robertses were there and after they left so that the villa could be cleaned. She had aged but was still spryer than one would think for a woman her age.

"*Buenos tardes*, Doctor. The lady, Ana, called me. *Lo siento*, Doctor Guillermo…doctor Bill." She crossed herself. "I am sorry my English is not so good. I changed the…how you say…*sábanas*"—she paused—on the beds. Lady said you like guacamole. I made"—she pointed to the kitchen—"in the refrigerator. Please tell me what you and the señora want to eat. I come every morning, and I cook."

"Señorita," Rainee said.

Delores nodded and smiled kindly.

"Thank you, but we can manage," Sam said. "Maybe sometime this week, you can cook. Talk to me when you come back."

"I have key. I come about eleven *de la mañanas*. I clean and cook then. Si lunes, Monday I cook."

"No need for lunch today. We want to go to the square for lunch. Maybe some chicken and rice for dinner one night, and those squash flowers?" Sam was intentionally rushing her out of the house.

Rainee rattled something in Spanish. She and Delores giggled.

Sam brushed it off. He smiled and winked at Delores and then looked at Rainee. "Your guacamole and pico de gallo are the best, but I ate so much guacamole last time I was here, I didn't think I could look at another avocado."

Delores smiled. "I cook the *calabaza*, ah, *flores fritas*, and make *arroz con pollo?*" she said, sounding somewhere between a question and a statement.

"Fried squash flowers and chicken with rice! Well, I love it, and we'll have her guacamole," she whispered. "Can't hurt her feelings. Or mine. I also asked for mangos and fresh tortillas. Delores is happy." She laughed.

"Sounds like you are too!" Sam smiled.

"Si, señor."

Sam rummaged through the house but was unable to locate any type of safe.

He dialed Ana's cell phone. Maybe she knew where her husband had put it, but the call was about his last resort. He hated the thought of perhaps opening a can of worms with the question, especially if Ana had had time to think about it and maybe had questioned his motives.

The cell phone rang five times, and then Ana's voice mail answered. Sam dialed it three more times, receiving the same automated response with each. Ana was on her way to British Columbia. Maybe she was in the air, or perhaps already on the train without cell service. Either way, he was not able to reach her, and time was of the essence.

Sam called out to Rainee. She was in the back courtyard trying to open the small guesthouse door. "Is it locked?" Sam asked.

"Yes, and the house key doesn't open it," she shouted back.

"Be right down." Sam grabbed a large knife and a screwdriver from the drawer in the kitchen and started down the stairs. He could see Rainee walking around the casita. As he caught up with her, she was standing on a pile of bricks peering into the only window.

"Very dark in there," she said.

Sam started to pry the lock on the door. The handle had a place for a key, but it appeared that the only lock was the large metal dead bolt. The handle easily fell off, but the door would not budge. "I'm going to look for something larger to take down the door. Maybe I can find something in the storage room over there. The yardman surely has tools somewhere."

As Sam walked away, he heard breaking glass. "I'm inside!" Rainee yelled.

Sam shook his head and ran hastily to the back of the property. "Open the door," he asked, feeling a little stupid for not thinking to break the window. He heard the bolt turn, and Rainee threw open the door. "You know, I could have taken down the door. I didn't expect you to break the window," he said.

"What's the difference? The door or the window?" she replied mischievously.

Sam laughed. "I'm just a bit embarrassed to have been taking the hard way around the problem. Anyway, my mother always told me that if I broke a window, I'd have to pay for it. It's posttraumatic stress disorder because growing up I mowed a hell of a lot of lawns to pay for baseballs through windows."

There was a flashlight sitting on the bedside table, and as luck had it, the light worked. Rainee had already started opening cabinet doors. Sam shone the flashlight in the small closets, but neither one found a safe.

"Perhaps it's in the floor," Sam suggested as he threw the colorful rug in the corner of the room. He shook his head. "Nothing here." He sat on the side of the bed. "We need to think. If Bill had something as important as we think in the safe, he wouldn't just leave it out in the open, and he also would not hide it in a conventional place."

"But where else could it be? We've virtually torn this place up. It's not in the house. It's not in the guest house." She paused, and her eyes met Sam's.

"The laundry room!" they both said in unison.

"No one would think to look in that old spider-infested shack," Sam said.

They weaved through the brick path to the block brick building. He pulled open the tall wooden door. The inside had a brick floor with small weeds poking their heads out between them. There was a stained ceramic sink and a few well-worn yard tools. There was a washing machine against the back wall. Sam pulled the light string. The glowing bulb swung easily in the fresh air that now filled the stale building.

"There used to be a large brick oven right here," Sam said, walking closer to the once cooking grotto. "It's been bricked in."

Rainee came closer. "Looks to me like it's newer brick and mortar than the other walls."

"Yeah, for sure, this is fairly recently closed in. I haven't been here for some time, but there was a large open oven, and I know it was right here." Sam pounded his fist against the large concrete bricks. "Sounds pretty solid."

"How big was this oven?" she asked.

"I'd say big enough to hold a whole pig or goat," Sam said.

"So pretty good size?"

"Yeah. You think this is the place, don't you?" Sam asked, but already knowing her answer.

"We have to tear into this wall," she replied.

Sam stood with his hand on one hip and his head cocked to one side. "We?"

Rainee grimaced. "Well, I can do whatever you can do—and better, Buster."

Sam started for the door mumbling "Buster" under his breath. "Yeah, well, we'll see about that." He acted put out with her.

Rainee giggled.

"Going to look for a sledgehammer." He walked out of the old building shaking his head, but nonetheless, he was amused at how cute the little Italian doctor could be.

"Apparently, Delores doesn't do the laundry here," Rainee said to herself, wiping a cobweb from her face.

Sam soon returned. "There are no tools here. A shovel with a rusted handle, a broken garden rake, and a mortar trowel is all I found. Yeah, whatever he had to hide and to tell us killed him. Now this is going to kill me. Mind you, I'm not underestimating the gravity of this situation, but hell, Bill could have made this easier for us."

Rainee huffed. "Sam, he was making it harder for someone else."

Sam nodded but said nothing more about it.

"Well, the safe has to be here." Rainee tapped the trowel against the bricks. "I don't think anyone looking to steal something would think to tear out a wall in an old building. Bill was clever. He even tried to distress these bricks and stucco."

Sam mumbled under his breath, "This distresses me."

Rainee tried to keep from laughing at Sam's whining over the task ahead.

Sam huffed, "We'll need tools. Maybe a pick and sledgehammer and something to pry out the bricks…a crowbar thing," he said, dusting off spiderwebs and dirt from his shirt and jeans.

"A crowbar thing?" Rainee laughed again, amused.

"Yes, a crowbar thing," he said defensively. "Give me a break. I bet a carpenter doesn't know what a trephine is."

"I hope a carpenter never needs to bore a hole in a skull. You kill me, Sam," Rainee said, laughing loudly.

The moment of Rainee's teasing did them both well. The tension was building to find the safe and Bill's documents. The days had been passing quickly since Bill Roberts's death. If Bill died and made that ultimate sacrifice so the Factor-7 plans could be exposed and thwarted, then possibly they had little time left.

———————

Sam found a small business near the center of town. It sold used tires and repaired them.

Rainee asked the owner, in Spanish, if he could sell them some tools. He had a crowbar and a very old wooden-handled ax in lieu of a sledgehammer. She asked to buy a pair of gloves. The owner of the tire shop pulled off the gloves from his hands and handed them to her. She took them with two fingers.

The elderly Mexican man shook his head in amusement at the Americans. He smiled as he counted his handful of five-dollar bills.

Sam heard the old man shut the doors to the tire barn as they walked to the car. He had made more selling them the old tools and gloves than he would all week fixing tires.

It was beginning to rain again. They rushed toward their parked car. El Jardin Square was buzzing with people trying to find a dry place to sit until the summer shower passed. Rainee caught a glance of a large Mexican man with dark-gray tinted glasses standing against the wall. He intently watched them as they passed. He wore a white cotton shirt with a squared hem that was not tucked into his pants and a white Panama-style hat. He puffed on a large cigar. His gold oversized watch gleamed as he put the cigar to his lips. He was a caricature of someone in a beer or rum commercial. Rainee slowed her pace and looked straight at the man, whose eyes seemed to follow their every step, but neither spoke.

"Did you see that man?" Rainee asked as she closed the car door.

"Which man?" Sam looked around.

"There, by the column." Rainee looked behind her. The man was no longer there. "He's gone now. He was really checking us out."

"You mean he was checking *you* out?" Sam asked.

"No, he was really looking us over," Rainee insisted.

"You're just jumpy. No one knows we're here. He was looking at a beautiful lady, that's all."

Rainee relaxed in her seat. "Thank you, but I'm not so sure."

The drive back to the villa was short. The afternoon shower had slowed by the time they pulled the car behind the walls and Sam closed and locked the double wooden gates. Inside the walls, no one from outside could see them or the house. Rainee felt secure once again. As tacky as Sam thought it to be, he was glad that the beautiful villa had broken pieces of glass cemented into the tops of the thick walls surrounding the property. It was a fortress.

The task of tearing down the newly sealed area was daunting. The entire building was constructed of concrete blocks and bricks. Although newer than the rest, the oven was no exception. The ax broke pieces off the bricks, but the enclosure remained sealed and was not budging as easily as Sam had hoped. Rainee held the crowbar between the blocks of concrete, and Sam would slam the end of the ax into the masonry. The wall seemed impermeable.

"I've got to take a break," Sam said, wiping the sweat from his face and neck. "I haven't worked this hard since I mowed forty lawns in one month." He smiled at Rainee. "Had to pay for those windows, you know."

She smiled back. "You'll get it. I have faith in you."

Sam picked up the ax and began to swing at the wall. He stopped. "What if this is all for nothing and the safe isn't in there?"

"It has to be," she said. "It would be insane for anyone to work as hard as you are for nothing."

Sam sneered at her.

Rainee grinned. "No, Bill wouldn't have gone to this much trouble for no good reason. He would not wall up a nineteenth-century brick oven. I hate that he did. The history here is incredible."

"Well, I hope Bill was sane and all this is not just some crazy man's paranoia." Sam wiped his brow and groaned, as if in pain. "Ana said he had been acting strange, and what he said to you…geez, he brought you into the middle of this. God, what if this is all some insane hallucination or paranoia. It could be that this is all some crazy, delusional man's labors."

"I think you're simply wishing. You know there's evidence that Bill knew something that was seriously dangerous, and we must know what all that is. Sam, get over your doubts." Rainee took the dirty cloth from Sam's hand. She grimaced at the feeling of sweat that permeated the dirty cloth. "It's too late to start doubting our task."

"I guess. So if what Bill wants us to find is in there, it's pretty sure no one could steal it," Sam said firmly. "Someone would have to know there was a brick oven in the wall. That would not be considered by just anyone. And, I mean, someone would need to know that Bill was desperately trying to hide something. So you're probably right. This bricked-in oven would be so ridiculous of a hiding place, that it really might be our one clue that this is, in fact, where he put the information. And he knew I knew there had been an oven."

"You're funny. You've stood here for five minutes talking to yourself and trying to convince yourself there's no safe, and now suddenly you agree with yourself?" She let out a small giggle. "Who's the insane one?" She patted Sam on the back. "And yeah, maybe the most ridiculous is what Bill knew we would recognize."

Sam looked at her strangely, not entirely confident that they were destined to find the safe because of Bill's unconventional camouflage. He regained his strength and began to chisel once again at the wall. A large piece fell, and rebar metal began to peek through. "Ah, geez. Bill put metal rebar between the concrete blocks. Look, there is still another layer of blocks behind this one."

"Be careful. The metal's sharp, and we don't have any tetanus shots with us," Rainee said jokingly, but it had a ring of seriousness. "Even I'm stunned at the effort Bill put into this," she said.

Sam wiped his forehead with his sleeve. "Maybe the effort was indeed to save his life or perhaps someone else's. What I want to know is why Ana had the combination but didn't say anything about this bastion of a hiding place!"

"She must not have known. Maybe the safe was simply a family container to keep things in when they were not here. And Bill moved it"—she paused—"I hope...and fortified the stronghold for secrecy and protection."

Hours passed. It was getting dark. "We aren't going to be able to finish this tonight," Sam said. "I'm exhausted, and it'll be dark soon. Let's close it down."

"Yeah, I agree. You need rest," Rainee said sympathetically.

Sam stripped off his clothes at the bathroom door. Concrete dusk filtered into the air. The warm shower soothed him, and he allowed the water to run over his tired body for longer than usual. Rainee's shouts through the bathroom door interrupted his solitude.

"Sam, I have a bottle of red wine that I found in the pantry and the guacamole out. You need to eat something, and *you* told Delores to not cook. So all you get is guacamole!" He heard her whisper, "Asshole."

In a few minutes, Sam was upstairs. Rainee was sitting on the balcony and sipping a glass of wine and eating guacamole with saltine crackers. The bells from the cathedral rang out seven chimes.

"Asshole, huh?"

"Oh, you heard that?" she said sheepishly. "Well, you are! We could have been eating like royalty, but no...you had to tell her to not cook, and these damn crackers are stale."

Sam started to laugh. "You are too beautiful when you're angry."

"I'm not angry, damn it. I'm hungry." She laughed.

"I promise tomorrow I'll have Delores bring in food. Better still, I'll take you for dinner at Chapelina, a small restaurant on the top of La Parroquia."

Rainee smiled. "And the man says don't cook for us tonight. And it gets better still—Delores doesn't come until eleven o'clock on Monday.

So let me see. That would be no dinner tonight, and no breakfast. No food!"

Sam started to laugh loudly, and it felt good. "The lady is hungry."

"Damn right."

"Guess what I know?" Sam asked, nudging her with his forefinger. "There's a pizza delivery right down the street, and the number should still be written on the inside of the pantry door. Yep…here it is. Extra-large all the way. The works?"

"Yeah, we're both exhausted. I'll go for that. I've died and gone to heaven," she replied.

"Oh, one thing. The crust down here is made from tortillas. It's called a pizzchalupa." Sam laughed.

"No, you're joking…right? Oh well, I'll eat anything right now. Even a what? Pizzchalupa." She tried not to laugh, but Sam was too amusing.

He looked at her. Tired or not, she was tempting. The lady was beautiful, funny, and smart.

———

Sam fell into a deep sleep just as his head hit the pillow. But the comfort of rest was only temporary. He awoke in less than three hours with his mind reeling over the events of the day. Every facet of the mystery left by Bill haunted him. Sam leaned back onto the pillow. Bill Roberts's last words obsessed him. John Albright's conversation unnerved him. President Winger's death troubled him. And the thought of Rainee in the other bedroom aroused him.

How did Bill achieve such an undertaking? He had to have had help. Sam wasn't the strongest man in the world, but he had far more stamina than a seventy-plus-year-old man. Sam had worked virtually all day making a few holes in the bricks. There was still no sign of a safe or an end to the formable task. He watched the moon move between dark clouds for over half an hour. There was something about it all that confirmed that he and Rainee were digging up danger. But that was the mission. Sam groaned aloud. He had to disassemble the block brick wall, release the steel bars, and remove the additional layer of bricks. It was far too much for him, and he knew it. He needed better tools. He had never wished for a Home Depot or Lowe's so badly before. León was the closest large town, but he hesitated to drive to and from León. It was a winding road, and much of it was sparsely traveled. There were few towns in between and a lot of wide-open spaces to be attacked by Mexican gangs just waiting for an unsuspecting tourist. He could perhaps hire someone to get the tools for him. Sam reclined again on the bed. He had a weak plan, but at least a plan. They would go into town early to see what could be bought.

Morning light broke through at 6:15. Sam was sore from the previous day's work out, and he didn't think he had slept. But in fact, he had a few restful hours after his 2:00 a.m. strategy session with himself. Rainee was already in the kitchen making coffee.

"Good morning," she said softly.

"Good morning," he replied. Sam stood at the bottom of the stairs, shirtless and in sweatpants. Suddenly he became embarrassed.

She was already dressed in jeans and a pink tee. The low-cut cotton shirt clung to her every curve. "Did you get any rest?" she asked.

"Maybe some. I dunno. I thought all night." He held his eyes on her too long.

She poured a cup of coffee for him and then one for herself. Their eyes met, and she smiled and then looked away. "Yeah, me too."

Sam wasn't sure if her answer was that she really had not rested, or she could read his mind and was thinking the same thing. He hoped for the latter.

They went over Sam's plans while sipping coffee on the balcony. The bells at the cathedral rang eight chimes. Sam thought of how easy it had become to talk to Rainee. Time had flown by. But now they had to get on with their objective.

Sam dressed quickly. He found Rainee walking in the back garden when he emerged from the house. He watched her for a few moments before announcing himself. "Ready?" he asked.

"I'm ready for most anything," she said seductively.

Sam was now certain she could read his mind and was toying with him. It was both alarming and satisfying. He shook his head and grinned. "Let's roll."

The square was busy with vendors and strolling men playing very large guitars. The El Jardin was decorated with big colorful paper flags and balloons. Young girls in fancy lace dresses and flowers in their braided hair paraded for the young men, who all sat on benches and whispered to one another. Old men and women held hands as they slowly meandered through the crowd. The ancient cathedral, La Parroquia de San Miguel Archangel, was decorated with banners and colorful streamers.

Sam looked at Rainee. "It's Sunday. There must be a festival today."

"Must be something, and I'm starving," Rainee said.

Sam shook his head in agreement. He pointed to an open café across the street. "Let's go over there and have some breakfast. Maybe the waiter or owner can help us find the tools."

They found a table halfway on the sidewalk and halfway inside the tiny café. A basket of hard rolls and a tub of pale-yellow butter sat on the table.

"Please," said the man standing at the door. "Please sit."

Sam nodded and pulled out the chair for Rainee.

The man who had greeted them came over. He was dressed in all white except for a very large green stain on the front of his apron.

"Buenos días," he said. "Bienvenidos. I am called José, and this is my restaurant." He glanced at the salsa stain on his apron. "I also cook." He smiled. "What you like to drink? I can bring coffee?"

"Café solo," Sam replied.

"Y usted Señora?"

"Señorita," she replied with a cordial grin. "Café con leche, por favor."

"Lo siento, Señorita. Café con leche y café solo. Un momento, por favor."

Sam handed Rainee a small paper menu. "What sounds good?"

"Hum," she replied, looking up at Sam and smiling.

Sam was sure she was flirting. Or maybe she was getting her kicks by seeing him squirm.

"Maybe eggs scrambled with ham?" she said.

"What the hell are divorced eggs?" Sam asked. "They have a dish here called divorced eggs." He laughed, pointing to the menu.

Rainee giggled. "I guess the yolk and whites are separated."

Sam laughed at her joke, but Rainee had already moved onto the task at hand.

She called to José. "Where might we obtain tools or perhaps someone to help with some work?" She explained in perfect Spanish that they needed a brick wall removed.

The owner and waiters knew of no one willing to work Sunday and especially not on the festival day. "Es el Festival de Expresiones Cortos," the owner of the café said. "There will be much music and food all day."

Sam took the last bite of his breakfast and sat back in his chair. He looked out on El Jardín, where the action was increasing by the moment. Dancers dressed in indigenous costumes and mariachi bands were lining up in front of La Parroquia de San Miguel Archangel for what appeared to be a parade. "Well, it's a party," he said.

"Yes, it appears so." Rainee looked around. "But…what do we do about tools?" she asked.

"I don't think we'll get anything today, and I really don't want to drive to Guanajuato or León. We might get there, and the same thing's going on. They all might have festivals today." Sam looked at Rainee, who seemed a thousand miles away. "Hey, are you there?" he asked.

"Sam," she whispered. "There's that same man, and he's watching us again."

Sam scanned the crowd. "Where?"

"He just went through that ochre-colored door." She pointed to Sam's left but kept her fingers flat on the table.

"Let's walk over there and see what he wants," Sam said, smarting off, knowing full well that Rainee would emphatically refuse the suggestion.

She turned her head slowly toward Sam. Her lips were tightly pursed, and her eyes squinted. "You can really be an ass. You know that?"

"I've been told that a few times. Hey, relax. He just lives here or something and is probably here for the festival. Again, you're beautiful and…well…I think he has damned good taste."

She smiled. "OK, so you have redeemed yourself."

"Looks like we're stuck here in the square for a while. I have an idea."

Rainee listened to Sam's idea with reserved optimism. She had become familiar with some of his ideas, and she was not about to agree to anything until he was finished talking.

"Let's walk around the square and burn off breakfast. Then we can find a spot to sit on the steps of the Parroquia and watch the parade. Oh, and we can get a couple of roasted corncobs and cervezas." His voice was filled with childlike excitement. "Seriously, maybe we'll find what we need if we hunt around."

Rainee laughed out loud. "Sam, I read you like a cheap novel. You amuse me. I know, you're trying to get out of your chore."

Sam paid the check and pulled out her chair. He brazenly put her hand on his arm and led her from the café and onto the sidewalk. They strolled commenting on the architecture and cobblestone streets. They looked at artwork, silver jewelry, and fine ceramic pieces. Sam stopped and bought her a colorful serape from a small indigenous woman with two toddler-age children playing around her and an infant in her arms. He followed the purchase by giving Rainee a history lesson on the origin of the blanket. "So now you have a real serape from the town where it was first made."

Rainee raised her eyebrow sarcastically. "Wow."

"I take it that you don't like serapes, or is it the history lesson?" Sam smiled.

"I love both, and thank you. I was playing with you. You're so cute and…well…despite our mission here, I'm really having a wonderful time."

Sam squeezed her hand as it lay on his forearm. "Me too." They walked a few more feet, and then Sam stopped. He removed her hand from his arm and grasped it firmly in his right hand.

She didn't object. They had reached the large wooden ochre-colored door, where Rainee had seen the man enter earlier. "There are usually shops and galleries behind these kinds of doors, kinda like a mall. Well, loosely kind of like a mall," he said as he cracked the door and peered behind it.

Rainee nodded. Hesitantly, she followed Sam inside the long corridor. There were no people around, and the inside shops were closed. "OK, let's go," she urged, pulling him back toward the street.

As they were about to turn around, the large man Rainee had seen before stepped out from an alcove in front of one of the jewelry stores. He began to walk briskly toward them.

"Señor, señora, pardon me," he shouted.

Sam stopped and glanced at Rainee. "It'll be OK," he whispered.

"Buenos días. I was going back to the café where you had breakfast. I was looking for you. This is a lucky day to see you here," he said in well-spoken English, but with a heavy Mexican accent.

Rainee squeezed Sam's hand so hard that he flinched.

"Buenos días, señor," Sam replied. "Why were you looking for us?"

"José Luis, the owner of El Jardin Café, the place you ate this morning, told me you needed workman or tools to fix a wall?" His voice trailed off, ending the sentence with a question. "I, perhaps can help you?"

"I need to remove a wall. Do you have tools that I can buy?" Sam asked.

"I have men to do the job."

"I thought no one would work today."

"Señor, my men will work when I tell them to work. Do not worry. May I ask why you need to remove a wall today?"

Rainee cut her eyes at Sam and turned back toward the man. Sam was obviously fumbling for the answer. Rainee glanced once again at Sam and back to the stranger with widened eyes. The answer from Sam was coming far too slowly, and the Mexican man was waiting.

"We need to remove it so we can put some new laundry equipment in the area. The washer won't fit without removing the wall. We want to help our friends sell their home here, and a new washing machine will enhance the price," she said nervously.

The man took a puff from his large cigar and turned his head to exhale the smoke. Rainee studied his gold-and-diamond Rolex and a ring on his right hand. The ring was over an inch wide with a circle of blue sapphires and one solitaire diamond that must have weighed at least five carats. He wore a large gold-and-diamond crucifix around his neck. He didn't wear a traditional wedding ring but had a very wide band of gold with what appeared to have cartouche-type symbols. She concluded that he was a very wealthy man by anyone's standards.

Sam interrupted her examination of the man. "We don't want to impose on you or your men on this festival day." Sam just wanted to do the job himself. Was it safe to bring in outsiders? Did he have reason to be concerned about a man who was being so cordial and offering to help? Sam thought quickly. *No way that anyone knows we're here or why, and certainly not this man.* He took a small step forward. "I would appreciate the help. But why are you offering two strangers help on such a festive day?"

"Señor, you are in my country. You need help. I can help. What other reason would I have? Mexico is a very friendly country."

Sam nodded and glanced at Rainee. She was motionless with no expression on her face. *Damn*, Sam thought. *I don't have a clue what she's thinking.* He freed Rainee's hand and reached out his hand to the man. "Thank you, sir. I would like your help. I will be sure to pay your men whatever you feel is right."

The man took Sam's hand and gave it a firm shake. "Good then. We will be there at two o'clock today, OK?"

"Yes, yes. Perfect. Let me give you my address."

The man pulled the cigar from his mouth. "My mother named me Gustavo Eduardo Galvan, but I am called El Espino." He took two steps backward, turned, and began to walk away. "I know the address."

Sam and Rainee watched the man disappear through a door at the rear of the corridor.

"What the fuck have we done?" Rainee asked. "I'm sorry for my language, but really?"

"Right. What the holy fuck have we done?" Sam mumbled. The man's reply had sent chills down Sam's back.

The festival continued down the street as Sam and Rainee drove slowly toward the Robertses' villa. Neither spoke for several minutes.

Sam broke the silence. "OK, so we're committed to El Espino's help."

Rainee interrupted. "Sam, do you know what El Espino means in Spanish?"

Sam shook his head. "No, can't say I do."

"The Thorn."

"Holy shit. Who is this man?" he shouted without thinking the alarm he was obviously showing. The last thing Sam wanted to do was to show fear in front of Rainee.

"I don't know, and I don't like this one bit," she said quickly.

"If we let them break through the wall and if I pay, he should take the money and leave." His words sounded like a mixture of affirmation and of questions.

"That's a lot of ifs, Sam."

"Yeah, I get that. But let's think about this. No one with the Factor-7 group knows we're here. We don't have anything of real value with us, and why would he just pick us out to rob or kill? Logic tells me we're overreacting."

"I hope you're right." Rainee turned and stared out the car's window. "I hope you're right," she whispered.

———

The bell buzzed at precisely 2:00 p.m. Sam walked down the stairs and wearily unlocked the large wooden door that opened onto the street. There were four Mexican men with tools and a bulldozer in the narrow street.

Rainee joined Sam. "Buenas tardes," she said. "Please come in."

A well-dressed man about forty years old stepped from the right in front of the workers.

"Hello, my name is Jorge. I am here to supervise the work." His English was equally as well spoken as that of Gustavo…El Espino."

"Thank you," Rainee said. She looked closely at the man. He seemed overdressed for a work supervisor, but she would not object or show her suspicions. After all, everything frightened her, and everything was venturing into an unknown. She brushed off her feelings.

Sam and Rainee sat on the wrought-iron bench in the garden and watched as the men slammed hammers against the block brick wall. Each time the hammer hit the wall, Rainee would flinch.

Sam put his arm around her and held her closely. He whispered, "Relax. They don't know us. This will be all right."

Rainee said nothing, but she pulled closer to Sam.

Less than two hours passed, and the crew had chiseled completely though the wall. They were working on cutting the final interior rebar. Sam had to go to the bathroom. Rainee assured him that she was fine and would wait for him to return. He stood on the stairs staring out the large windows. She was fine. She was oh so very fine.

Several minutes went by when Sam heard Rainee. "Sam, please come out here." She stood at the bottom of the stairs. Her words were staccato and breathy.

"What is it?" Sam shouted from the bathroom.

"Just come."

He emerged from the bathroom. "What? What's the matter?"

"The man…Jorge…has a gun."

"How do you know?"

"Geez, Sam, what do you think? I didn't frisk the motherfucker, if that's what you're thinking! The wind blew open his jacket, and I saw the gun in a shoulder holster."

"Well, that can't be good. OK, I'll go out there and tell them they have finished the job. Hopefully he and his men will just leave. Can you go get my wallet and meet me outside?"

She nodded.

Sam walked up to the boss. "Jorge, Señor, looks like your men have done a great job. I can take it from here. How much do I owe you?"

"El Espino said that you do not owe anything. This is a gift."

"Oh no, sir. I can't take this work as a gift. Please…I want to pay."

"El Jefe says no money. That's means no money, señor."

"Well, thank you, but this just isn't right." Sam didn't know what else to say.

"El Jefe says he will be in touch."

Sam put out his hand to the man. "Well then, I owe him."

Jorge shook Sam's hand. He looked like he was about to break out laughing.

Damn, why the fuck did I say that? Owe the man? You idiot…stupid jerk! Sam cursed himself.

The group gathered their tools and machinery and left.

Sam locked the front door to the property. He pressed his back to the door and slid down to a sitting position. He pulled his knees to his chest and buried his head in his hands. He reiterated what Jorge had said. "El Jefe will be in touch." *I have no doubt that he will,* he thought.

Rainee stood at the end of the stoned sidewalk. "Sam are you OK?" she asked.

"Yes." He pulled himself to his feet. "I know you want to get to the bottom of this Factor-7 deal, but babe, your safety is my utmost responsibility. We need to get into the safe and out of Mexico, ASAP."

"Sam, we've gone this far. We're burning daylight. Let's get to it."

Sam took a deep cleansing breath. "OK, let's do it."

Most of the block bricks were freed. Sam and Rainee pulled the few remaining out. Ragged pieces of steel protruded from the walls, and pieces of brick littered inside and outside the opening. But there it was. The safe was indeed there, and the combination panel faced up. He reached into his pocket, pulled out his wallet, and retrieved a small pink sticky note. He punched in 5, 9, 3, 1, #. He looked at Rainee. "OK, here we go."

She nodded. "Do it."

Sam pushed the silver handle down, and the door to the safe released. He opened the small door as far as it would go given the small open space. There were several file folders and a legal pad that had been folded in half. He handed each item to Rainee as he took it out. When the safe was empty, he shut the door but saw no reason to lock it.

"Let's go upstairs and start reading," she said. "It'll be dark soon, and we aren't going to get out of Mexico until day after tomorrow."

Sam agreed. The bells of the Parroquia rang seven times. He glanced at her. "Seven."

"Let's hope that's a good omen," she said as she laid the stack of files on the wooden dining table. "How do you want to do this? You want a file and I take one, or do you want to read aloud for a while and then I?"

"We both need to know every word in these. I think we should read it out loud. I'll start." Sam opened the file folder on top.

"I agree," she said, opening other files and checking dates. "Seems he has the files dated. According to the dates, the one on top is the latest thing he wrote."

"So let's start from the bottom," Sam suggested.

The first file contained several sheets of typed paper. Each page was numbered and dated. "This was written on June fifteenth," Sam said. "What's today's date?" He glanced at the date on his watch. Then he answered his own question. "August fifth. Time has sure flown."

CHAPTER FIFTEEN

Sam began to read.

I begin with the sincerest apology to my wife, Ana, whom I love and cherish. I apologize to the world for what I am about to reveal and state my involvement. My association with what I will expose was intentional, premeditated, and insidious. Today, I know that the agenda originally set forth cannot be possible and that it must be stopped at all costs. This information must go to the able and correct hands. It is imperative that this information be privileged and protected. You will understand as I tell you more.

A highly secretive organization, as old as the Freemasons and perhaps the Illuminati. Some believe the transcendental fraternity dates back centuries or as far back as the middle ages. Although it was shrouded in mystery and codes of extreme silence, I first heard of them in 1961. It was while I was in the Army Medical Corps as a young man in Germany. I was privileged to information divulged by a man who was being treated for severe burns. He was in tremendous pain and was mumbling incoherently with claims of membership to the Keepers. Then he spoke Latin. I knew it to mean, "I am my brother's keeper." He touched my hand, and tears ran down his cheek. "We are the Keepers," he moaned. He ranted a short while about hunting remaining Nazis or sympathizers and watching for any resurgence of the ideology. He claimed the fire that burned him was set by the Aryan belligerents, and he was going to hunt them down like wild boar. He expired within a few hours and said little more before his death.

I gave the event very little, if any, thought until that afternoon in Washington when it all started, and my life and freedom ended. I had heard bits and pieces about the Keepers over the past many years. Mostly conspiracy theorists spoke of them. If they really exist, it is my understanding that the original Keepers—the men and perhaps women—are honorable. They live by a strict rule of ethics and moral conscience. They are fighters for justice, supreme knowledge and freedom. They are covert in their actions but take on challenges that perhaps they alone could defend. They join freedom fighters across the globe and often are the catalyst that push people to freedom, civility, and justice.

My first introduction to another group of people who called themselves by multiple names, but mainly the Keepers Collegium or the Keepers Brotherhood, was in early 2001. This evil group I will tell you about have bastardized the secret society, the Keepers. They should not even use that revered name. I will tell you all I can, and it will be up to you to stop them or find someone who can.

———————

Sam looked at Rainee. "Wow." His eyes widened. "This is already weird." He continued reading.

I don't recall the exact date that Steven Roberts, my younger brother, introduced me to Kenneth Guidry, but as I said earlier, it was early 2001. Guidry was military, now assigned to a foreign counterterrorism unit. He was in a special-operations unit called Ghost Agents. Steven was introduced earlier and somehow was convinced that these people possessed knowledge that others, even in governments, did not have. He saw a huge threat to our nation and the world. He was convinced our country and others were on the precipice of some major occurrence from outside our borders. He spent months talking to me about this imminent threat and said that he and I should talk about it with some people he knew. I now know he meant the Collegium. And that's where my horrors started.

Finally, just before summer of 2001, I met Steven at a hotel in Washington, DC. When I arrived at the suite, there were two other men there, and that surprised me. Steven had not told me that I was meeting anyone but him. That meeting lasted about twenty minutes, and I was more confused than ever after it was over. There was no conversation about these imminent threats or anything about who they were. I was offered brandy, and we talked about my work and my thoughts on how President George W. Bush was doing. After the meeting, Steven and I went to dinner. He told me much more about the group and that he had been advised to offer membership to me. I told him that I was busy and had no time for some club. It became tense between us, and he finally said that I was needed to complete a massive plan, and my cooperation was not an option. He said that I had been "chosen."

Sam looked at Rainee. "This sounds like some communist concentration indoctrination club."

"Bill didn't have a choice, it appears. Read on…"

––––––––––

I was told a lot about the threats that they knew were going to occur. I was told about problems in and around where my boy was stationed and that our men in that region would be targets in the near future. Bin Laden was gearing up, and they explained much of what he was planning. What they said did indeed come about.

After many conversations, I was truly convinced that they had the only answer to how to save our freedoms and liberties. I was convinced that forces throughout the Middle East, China, Russia, and North Korea were rallying to take away the United States as we know it, and along with our downfall would be that of our allies.

They counted on my patriotism and love of country. In late summer of 2001, I was attending regular meetings but had not yet been assigned to any specific duty. But by September 11, 2001, and the tragic events of that day, they brought me into the fold. It was because of my background in viruses, bacteria, and cancer research, compounded by my association with many scientists around the world, that they needed me. Perhaps Steven knew I could be trusted, and he persuaded the principal figures to accept me—or, rather, draft me—into the biological sector of the organization. Looking back, I had been jaded by their rhetoric. I was given no choice but to assist them in finding the perfect weapon, a pathogen that was so refined that it would be swift, silent, and more deadly than anything known to man at that time. It was called Operation Nemesis and they had a specific mission.

I was a compliant player in their scheme. I tell you these things not because I want you to sympathize with me or because I am somehow trying to justify my actions. I am not and could never justify the dangerous actions that I set in place by my aiding them. The strategy meeting was set for September 14 at 7:00 p.m. It was to be at a hotel near Dulles. That became our meeting place for several months to come. I recall the date of that first meeting as the day my life was ruined by my wrong decisions.

———————

Rainee stood up and walked to the window. "Well, it's all true. Now what?"

"We read the rest and then *we* make some very difficult decisions," Sam replied with an unrecognizable tone. "Sounds like a doomsday scenario."

———————

Guidry had a partner who was former CIA. They had gathered a cadre of rogue military and intelligence personnel and private contractors from all corners of the earth who would carry out a plan to have no boots on the ground yet wage war on the jihadists and other threats to the United States and her allies. The targets would be known terrorist cells at the time. Precisely, the name al-Qaeda was mentioned at the first meeting. Guidry was disgruntled. He had seen more death and destruction in the Middle East regions than he could tolerate. Although the man Guidry had aligned himself with was not at that September fourteenth meeting, Guidry told us much about his associate, Mr. Z. I now know he was setting a stage of fear with each story he told of Z.

It would ultimately be self-preservation that Guidry and Z held over Steven and me. The thought of double-crossing this man called Mr. Z would surely bring down his wrath, and we and our families would be its unfortunate recipients. Mr. Z was all he was ever called, and to this day, I do not know his real identity.

I was in that first meeting with Steven and Guidry all night. It was all interesting yet frightening.

On the morning of the second day, I met the notorious Mr. Z. Steven drove me to that same hotel south of Dulles Airport. We met in an adjoining suite to the first meeting room, on the sixth floor. Mr. Z was probably in his mid-sixties, a tall man with gray hair and a scruffy beard, and he always wore dark glasses. He said very little at first.

Mr. Z began to talk directly to me after about an hour. He told me that he was soliciting patriots for a cause greater than we. He wanted men and women who would risk life and limb to serve the betterment of mankind and secure our homeland. He memorialized the almost divine attributes of the ancient Keepers. He said his plan was righteous and sanctioned by God through the ages. I knew he was overstating his relevance, but on the other hand, I felt he had a point. I knew that they, the terrorists of 9/11, and those before and those who came afterward, must be stopped. Nuclear proliferation, chemical and biological attacks against innocent civilians, and other threats to our freedoms and liberties were to be eliminated.

At first, I thought this clandestine group was in some way associated with the secret agencies of the US and allied governments. Perhaps some deep secret agency at the Pentagon. That made sense to me because Steven worked there. I thought what they talked about was somehow a government-backed operation, or at least that the "project" had their blessings. But as the details developed, it became clear that the plan would be considered a crime against humanity. That soon told me that no legitimate government was involved, or at least would admit to it. I was stunned at the complexity of what Guidry and Z laid out. Later, I would discover that it was indeed international. There are some obscure persons within the various governments, some very high up, and some well-heeled businesspeople from around the world in the Keepers Brotherhood. One might call them a shadow of angry strength and power.

Z is apparently the United States boss and is knowledgeable, to state it mildly, in international fusion centers and espionage. He knew the covert collaborative efforts between all branches of the intelligence communities was vital to the United States fusion centers and continued his efforts of gathering information in order to detect terrorist activities. But his involvement in fusion centers went much deeper and was far more diverse. I'll try to stay here within my timelines, so you will follow how this all transpired. So I'll get more into fusion centers later. He had fought in the Vietnam War and is still angry that the war ended as it did, without a clear victory. He had been in the Central Intelligence Agency since the late seventies. Mr. Z had been a part of the Iran/Contra affair but was able to keep his anonymity and his job when many high-profile careers came to an end. Desert Storm and other battles had wreaked havoc on the Middle East. Hostile governments were in control. Israel and Palestine were bubbling caldrons. Much of the Middle East is presently consumed with hatred for the so-called infidels, and Z and Guidry were convinced that simple fact alone posed an impossibility to reason with any of them. They therefore must be destroyed. Z let me know that he had been undercover in Libya and could tell volumes about the Benghazi attack that killed our diplomats. He was in Iraq when Saddam Hussein was executed in 2006. He had been in the middle of multiple ally-backed attacks on terrorist cells. He pulled up his pant leg and showed me his calf. An IED had exploded and killed his buddies. It had torn his leg to shreds. He walked with a cane. He would not elaborate but only said there is self-righteousness and fear among the ranks in our government…more than you will ever know. I saw him glance at Guidry before he said, 'But the world's complacency will not be seen in this room. We take action for what others walk from.' The look in his eyes sent cold chills down my back. Mr. Z's and Guidry's attitude was that everything the free world had done thus far to stop the expansion of terror had been virtually worthless, but at a cost of far too many good lives.

I'll begin with some background on Mr. Z. Perhaps this will help identify who is really is. He held his job and apparently did his personal undercover work, Collegium business, until mid-2015. That year, the director of national security had advised the director of the CIA to release Z from his lofty yet clandestine CIA position. Apparently, Z had been involved in too many shady undercover deals, or maybe they had gotten a whiff of what he was really doing. He had suspicious knowledge, which I felt certain was obtained from the fusion centers around the world that still exist today. He supposedly told someone in 2001 at the NSI that the Twin Towers in Manhattan would be attacked. The scuttlebutt that Steven heard was that he was going to tell the media if someone did not take preemptive appropriate action. No action apparently was taken, and indeed we know that tragic outcome. They kept him in the agency until he was out of control, which is where we are today.

He clearly believed the Middle East was so hot that it would soon explode, and in fact, he was right.

Steven had heard of a man with a reputation such as Z's while working at the Pentagon. Z was known as a rogue as far back as the late nineties. He must have had something on someone, because it took so many years to get him fired. I was never privy to all of that information.

But Mr. Z had no shame. He laughed after one of his long-winded stories about his experiences. "They didn't know who they were dealing with. There might be a President, but I am now the CEO."

Supposedly, Z and Guidry met in 1994, and they got deeply entrenched into the espionage of tracking terrorist cells. They utilized the old fusion centers and had been quite successful in locating deeply hidden jihadist strongholds. Guidry explained that the international centers had been in existence since the Reagan administration. There were estimated to be over forty centers in other countries. Most of the centers were in old abandoned buildings or homes. The operatives knew how to adapt, keep cool, and blend into society. Many of the operatives had lived in the towns for over twenty years and had meshed into the communities. They were cloaked in a blanket of secrecy. Each location contained sophisticated high-tech equipment for tracking and monitoring. The best of the best special agents, spies, and technology were all in these centers. International fusions were top secret for about ten years, when in use, but the United States stopped their overseas use and staffing in mid-1996. But that did not stop people like Guidry, Mr. Z, or the Collegium because, as he stated, their usefulness had just begun. They enlisted many of those people into their cause, and they are still actively working in their secret capacities. So their intelligence is superb and ongoing.

Kenneth Guidry was clearly livid that the international community would not recognize and address the direct threat of terrorism and the nuclear threat of countries such as Iran and North Korea. He added that the United States government and her allies had known for years that there was a real threat, and they did nothing. His pet peeve was that a few guns and a few air strikes were made on terrorist groups only to satisfy the international media and the public. It was a ploy to divert attention from the seriousness of the terrorism matter, a threat against which no one seemed willing to do the one thing that would stop them in their tracks. The terrorists would lie low and then make a strike. Allied and United States retaliation was below the Collegium's level of warfare for such crimes. That one thing, according to Z and Guidry, was complete and utter annihilation. He clearly told me that no progress had been made in slowing the jihadist groups, nor did it appear that any would be made under the same military agendas. The terrorist attacks would continue to ebb and flow. Sanctions, summits, or conversations would never stop the evil of radical Islamists or the insanity of someone like Kim Jong-un. And after one murderous dictator, there would be another, and another, unless the entire ideology was wiped out. So finally, I knew the full agenda. I knew what Project Nemesis was and it was international and enormous. Nemesis is the mythological god or revenge and retaliation. It was a fitting name for what they planned against those who are hell bent on our country's destruction.

Guidry made it even clearer. He told me at that first meeting that the world would soon change, and accordingly, the world would have to reinvent how it protects its citizens against terrorism and hostile governments. Man-made pandemics, cyber theft, and other terrorist threats were the next wars. He kept saying, "We will find the terrorists' Achilles' heel, and we will win this war once and for all." He also told me in that meeting to commit everything said to memory. I did not understand that but found out later that nothing said in meetings is written, and what was written was destroyed. I did learn of a building somewhere in Texas where they had set up vaults and secret rooms, which Steven and I presumed contained the top-secret files. Find those hiding places and you will find the documents. I couldn't disagree with anything I was told. But I didn't know specifics. I needed to understand what, and how, and with whom, I was to work. Finally, I got my answer.

Z stated that I was a pillar of the community and thus would be able to do whatever needed to be done without suspicion or exposure. He knew everything about me. Talking to him was like hearing my bio. It was both frightening and intriguing. He told me that they wanted to gather the best scientists to develop the new weapon. I recall becoming very uneasy at that point. I knew what he was referring to. But I wanted to hear exactly the words from his mouth. So I asked if he meant a biological weapon. His eyes burned through me, and his words were blunt and searing. "Of course, I mean biological." He then calmed and said that he wanted me to work with one of my associates, Dr. Andres Rodriguez, who was already working on a new strain of bacterium. I was beyond stunned to hear Andres was part of the group.

Z's transparency confirmed to me that he had no fear of the outcome. His vision was razor sharp, and anything in its way would be severed to bits. People were removed to make way for important positions to be filled by the Collegium. Andres replaced Ben Whitten at the Federal Laboratory. I fear Whitten is dead. Working with Rodriguez was not a choice, but a command. These were serious killers. You did what they demanded or risked becoming the one they removed... permanently.

Sam stopped. "Damn it, I get it now! Somehow, Rodriguez and those Collegium people weaseled his way into Chairman Whitten's position at the Federal Lab. The day you saw me there, I had just left Rodriguez. He must have been using the stored viruses and biological materials in the lab. Damn, he knew why Bill's specimens were removed from the lab, and that's why he threatened me when I left his office. Son of a bitch!"

Rainee took the file from Sam. "Weaseled? More like he was placed there by a very strong arm, and they probably eliminated Whitten entirely. Apparently, murder of an innocent person is acceptable if it makes way for their plans. I'll read for a while." She said shaking her head in disbelief and disgust.

Sam agreed. "This is just beyond comprehension. Bill is telling us how he got involved, but nothing about how to fix this thing or what he did. It's a lot of stuff that looks like he's trying to redeem himself for getting involved with these crazy people."

She nodded. "There's a lot more. Let's see." She started to read.

———————

His perspective was that what the Collegium was doing would be far better than if it were a government. The United States, Great Britain, Germany, France, or any of the allies could not be blamed, yet the job of eliminating terrorism would be achieved. I went on with my work, but it was always nagging at me. I wondered when and if they would contact me.

I remember that the house was beautifully decorated for Thanksgiving. It was a cold holiday. Ana had set a fire in the fireplace and a fine dinner for us. James was to be coming home two days after Thanksgiving, and we were going to have a little turkey and then throw a huge banquet when he got home. The doorbell rang about eight thirty. I turned on the porch light, and my heart sank. No one needed to say anything. Men in dress uniforms stood somberly in the dim light. James had been killed in Afghanistan. It had been a terrorist bomb. He was only twenty-two years old and a medic. He would have been a fine doctor someday. My boy never had a chance.

"Oh God, I remember that night. Bill called me about midnight. I went over and stayed with them until daybreak." Sam bowed his head. "It was a horrible night."

Rainee resumed reading.

Ana was devastated as was I. She had to be hospitalized, and I would never be the same. The two weeks after, I kept her in an institution and in professional care for years following. She recovered but never was the same. She and I both had deep hatred for the jihadists. We despised the radical Islamic terrorists who had killed our boy. I was overcome with grief, and I thought that, as the Collegium, I had also found my reason and my revenge.

I called Steven. All he said was "It's time to stop the enemy and settle some scores." He called Guidry.

If the Keepers Collegium's intelligence was such that they knew in advance of what was going to happen on September 11, 2001, why didn't our government? Then it hit me, and I replayed things Guidry and Z had told Steven and me. The governments of the world did know. They had the intelligence. The United States, Great Britain, France, Germany, Canada, Russia, and China…they all knew what was happening. They just didn't know when and some countries had more at stake than others. Indeed, some countries perhaps welcomed an attack on America and longed for a change in the balance of powers. Maybe nothing could have been done by the various governments, including the USA, if the intelligence was sketchy or withheld from the proper departments. But I knew Z and Guidry had a plan, superior surveillance, information gathering intelligence; and that mixed with their fortitude, would make it a success. I suddenly had a changed heart. I don't recall ever being so angry and hurt at one time as I was after James's death, and I realized it all could have been different. The anguish of 9/11 was greater than we as a nation could bear; that horrific event and James's death were greater than I could bear. I vowed, at that moment, I would do all in my power to never allow it to happen again.

———————

Rainee paused. "Bill had a terrible time after September eleventh. I can't believe James was killed so quickly after that. No wonder Bill was out of his mind with grief." She continued to read.

———————

About the same time, I remembered a young doctor, John Albright, who had made great strides in the study of viruses, DNA, and RNA. I hesitated to contact him for multiple reasons. Albright had a reputation. He was an arrogant, self-consumed hothead, yet one of the sharpest minds of our time. I wasn't sure how to approach him, but Z insisted. He was adamant that the risk of terror exceeded any of my fears and that he would protect the exposure of the brotherhood's agenda from the public. In other words, he would deal with Albright.

———————

Sam growled. "I introduced them." He grabbed the files from Rainee.

———————

John and I met in Houston in August 2002. He was something between arrogant and insane. Later, I realized he coveted recognition.
After hearing my story, he looked straight at me without emotion, and
the first thing he said was "Anything we study can become a weapon."
I knew at that point that he was in. I considered what we would be
inflicting, but I rationalized it by comparing the differences between
a gunshot to the head or a germ that killed swiftly. Death was death.

During the next few months, we gathered a few associates and explained carefully the plan. We had five who were ready to help. We
knew them well and chose all of them very carefully. It was now mid-
2002, and a few minor glitches arose with the operation. The weapon
had to be undetectable, and so far, the delivery systems were not perfect
in Mr. Z's mind. "Undetectable" was the word that had become the
mantra. It had to be swift, clean, and undetectable. Time was flying
by, and more global terrorist activities were taking place. Al Qaida and
the Taliban were no longer alone. Small factions of terrorists were filling up the entire Middle Eastern region and spilling their terror into
Europe and elsewhere. We were still without the definitive weapon. Z
wanted to test what we had and without our knowledge then, he and
Guidry worked out a plan. He tested the virus in Sierra Leone, the
Congo and a couple of other places. It did not do what he had hoped.
He wanted it to directly affect certain ethnicities with specific DNA.
It killed everyone infected instead. Guidry and Mr. Z were contacting
me daily. There was a man from China. He and his group supposedly
were primarily working on extracting faulty DNA from a person's genome and changing the progression of genetic diseases. Dr. Hui Wong
was somehow with that group. He had jumped at the opportunity to
become part of the brotherhood. He knew there were some distin-
guished scientists involved and that incredible research was being done.
The research was for a weapon, but even so, I knew that parts of it

could someday be miraculous cures for many diseases. So out of the bad could come good, I hoped. Manipulation of a human's DNA is the next new science and it might be used benevolently or could result in sheer evil. We can make people stronger or weaker. If used properly many illnesses could be eliminated. If used improperly, it could result is a master/slave/ superior/inferior human-race. I don't know what the Chinese were actually researching. Wong gathered a few Chinese scientists to come with him. I still believe he wanted the shared scientific knowledge rather than to help the Collegium.

"Chinese...the Chinese are notorious for jailing and persecuting Chinese Muslims," Sam casually said.

Rainee grabbed a pen and wrote "Kenneth Guidry, Mr. Z, and Hui Wong" on the back of one of the file folders. "I want to keep track of names."

"I wonder if Wong had a brother," Sam blurted out.

"I don't know. Why do you ask that?"

Sam couldn't help himself. Mimicking Bugs Bunny, he spoke softly. "Well, two Wongs can never make this whight!"

Rainee glared at him. "Really, Sam?"

"I'm just trying to keep my sanity. Bill's confession is giving me heartburn. Sorry. I totally get it. This is super-serious shit."

Rainee knew when Sam spouted off one of his sillies, he was concealing either fear or nervousness. It was now probably both. "Well, your sanity's gone. How about trying to keep your focus." She smiled at him as she began to read.

By 2004, John had developed a weapon that was virtually perfect. It was a bacteriophage, and nothing like it had ever been seen before. It is a virus that is encased within a bacterium. It housed the lethal virus that targeted DNA, certain ethnicities' DNA genomes. It also targeted the liver in all subjects. The factor VII protein, also known as proconvertin, is vitamin K dependent and produced in the liver. When depleted, compromised, or destroyed, the f7 cannot initiate blood coagulation in conjunction with tissue factor III. You know the results of a deficiency of that protein, so I will not get into his intentions for that part of the virus, other than when bleeding starts, it will not end, and death is imminent. I helped with its efficacy, and it seemed to work in every test. It worked similarly to diseases that only affect certain ethnicities (e.g., sickle cell, certain cancers, etc.). The target groups were, at that time, anyone with at least fifty percent Middle Eastern DNA. Albright was supposed to be working on other specific ethnic DNA sequences. I knew that North Korea was considered a target, and anyone who was helping that dictatorship was also in the crosshairs, which meant China. So my mistrust of Hui Wong grew.

"See, that's what he told me and I told you. It is a DNA and a factor XII protein thing." Rainee paced the floor as Sam began to read again.

John Albright was working on two more delivery systems. It was stacking up to be a fail-proof agenda. He had virtually left the other scientists in the dirt, as far as Z was concerned. There would be need for whatever the foreign scientists created, but Albright was the man of the hour. He called his lethal pathogen Factor-7 for what it precisely did. He had created what Z wanted.

Dr. Hui Wong was there when Albright told Z how his bacteriophage operated. Suddenly, after that meeting, I feared Wong. I expressed my concern to Z. If Wong took the weapon back to China, it might be shared with North Korea or any of the free world's enemies and be used one day against us. I did not trust the Chinese or him. Guidry and Z promised they would keep a close eye on him, but he had given them intelligence on North Korea, and they were not ready to eliminate him.

I didn't want innocents involved. Guidry told me that the intelligence was such that the targets would be clear and concise. All the Collegium needed was the biological weapon that Albright and I, to a lesser degree, were making, and it was done. When the pathogen was refined and ready, Albright would develop a vaccine within a few months because, of course, he created the pathogen and knew the virus's gene sequence. Although the vaccine would not be available to the intended targets, it would be needed if somehow the bioweapon moved outside of the target area. If the need for a vaccine—say in the US—arose, there would be urgency to get it to the people. Therefore, clinical trials and tests would be rushed through. Albright would be the genius who developed it and saved the world from what could be the worst deadly pandemic known to earth.

———————

"There it is," Sam shouted as he threw the file across the room. "That's what that motherfucker wanted. That's why he's doing this. It's purely in his selfish, narcissistic self-interest. That's what he basically told me at La Playa! Well, that son of a bitch motherfucker!" Sam kicked the chair. "He wants fame, fortune, and the Nobel Prize."

Sam's reaction startled Rainee. She was as angry as he. It was abominable. "Yeah, that bastard." She picked up the file of papers that Sam had hurled in his rage. "Albright was going to manufacture a pathogen, release it into the world, and then be the hero who developed the vaccine. He would get global recognition, accolades, and a hell of a lot of money."

"And the Nobel Prize. Don't forget that. He's never given a rat's ass about humanity."

"I'll read now. Cool down before you stroke out." Rainee began to read.

They planned to have an abundance of both the germ and the countermeasure stored in several secret locations. I would not know when or where it would be delivered, to exonerate me from anything. But I also knew I could not stop Operation Nemesis once it was in motion. I, in all practicality, would know nothing once the germ was produced.

Rainee took Sam's hand. "Without question he was desperate to tell someone or get help at the end."

Sam squeezed her hand to either comfort her or himself. "I can see how a person could become consumed with hate for all the devastation and death brought by terrorism, but not so swallowed up by that hate to resort to bioweapons."

"I don't know how Bill thought they could get away with such a thing." She shook her head and sighed. "I guess they really might still get away with it. We don't have a way to stop them."

Sam nodded. "So far I don't see any clues or directions from Bill on how to stop the madness." Sam huffed. "He's still just telling us about them, and he's making a case for why he became involved. I'm beginning to not give a shit about why. I need to know how to kill this threat. I hope he tells us more than this, because right now, I'm pissed as hell at Bill."

Rainee rubbed her eyes. "There's only a bit left in this file." She resumed reading.

———————

Within six months, John Albright was to refine a therapeutic that would stop the virus, if an unintended group was infected and not vaccinated against the virus's wrath. He and I held a dangerous secret, and I did not know how to tell Mr. Z about it without being a recipient of his wrath—meaning his lethal hand. The therapeutic was and is today useless because Factor-7 has a ninety-five to one-hundred percent mortality! And it kills in less than twelve hours. Later I realized that Z, along with others, would not care about the mortality of innocents, because if they shared the specific DNA of those he hated, then—in the sick mind of the Collegium—they should die, whether terrorists or not.

———————

Sam stood from his chair, as if he wanted to run somewhere. "Albright's bioweapon could already be in the hands of our enemies. Anyway, I don't totally get how this works. I'm not really trained in this infectious-disease stuff, but you are."

Rainee placed the folder on the table. "Sam, this is what I've been telling you. They've developed something far more sinister than any nuke or weapon known to man. I'm not certain how it works, but I'm certain it must be destroyed. If these guys can target our enemies, then in time, the enemies can target us, and that would be the end of the world as we know it. The plague in the thirteen hundreds or the Spanish flu or HIV—even Covid-19 and its mutations—would be a tea party compared to the death toll of this bioweapon unleashed on the world. I don't know how Bill Roberts could get involved. That virus could so easily mutate and jump to other persons with other DNA genomes. Hell, it could jump to all DNA genomes and infect everyone. Viruses mutate. That's what they do. Albright's vaccine is worthless. Ana told you that Bill felt bad after dinner, and he died eight to ten hours after that. Bill said max twelve hours. Imagine if it mutates away from their specific DNA targets. A therapeutic is worthless, too, when Factor-7's efficacy is a hundred percent of the infected die. That can't be fought! There would be no time. Three hundred and fifty million people in the United States alone could be dead in a matter of hours, or perhaps days. Any cure or therapeutic, so to speak, couldn't even be transported to all the world in that period of time." Rainee began to hyperventilate, and it was evidence of her near panic. The knowledge was bad enough, but her analysis of what could happen scared Sam to his core.

Sam put his arm around her. "No doubt, it would be impossible to handle. Hospitals would be overrun, supplies gone. Hell, we saw what happened in 2020, and that was nothing compared to the possible loss of life with Albright's little friend. Other countries, our enemies, may also be testing novel viruses on the world already, but those have not shown to be as deadly as the Factor-7 is supposed to be. Let's hope that the intelligence of the Collegium is as good as Bill states and they can police their own. Otherwise, it's unthinkable." Sam tightly closed his eyes and resolutely nodded. Words barely left his lips as a whisper. "It's unthinkable in any regard. We won't be fighting the immediate viral threat, but future viruses too. Come on, let's be serious. This shit is too big for us."

Rainee exhaled slowly and then nodded reluctantly, trying to assimilate the truth in her own mind. "Catastrophic. It's too big for anyone. They have worked on this weapon over twenty years, and a lot of that time Bill was among them. Bill knew how big this was. I'm angry too, Sam." She began to read again.

I was never privileged to know the source of funding, except that Steven said that all governments had black budgets, and some of the brotherhood had infiltrated the agencies and gotten their hands on money that had no traceable capability. Black budgets were used to fund covert military attacks or operations and hostage payoffs, secret missions, and bribes. Billions, perhaps trillions, of dollars are in the black budgets at any one time. But spending too much of those funds would alert the president and others. So an alternative source had to be engaged. There were unlimited amounts of undetectable funds, unaccountable to foreign governments, our Senate and Congress, and, of course, the American people. Steven was told that major funding came from someone of great wealth. So we concluded the money was arranged from a single individual, black budgets, and shadow governments that were walled in secrecy. To this day, I'm not sure if they ever knew the true scope of what they were funding.

There are paid and unpaid personnel. There are scientists, military, and officials from all levels of governments, and from every corner of the globe. There are independent contractors of both genders. I'm watching my back at every turn. I cannot trust anyone. The fear of God had been put into the minds of everyone. If one accepts the mission of the Collegium, you are expected to keep a solid code of silence. Many of the workers are paid large sums of money simply to do a job and keep quiet. Many are doing jobs for large sums of money and don't even know for whom or what they are working. Private contractors are not subject to the Freedom of Information Act. They can do whatever they're instructed and never be required to tell anyone anything. And there is no paper trail. But Steven was quick to tell me that most of the workers were ignorant of the true agenda. They were just doing a job and being well paid for it.

Many other world leaders and people involved in the Collegium are also just as in the dark. But no one in the brotherhood cares. To them, the end justifies the means.

I asked Mr. Z if the president knew what he had planned. His reply was simply that he didn't care who the president was, but the information flowed to the top. There would be controlled leaks to divert attention from the true issue. He seemed totally in control and unconcerned. He is an ice cube. Mr. Z looked straight at me and calmly stated, "Don't you know that all behavior can be justified with the right spin?"

So that meant that President Walthers had knowledge, but the Collegium had given the project some form of credence, some spin of acceptability.

I asked him when legitimate secrecy ends and political cover-up begins. The latter would have dire implications. Mr. Z gazed stoically at me from behind his dark glasses and firmly said, "Never."

I knew then the madness in which I had become involved. There were no rules and no governing body. The Collegium has the government and the president by the balls. These are murderers and lunatics.

Guidry told me that all papers were purged from the records, and no names were left to implicate in a strike against Al Qaida, ISIL,

Iran, North Korea, and the other targets. There were no manuals and no written records. The president, now only referred to as "the Tree," would not be involved or implicated in any assassinations or secret wars, including covert operations against terrorists. The brotherhood was on its own, and I was told even the president sanctioned the secrecy. No government was going to become directly involved. Each would claim ignorance of the Collegium's existence. They would turn their heads. Honestly, they had to.

Guidry called one day in the early spring of 2014 and summoned me to see him and Z. Mr. Z. was enraged when we met. He told me that we had no more time. Iran had been a threat since 1979, and North Korea had been a continuing threat since we had boots on the ground in the Korean War. Nuclear proliferation was at an all-time high. ISIS or ISIL was killing at historical rates, and the brutality was like no other terrorist group. Syria and Iran were killing thousands with biowarfare and chemicals such as sarin gas and chlorine. A prominent archeologist had been beheaded, and archeological treasures were being destroyed. Terrorist attacks were escalating. History was being erased. Z was ready to act. I was not sure we were ready even for the original plan, but I was not in control.

The Collegium's long arm was engaging people from all parts of the globe, and information was filtering outside their grasp. John Albright's arrogance and big mouth were getting him in serious trouble. Some of Albright's work had been published in a small European medical journal by a Swedish journalist. I think Albright leaked it to boast his accomplishments. The story was sketchy but said enough to expose the plan, and that scared me. He only wanted recognition and now was playing a very dangerous game with Mr. Z and the rest of them. A copy of the journal was given to me at a conference in Geneva, Switzerland, that same spring. I kept it secret and put it with my journals. The man who gave it to me was Dr. Frederic Arienzo from Naples, Italy.

Rainee gasped and glared at Sam.

Knowing that both John Albright and I were from Texas, Dr. Arienzo asked me about Albright's work. I told him as little as possible, but I know now, after his unfortunate death, that he dug deeper. He was murdered by the Italian fingers of the Collegium.

Rainee laid the papers on the table. Large tears welled in her eyes. "I knew he was murdered, and those Polizia di Strato sons of bitches covered it up."

Sam took her hand. "We don't know who covered it up. Maybe it was simply a job...a hit...well done, or those investigating were inept. But as God is my witness, we are going to expose the Collegium's Operation Nemesis and the Factor-7 and somehow annihilate their agenda and perhaps them."

Rainee needed a break. She poured a glass of red wine and walked to the balcony. The lights on the square and those on the Parroquia were sparkling in the distance. "Look, Sam, the cathedral is lighted for the night's festivities."

Sam put his arm around her. They stood for several minutes just listening to the distant beat of drums and bells from the many churches that were joining in on the day's celebrations. There were no words for what they were learning from Bill's letters. Sam found himself questioning his old friend and wondering if Bill had hoodwinked him from the first day they met. Sam had honored him and considered him to be the finest man he had ever known, short of Sam's own father. Now he knew Bill was weak and vindictive to the point of becoming involved with a group of murderers. The Keepers Collegium, he thought…more like the Killers. He stared into the distance and then turned to Rainee. "You know, I just had a thought. Bill mentioned the money he gave you in his will so I would know your name. He knew Ana would consult with me on his final wishes. It was a clue, and it was maybe his way of saying you were OK." Sam looked at her and gently smiled. "You *are* indeed."

They were both overwhelmed. The information was hard to process, and it was taking an emotional toll on Rainee. She had lived with the knowledge much longer than Sam. The death of her father put her closer to the issue. It was no longer some foreign unknown organization. She had the awful proof, and it had hit too close to home. Sam tenderly touched her arm. "I know this is very hard for you, but we have to finish the journals and get some rest. I really want to get copies made of all of this in the morning. Perhaps we hide a set somewhere in the event our originals are…" Sam stopped in midsentence.

"You mean, in case we're murdered too," she said.

"No, I was *not* thinking that," Sam answered emphatically. "Lost or stolen is what I was going to say. I won't let any harm come to you. I promise."

Rainee looked at Sam. She postured her head to the right, indicating that she questioned what he had said. "I'll keep you to that promise."

Sam picked up Bill's papers again and began to read.

I had seen a list of the Masters of the Keepers Brotherhood / the Collegium. These people have been involved for some time, some as long as sixty years. They are the leaders, members of several shadow governments, an international faction that advised from a distance. They have achieved trust with high officials in many countries. There are many, but these are a few of the main players. And you need to know they are the most dangerous and skilled in their specific killing arts. Of course, there are Z, Kenneth Guidry, Simon Rezinck, and a man named Abel Cote from Ontario. There is a scientist with a past of being one of many Nazi sympathizers from Argentina named Jorge Mata Santos; a Russian biologist, Kondeski; a Russian former Soviet KGB man named Lipinski; a French scientist named Calleis; and a German doctor named Klement. As I understand it, there are three main players from Great Britain: Jonathan Whalen, George Killian, and Wenchel Waterman. Jude Tanamachi and Mr. Sato are from Japan. Although not considered one of the Masters, Hui Wong is from mainland China, and he had a few scientists in his entourage, but I never met them. They are dangerous on their own. There are many more. My fear of the group has been raised to new levels. I took a gamble one day, while Guidry was out of the room, to take a poor photo of the list with my cell phone. If I had been caught, I know I would not be writing this. He destroyed his list that same meeting in accordance to their rule of no paper trails. The photo of names will be with my entire journal. It shows names, countries, and involvement of many of the key people.

Guidry and Mr. Z were insistent about expanding the plan to include other problem hot spots in the world, other than the terror-ridden Middle East—namely North Korea, Venezuela, Beijing, and even Moscow. I knew when China was included, they would be watching Hui Wong closely. I heard no more about him after that day.

Any region of the earth that had an ideology that differed from Mr. Z was suddenly a new target. It had gone from taking out the radical Islamist terrorists to eliminating any group or government that disagreed with him. He had become lord and master and was more dangerous than I can put into words. He was judge, jury, and executioner, all wrapped in a fine little package he called "taking care of his brother."

Simon Reznick acted as if he was my new best friend. I did not realize the extent of his hatred for all people of the Islamic faith. It was unparalleled. He wanted all Muslims dead and their lands regained by the Jewish people. I soon found out he was part of the Israeli intelligence organization Mossad but had become disenchanted with the military's lack of controlling the movement of the Palestinians, as well as the jihadists in Israel and the Middle East. He spoke often of rebuilding the temple on the Holy Mount, stating that the Jews were ready for the rebirth of Judaism. He considers himself to be the Jewish Messiah. He would take back all their land, and he would rebuild the temple as prophesied in the Torah. He had also lost his wife to a terrorist. His daughter was maimed and crippled for life. He has a deep-seated hatred for Islam. He claims to be an orthodox Jew but has become fanatical and fixated on the demise of anything Muslim. Hatred spewed from him like a volcano. According to Simon, the Jews are God's chosen people, and man's laws do not apply to him. It is a religious war, and there are those to be protected and those to be destroyed.

Small test sites were engaged again in 2014. An outbreak of Ebola was happening in Sierra Leone. The Collegium had successfully run their previous tests without repercussions, so they expanded it to also include parts of Liberia, Senegal and the Congo. The virus test was to see if this time the DNA was affected as planned. It sickened me, but I had no control at all in these matters. Thousands died, some from Ebola and other diseases, but many from the Factor-7 virus. The aerosol containing the Factor-7 had been released, and it was successful. The initial results were so similar to the Ebola symptoms that were already killing in parts of Sierra Leone that when the Factor-7 was introduced, it was never considered to be anything but Ebola. The WHO never even looked into it, for whatever reason. With the massive death toll and the highly contagious Ebola disease, the bodies were destroyed, and sadly, but to Mr. Z's delight, the second virus, the Factor-7 virus, was never detected. That test was on innocent humans. It sickened me to consider how many more tests they had done or were going to do before the final stage of their plan. I could no longer stand by and allow this sort of barbarism to happen. The original plan, the one I had sanctioned, was to only hit the terrorist cells and be done with it. What if next time the test went sour and a world pandemic occurred? Don't think I didn't consider these things. I was now deeply entrenched in the black hole and could not get out. All I could do was buy time. Steven was also feeling the pressure. What we each thought was a plan to rid the world of terrorism and not put our men and women in harm's way had morphed into a nightmare run by hate-mongering maniacs.

In December 2016, I received a call from Simon Reznick. I reluctantly met him alone at his hotel room in downtown Houston. He had summoned me to assist him in securing a meeting with Dr. John Albright. Albright had become a loose cannon, and Reznick was unable to track him down and, as he put it, "shut him up." Since I had been the initial contact between the Collegium and Albright, they considered me the one to find him. I think my life depended upon me locating him. Apparently, he was talking to various medical magazines about his work with bacteria viruses, and the brotherhood thought he was getting too close to exposing his part in the project.

I finally found Albright in New York City at a mutual friend's apartment. I told him he had to get back to Houston, or he would be in serious trouble. John is an arrogant bastard, but stupid he is not. He knew the consequences. The Collegium did not play games. I picked him up at Bush International Airport the next morning.

We went directly to Simon Reznick's hotel. Guidry and Mr. Z were also there. Reznick did not mince his words, telling Albright that he would never see another day if one more word was to leak out about his research or discoveries, its intended use, or where the labs were located.

Mr. Z handed Simon a pistol with a silencer attached to the barrel. He put the gun to Albright's temple and told him that nothing having to do with Factor-7 or the Collegium was to leave his mouth. Reznick pulled the trigger. The gun clicked. There were no bullets in the chamber.

John Albright fell to the floor, sobbing. Urine ran out of his trousers. He lay on the floor covered in sweat and urine, begging Reznick and Mr. Z to not kill him.

Reznick backed away from Albright and glared at him. He clenched his teeth together, and I recall his exact words: "Next time, you will not hear the click of an empty chamber. I will see your brains splattered to the wall."

I knew these men were deadly players in a hideous chess game, and all the rest of us, including Albright, were just their pawns. I wasn't sure if that display was for only Albright or for me and everyone else in the room.

There's always the one or two people who want to have the glory, and Albright was that one person. Simon Reznick shut that down. Albright was to not leave Texas and was to carry a cell phone that was tracked so Simon and his people could monitor him on a regular basis.

Somehow, my allegiance to the Collegium had not been questioned. But I was scared. There is no way out, and there is no way to tell someone who could stop the madness.

After that, Simon Reznick and Albright were inseparable. Albright would not be allowed to screw things up.

Sam looked at Rainee. "So that's why he was at the hotel the night I took Albright home…drunk." Sam continued to read.

They came to my house too often. Reznick said that it made them blend well into the community to be seen with Ana and me. I believe he was keeping an eye on me.

By the summer of 2017, the heat from Washington was bearing down on the Collegium. Apparently, Walthers had different thoughts about the "project." He was doing all he could to shut them down without exposing them or himself. It was a futile effort, which enraged the Masters.

Steven called me the morning of August 1. He had overheard Z tell Reznick and a man on the phone that "there is a drought. That big tree had to get wet."

I had no idea what that meant, but Steven quickly said, "Watch the news." He hung up.

The president had suddenly died from what was reported as a heart attack. I knew then what had happened and what Steven had told me meant. The word "wet," meaning to kill, has its origins in the early days of the Russian KGB, and the Russian, Lipinski, was on the phone. The old phrase took on modern meaning. The Collegium's hand covers a lot of territory and has touched a lot of people who think there's no other way but this to cleanse the scourge of terror, nuclear proliferation, genocide, and all the other sins of this world. It got me, but I wised up too late. I knew that there was no getting out and that the brotherhood would go to all extremes to finish their project, Factor-7. Anyone who got in their way was subject to assassination. They were strong and out of control.

The in-fighting among the brotherhood was at an all-time high. Several of the players had their own agendas, and others didn't think the plan was moving fast enough or would even work. Every facet of the plan was getting out of hand, and the once-cohesive strategy was unraveling at the seams. I was terrified that it had already ruptured. Power is poison when put in the wrong hands. The Collegium had too many bosses.

The new election took place in November. Miles Winger was our new president. He seemed to be an independent thinker, and perhaps he had strong allies in and out of the White House. All I knew was that the Collegium had to be stopped. Everyone and everything that got in their way would be eliminated, and that also meant the new president.

My only hope to redeem myself was to expose the Collegium to the highest office in our country, so Steven and I planned to contact President Winger. We were not sure if we could trust him, or if we were putting him in danger. After President Walthers had died so abruptly, I feared for his safety too. It was a life-or-death risk, but we also knew that we had to take that chance. Since there were rogue FBI, CIA, Mossad, MI6, and who knew who else from governments around the world, we didn't know how far up the chain this thing went.

Steven arranged a meeting through special top-secret channels. He did not have to tell why or what the meeting would be about. His clearance and his military training worked, and I met with the president on February 2 of this year at the White House. There was President Winger, Vice President Housier, and Secretary of State Julian Poole. After a brief introduction to why we were there, Winger then dismissed the other two men, stating that for their safety and security reasons, they should not be involved in the conversation. He furthermore told us that the meeting was not being taped. Winger already knew more than I expected. He would obviously take all the heat, if ever needed. We, of course, also said that we were never involved. But at this point, we feared the Collegium more than the judicial system. I told the president of how I knew Albright and that I suspected he was the head scientist. Steven explained that he had discovered the clandestine group by hacking into some email accounts and by obtaining top-secret documents while working at the Pentagon. We turned over the names of the people we knew who were involved. The president had everything he needed to close down the operation. But exposing it would be tricky and very risky. It could certainly look as if the United States was covering up something. I didn't know how he would avoid the appearance of the US implication if he identified the threat. I furthermore knew how hard it would be to suppress all leaks before he had dotted every i and crossed every t. If there was a leak, it would certainly set off a media frenzy and, consequently, a world panic. As I always feared, the truth could be worse than the weapon. And I was between the two, not sure I had made the right choice by going to the president. But time was of the essence then, and more so now.

Sam raised an eyebrow. "Well, I guess he tried."

A few days passed, and I got a call from President Winger. He asked me to come see him. The day before I was to leave for Washington, DC,

I got a call from Secretary of State Julian Poole. He told me that I did not need to see President Winger. He made a very strange statement. He said in a low but intense voice, "The president cannot and must not become involved in anything you might have suggested to him. He cannot, because if asked, he must be able to say with conviction that he doesn't know about any 'doomsday' operations. Dear Doctor, this is the last communication."

I found it all very strange, but later that week I got another call from Washington. It was the president calling from a secured phone in a private area of the White House's situation room. He whispered, "Do not say anything. Listen." He said that the Secret Service was outside the room and he was being watched closely. He was being contained, and he told me to go to another authority. He hung up. I have been unable to reach him since. I cannot trust anyone.

Steven called me in late March. He had been contacted by Mr. Z and was to meet with him in an hour. He said Z did not say why he wanted to meet. Steven indicated that he was concerned. He told me that the bacteriophages and vaccine were in a biorepository stored in an underground bunker that Lyndon Johnson had built for other reasons in the sixties. It was somewhere near NASA. He wanted me to know that. We knew then why so many of the Collegium were hanging around Houston. They were filling their arsenal. That was the last time I spoke to my brother.

Steven's car was hit from the rear by a large truck just moments after he left the Pentagon. His car was pushed against the esplanade and ended up completely under the truck. Steven was decapitated. I am certain it was murder.

Our visit to the White House had drawn attention to what Steven was doing. Steven was defecting from the Collegium. His house and office were ransacked. All his papers, files, and hard drive had been erased or stolen. His name was apparently erased from all records. It was as if he never existed in the government.

I am under constant surveillance. The only reason they haven't killed me is because they still need me. We are about to engage in tactical unconventional warfare, and I cannot stop it. There is less than six months left before it will be all over.

———————

Sam looked at Rainee. "They killed Winger."

"I wish I had never heard of Factor-7," she replied.

Sam flipped through the next file. It contained names and contact addresses or numbers beside some names. "This must be the list that Bill gave to President Winger," he said.

Rainee sat frozen to her chair.

He thumbed through another file. He read aloud.

———————

APRIL 5

More test sites have been penetrated. They tested for efficacy and used unwitting humans for their test trials. Poor nations are unable to detect new diseases, and rich nations show marginal interest until the outbreaks directly threaten its citizens. This is what the Collegium was counting on. The stories of an outbreak of Ebola in Nigeria have been put on the back burner. The WHO's network of Global Outbreak Alert and Response has been further stifled. The Collegium is moving forward and covering their tracks with every step. And no one has yet to realize that Albright's vaccines will be of minimal or no help with such a deadly and quick bioweapon as Factor-7. They despise John

Albright but still do not know that he is scamming them once again. A tweak here and there of the virus could cause it to mutate or change in a manner that could be stopped with a vaccine. I emphasize *could*. Albright could have this planned for his own rewards. He has his own plans, and I am certain they are as treacherous as he. But what Albright has now will kill too quickly.

———————

Sam took a deep breath. "Going to say this again…and again…it's too big, Rainee. I don't know how we can stop this or whom to tell. I'm not equipped to end something this big or sinister."

"Read on. Maybe Bill tells us," she said.

Sam grimaced and began to read.

———————

JUNE 10

Today, I was diagnosed with pancreatic cancer. I have known for some time, but it is confirmed today. It has spread, and my days are severely numbered. It will be a painful death but a welcome relief, and I will not put Ana through my last days. My time is shortened by the cancer, and soon the Collegium will no longer need me. They have their weapons. I have less than a month to do everything I can to stop them. I am writing everything that I know and names of people, but I have eliminated most government officials from the list. Some higher up in governments are involved, but they may or may not know the true intentions of the Collegium. Furthermore, some were duped or blackmailed into becoming a part of what they did not understand. The governments must be nervous. If people in President Winger's administration are implicated, he will also be accused of being a part of this madness. I know he is not. His predecessor, President Walthers, was murdered. That I know, but of course I cannot prove it. If the Justice Department, CIA, or FBI opened a probe into how he died, they would certainly expose the Collegium and perhaps people here or elsewhere in the world who should not be identified. Walthers knew about them. It would be a huge scandal inside the government if the probe into his death were to expose too much. Too much information can become misconstrued information, and those facts could bring down a government. No one is willing to take that chance. So it's simply being called a heart attack and brushed under the rug, perhaps forever, something like Kennedy. Too much information is often dangerous. Winger is in danger as well.

It's common knowledge that I was adopted at birth. But what no one knows was that my birth mother was Persian and born in that country, which is now Iraq. Her brother killed her under Sharia Law because she had gotten pregnant by an American soldier and out of wedlock. Thank God, her grandmother saved me and took me to a Christian church. I was adopted by my mother. She was an army nurse stationed at the United States research unit in Kuwait.

I have obtained a vial containing the bacteriophage that Albright created. I will administer it to myself when I deem it to be the right time. I have contacted a doctor in Italy. She has been instructed to contact my trusted friend. I hope that you are reading this now. I have also given this information to a dear and trusted friend on a USB flash drive. So you have a copy, and another has the flash drive. I cannot give you specific instructions on how to handle this threat, but I hope I have given you reason to handle it in a surreptitious manner. Your life, as well as much of the world, now depends upon how you deal with it. I realize you are not normally equipped to manage something so dire. I was a part of this, and I could not handle it. Forgive me if you can. And if you can't, please find a solution to eliminate the Collegium. My fate is sealed, and my eternity is without redemption for my sins.

"So someone else has this information," Rainee said. "I wonder who."

"Damn him. I have no idea who he would have given the flash drive to."

"I think he damned himself, Sam."

Sam put his head between his knees. "I'm so pissed at him."

"He was a deeply troubled and desperate man. People do a lot of things when they are without hope."

"I guess, but it doesn't change that without his input, they might not have ever gotten this far. For God's sake, he introduced Albright to them…the most morally bankrupt human I have ever known. And geez…the fucking awesome commission he placed upon us. But he's right about one thing. I don't have an answer or even a clue of a solution." Sam bowed his head. "I never knew Bill was adopted. I don't know why I should have known that. I guess there were a lot of things I didn't know about him," Sam said regretfully.

"Yeah, a ton. But it explains how the Factor-7 virus killed him. He carried her DNA," Rainee said. "We have to be very careful. Should we destroy the part about President Winger?" she asked.

Sam paused. "I dunno. We can't become invisible or stupid. We have Cameron's findings. We have Bill's journal, such as it is…and we have"—he took a quick breath—"nothing. We have fucking nothing."

"We need to calm ourselves and think this out." Rainee poured another glass of wine. "Bill was sick. He told no one. You know…"

Sam stared at Rainee. "You and I had discussed the repercussions of a leak of information about the Collegium. It made sense then, but now, it comes together like glue. Walthers was killed because he was going to reveal them. He wanted transparency. But for their sakes and because of the risk of total world annihilation from the fallout, someone did him in. The Collegium might not have even been his killers. It could have been an inside job, to bury the truth…no pun intended. Bill just confirmed it. If the truth goes viral and the United States and its allies are unjustly implicated—and we most certainly would be—it will give all our enemies the right to go to war. If knowledge of this mess gets out, the world would have to blame someone. I sure hope the Collegium is damn good at being covert. I know what Bill was saying. The USA and/or our friend nations would be blamed, and the world would retaliate, either in kind or in some other devastating manner. What the Collegium is doing is already war. The enemies of the US will only be defending themselves, and the world will see it as justified. Talk about being between a rock and a hard place. Nobody is right and everybody is wrong, and it could lead to total devastation. Secrecy and cover-ups are the only answers for governments. China is a prime example. Its propaganda machines have done it numerous times before and are still doing it today. And there are others out there doing the same thing. The world is full of evil and lies." Sam bowed his head. "Makes me nauseous."

Rainee groaned. "Bill died without knowing that President Winger was also assassinated. So, the brotherhood—god, I hate that name— have murdered two presidents, either directly or by proxy. They killed Bill's brother, and who knows who else. They'll obviously do anything to see their demonic plan executed…" She paused and made a low guttural moan. "Poor choice of words." She continued her thought. "And anything to keep it secret."

Sam shook his head in disgust. "Rainee, they're willing to execute perhaps millions of innocents just because they share the same ethnicity and they carry the same DNA. Hatred is as much of a virus as the Factor-7. It took hatred and greed to create Factor-7." Sam's voice got louder with each word. "So if kids in Iran, or Syria, or wherever carry at least fifty percent of the genome as other persons of Middle Eastern dissent, then they die. These are not the Islamist extremists. These are children and families…people who most likely are peace-loving Muslims." He took a deep breath. "And what about North Korea? It's not the people we have the beef with, for crying out loud! There are millions with that same DNA ancestry in South Korea and around the world too. All disposable to these monsters."

Rainee walked to the kitchen and poured two glasses of red wine. She mumbled as she returned to the chair, "Sam, are these people sheer idiots or pure evil or both?"

Sam took the glass and drank a huge gulp. "I don't know. There're people all over the world with these genomes in their DNA. They can't eliminate those they hate and not eliminate huge masses of innocent people with the same ancestral DNA. Sadly, I propose they have known this all along."

"Obviously they don't care. In fact, that might just be part of the plan. Maybe this is really ethnic cleaning in the name of eliminating terrorism. I'll bet they justify the collateral damage because they will wipe out a few terror organizations or warmongers."

"It's genocide," Sam shouted. "We now know their plan encompasses a much broader scope, and it can backfire in a moment. We know the virus can mutate again. It could wipe out the planet if it's as quick a killer as Bill says it is."

Rainee leaned back and rubbed her forehead. "Bill was right: there would be no way to stop its path of death. How do we begin to think like these maniacs and head them off? I say that's impossible for us." She paused. "We only know enough to be afraid. We have no clue how to end this."

Sam knew as well as Rainee that Bill Roberts had not given them as much information as they really needed. All he knew was that no one could be trusted. And that left them with nothing and very alone.

"There's a small file left. I'll read it," Sam said firmly.

The dark organizations, the financial backers, and the rogues are the ones who must be stopped. Formulas and storage locations for the Factor-7 are listed. I'm not sure if I wish I had never known or glad that I do. If I had never known, then I would not have this last opportunity to stop it. If it can be stopped at all.

Steven knew people who could begin the process of eliminating the Collegium, but he is dead. The military knows how to keep secrets, and they might be the only people to kill off this plague. The US Congress, Senate, and the Justice Department, as well as the president, must deny knowing anything about this. Hopefully the militaries of the free world can wipe out the leaders I have exposed in here and destroy their mission of death and the Factor-7. That might be enough to cause the rats to jump ship and hopefully go back into the holes from which they came.

Sam groaned. "*Hope* has never been a strategy."

But more importantly, if the enemies of the US or its allies think that these governments had planned or were planning an attack with biological weapons, then the entire world is at risk of World War III. Every adversary would justify war, and all hell will break loose. There will be no rules in that war. Factor-7 is that dangerous. It is dangerous for the destruction that it can bring about itself and for the devastation it can bring by literally being the single cause of World War III. The fallout from a leak would be opening the proverbial Pandora's Box. Even though it is not directly the United States government or that of the UK, France, Germany, China, Russia, or any number of smaller countries, the buck will ultimately fall on the United States and our allies. It reminds me of the old movie *Fail Safe*. There will be no way to explain it away if the United States is exposed and implicated, and there will be no way to survive the fallout. God be with you, and God forgive my soul.

———

Bill's confession was not only a disclosure, but also a confirmation of what Rainee already knew. Sam knew now as well. Sadly, people in very high places also knew. It confirmed that the government had to keep this secret at all costs, and they would have to keep the secret of murder in the White House. It would be buried from all eyes forever. Sam and Rainee knew that the risk of exposure of either the Factor-7 virus or the assassination of the president who knew of the plan was too big for any government to assume.

CHAPTER SIXTEEN

Rainee fell asleep on the sofa. Sam put a pillow under her head and put his head next to hers. It was almost 3:00 a.m. He was glad she could sleep. He ran Bill's words through his mind over and again. Finally, he also fell asleep.

He awoke abruptly, but somehow during the night he had put his arm around Rainee. She was soft, smelled wonderful, and slept quietly. He was hesitant to wake her because she needed her rest and because he found solace and pleasure in holding her in his arms.

She roused and looked at Sam. She smiled "What a night, huh?"

Sam looked at his watch. It was 11:45 a.m. "Come on. I want to get copies of this made right now. Maybe we can get copies made at the St. Anthony Hotel."

They dressed quickly. Rainee fixed a French press of strong coffee and handed him a cup with a day-old pan dulce.

"You were beautiful to wake up to," Sam admitted nervously. His eyes stared into hers like a cocker spaniel.

Rainee smiled and took his hand. "I agree."

Sam bent down and took her face in his hands. He stared at her for a moment. Then he kissed her softly and tenderly. "Well, good morning."

Rainee kissed him back, and it got more intense as he pulled her closer to his body. She ran her hand down his back and put her hand into his jeans and touched his buttock. He pulled her hard into his groin.

"This can't happen right now," Rainee breathlessly said. "Your jeans are not going to fit if you get any bigger. I like that."

"Oh hell, I know…why not now? I'm crazy about you," Sam whispered as he hugged her tighter. He kissed her again. It was a gentle, soft kiss, and Sam's broken heart was immediately healed by her soft lips.

She began to talk as he kissed her, and she kissed him back between her words. "We have things to do. Ah…yeah, we can't do this, Sam."

He put his forehead to hers. "I wish we could." He took several deep breaths and threw his head back. "You're going to kill me, woman." Sam grabbed the files and put them in a brightly colored Mexican shopping bag.

She smiled and winked. "In time. Do we really want to take Bill's letters out of here?" she asked.

Sam didn't respond at first. He was trying to rid himself of his desire for unbridled sex with her. He pushed the files into the mesh Mexican shopping bag. "We've got to do this, I guess. We have to get copies of this confession and find a safe place for them tonight. It would take too long to take pictures on our cell phones and they might not be as clear as clean copies. Let's old-school this one and make copies." He was preoccupied with her but insistent on the task he knew was inevitable. He took her by the hand and led her to the car. The hotel was only a few miles from the villa.

"Sam, slow down. You're making me nervous."

He pulled into the parking lot and quickly found a space.

"Geez, Sam, do you think you drove fast enough?" She threw her head back in a gesture of relief to have arrived safely.

Sam opened the door for Rainee and patted her sweetly on the back. "Sorry. I didn't mean to scare you. Remember, I drive a Porsche."

She shook her head in disbelief that he had said such a thing. "And that makes me feel better…how?"

Sam ignored her. "OK…we'll go in and order a drink and maybe some nachos or whatever you feel like eating. You ask the waiter in Spanish if they have a copy machine. I'll take it from there," he said forcefully. Then he gently kissed her cheek.

She was not going to argue. Anyway, she didn't have a plan, and right then, any plan was better than none.

"What may I get you?" Displaying a slight Cajun accent, the young woman spoke perfect English. She held a white pad in her hand.

"You're American?" Sam asked.

"Yes, sir. I'm a student at the instituto. I'm studying art. Working to make my rent, you know."

Sam smiled. "Where's home?"

She looked at Sam and then to Rainee. "New Orleans was my longest home. Army brat—we moved a lot."

Rainee nodded. "I live near Naples, Italy. Sam's from Galveston. Guess we're an international crowd here. Have you ever heard of Sorrento? That's actually fairly close to my home."

The young woman shook her head. "Oh no, ma'am. But I'd love to go to Italy someday. It's been my dream. All the art to see. Have you ever been to Capri?" she asked, mispronouncing the island's name so it sounded like a pair of lady's summer pants.

"Yes, I have a home there. Not that it matters, but you might want to know it's pronounced, Cap-pri," she said nonchalantly, but not arrogantly. It was as if everybody had a home there and that the correct pronunciation was imperative. "I hope you do get to go to Italy. It's beautiful. The southern part is not Italy's only beautiful area, but it's my favorite. It's all beautiful. I miss it greatly. Try to see it all as soon as you can, because someday you might not have that opportunity."

Sam glared at Rainee. "You sound too doomsday already. The poor girl has no idea. I want to go too, and very soon." He paused and blurted out without consideration of his tone, "You have a home in Capri?"

Rainee rolled her eyes. "Yes, it's been in my father's family for a very long time. I don't get to go as much as I would like."

"I've got it. You work, and I'll live on Capri like some international rich spy," Sam joked.

Rainee shook her head and pointed playfully at Sam. "Order. The lady is waiting."

He smiled. "I'll have a dirty Gray Goose martini."

Rainee whispered in his ear, "So glad you didn't say shaken not stirred. You international rich spy."

Sam could barely control his enjoyment of Rainee's quick wit.

"I'll have the same," she said, breaking out in laughter. "Wow, it's good to laugh."

The waitress soon brought the drinks.

"I didn't know you liked martinis at noon," Rainee said.

"Bet you didn't know I like piña coladas, either."

"And getting caught in the rain, I suppose."

Sam held up his glass to Rainee's. "If I'm caught with you."

Rainee was taken aback. She became speechless, something not akin to her personality.

"I'm sorry. Am I being too forward?" Sam asked sheepishly.

"No, I just wasn't expecting that from you."

Sam took a sip of his drink. "And why not? Have I not given you enough hints the past few days? I like you, Dr. Rainee Arienzo. I really like you."

She bowed her head for a moment. Then she looked Sam straight in his eyes. "I like you too, Dr. Sam Hawkins."

The vodka went down well, and both Sam and Rainee felt a slight sense of relaxation.

Sam took her hand and kissed it. "We're going to be all right."

Rainee pulled her hand away. "You sure say that a lot. Who are you trying to convince?"

The waitress returned. "May I bring another round?"

Sam glanced at Rainee. He raised his eyebrows and smiled. "Another?"

"Oh, why not?" She smiled, softening her tone. "And chips and salsa?"

"Yes, two more. May I ask if you know where there might be a copy machine I could use?" Sam asked, looking up at the waitress.

"I think there's one in the reception area. Please ask the man at the front desk. I'm sure he can help you."

Sam excused himself, leaving Rainee in the dimly lit bar. He walked into the sun-bathed corridor that led to the front of the hotel. There was a nice-looking young man behind the counter. Sam inquired about using his copy machine, but the man didn't understand Sam's request. Sam held up the papers and as in a game of charades showed him what he needed. Laughing, he led Sam to the office where the small anti-quated machine sat.

Sam laid one paper on the glass at a time and pushed the button. The single copy slowly rolled out. It was going to take much too long, but he had no options. Midway through the files, Sam realized that he needed to let Rainee know what was taking him so long. He grabbed the files. A young woman was now attending the front desk. She was engaged in a serious conversation with what appeared to be a woman from housekeeping.

Sam spoke slowly. "Señorita, I am using your machine in the office. I will be right back. OK?"

The young woman appeared to understand him and nodded, but she promptly returned to her conversation.

Sam tried to focus his eyes when he stepped into the dark bar. Rainee was not there. The two martini glasses remained on the table. Where had she gone—or had she been taken? His heart pounded, and beads of sweat erupted on his forehead. He ran to the back of the bar where the bottles and glasses were stored. The waitress was nowhere to be found. The bar was eerily quiet. "Rainee, where are you?" Sam shouted as loudly as he could. "Please tell me where you are."

There was no reply. He shouted again. Still nothing. He ran outside the front door. The streets were wet from the afternoon shower. The sun reflected off the standing water, which temporarily blinded him. He shouted for her. People on the street turned and stared, but Rainee was not around. Sam was in full panic mode. *Why, why…why did I leave her alone? Stupid fuck!* He cursed at himself.

He checked the bathrooms and several open rooms on the first floor. The back of the hotel was a garden with winding paths. Sam ran the length of the garden, shrieking her name. But nothing. There would have been no reason for her to go upstairs, and if someone had taken her there, which of the four floors would Sam check first? The combination of the known violence against Americans and others in Mexico, Jorge's gun, and the newly revealed information from Bill Roberts's notes had heightened Sam's fears into sheer paranoia.

A short fat man wearing a bloody apron stepped from an open doorway. He held a butcher knife in his right hand and a leg of a small goat in the other. Sam's heart sank. "Have you seen a woman with long dark hair?" he screeched loudly at the man. Sam's Spanish was poor all the time, but in his anguish, it was indistinguishable. Then, he winced. *Every woman had long dark hair—they were fucking in Mexico!*

The man flinched. He pulled the severed piece of meat to his chest, as if the goat's leg would protect him against the American madman.

Sam shouted, "A lady—have you seen a lady?"

The cook's eyes widened even further as Sam stepped closer to him, still shouting his question. That was enough to cause the poor man to make a low guttural sound and flee behind the kitchen door.

Several men ran down the corridor toward Sam. He recognized one of them as the young man who had helped him with the copy machine.

"Señor, señor, que paso? Señor, silencio," one of the men shouted as they approached.

Sam stopped in his tracks. He had to get a grip, and perhaps these men would help him find Rainee. "Do you speak English?" he asked.

One of the men walked closer to Sam. "I speak English, señor. What is the problem? You are interrupting the hotel, sir. You are frightening the guests."

Sam looked around. He had not seen any guests. "I'm looking for a woman. I left her in the bar, and now she's gone!"

The young man who had helped Sam earlier began to speak softly to the English-speaking Mexican man. They both would say something in Spanish and then look at Sam.

"What the fuck, man? My friend is missing while you two have a reunion," Sam said angrily.

"Manuel told me that she came to the front desk looking for you."

"So where did she go? Was she alone? Why didn't she go to the office where I was?" Sam asked rapidly.

"He said…" The man paused and pointed behind Sam.

"Sam!"

Sam wheeled on his heels.

Rainee quickened her steps.

Sam ran toward her. "Where have you been? I've been so scared something happened to you." He pulled her into his arms and held on tightly.

"I went to the farmacia next door. I told the man at the front desk to tell you that when you came out. I needed some antacids, that's all."

The bilingual Mexican man came closer to Sam and Rainee. "I was about to tell you that Manuel knew where she was."

Rainee pulled away from Sam. "He didn't tell you until now?"

"No. I've been frantic for over ten minutes. Don't ever do that. Please."

"Perhaps you should not leave me alone then." She gently touched his arm. "I'm fine. I didn't mean to worry you."

"Señora, we are happy you are all right. Manuel was not there when the señor left the office. It is just a misunderstanding."

"Sam, they had a shift change, so my message got lost. I'm fine." Rainee took his hand. "Let's go back to the villa."

"I'm not finished with the copies," Sam said.

"I don't think we're particularly welcome here. We'll find somewhere else." She pulled Sam closer to her as she took a step toward the front door of the hotel. "Gentlemen, we are sorry for the disruption. Thank you for your kindness," she said in Spanish.

"What did you tell them?" Sam asked.

"That you are insanely in love with me and just couldn't bear to be without me, even for a few minutes."

"You did not!" Sam smiled and let out a heavy sigh of relief. "But that would be pretty close to the truth."

Rainee smiled wearily. "That's strong talk and very quick, Sam."

"Well, doesn't take me long to look at a horseshoe."

"What?" she asked, not familiar with another one of his colloquialisms.

"It means that I know something when I see it. In this case, I know something when I feel it."

She bit her bottom lip. "Let's find a copy place." She pulled Sam closer to her and kissed him slowly on the mouth.

Sam stood paralyzed by the kiss and the possibility that she too might feel the same about him. There was a slight kick in his step as he rounded the car to the driver's side. He momentarily gazed at her through the car window before opening the door. He could smell her scent on his lips. He ran his tongue over them, sucking up her flavor. He desired nothing more than to become entangled in that fragrance. He breathed deeply, filling his senses with her. She had a grip on him, and he was not about to let go.

Sam drove to the square and located a tiny parking space on a side street. He pointed toward the cathedral. "I'm taking you to La Chapelita for our last night in San Miguel. It's up there on top. But I'm not eating cabrito."

"Why not? Roasted young goat is a Mexican tradition."

"Just because." He laughed to himself. "Yep, just because."

They found a small store near the square. It had fax machines, printers, an internet connection, and two copy machines. Between the two of them, they got all the copies made in less than a half hour. Sam wrapped the new copies in a bag he bought on the street and secured them all in the trunk of the car.

"OK," Sam said, "it's our last night here, then back to business. It's just you and me, kid." He squeezed her hand. "What's your pleasure? Just name it."

"Well…" She thought for a moment. "I'd like that turquoise ring and bracelet we saw the other day, then a cold bottle of champagne, and a traditional Mexican dinner. But not cabrito." She laughed without knowing the true reason why Sam had suddenly gotten an aversion to goat meat. "And I'm buying my jewelry."

"Not on my watch, you're not. I'm buying your jewelry, and maybe more than just the turquoise. I saw a cat's eye I liked. It would look beautiful against your skin." He stopped and looked into her eyes. "Anything or nothing would look beautiful on you."

"You embarrass me." Rainee bowed her head, visually uncomfortable with Sam's advances.

"I'm sorry. I'm coming on too strong. Please forgive me. I'm just being playful, but I know that came out a bit forward."

"You think?" She laughed. "More like a bit horny."

He gave her a smirk. She had a way to one-up him every time, leaving Sam dumbstruck.

She took his hand and gave it a long squeeze. She giggled as they wandered down the cobblestones. Rainee was quick witted, and he had, perhaps for the first time, met his match. He loved every minute of it. He felt things he had never imagined possible.

They shopped and walked around the quaint town for hours. Both seemed to relax and perhaps bury their troubles for a brief time. They didn't have to wait for a table at La Chapelita, or the Little Chapel, as the Americans who had made San Miguel their home called it. It was open air and above the famed cathedral. The food at La Chapelita, although anything but quick, had always been outstanding. Sam believed it was a combination of preparation time and the opportunity to sell a lot of wine and liquor. That night was not going to be the exception. Sam was there to show Rainee the night of her life in Mexico. He kept getting the sick feeling in his gut that it might indeed be one of their last days. He would not waste a moment. What they would face when they got to the United States haunted him, but for one night, he was trying to forget it all. If Rainee wanted a traditional Mexican dinner, he knew this would be the place for fine dining and a few specialties.

"What do you suggest?" she asked, perusing the menu.

"Well, I think we should start with an appetizer. Have you ever had huitlacoche?"

"No, and it sounds like something smoked in a teepee or the back seat of a car."

"Kind of tastes likes smoke." Sam laughed. "It's a fungus that grows on corn and goes back to the Aztecs. They call it Mexican truffle. I had it once in Mexico City and threw up my guts for a week."

"Oh, then by all means, let's eat that."

"No…it really is a Mexican specialty, and I think I ate some bad fish that night. Not the huitlacoche," Sam said assuredly.

"Who orders fish in Mexico City, anyway?"

"An idiot, I guess. Anyway, I think we should do that. And for our entrée, let's do the roasted pork with mole sauce on the side, fried squash flowers, rice, cold fresh mangos, and fried plantains. Can't get any more Mexican than that."

She agreed. "As long as it's not huevos rancheros. Seems that's about all I've heard."

"Hey, you got a pizzchalupa, didn't you? And I like beans."

Rainee laughed. "You're full of beans. Wine. I need wine!"

Sam and Rainee tried to forget the day—or, more importantly, the reason for their being in Mexico. If it was not spoken, it would, at least for a few hours, disappear.

A bond between them had formed. Sam hoped it was more than their mutual involvement in something much larger than they could have ever imagined. They were alone with the overwhelming task.

But tomorrow was soon enough to tackle what was obviously way over their heads. Sam held Rainee close and toasted their future success. The champagne flutes remained filled, and the flicker of candlelight consumed the darkness around them. They sat in obscurity and anonymity for those few hours. It was not to last, and Sam knew what had become their duty, if not, their destiny. Words were not important.

He felt her breath on his neck. Her soft face lay against his skin, and again he became intoxicated by her scent. He knew she was frightened. He was as well, but Sam was determined that Rainee wouldn't sense his fear. He meant what he had said at the villa. Her safety was his utmost responsibility. To hell with the world that had gone crazy. He had her with him, and he was not going to allow anything to happen to her. But what was their next step? What would they do when they got back to the US? It was only hours away. Sam had no real plan, and this time, winging it was not an option.

"You're thinking too much," Rainee whispered.

"About you," Sam replied, stroking her hair with his left hand.

"If only that were true and the extent of it. I feel the tension in your neck and chest." She put her arm around his torso.

Their bodies were tightly fused for a moment. Sam breathed deeply as he pulled her closer to him. He slowly touched her chin, moving it upward toward him. His mouth found hers. She held on to him tightly. Sam opened his mouth and slowly kissed her, his tongue lightly licking and teasingly biting her bottom lip. She kissed him back with the same intensity and tenderness that was in his caress. They held each other's lips with soft sucking motions of open and then closed mouths. Their tongues touched gently, and then they ran them over each other's lips, as if tasting the sweetness of the moment.

"That was perfect," she sighed, breathlessly.

Sam kissed her softly. "Do you want to leave?" His invitation was as easy as his kiss.

She sat straight in her chair, pulling gently away from Sam's embrace. "Yes. I'm ready now. I'm ready for you, Sam."

Sam gazed into her dark eyes, which were glimmering in the candlelight. "I'm ready for you too, Dr. Rainee Arienzo."

He paid the waiter for their meal and ordered a bottle of champagne to go. Rainee took his hand as they walked down the narrow stairs from the restaurant to street level. Several couples sat on the benches in the square, all apparently enjoying a night's romance. Music played softly from a distant bar, but otherwise, there were no sounds. Hand in hand, the two meandered down the cobblestone street.

"I hope I don't come across too mushy," he said, "and I need to apologize for my silly behavior. I monkey around when I should be serious, and I'm accused of being too serious when I should be monkeying around."

"Well, it's all OK. You're a pretty *guapo* monkey." She giggled.

"I know what that means. You said I'm the most handsome monkey you've ever met."

"I didn't go that far." She giggled again. "This is truly a beautiful town."

"It is, but I have never seen it or felt its beauty until now. Honestly, I feel like I'm seeing all this for the first time." Sam paused and turned to look into her eyes once again. His tone became serious and deliberate. "It's been a long time for me to feel anything at all, especially what I feel now. For years, I've been numb to all emotions. It probably sounds corny, but one is never more alone than in a house without love. I've just been going through the motions of life, but I haven't been living. You have made me feel alive again."

She squeezed his hand. "I know what you're saying. Thank you, Sam. Thank you for tonight and your honesty. I know we have a lot ahead of us, but together, I think we just might make it."

Neither one spoke as they approached the parked car. Rainee allowed Sam to open her door. Before she slipped into the seat, she leaned into him and gave him a soft, wet kiss.

"You are teasing me, my dear," Sam said playfully, with one eyebrow raised.

She laughed. "I am indeed."

Sam started the car, and they slowly pulled from the parking space.

"Sam, look over there." She pointed to the corner of the Chapelita entrance. "Isn't that Jorge, El Espino's guy?"

Sam slowed as they passed the man. He tried to not look directly at his face, but he knew who he had seen. "Yep, that's Jorge."

"Do you find that odd?" she asked.

"I'm not sure. He might just live here and be out for dinner like we were. It's a fairly tiny town." Sam turned onto Calle De Leon toward the villa. *Or he could be watching us*, he thought.

Sam opened the car door for Rainee and then the trunk. He pulled out the brightly colored bag containing the originals and the copies of Bill Roberts's letters. Nervously, he fumbled with the front gate keys.

"It's really dark out here. They need some streetlights." She exhaled quickly. "But I guess not. This is Mexico, after all."

Sam huffed but didn't answer. Jorge consumed his thoughts.

"I'm reading you like a cheap novel again, Dr. Hawkins. You *are* concerned about seeing Jorge, right?"

Sam opened the front gate and shuffled Rainee inside, locking the massive double doors behind them both. "I don't know if I would say that I'm concerned," he replied. "I just find it a bit disconcerting. But we're safe in our little fortress now." He pulled her close to his body and wrapped his arms around the small of her back. He kissed her neck and then up her chin to her lips.

Rainee arched her back as Sam pushed himself harder into her lower body. They desperately wanted each other. Holding her off the floor, Sam carried her to the bedroom. His mouth held tightly to her mouth. He gently laid her on the bed and crawled to her. She rolled onto her side, grasping his shirt with one hand and his belt with the other. She moved one leg in between Sam's and pulled closer to his groin. He kissed her hard with an open mouth, swirling his tongue around her mouth. His hands ran down her body, following the line from her breasts to her hips. She slid her hand into his jeans and gently touched the skin of his lower abdomen. He flinched as she moved her hand closer to his penis, but she did not touch it.

Sam pulled her to a sitting position and, while still kissing her, pulled her T-shirt over her head. His hands reached her back, and he easily unfastened her bra and threw it to the floor. As she sat facing him, he held both of her breasts in his hands, massaging them both tenderly and methodically. He gazed a moment at her naked breasts and then leaned into her.

"You are so beautiful," he whispered.

She bent forward and kissed him but said nothing. He gently pushed her to a reclining position and then laid his body on top of her, supported by his elbows and bent knees. His mouth found her nipples and lightly tugged on them. Sam held her breasts with both hands and sucked while encircling this tongue around her areola. As he wrapped his arm under the small of her back, Rainee pushed again harder into his body. He slid down her body, streaming wet kisses from her neck to her breasts, then to her stomach. He unzipped her jeans and pulled them to her ankles. Her scent was intoxicating as he kissed her stomach and down to her pelvis. Sam moved farther down the bed, kissing the inside of her thighs and running his hand inside her panties. She gently pulled them off and let both her panties and jeans drop to the floor. He sat up and admired her naked beauty.

"I want you," Sam whispered. His fingers found her pelvic area, and with smooth circular motions, he found the lips of her vagina. Rainee's body quivered with Sam's touch. Still kissing the inside of her thighs, Sam softly traced the outside of her vagina with two fingers. She thrust herself hard into his hand, and he entered her with one finger, softly finding the sensitive spot. She sighed with pleasure. He pushed his fingers against her wet clitoris and then quickly inside her vagina and again to the clitoris. He alternated the movements as Rainee sighed in orgasmic ecstasy.

"Sam," she breathlessly whispered as she pulled him up to her. She began to unbutton his shirt, but Sam jerked it off. His exposed naked chest pressed against her breasts. Sam hastily slipped off his jeans and boxer shorts. Their naked bodies lay wrapped in each other.

"You feel so good," Sam sighed, kissing her throat.

She bowed her neck backward, allowing his kisses to run the length of her neck. He ran his tongue down her body, kissing and sucking her skin. Sam pushed himself to the foot of the bed and pulled her to the end. He sat on the floor with his knees bent and his head between her outstretched legs. His tongue slowly moved into her vagina, and he softly nibbled at her clitoris. He circled his tongue and fingers around the outside, then inside. As she verbally exhaled with desire, Sam pushed his entire tongue into her with quick staccato movements. Her body began to tighten, and she released a low moan of pleasure. Sam pulled himself on top of her, kissing her as he reached her lips. Her legs wrapped around his lower back, setting her higher and ready for him to enter her. She pulled his buttocks toward her, so as to push him tighter to her. She breathlessly whispered, "Don't stop. I'm on the pill. Don't stop." He had a full erection, and his hardened penis sat between her legs. He pushed himself slowly into her. She was tight, wet, and warm. Sam was in a euphoric state, as if he were in a dream, out of his body and immersed in hot spring water. He arched his back and plunged deeper into her. He set her arms above her head and placed his hands in hers, locking their fingers as their bodies fused into one. Rainee groaned again, drowning in the rapture of the moment. Sam pushed himself inside her with the full length of his manhood. He moved in rhythmic motions up and down as he ground his loins into her until he could go no deeper.

Rainee wrapped her hands under his buttocks. She alternated rubbing his balls with the palm of her hand and gently massaging his prostate area as he slowly pumped himself inside of her.

"I'm going to cum, babe." He gasped for air.

She released her hold and tenderly pushed him off her and onto his side. His penis slipped from inside her.

"Woman...what *are* you doing?" he asked breathlessly.

She didn't speak but began kissing his mouth and holding his engorged penis with her right hand. She kneaded his balls and then moved her hand up and down the shaft. She placed his penis on the outside of her vagina and slowly moved the tip up and down without allowing it to penetrate her.

"Oh, baby, you're driving me crazy," Sam shouted.

"Shhhh," she whispered. She moved slowly down, kissing his chest down to his groin and then licking the top of his penis. She ran her tongue down the shaft and around the tip, all the while holding on to his balls and massaging them with tender motions.

Sam was barely able to hold himself back when she slipped the entire penis into her mouth and began to suck on it and pump it up and down with her lips. When Sam could hold it no longer, Rainee moved to a sitting position on top of him and slowly inserted his penis into her wet vagina. Sam pushed harder, making himself enter deeply inside her. She gasped, and he pushed himself to the limit. She moved forward and backward while sitting on him. He could feel her begin to tremble and her body become tense. Her vagina was in a spasm of orgasmic ecstasy as Sam's pelvis lunged, and with one strong thrust, he released himself. Mutual intense pleasure exploded as they climaxed together. Rainee fell onto his chest, squeezing her legs together so as to hold him deeply inside her. Her entire body shivered again while the orgasm continued. They lay that way until Sam naturally receded from her. She rolled off him, and they held each other closely, legs entangled, breathless.

Rainee quietly got out of the bed. In a few minutes, she returned with a warm cloth and began to wipe Sam's penis and legs.

"That feels wonderful, but you're wiping you off of me." He pulled her close and gently kissed her.

She snuggled closely to him, and they both fell into a deep, relaxed sleep.

CHAPTER SEVENTEEN

The sun broke through the clouds, and light streamed onto Rainee's face. Sam was awake and was watching her sleep when she opened her eyes.

"Good morning, gorgeous," he said, running his hand over her breasts and down her body.

She smiled. "Good morning, sexy."

Sam pulled her close to him, and she felt his hard penis press against her.

"Someone is ready," she said.

"Yes ma'am," he said, placing his hand on her vagina and slowly inserting his fingers.

She rolled onto her side, placing her left leg over Sam's hips. He rolled onto his side. She took his extended penis and began to slowly rub the tip on the outside of her vagina. Unable to hold his excitement, he pushed himself inside her and began to move himself deeper and deeper. She pushed hard into him as he pushed himself entirely into her. With an explosion of pleasure, they both came at the same time, with intensity neither had known before.

"It just keeps getting better," Sam said.

"Morning sex is great!" She rolled over and laid her head on his chest. "And the nights are wonderful." She giggled.

His heart was pounding.

"Will I need to get an oxygen tank?" Rainee laughed.

"Keep this up, and I'll need an entire oxygen truck." He kissed her. "But don't stop. Don't ever stop."

She pulled playfully on his chest hair. "I won't if you don't."

———————

It was 8:00 a.m. and the plane was not scheduled to pick them up until 3:00 p.m. Sam suggested they go into town and have breakfast. They packed up their things and dressed for the day.

They found their little café open. José Luis greeted them and promptly brought coffees the way they had previously ordered them.

"Good memory," Rainee said as he set down the coffee and rolls.

"You're hard to forget," Sam added with a smile.

She just shook her head and sipped on her coffee.

Breakfast was served. Sam and Rainee chatted about anything except Factor-7. That would come much too soon. The difference was that they knew what they were truly up against now. Sam would go to Washington and speak to his friend in Congress, but other than that, he had no clue what they would do. It was even more important to him to keep Rainee safe. He knew he was falling or already had fallen in love with her. He wasn't sure how she felt, and it was so quick that he was reluctant to say the word out loud. He had only loved one other woman, and that was the biggest heartbreak of his life. Could it be that he was rushing into this because he was rebounding from Lauren? He questioned his emotions. But it didn't feel like a rebound. It was so easy to be with Rainee. They were so compatible now. She was witty, smart, and always one step ahead of him. Sam liked that in her. She never ceased to amaze him with her insight and humor. *And the sex…* he sighed. *Wow,* he thought. The sex had never been better. She surely would be going back to Italy, if and when they had done what they could to expose the Collegium and Factor-7. Then what? Was he going to ask her to marry him? Sam shuddered at that thought—not because he wouldn't, but because he knew she wouldn't marry him so quickly. And why would *he* marry again so quickly? His thoughts swirled around in his head.

"What are you thinking about, Sam?" Rainee asked. "You seem a million miles away."

He stared at her, studying her every feature. "I was wondering what you will do after the Factor-7 threat." His brow furrowed.

"After Factor-7, Sam? There may never be an after the Factor-7. I know you think we can expose them, but I'm not so sure that simply exposing them will stop them. We have no strength against them. They have money, power, and—let's face it—they have operatives that are so far advanced that they could hide under rocks for decades without detection. There are eyes everywhere, according to Bill Roberts. We can't trust anyone."

"I'm sorry; I didn't mean to bring it up. We were having such a pleasant breakfast. This thing will happen soon enough. Let's try to enjoy what time we have left here in San Miguel…together."

She took his hand and smiled. "Yes, Sam, it has been wonderful, even with the threat. You didn't particularly like me at first. I remember you were very rude to me. But you thought I was a lunatic, so you're excused."

"Not really. Can't go so far as to say I thought you were loony, but maybe a little bit of a whack job." He laughed.

She again just shook her head and smiled. "I guess I can understand that."

"But I always found you incredibly attractive, sexy, witty, and… well…I did then and I really, really do now. Wanna go back to the villa?"

"You're too funny and insatiable. I like you too, Sam."

Sam took a bite from his buttered roll. *She likes me too?* That was not exactly what he had hoped to hear. It was such a nonchalant statement. You like chocolate cake; you like the beach…you don't have a night like they had and say that. He didn't have wild sex with just anyone. In fact, he couldn't recall ever having such intense sex, and then awakened wanting more…maybe wanting a lifetime of lovemaking and her. His ego was bruised, and he was longing for her to say something that would change that feeling, but she didn't.

The waiter brought sweet breads and they picked off bites of each of them. Sam watched her while she tasted each pastry. Even when she ate, his penis had a mind of its own. Her mouth mesmerized him. He sat quietly hoping for some glimpse of how she was feeling. *Damn it,* he thought, *what has this woman done to me?*

"Sam, when we get back to Texas, are you going to call your friend in Washington?" Rainee asked.

He cleared his throat. "Yes, probably tomorrow."

She continued. "If he will see us, then I think we should fly there tomorrow. We don't have a lot of time, according to Bill."

"Yep, stage four. Six months max…and that was a couple of months ago."

Rainee's thoughts were strictly on Factor-7. "One leak…just one leak, and it could explode. No one will survive that apocalypse. This world is in a hell of a mess."

Sam took the last sip of his coffee. "Yes, it is. It has been for some time. This revelation from Bill only gives credence to the total plight the world is facing. But I've had an incredible time with you here, and I hope it's not over. I want to be with you more." His words stung when they left his lips. He was revealing how he felt too much and too soon.

"Me too, Sam. We will have more time together, and I hope it will be easy and without this cloud hanging over us."

Sam smiled. He had gotten his glimpse of hope.

People were opening their shops, and the little town was coming alive. Sam and Rainee had been engaged in themselves, without noticing the hustle of a new day.

Sam would have done anything to stop what they were getting ready to encounter upon their return to the US. "Are you packed and ready to go?" he asked, pulling out her chair.

"Yes. Just pick up the bags, and we can go to the airport." She glanced at her watch. "We still have about three hours."

Sam looked seductively at her. "Whatever shall we do?"

"Sam, you're incorrigible. But as nice as that sounds…I'm showered and dressed. You will mess me up good."

"Mess you up?" Sam put on the southern accent. "Yes, ma'am. I intend to do that a lot."

Storm clouds darkened the distant skies, and a light rain had begun. They walked under the roofs of the shops that lined the streets until the rain was so intense that they popped into the first store they saw.

Sam asked to see some boots that were in the window. The young man promptly arrived with a pair in Sam's size. He slipped them on, and they were beautiful. "I like these," he said. "But at close examination, these are turtle skins."

Rainee winced. "No!"

Sam removed the boots and asked to see something in cowhide. "I donate to save those poor creatures. It's just wrong to make boots out of them."

"Peculiar how a person can justify almost all wrong if it fits one's needs," she said. Then under her breath, she said, "Even the Collegium have justifiable motives."

The young man returned with a pair of boots for Sam and one for Rainee.

She held up her hands. "No, I don't want boots."

"Yes, I'm buying you a pair of western boots," Sam said.

Rainee reluctantly put on her boots. "How did he know my size?" she asked.

"Apparently, beautiful women wear size seven."

"Ah-ha, sure. And you would know this, how?"

"I looked in your shoes this morning," he said shyly.

"Kinky! Good thing those shoes were made in the US, or you would've had a time deciphering the European size."

"I bet I could have figured that out too. How do they feel?"

"I must admit these are very comfortable." She slipped on the left boot and stuffed her jeans inside both. "I really love these."

Sam paid the man for both pairs of boots, and they walked out wearing their new finds. "I look like a cowgirl now, huh pardner?" Rainee joked.

"Yep, you shore do, but do you own your cattle outright, or does the bank own them?" Sam asked, seriously staring into her eyes.

Puzzled, Rainee stopped and looked hard at Sam. "What the hell are you talking about?"

"Well, in Texas, it's said that only those who own their cattle outright can wear their jeans inside their boots. I guess I have to buy you a cow."

"Make it a bull, because that's exactly what you're full of."

When they rounded the corner to go back to where they had parked the car, a man stepped out of a dark alley. He pointed a pistol directly at them.

"Alto," he screeched.

"What the hell?" Sam yelled, pulling Rainee to his side. "What do you want?" He pulled out his wallet. "I have money…here, take it!"

The man began to laugh. "You think I want your money, white bread?" he said in broken English.

Sam quickly turned around to see if there was any way to escape. There were four men behind them, with guns drawn and sinister smiles on their faces.

"What do you want?" Sam shouted again.

"Silencio, señor, I do not wish to harm you and the lady," a man said softly from behind them.

"Then what is this?" Sam asked.

"You will come with us now," the man said forcefully.

"You tell me why," Sam said.

"So, you and your lady will not die here on the street. We do not like blood on our streets." The reply came from far behind.

Sam recognized the voice. He turned quickly to see the man holding a gun in his hand, but not pointed at either Sam or Rainee. Sam pulled her closer to him and whispered, "It's Jorge. We have to do what they say."

"No, Sam. They'll kill us."

Sam squeezed her hand. "We'll have to take our chances, because otherwise they'll shoot us dead right here."

She reluctantly nodded. "We don't have a choice. They're going to kill us no matter what we do."

Jorge approached the couple and put the barrel of his .357 Magnum firmly against Sam's temple. Defiantly, Sam stretched his neck until it was tense, but he didn't speak.

"You will come with us now," Jorge said, nudging the pistol harder into Sam's head.

"Take me and let her go. I'm the one with money. You don't need her." Sam pushed Rainee away from Jorge and the gun.

Jorge began to laugh almost hysterically. "Money? You fool. I don't want your fuckin' money!" He looked at all the men and said something in Spanish, and they all began to laugh. "I want the papers." His Mexican accent was stronger than before.

"What papers?" Sam asked.

"Don't fuck with me. I want the papers you have," Jorge said. He held his hands up, shaking the gun in Sam's face. He repeated himself. "The papers, señor, or you and the pretty lady die!"

"I don't know what you mean." Sam ran to Rainee and pulled her again to his side.

"He wants Bill's papers, Sam," Rainee said, crying.

Sam looked at her. Bill Roberts's letters were all they had as real proof to expose the Collegium and the Factor-7, but now some street thugs wanted to take that only piece of evidence from them. They could either give them the papers or die. Sam looked around at all the guns pointed at him and Rainee. The world was not worth having her slaughtered on a Mexican street. To hell with the assholes who had gotten them into this. Sam wanted out. "OK, I'll get you the damned papers."

Jorge pulled out his cell phone and texted something. Two men moved in closer and pointed their pistols at the two doctors. "You are a wise man to not fuck with me," Jorge said as he replaced the phone in his pocket. "We will be leaving soon."

"Where are you taking us?" Sam asked, clinging to Rainee.

"You will tell *me* that. I want the papers, and I want them now." Jorge stepped closer to Rainee.

"I don't want to hurt this pretty lady." He gently ran the barrel of the gun down the side of her face. "She has not done anything to me.

But I will if you make me." He sneered at Sam and pushed Rainee away from Sam's side. He motioned with the gun for them to move farther down the street.

Rainee began to sob. "Sam, do what they say, please." Then she whispered, "Don't try to be a dumbass hero."

Sam grabbed her arm, securely holding onto her. "I'll do what I can." He looked around again. There was no way out. Men with guns surrounded them, and he knew they would kill as fast as they would look at them.

"Are the papers at the house where you are staying?" Jorge asked.

"Yes, I have them there," Sam said. "Are you part of the Collegium?"

"Quiet. You will answer *my* questions. Give me your cell phones… now!"

Rainee handed her phone to Sam, and he gave both phones to the burly man standing next to him. "You better hope my location services are off," Sam shouted as he jerked his hand away. The man laughed loudly. He threw the phones onto the sidewalk and stomped both with the heel of his boot. He stared into Sam's eyes, shrugged arrogantly, and laughed again.

Suddenly, a black Suburban turned the corner and stopped beside them. Jorge motioned with his gun for Sam and Rainee to get inside. Rainee crawled into the back seat first, then Sam. Two men flanked them and held guns to their heads. Jorge got into the front passenger seat. The driver never said a word, but he pulled out of the side street, leaving four armed men on the sidewalk.

"I told you that it would be smart to not fuck with us. Your questions might be answered later, or you might die…if you fuck with me. That is up to you." Jorge shook his gun toward the back seat.

"*Bonito reloj*, Doctor," said the burly man. He was staring at Sam's Rolex Submariner.

Sam quickly removed it from his wrist. "Here, take it…let us go."

The car broke into laughter. The burly man, now called Juan, stuffed his pistol into his pants. He unbuttoned his shirtsleeve to reveal a gold Rolex with the bezel encompassed in diamonds. "*Pendejo*," he snorted.

"We do not want your money, Doctor. Now, shut up!" Jorge said firmly as he motioned to the driver, instructing him to go. They parked in front of the Robertses' villa. "Open the gate and get me the papers," Jorge said.

"I will, but she comes with me," Sam said.

"No, she stays here to be sure you return with what I want. Juan goes with you."

"No deal. She comes with me. How do I know you will not leave with her?"

"You don't, but you both will be dead if you wait another minute. I want only the papers, señor, but now I know they are here. I will kill you both before your next breath if you continue to waste my time."

"Get Bill's letters…the journal, Sam. He's serious. Go get the files," Rainee said.

Sam reluctantly got out of the car and walked with Juan into the villa. He quickly went to the bedroom and retrieved the bag with both the originals and the copies from beneath the mattress. He should have separated them earlier and hid them in two places, but it probably did not matter anymore. They would be killed, and no one would find Bill's letters. He was fucked, he thought. He handed the bag to the man. Sam almost ran back to the Suburban.

"OK, you have what you want. Let us go," Sam demanded as he pulled Rainee toward him.

"Get in," commanded Jorge.

"I got what you wanted. Let us go. Please, we have nothing you want."

There was no reply. The Suburban drove from the town of San Miguel de Allende and onto the back roads. Juan put a blindfold on Sam, and the man next to Rainee placed one over her eyes. Rainee gasped and trembled as the man touched her face and the blindfold tightened over her eyes.

Sam squeezed her hand and whispered, "I love you."

Rainee and Sam sat quietly waiting for their doom. These were killers, and they had no defense against such men.

Sam blamed himself. They must have been watching him make copies. Maybe they were part of the Collegium in Mexico. Perhaps they thought he was police, or someone sent by the United States. Or maybe they were simply thugs looking for Americans with valuable documents. His thoughts flew in every direction, and nothing made complete sense. If it wasn't revenge, their money, or a big ransom, then he had no idea why he and Rainee had been kidnapped.

No one spoke a word as they traveled for at least an hour. Sam could take no more.

"Can't you tell me where you're taking us?" he blurted.

"Either to your salvation or to your death" was all Jorge said. "Take off their…" he motioned for the men to remove the blindfolds. "You can't see where you are now."

"Pendejos! Gringos locos," mumbled Juan. He stuffed the blindfolds into the front seat back pocket.

Rainee's face was stained from tears, and they had caused her mascara to streak down her cheeks. Sam touched her cheek and whispered, "I will take care of you." But he knew that might not be possible, and as the words left his lips, he felt weak and inadequate. He wanted to be brave for Rainee, but she was no pushover, and he was certain that she knew as well as he that their destiny was bleak.

"Sam, there's nothing you can do. It's over," she said, confirming Sam's thoughts and reemphasizing that she *could* read his mind. They drove without speaking for at least another hour. Jorge occasionally turned around to look at Sam but mostly stared straight ahead. Sam held Rainee's hand and stroked it, but it was not enough to calm her, and it would not be enough to save them from the kidnappers. Sam had convinced himself over the hour that they had some affiliation with the Collegium and Factor-7; otherwise, they would not have known about or wanted Bill Roberts's journals and notes. He reasoned that they wanted Bill Roberts's files so as to erase any written document showing their involvement. Was it the Mexican government or perhaps a faction of it? Sam knew there were members of the Collegium all over the world, so this certainly must be the Mexican group. If that was the case, Rainee was right. They would have no use for them after they got the information that they needed. They certainly would eliminate any roadblocks.

Suddenly the Suburban made a hard right turn onto a dirt road. Sam bent forward to see the surroundings. There was nothing but small trees, rocks, and a fairly large hill ahead of them. As they approached the hill, Sam noticed several armed men walking around. Most of them were carrying semiautomatic weapons and were dressed in civilian clothing.

Rainee began to cry. "This is it, Sam."

"Maybe not," he whispered. "If they had wanted us dead right away, they would have gotten Bill's notes and killed us on the spot." *Or they could have dumped our bodies on the road, and they didn't... yet.* He turned his head away from her and surveyed the surroundings again. But in reality, Sam had to turn away from Rainee so she wouldn't see that he was only placating her. He didn't know anything about the goons, but in his gut, something just didn't seem like a normal kidnapping. "There's got to be something else, and I'm going to try to bargain with them," he said under his breath.

She frowned and nodded, but she knew it was hopeless.

The Suburban stopped in front of what appeared to be an old silver mine entrance. A sign covered most of the entrance. It was a hand-painted sign on what looked like a large sheet of plywood. The sign hung crookedly from the top of an opening. It read, simply, PELIGROSO.

Sam thought, *Fitting statement: DANGER.*

Jorge stepped out, as did the two men who flanked Sam and Rainee. There was a verbal exchange between them and the group carrying the semiautomatic weapons. Jorge pushed the large sign to one side and went into the opening of the mine. He disappeared into the darkness. The two men who had ridden in the back seat picked up more guns that were leaning against a rock wall. They walked out of sight behind some brush. It was just Sam, Rainee, and the driver left in the Suburban.

"Hey, do you speak English?" Sam shouted to the driver. The dark-haired man behind the wheel made no movement and continued to stare straight ahead. It was as if he didn't hear Sam at all. "Ask him in Spanish where we are."

Rainee did, and they received the same lack of response. She shook her head and wiped her cheek with the back of her hand. "There's no use in trying to talk to him," she whispered, tucking her head between her knees.

Sam turned around to get a view of the area behind them. There was no way to escape. Over a dozen armed men were within twenty-five feet of the Suburban. No one seemed particularly interested in its cargo, but Sam knew that if he and Rainee were to try to run, they would be filled with bullets. And if they didn't kill them immediately, they would certainly chase them down in the brush and slaughter them for no other reason than for their escape…or for fun and amusement.

The tailgate of the Suburban swung open. Sam turned around quickly to see what was happening. Two men threw something in the back. Sam leaned to see what it was. It was his and Rainee's luggage from the villa. "They brought our bags," Sam said in a low voice.

"Yeah, get rid of evidence at the villa. That's all that means, Sam. Don't you get it? They're going to kill us." She laid her head on his shoulder and sobbed. "I'm so frightened."

Sam pulled her closer to him. "I know, baby. I know." Sam looked once again at the bags in the back seat. Why didn't they just throw the bags into the river or something? he thought. There was no making sense of anything. Sam was scared too, but now was the time for him to man up to everything. He had promised to take care of her, and he would stay strong, for her sake, to the bitter end.

He suddenly felt a calm come over him. He had resigned himself that it was, indeed, the end. There were some things worse than death, he thought. Perhaps the Factor-7 is that thing.

———————

Sam figured they had been parked for a little less than an hour when Jorge emerged from the dark hole in the side of the mountain. He walked straight toward the Suburban. "Sam?" Rainee cried.

"Shhh, let me handle this." Sam tried to open the door, but the driver had it childproof-locked.

Jorge came to the back door and opened the side closest to Rainee. He motioned for her to get out. "Please," he asked politely yet sternly.

She slid toward the door. Sam followed her, sliding to his right and as close to her as possible.

"Step out, señorita…ah…Doctora," ordered Jorge.

She stepped onto the moist clay, glancing back at Sam. Sam tried to get out of the Suburban behind Rainee, but Jorge angrily pushed him back.

"Noooo!" Sam screamed.

"Follow me, please," Jorge said, taking Rainee's arm.

"Sam!" she screamed. "Please let Sam come with me," she pleaded with Jorge, but he slammed the door closed. She could hear Sam yelling for her and pounding on the window. She screamed again for Sam. Annoyed at the delays, Jorge bent her arm against her back. He had her in a tight grasp. Then he pushed her hard, causing her to stumble. She fell at the opening of the old mine. Jorge helped her to her feet and said something to her. She turned one last time toward Sam. Jorge then forced her to walk into the entrance of the old mine.

Sam saw the fear in Rainee's face, and then they disappeared into the darkness. Would it be the last time he saw her face? Sam screamed her name and began to shake all over. Perspiration poured from his forehead, and nausea overcame him. He vomited violently onto the floorboard of the Suburban. When he sat up, the driver had gotten out of the Suburban and was standing at the side door. "God," Sam yelled. "My God, please help her!" He pounded on the window. "Let me out. Damn you…damn you, motherfuckers…let me out!" Sam threw his head back against the seat. He had let her down. *Why didn't they take me? Why didn't they take me?* The calm he had felt minutes earlier had turned into sheer panic, but not for himself. His entire being focused on Rainee.

Minutes seemed like hours. Sam waited for Jorge or anyone to show and perhaps take him to his death. He was sure they had killed Rainee. He had never felt such pain, hopelessness, or unmitigated fear. Their captors were true monsters. The mental anguish they were instilling was something akin to torture. He prayed that if they had killed Rainee, it had been quick. He blamed himself for everything. He should have adamantly rejected her idea to go to Mexico in the first place. They were doctors, not spies, and all they had been through trying to find their smoking gun against the Collegium was so out of his league. And now…he shrugged and shook his head in desperation. It's probably all over, and all their labors, tears, and fears would not have accounted for a plug nickel. It had all been in vain.

Sam had given up all hope by the time Jorge emerged from the veil of darkness. It didn't faze him. Sam was numb and resigned to his fate.

Jorge stepped into the sunlight, paused for a moment, spoke to a couple of armed men, and then proceeded to the Suburban. He pulled his gun from his shoulder holster and opened the passenger side door. "Get out!" he said forcefully. His tone was far less cordial than it had been when he took Rainee. Sam did not move. "I said, get out!" Jorge reached into the Suburban and jerked Sam's arm, sticking the gun to his head. Sam fell out onto the ground.

"You son of a bitch! What have you done with Dr. Arienzo?"

Jorge kicked Sam in the ribs, but not hard enough to break a bone. "You may wish you had not talked to me in such a manner. Get up."

Sam groaned and stumbled but finally got to his feet. The wind had been knocked out of him, and his words were low and breathy. "I want to know what you have done to Rainee."

"And I want you to shut the fuck up!" Jorge shouted.

"You killed her, didn't you?" Sam shouted, having regained his breath. "You fuckin' bastard…you killed Rainee! Why don't you just shoot me right here and be done with it."

"Do not think I would not want to do that right now," Jorge said, pushing Sam closer to the entrance of the abandoned mine. His accent became more apparent as the Mexican became increasingly angrier with Sam. "Cállate, you would be wise to shut your mouth."

"You don't scare me, you motherfuckin' gorilla," Sam shrieked.

Jorge found sick humor in Sam's words. "A motherfuckin' gorilla?" He smirked. "I have to remember that one." He then frowned and violently pushed Sam into the darkness. It was a short few steps until a dim light shone through a doorway. Jorge opened the door and pushed Sam into the coolness of an underground maze of hallways.

Sam managed to remain on his feet despite Jorge's shove. He calmed, giving in to his fate, as he entered into a narrow hallway. The floor seemed to be made of pale gray marble or highly polished stone. Gold-finished electric lamps hung on the smooth rock walls, and various marble sculptures lined the sides. A cool breeze engulfed him.

Jorge nudged him on with the barrel of his pistol. They walked for what seemed to be approximately three or four city blocks. The view was the same the entire way; only the sculptures changed, and a few fine works of art hung between the shiny gold lamps. Sam recognized some of the artwork as being museum quality. A sickeningly sweet smell of cigar tobacco occasionally wafted in the air.

Jorge stopped outside a large metal door. He knocked three times. An intercom answered with only a computerized voice. Sam did not understand the Spanish words, but soon the metal door slowly opened. Jorge pushed Sam inside. It was a small room, perhaps the size of an entry in a fine home. The floors were carpeted in dark burgundy, and a pale-pink and gilded-gold sofa sat against the wall. Fine impressionist paintings hung from eye level to the ceiling. The ceiling was at least twelve feet from the floor and was painted in frescos like one might see in a European cathedral. It was something between elegance and a whorehouse.

Sam turned around, and the door shut with a loud clanging sound. Jorge had left him inside the room. He was alone. Sam walked around the room. There were three surveillance cameras and what appeared to be speakers on the wall. He walked by each, yelling at the cameras and shooting the finger. "You sons of bitches. I hope you burn in hell!"

Time stood still for Sam. He paced, then sat, then paced again. He banged on the rock walls and the door, but to no avail.

After almost an hour, a male voice speaking fair English, yet revealing a strong Mexican accent, came across the speaker. "Dr. Hawkins, I know you are upset. Please calm yourself."

Sam thought he recognized the voice, but it was muffled, and he couldn't be sure. "Who are you? What did you do with Rainee? What do you want from us?" Human trafficking consumed Sam's thoughts and he knew the torturous and hellish existence that would be.

The faceless voice replied, "All in good time. There is cognac in the bar. Please help yourself."

A cabinet door opened automatically at the sound of the voice. A fully stocked bar sat behind the door.

"I don't want your damned cognac. I want to know what you have done with Dr. Arienzo."

There was no reply.

Sam yelled again and again, but no one answered. Finally, giving up, Sam sat down on one of the pink sofas and put his head in his hands. It was all so unreal...like something in a nightmare. Who were these people? What was this place? It was like a bunker decorated for prostitutes. He gasped and his body shook as he could not dismiss the thought. It seemed more probable than ever. "Human trafficking...oh my God, they have Rainee for God knows what." His heart raced and he could barely breath. A sick feeling consumed him. Whatever these thugs did, it must be very lucrative, he surmised. The paintings were obviously stolen or purchased on the black market, which was the same thing. And they perhaps were fakes. Looking around, he saw that there was a Picasso, two Monets, a Chagall, and one da Vinci lithograph. The

261

stone walls had been smoothed out to a fine sheen. Fresh air was being pumped inside, and the electronics seemed to be state of the art.

Sam leaned back and ran his hands nervously over the velvet. He felt something. Looking down, he saw a cat's eye silver ring stuck into the tufting. Rainee had been there! It was the ring he had bought her the day before. He put it on his little finger, turned it a few times, then stuffed it into his jeans. "Oh God, please let her be alive," Sam prayed. He had a bit of hope. Maybe they had not hurt her. Maybe they would not harm her if she was to be among their stable of kidnapped women. But Sam suddenly visualized what she would be doing for the demons, and he knew it would be worse than death. He didn't know which he should pray for, because being set free didn't seem to be an option. He walked over to the bar and poured a crystal brandy glass with cognac. He drank the entire glass in one gulp. He had to think and think fast. If she was still alive, how could he get her out? How could he find her in the enormous rock-walled prison? Hell, he thought, he couldn't even get out of the pink room, much less find her.

Abruptly, the large door opened. A thin gray-haired man dressed in white pants, a white cotton shirt, brown leather sandals, and black-rimmed glasses called his name.

Sam stood up but did not move.

"You will come with me," the man said, pointing to the outside.

Sam said nothing. He walked outside the door.

"Please follow me."

The man did not have a weapon that Sam could see. Was this his chance to escape? Sam knew it was not. There were dozens of heavily armed men outside, and the entire inside of the hollowed-out mountain seemed to be wired with cameras and...who knew what else?

The thin man led Sam farther into the maze of hallways. His sandals crackled with every step. One leg seemed shorter than the other, so his gait was more of a bounce than a stroll.

Sam suddenly heard a female voice in the distance. He screamed, "Rainee?"

Faintly, he heard her voice. "Sam, Sam, are you all right?"

"Yes. Are you OK? Where are you?"

She replied, but it was a faint mumble. Sam was no longer able to hear the words, but he knew she was alive.

The older man guiding Sam seemed to not care that the couple was yelling and trying to communicate. He just kept walking, occasionally turning back to look at Sam.

There were halls to both Sam's right and left that ran off the main corridor. He yelled again as he passed each opening, but he no longer could hear anything. "Oh God, please let her be OK."

The older man stopped outside another large metal door. He again knocked three times, and instead of an automated voice, Sam heard clearly a familiar sound. It was the deep voice of El Espino. The door opened, and Sam saw a very large room. It was solid white. There were white marble floors and walls and a white marble desk. Gustavo, a.k.a. El Espino, stood behind it.

"Welcome, Dr. Hawkins," he said, puffing on his cigar.

Sam stood quietly, staring stoically at the man dressed in white and blurred in his solid-white surroundings.

"I hope you have been treated kindly," the Mexican said.

"Kindly? You son of a bitch. What have you done with Dr. Arienzo? You kidnapped us!" Sam snapped.

El Espino sat in his chair and motioned for Sam to sit. Sam continued standing.

"Have it your way, Dr. Hawkins. Would you have given me Dr. William Roberts's papers if I had asked? Would you have come here if I had asked? I think not."

"You have not told me. What have you done with Dr. Rainee Arienzo?"

"She is alive and well for the moment…just as are you." El Espino took a puff off his Cuban cigar and blew the smoke into the air above his head.

"I want to see her," Sam demanded.

"All in good time."

Sam took two steps forward. "You do not scare me, you son of a bitch. There is no better time than now. I demand to see Dr. Arienzo."

"Dr. Hawkins. Love is a strange thing. It is like money. I should know because I have both. Love will give you certain fulfillments, and money will do the rest. She is your love, no doubt. I give you my word that she is not harmed. With your cooperation, she will remain safe."

Sam walked over and sat down. "All right. I do not trust kidnappers or gun-carrying thugs, but I have no choice. What do you want from me?"

"Now we can get to business." El Espino opened the folder that contained Bill Roberts's notes. "I have read all this twice and even had an interpreter in the case I was not understanding everything."

"What is your involvement with this?" Sam moved closer to the desk, leaning in to hear El Espino's answer.

"Dr. Hawkins, you do not know who I am. I run the biggest drug operation in Mexico and Central America. I supply ninety percent of all cocaine, meth, and marijuana to the United States. I supply seventy-five percent of all other countries with what they want. I am not an evil man, sir. I give people what they want and would buy anyway, if I was not the seller. When people want to ruin their lives, that is not my fault. But I choose to be that supplier." He laughed. "If they didn't buy or if your government legalized the drugs, then I would not have a job." He laughed again even louder. "Neither of those things will happen, so I am a very rich man. I am so rich that I could wipe my butt every day with American dollars and not make a dent in the piles of cash."

Sam stared at him. "You *are* the cartel. You *are* killers."

"Only when necessary. I am not the Zetas or the Gulf Cartel or any of the other little guys. You do not hear about me, but I own Mexico. I am bigger than the Mexican government. I *am* the Mexican government. I do not kill innocent people. I kill those that betray me. My people love me. The poor have homes. Their children go to school. They protect El Espino, and I protect them. They do not know me, but they know who I am."

Sam threw his head back in disgust. "You think you're Zorro or Robin Hood? You arrogant prick! You are a drug lord, and that's all you are. Your drugs kill daily. You say you're the biggest? La-te-fucking-da, El Espino. That makes you the biggest murderer." Sam took a belabored breath. "I demand to see Dr. Arienzo now."

El Espino smirked, as if almost amused at Sam's rant. "I understand. I will bring her to you soon. You must hear me out. It is to your and her benefit that you hear me."

"How is it that you can help me?" Sam asked.

"You want to stop the Keepers Collegium?"

Sam's eyes grew wider, and he almost choked on his words. "Yes, but right now I want to be free and see Dr. Arienzo." Sam coughed. "I don't know what your interest is with those people or with us, but we are not involved at all. We were just told to get Dr. Roberts's journals. Please bring Dr. Arienzo to me."

"All right, Dr. Hawkins. I will have her brought here. But women are not allowed in negotiations."

"Tough shit, Gustavo…El Espino…whoever the fuck you are… Dr. Arienzo knows more about the Keepers Collegium and the Factor-7 than you or I ever will. She sits with me on all talks, or you can shoot me right now." Sam swallowed hard. *Damn, if he takes me seriously,* he thought. But he had to play the high card, and that was because both he and Rainee had information that perhaps El Espino did not. Sam was counting on that.

"I admire you, Doctor. You have balls, as you say in English! You are strong. Your woman is feisty too. Is that the right word? I am sorry my English is not always correct. But I repeat, negotiations are between men."

"Just bring her to me," Sam said forcefully.

El Espino huffed but maintained a calm demeanor. He made a call on some kind of internal system. He spoke in rapid Spanish, and Sam was only able to identify the word *doctora*. Five minutes later Rainee was in the room.

Sam ran to her. He held her in his arms. "I thought you were dead."

She was trembling, and her voice was raspy from crying. "Sam, I thought we both would be dead by now. What's happening?" Rainee looked up and saw the man she had talked to in the shopping corridor in San Miguel de Allende. "You are El Espino!"

"Yes, Doctora, I am."

"Why did you bring us here?" she asked timidly.

El Espino took a puff off his cigar and blew the long trail of smoke upward as if beckoning a higher power. "Do you like my artwork? They are originals, you know. One of my South American dealers lied to me about how much money he made. My men went to Argentina, and they got what was owed to me. I think these were stolen by Hitler and brought to Argentina." He held his hand up and in a sweeping motion, like a game show model might do revealing a prize, he drew attention to an array of exquisite art. I am a proud man to now own such priceless works. The man who fucked with me...well, he is not so lucky. I get rid of problems. Sometimes I stand and stare at their beauty." He took another puff and blew it into the air. "I tell you this because no one does me wrong and gets free of my wrath. You both would do well to remember that." He laid his head on the neck rest of his oversized desk chair. "Yes, I always get what I am promised and what I demand...even when someone breaks that promise. I have already told some things to Dr. Hawkins, and he can explain to you later. You must sit, and we will talk." He laid the cigar in a large marble ashtray and picked up a rosary. Fumbling with the beads, he said softly, "I am a peaceful man, Doctors. I only do what is necessary."

"And that is what?" Sam asked snidely.

"You will soon know. And you will understand. Your friend, Doctoro Robertos, was part of this group called the Keeper Collegium, no?" He hung the rosary over a picture frame. The photo inside faced only him. "He and I did not have the pleasure"—he cleared his throat—"opportunity to meet. But I knew he was involved. I knew he had a house in Mexico, and I knew he had brought something there a few months ago. I had my men watch him. He gave himself away, and it was easy to know why you and the pretty doctor were there too." He bent over and retrieved a bottle of tequila from the floor.

Sam pulled Rainee to him and whispered, "We have to listen to what he has to say. I don't think he wants to hurt us." *Not right now anyway*, he thought.

She relaxed in Sam's arms. "I'm so scared, Sam."

"Yeah, me too. Sit down." Sam pulled the chair out from the desk, allowing her room to sit. He pulled the other chair closer to hers. "All right, why have we been brought here, and why did you want Dr. Roberts's letters and files?"

"May I offer you my best tequila?" El Espino asked, drinking a full glass. I am sorry if my men were rough with you, Doctora," El Espino said, addressing Rainee. "They do not know why I ordered them to bring you to me."

"Well, yeah, Jorge is an asshole, and we don't want tequila," Sam blurted.

"He is under orders, and he has his own way of doing things. He is a good man and follows orders well, having been trained by your military."

"What, the United States military?" Sam shook his head. "Why would our military train a thug like him?"

"He was with a group that was all trained at your Fort Hood. Most are now my enemies. Doctora Arienzo, have you heard of Los Zetas?"

"The cartel?" she asked, fearful that she asked the question and more afraid of the answer.

Sam took her hand. "Yes, one of the drug cartels. And this man is head of another cartel."

"Yes, the Zetas are only one organization, Doctor." El Espino frowned as the word *Zetas* left his clenched teeth. "I also have an operation, and as I told Dr. Hawkins, I run the biggest in all of Mexico and Central America. I have men in Europe and Asia too. Perhaps… no, without doubt…I run the biggest operation in the world. I run the Prima Costas. We do not kidnap for money. I say this so you know that you were not ever in real danger. And I can keep you safe. If you cross me, however, I can kill you as fast. If you work with me now, I can keep you from further danger from the men that Dr. Roberts writes about. I know why you are in Mexico."

Rainee quickly turned to face Sam, then turned back to face El Espino. Her eyes squinted as she spoke. "So, if you know why we are here, why all of this? I mean, what can we possibly have in common with you?"

Sam took her hand again. He squeezed it as if suggesting that she be silent.

The Mexican picked up his cigar and took another puff. Smoking his Cuban was a delay tactic as he calculated his words carefully. "Apparently, we *will* talk in front of the woman." He smiled and shook his head. "Never in my culture." He turned his neck from side to side as if trying to loosen tense muscles. "You wash my hand, and I will wash yours. I gave the Collegium billions of dollars to bring me weapons, a helicopter, and safety to transport cocaine across five US borders. That should have been an easy job for such a large operation. We agreed that my money would further their plan, and they would do many things to help me. Andres Rodriquez betrayed me. No one fucks with El Espino and lives. I got one small shipment of guns, and he said he was not able to deliver on his promises."

Sam interrupted. "You funded this thing? You were working with Rodriguez…the one who's now at the Federal Laboratory? How do you know him?"

El Espino laughed out loud. "I will get to Rodriguez. Americans are in such a hurry." His eyes moved to the walls and his array of artwork. He seemed to admire them as he considered what he would say next. "Does that amount of money alarm you?" He cackled and puffed hard on the now-extinguished cigar. "Damn thing is out," he cursed, throwing it into a can by the desk. He unwrapped a new Cuban. "Andres and I were both born in a small village just out from Mexico City. His family took me in after my family died. I was about twelve years old. I worked very hard for them in their house and ranch. I got a bed and food. It was bad, but better than living where they put garbage. When his father found me, I was living there, stealing what I could and eating *basura*…sorry, I forget the word. I ate…how do you say…trash? Food that was thrown out in the trash."

Rainee winced. "I am sorry. That must have been terrible for you."

Sam looked at her with raised eyebrows as if to tell her to not be sympathetic to the killer.

The Mexican leaned back in his large desk chair, chewing on the end of the new cigar. His words came out muffled as he sucked and gnawed on the wet tobacco. "Dr. Hawkins, what is it you Americans say? What does not kill you will make you stronger?" He lurched forward, firmly placing his elbows on the desk. His hands were clinched together in fists. His eyes filled with what looked to be a mixture of anger and resignation. "It made me the strongest, and I am still the strongest in all of Mexico." He pounded the desk with one fist when he said "Mexico."

Sam took a deep breath. This man had said he was not going to hurt them, yet he was anything but comforting. Sam knew they were amid some of the worst that mankind had to offer. The Mexican had helped the Collegium with the Factor-7 bioweapons, and Sam had to contend with his stories and satisfy him. Working with El Espino was not an option. He and Rainee were prisoners, and they had very little bargaining power. "So, what can you do to stop the Collegium from using the biological weapon?" Sam asked, as cordially as he could muster.

"I have people that will dig them out and expose them. I will make sure they are shut down."

Sam leaned forward in his chair. "With all due respect, how will you do that? You cannot involve the United States or any of its allies. You realize disclosure of their plan could result in all-out war, and then, even you will lose everything."

"Dr. Hawkins, you have no say in what and how I do things, but I am not stupid. When I say that they will be exposed, I do not mean that the media will know. Soon you will understand. I know the consequences of publicly exposing this. I live on this earth too. So you do not have to worry about that end of it. I take care of what I say and what I will do, and I expect that you and"—he nodded his head at Rainee—"Doctora…will do what I require. I have planned it well. And you must know that I have more money than most countries. I cannot spend all my money. I want to help you, and I will be helping myself. I was…*como dice*? How do you say? Double-crossed? I will have my revenge, which I will enjoy. But I also want to put my money into legitimate businesses. I want my sons to have businesses in Mexico. You can help me. I want to buy pharmaceutical companies, build hospitals in my country, and maybe a winery. I like wine. Do you like wine, Doctor?" His voice trailed off as if in a trance imagining that he was indeed working in a winery. "You can help me do this. I cannot buy things alone and not be exposed. But I think you can help me buy things. In trade for your help, I will make sure the Factor-7 weapon is never used, and I will make sure that the people who call themselves the Keepers Collegium are eliminated."

"How can I trust you?" Sam asked.

"Dr. Hawkins and Dr. Arienzo, how can I trust you?" El Espino said.

Sam shook his head. He really didn't have any other allies, and if this man had anything, it was money and power. But the biggest reason Sam asked about their task was that he knew that he had no choice. "What do we do?"

"Right now, my men are at war with the other cartels. We will wipe them from Mexico very soon. I will control all drugs in and out of Mexico by the end of the year. I want tourism to return to my country. I want my people to thrive." He gazed over Sam's head. His eyes squinted as he recalled his past and began another of his stories. "I was so poor as a child that I ate trash with maggots and worms from the ground and bugs from the trees to survive. My family had no clean water to drink. I walked a mile every morning to get water from the mountains. My mother died from drinking dirty water and no medical care. My father died from working in the silver mines in Querétaro without enough food or water to survive. Now my mansion and my warehouse are an old silver mine. Imagine, Doctors, I might own the mountain where my father died. Rather ironic, as you might say. My brothers died from working for rich people who paid them nothing. My sister died at the hands of a pimp, working as a prostitute only to feed her children. No one could go to school because we were so poor. But I learned how to survive on the streets when very young. When I was eight, I was alone. I stole food to survive. Hunger is a strong motivator, and when you are starving, you will do anything. You see, Doctors, I am not like you. I did not have food, clean water, clothing, or education. I made it all by necessity. I became smart, or I would die. I saw what money could buy and do for a man when I worked for Andres's father. I wanted that life and position. I worked hard to get where I am. I will not allow my countrymen—good, hardworking people—to go hungry. I will run this country with the fist and the gun, but it will be for the people."

Rainee leaned forward in her chair. "This is all a very sad story, and you obviously have good intentions for your people. I believe you are strong and wealthy, but none of what you have said specifically tells Sam and me how you will stop the Collegium."

"In such a hurry." El Espino laughed heartedly. "How I do things is something you do not need to know. You cannot know the details. Only the trust is required," he replied.

Sam blew breath through his clenched teeth. "I don't know how I would be able to buy hospitals and drug companies. I don't have that kind of money, and if you gave me your money, it would surely leave a trail straight back to you. And I would be your accomplice and thrown in jail. They'd throw away the key." Sam was raising any objection he could think of. There were many questions. Sam rubbed his eyes. "May we have some water?" he asked.

"I have food and drinks coming very soon, but there is water over there. Please help yourself." El Espino pointed to a small alcove.

Sam got up and stretched his back. There were cold bottles of water and juices and small vodka and tequila bottles in a glass-front refrigerator. He retrieved two bottles of water. "You know, the Gulf Team Aviation people will be wondering why we were not at the airport at three o'clock today," he said, handing a bottle to Rainee.

"Dr. Hawkins, you so underestimate me. I knew when you arrived in San Miquel, and I made sure they were not coming back for you at three o'clock."

"Guess I should have figured that," Sam said under his breath.

El Espino dismissed Sam's remark and continued his speech. "The Americans buy most of my drugs, so it is only fitting that an American assist me in finding ways to use that money to help my people. I have warehouses filled with American dollars. This is your choice, Doctor. Either we wash each other's hands, or you find a way to fix your problem. I don't need you, but I do need you to do what I have in mind. You, on the other hand, are in no position to deny me this. You are in desperate need of me."

Sam looked at Rainee. He shook his head. "We have no other way." Sam was keenly aware that he was between two evils and without any way out. He was entrenched in two secret worlds, and both were deadly.

"Doctor, I ask you, with lack of military support to stop the terrorists and the lies from those supposedly in charge, do you trust me less than them?" El Espino smiled sinisterly. "We all have good, and we all have evil gnawing at our guts. It all depends upon who is the stronger and who is most determined. I once had hunger gnawing in my gut. I now have hunger, like the bird gnawing in my craw, as you say, for my countrymen. They should not struggle to leave our beautiful Mexico to find happiness. We will, with your assistance, find it here in our homeland. I can run Mexico, and I have the money to do it, with or without you and the United States."

"So how do I buy these things you want?" Sam asked.

"The details will come in time, but you will need to put together a group of trusted people and make a corporation. I will funnel money to other countries and then back to the US for your use. You will buy the companies and then give them over to me in a takeover-type operation. By that time, I will have control of the Mexican government, and I will be in charge. Just know I can do what I say."

"You have mighty lofty plans, señor," Sam said.

"You can joke, but you have not seen El Espino's strength."

"Oh, but I believe we have tasted it," Rainee said.

El Espino smiled at her comment. "I have men in every country. I now have the names of those Collegium men that are leading this. As we speak, Rodriguez is dying at the hand of one of my men."

Sam felt like he was jumping from one fire into another. "What? He's dying? Where?"

"Dr. Hawkins, please. As I said earlier, you do not need to and cannot know everything. It is for everyone concerned, especially yours and the lady's safety. Anyway, you will be back home by midnight, and it will surely make the news. When you hear, you will know that I have done what I said."

A buzzer sounded. The Mexican boss pushed a button on the side of his desk, and a large door opened from inside the small alcove. Two Mexican men entered with trays of various fruits, cheeses, and hard bread. Two more followed rolling a table set with plates and silver flatware. In the center of the table was a large caldron, and on each side lay platters of various grilled meats and vegetables. The other platter held fresh tortillas and an array of sauces. The workers set up chairs. El Espino invited Sam and Rainee to sit and eat.

"You must be hungry," he said as one of the men dipped into the caldron and took out a large cup of a soup-like substance. "*Menudo*," El Espino said. "It is the best in Mexico."

Rainee looked at Sam. "What is it?" she asked.

Sam simply frowned and said, "Cow's stomach soup."

"Yes, and very good. You must taste it, Doctora," El Espino said in reply to Sam's apparent disdain.

She nodded as the man dressed in a white chef coat and hat set the bowl in front of her.

Sam also agreed to taste it, but only because he feared any wrath from Gustavo. "How did you get the nickname El Espino?" Sam asked, hoping he had not infringed on something he was not to know.

The man laughed. "Have you ever gotten a big thorn in your foot? And you can't get it out? It festers and hurts bad. You try to pick it out, but it gets worse and hurts worse. It consumes your foot with pain. I am that thorn in the side of anyone who crosses me. I will be a continuous problem to anyone who does."

"Yes," Sam said. "I get that."

"But my friends still call me by the name my mother gave me, Gustavo."

Sam took a sip of his soup and spoke before he had considered his words. "I will work with you, señor, but I will never be your friend."

Rainee flashed her disapproving eyes at Sam. How could he be so rude and to subject them to the anger of this man, who would clearly kill them as easily as serve them lunch?

But to her astonishment, the Mexican simply smiled and said, "You have cojones, doctor. I like that in a man."

Rainee smiled. Sam had balls, all right, but he was just damned lucky that the Mexican had not taken offense and castrated him right there at the dinner table. She breathed a sigh of relief. The food and the light conversation were taking the edge off the entire day. But she, as did Sam, knew the danger from the cartel boss, and the Collegium were always going to be biting at their heels like a pack of rabid dogs.

"So, this is your home?" Sam asked.

"*Otra vez*, Dr. Hawkins, you so underestimate me. Again, you think I am like other people. I am not. I have homes all over the world. This is a safe place. We are at war with other cartels. I am safe here. We have exits from all sides. I have tunnels that go deep into the earth. I even have a helicopter. I have an entire army of men. We have high-tech equipment and know when anyone is even five miles away from me. We own the military here, and they will not bother me." He laughed, as if mocking Sam. "You really *no entiendo*? You will understand soon."

El Espino ate silently. He smiled occasionally, but it became apparent that he was finished with the conversation and was leaving the details encrypted in his mind.

Sam knew that his times with the Mexican were far from over. He now owned both Sam and Rainee.

El Espino wiped his mouth and took a large sip from his glass of tequila. "And there is one more thing before you are taken to your waiting jet. I want you to remake my face. I want to look like a new and different person."

"Plastic surgery?" Sam and Rainee asked in unison.

"Si, yes," he replied with a stern smile, and one eyebrow rose. "Be sure you pick a handsome face." He smiled and laughed out loud.

But Sam and Rainee knew he was dead serious.

"Neither of us are plastic surgeons! With your money and power, surely you can get a highly qualified surgeon in here to do this!" Sam blurted.

"Perhaps, but I do not know any and how would I trust them when they have nothing at stake? But perhaps their life." He laughed. "You have everything at stake. You will not double-cross me because you know what I can do and soon you will know how I handle those that betray me. Anyway, I decided that I want *you* to do this. It is my decision and my desire. So it will happen as I want. You are both surgeons, and good ones, if I correctly did my research over the past two days about you. Whatever you need to learn, do so quickly." Smoke rose from a newly lighted cigar. "Si, learn quickly. And know this fact: if you do what I tell you, you will be safe. And your enemies...the Keepers Collegium...I will have their heads."

CHAPTER EIGHTEEN

Sam and Rainee were escorted from the mine to the waiting black Suburban. This time, Jorge did not join them. Only the speechless driver and Juan were in the SUV.

Juan looked at Rainee. "So, you are a lady doctor?"

She answered curtly. "I am."

"I have a problem with my eye." He removed his dark glasses.

Rainee leaned toward the front seat to take a better look at his eye. "You have cataracts, sir. Your lens is cloudy. I'm not an eye doctor, but I can see without equipment that you have cataracts."

"So what do I do?"

"You see an eye surgeon. It is an easy operation, and you will see again clearly."

The man smiled. "I thought I was going to be blind," he said in Spanish.

Dr. Arienzo smiled at the man sympathetically. "You will see fine."

Sam huffed under his breath. "The bastard's nearly blind. He wouldn't have been able to hit a football field with his pistol."

"Ah, don't be so sure." Rainee leaned back in the seat. "Señor, how long to the airport?" she asked in Spanish.

"Una hora, más o menos. Use your blindfolds, please," he said in broken English.

———————

They pulled the Suburban up to the waiting jet within the hour, as Juan had promised. He got out and opened the door for the two doctors. Rainee thanked him, but Sam simply nodded and took her hand.

The freshly starched suited man stood at the end of the stairs and welcomed them back to the jet.

"I trust you had a wonderful trip," he said.

"Oh, just peachy," Sam said facetiously.

The young man looked away, apparently instructed to never ask. He motioned for them to board the jet.

Sam watched from the window while the Suburban left. Dust boiled from its tires as it sped away. He heard the engines start, and the speaker rang out the seat-belt instructions. "I can't believe we're safe and going home," he said, exhaling the horrors of the day. Sam pulled the ring from his jeans' pocket and slipped it on Rainee's finger. "This gave me hope when I found it in El Espino's pimp pink sofa."

Rainee held her head in her hands. "I was so frightened. I was fidgeting with it. I didn't know where I lost it." She smiled. "I never was taught to pray, but I learned to do it today. There's something to that praying thing."

Sam pulled her to him. "Yes, ma'am...there sure is."

———————

Sam held Rainee close all night, but both were too spent, too tightly wound to make love. It was good enough just to lie in each other's arms. Neither wanted to even discuss what they had been through, hoping it was a bad dream or would perhaps be erased if not spoken aloud.

Morning came too quickly. Sam reached for the remote. The TV was set on a news channel, and they were talking about the weather beginning to cool. "It's been a season since we got involved in this shit," Sam bluntly exclaimed.

"Must be the season of the witch." Rainee turned her head toward Sam.

"Well, certainly been a bitch of a season." He forced a smile. "I don't have any training to speak of in plastics."

Rainee pulled herself up onto her elbows. "We'll figure it out."

"And if we screw up?" Sam asked.

"They'll kill us."

Suddenly a news bulletin interrupted the morning talk show. Sam turned up the volume. "We warn you that this bulletin contains sensitive information and should not be considered viewing for some people and small children. The decapitated body found yesterday tied to the buoy off the jetties at South Padre Island has been identified as Dr. Andres Carlos Rodriquez, medical professor and new chairman at the Federal Laboratory in Galveston, Texas. As we reported yesterday, sport fisherman spotted a decomposed body hanging from the buoy. Officials with the sheriff's and Cameron County coroner's offices say it was badly destroyed by perhaps sharks and the high waves that hit the end of the jetties. The head has not been recovered, but certain markings and identification in the pockets of the man's pants confirmed his identification. His wife has identified certain markings on his legs to confirm his identity. She had reported him missing yesterday. It is being investigated as a homicide."

Sam looked hard at Rainee. "It's started. He said we would know when he had his hand in finishing them. He wasn't joking."

"Hideous. It's just hideous." Rainee turned away from the TV.

Sam started making the coffee.

Rainee slowly walked onto the deck overlooking Galveston Bay. "It's just too much." She stared into the distance. Then she shuddered as if a cold breeze had engulfed her. "We have no choice but to let Gustavo work his demonic plan. Actually, we have no choice either way. We have never had choices." She took a large drink from the cup. "As hideous as this is, he says he will do away with them. I've given this thought. Sam. There was no one we could trust. We have the facts, but if we couldn't trust anyone…hell, we still don't know who's involved and who isn't. Two United States presidents have been assassinated before they finished their terms. Three years ago, the prime minister in the UK was killed. I recall that two men in the French cabinet went missing. And the list goes on…all this has become clear after reading Bill's letters and meeting with Gustavo. Media reported all the murders of people in high places, but no one seems to put together the dots. You'd think that these hotshot journalists would have figured out that there is something big happening, but apparently not." Rainee seemed resolute to the horror.

Sam gazed out over the bay. "Maybe they feared for their lives just like us. If they had a clue or inkling, they would have also been putting themselves and perhaps their families in harm's way. This is not some small-time operation. This is too big for the media. It's too big for most anyone."

Rainee nodded. "No argument there."

Sam and Rainee escaped for a few hours and went to their fish place, Charlie's. They ate and tried to talk about anything but Nemesis, Factor-7 or Gustavo. Occasionally, the subject would poke its ugly head into the conversation, and both would kill it before it took them over. But keeping it under wraps was virtually impossible. They had been through too much. Sam had witnessed his friend dying from a terrible illness; he had been shunned by Dr. Rodriguez, and now that man was dead; Rick R. Morris, the coroner, was murdered; his conversation with Albright had been enlightening but cryptic; they were kidnapped by a drug kingpin; and now they had no idea of their future. And above all, Rainee's father had been murdered for his knowledge long before either of them knew the existence or the severity of the Factor-7. Now both were in the middle of a dance between two devils. If El Espino were to lead the dance, there would be multiple homicides. If the Collegium led, the world would see horrific death. It was a fairly easy answer, albeit sinister and the epitome of evil. El Espino had to be the devil in charge.

CHAPTER NINETEEN

Upon returning to Sam's house, he noticed a parked car at the end of the two-lane gravel road. He said nothing to Rainee, but as they passed the car, he tried to see inside. There was nobody sitting behind the wheel. He shook off his paranoia and pulled into the carport.

The sun was beginning to set, and a cool breeze pushed through the open carport and adjacent boat dock. Sam pulled Rainee to his side. They ascended the stairway to the upstairs deck.

"I'll get the door," Sam said as he fumbled in his pockets for the house key.

Suddenly he heard Rainee gasp.

Turning rapidly toward her standing at the top of the stairs, he also saw his worst nightmare holding on to her arm. "Let her go, Albright."

Strangely, John Albright did what Sam ordered and released Rainee. "It's your fault, Sam; it's all your fault."

"Get out of here, Albright. We have nothing for you. There's nothing for you here," Sam shouted, still fumbling with the keys and only thinking of getting into the house, where his .380-caliber Colt sat on the entry table.

Now able to escape John Albright, Rainee moved closer to Sam. "Dr. Albright," she said calmly, "we know what you have done. Leave now, or the police will be here."

"Oh, my dear, Simon knows all about what you have done, and I realize you know all about me and my associates, but there won't be any police. You haven't told anybody anything, have you? You're both scared as rabbits of us. I can't do anything about it, but you have caused me great distress. Simon is pissed. There have been things happening. And you won't like Simon when he is pissed. You have forced my hand. Why didn't you just mind your own damned business?" Albright's voice trailed off, as if he were reminiscing about something in the past. "I told you too much at that Mexican restaurant. You figured it out, and Simon knows. It was so perfect. I was the genius. You fucked it up." He snapped his head to the right as if bringing himself out of a trance. "I'm here for Bill's files. You see, without those, no one can prove a damn thing." His eyes glazed over, his nostrils flared, and he hit the wooden railing with his left hand. "Get them now!"

"You're insane. We don't have any files!" Sam shouted again, louder than before.

"Don't lie to me, you asshole. Bill told Simon the day he died that he had documented everything, including names and places. He died. The son of a bitch killed himself before we could get them. Why the hell do you think we were there the morning he died? He told us! We searched his house, too, that night. You have his journals, and you know all about the Collegium and my genius work. Simon sent me here to get them. I'm not leaving without Bill's journals."

"You killed Bill Roberts! He might have done it, but it was your fancy-ass virus that killed him." Sam shouted.

Albright laughed. "I said...he killed himself! But Simon wanted to eliminate him and would have. Bill just did it before Simon could. Now get those documents. You and the lady are Simon's responsibility. I don't envy you, because Simon is not the kindest man around. And he most definitely will take care of you. Unless, of course, you don't do what I say. Then I *will* kill you right here, right now."

Sam pulled Rainee toward the door. "I'm telling you again, we do *not* have anything."

"You've been a pain in my ass since med school. So, honest...so kind...so good. The good Dr. Hawkins. Well, you do lie, and you're lying now. I know you went to Mexico. You are so stupid, Sam, telling Ana you were going to Mexico. Do you really think that Simon couldn't get that out of her?"

"What have y'all done to Ana?" Sam shrieked.

"Don't get your panties in a knot, you wimp. No one has hurt Ana. She's not in the way of the Brotherhood. If she was, she would have been dead right after Bill, but she's not." Albright huffed. "At least not yet."

Rainee looked at John Albright and then directly into Sam's eyes. "Open the door, Sam. I'll get him what he wants."

"Smart lady," Albright said, smiling the same sinister grin that Sam had seen more times than he wished. "I can kill both of you right now and still might."

Sam flashed his eyes questioningly at her. They didn't have any papers. Gustavo, El Espino, had both copies. What was Rainee doing?

John Albright held his hand inside his jacket, indicating that he had a weapon. "I really don't want to hurt you, but you see now that I can. I don't want to get your blood all over my nice jacket, but if you don't hand over what I want, I'll kill you both right here. It's only a matter of time until someone kills you. You don't know who you're dealing with. I'll leave that to Simon and the Brotherhood. And they *will* get you! You see..." Albright had begun to sweat, and his words became angry and staccato. "I have nothing to lose anymore."

Sam opened the door, and Rainee stepped inside. She grabbed the pistol from the table and held it behind her back. "Sam, you and John come inside."

"No," Albright wailed. "Bring the fuckin' files out to me, and do it now!"

Sam took a step inside the doorway. Rainee handed him the loaded pistol. Sam whirled on his heels and took one shot toward Dr. John Albright. The gunshot reverberated through the air, as if it was cannon fire. Wood splintered off the deck railing. Sam saw Albright stumble.

Albright dropped a large knife from the inside of his jacket and gave one last haunting stare at Sam. Then he groaned. "You will pay for this!" He ran down the stairs. Drops of blood fell onto the deck and followed him down the stairs.

Sam ran to the top of the stairs. He watched while Albright got into his car and drove quickly away. "He had a knife...no gun," Sam said as he hugged Rainee. "He's desperate and unprepared for this. He didn't know what he was doing here. Brought a knife to a gunfight. He's running. I don't think he'll be back here. He knows his time's up."

"He's crazy, and he might do most anything to save his skin. And Simon and"—she paused—"the rest of them..." Rainee poured a large glass of ice water. After taking a sip, she handed it to Sam. "You could have killed him."

"I have never even shot at a man, much less killed one. If I had wanted to, I would have. I'm a damned good shot. He's what we used to call *big truck, little belt buckle*. Albright could only kill with a manufactured germ. He doesn't have the balls to murder in cold blood. Anyway, we don't need police here." Sam took several long sips of the water. "Good thing there was a bullet in the chamber. I do that at night. I just left it that way this morning. Providence, I guess. Saved me that second or two. I only wanted to stop him, scare him off, perhaps wound him, but I couldn't kill him. He's the mad scientist and the potential killer. Not me."

"I don't think he would have hesitated to kill us." Rainee seemed annoyed and shaken.

"Are you angry that I didn't kill the man? I'm confused."

"No, of course not. It's just...oh, never mind. Albright's time is short. Gustavo will take him out, even if we didn't." She walked over and hugged Sam for a long moment. "Shouldn't we call the police anyway?"

Sam replaced the spent bullet and slipped the newly loaded clip into the pistol. "And tell them what? That Albright is the man behind the production of a biological weapon and that he and others plan a doomsday attack on our enemies? Do I tell them he came for notes that we found in Mexico but don't have anymore? Tell them that they were taken by the world's biggest drug lord? Tell them we are in cahoots with El Espino? And that I shot Albright? But he ran off?" He smiled. "Who's going to sound crazy then?"

Rainee nodded. "I guess you're right. Sounds pretty incredible when you put it that way. But what if he goes somewhere for treatment and makes up some story about you and you get arrested?"

"He wasn't shot bad enough for treatment. There's not enough blood. I just grazed him. Anyway, he's scared of Simon and *Simon* is waiting for him. He won't go for treatment." Sam picked up the knife and threw it over the balcony into the bay. "There, no more John Albright."

"I hope you're right. But Albright just corroborated Bill's documents."

"Yep, he did at that. And that's why this gun is going to be my best friend and bedfellow—for a while, anyway." Sam breathed out a cleansing breath. "You and this warm gun."

Rainee stared out the large plate-glass window. The sun glistened on Galveston Bay. "What did you mean 'big truck, little belt buckle'?"

"Big show, but the man ain't got no balls."

CHAPTER TWENTY

John Albright wrapped his left arm in towels he found in the bathroom of his dingy motel room. The bleeding had stopped, and it was only a graze of his upper bicep. Simon Reznick had moved them both from the Four Seasons the day before, fearing that they would be discovered in such a high-profile hotel. Albright surveyed the room. "I'm the best scientist in the world. I'm the brains behind this, and Simon thinks he can control me. How dare he stuff me into a scumbag motel?" He pounded on the wall to the adjoining room. "Hey, Reznick, get me some bandages and food!"

No answer came from the next room.

"I know you're in there. Your rental car is parked out there, and I hear the TV. You must be deaf, because I can hear every word that the newscaster is saying. Come on, man. Answer me." Albright got up from the bed and rewrapped his left arm. "Dammit, Simon." He pushed the old wooden door that connected the two rooms, but it was swollen from water damage and didn't budge. Albright leaned into it and shoved hard with his right shoulder. The door slightly opened, which allowed him to step inside the other bedroom. He leaned his head into the room. The blaring audio of the TV was near deafening.

"Simon?" he said as he entered the room. "Hey, man, you in the shower?" He walked toward the bathroom. There seemed to be no water running, and he heard nothing. He turned the bathroom door handle and cracked the door open. As he did, blood ran out from beneath the door. He swung it fully open. The bathroom was flooded with blood. He stepped inside and slipped. He fell to his knees, and the door shut behind him as if a ghastly presence had locked him in the horror chamber. From the corner of his eye, he saw a decapitated body hanging on the back of the door. A meat hook secured the body to the wooden door. The corpse's clothing was soaked in what was apparently its own blood. Albright tried to stand but stumbled. His belly churned with nausea. He couldn't breathe. He gasped for air as he tried to stand but, in his panic, slipped on the blood and fell to the floor once again. His hands were covered in blood, as were his pants, shoes, and shirt-sleeves. Then his eyes grasped the grisly sight. He couldn't move. There, perched upon the back of the toilet, was the severed head of Simon Reznick. It had been set there like some gruesome statute. His fixed dead-man eyes stared straight at Albright. Stuffed inside the toilet was a Kilij-type saber. Albright slipped again but caught himself by holding on to the door handle. He ran from the room, grabbing his small duffel bag on the way to his rental car. He was bathed in human blood. He rubbed the blood on his pants legs, as if he could, somehow, remove it. The revolting smell of human blood and bodily fluids permeated the interior of the car. He tried to get a clean breath, but there was nothing clean to inhale. There was only the disgusting stench of a violent death.

Hours passed while he frantically drove southward to escape everything. John Albright had nowhere to go and no one to call but, perhaps, Guidry and Mr. Z. He was crazed with fear, and the sight of Simon Reznick's detached head was burned into his brain. It was a like a haunting nightmare that he couldn't forget. He feared Mr. Z and Guidry almost as much as whoever killed Reznick, Rodriguez, and the others. Radio news channels were reporting more strange and bizarre deaths. The killers were making some hideous statement with their slaughtering methods. They were butchering, not just ending lives. But no radio news channel had reported Simon's death yet. Albright sneered. "He was Israeli and one of the elite Mossad, and he can't even make the news." Albright seethed with hatred for Sam. He hated and envied him more at that moment than ever before. Sam was free, he thought. Albright had convinced himself that his work, *his* Factor-7, was going to make him a shoo-in for the Nobel Prize in Medicine. He had planned it all. Everyone would know who he was, and he would, for once, finally get the respect he believed he deserved. World recognition and all the trappings that went along with that had been at his fingertips. Sam Hawkins had ruined it. But he would achieve what he knew he was entitled to, and he would finally get even with Sam and those who had been a roadblock to his successes. He vowed to one day get revenge.

Albright had to get out of his bloody clothes and find a safe place to stay. Daylight was breaking through the clouds as he pulled onto a dirt road that apparently led to a cattle ranch. Hiding his car behind a large mesquite tree, he shed his clothes. He quickly replaced them with fresh pants and shirt from his duffel. A windmill with a large round cement water tank was near. He rinsed his shoes in the green mucky water. He washed his face and hands but couldn't feel clean. He scrubbed them with his fist to cleanse himself of the blood and the memory. Unable to collect his thoughts or drive the horror from his mind, he sat on the edge of the tank and put his head between his legs. He didn't know how long he had been sitting there when he was startled from his trance by the sound of a truck coming down the dirt road. He grabbed his shoes and ran barefoot back to his waiting car. He revved the engine and left the truck in his dust as he pulled back onto the highway.

Another couple of hours passed, and then he had to make the decision to go farther south or take the highway to San Antonio. He veered to the left onto Highway 77 South. Mexico was south.

John Albright had credit cards but not a lot of cash. He couldn't run the risk of using a card or withdrawing cash from his personal bank account. That would most certainly enable the authorities, or perhaps the killers, to trace his steps. He had to get more cash. He pulled his cell phone from the glove box. It only had two bars of signal. He dialed Mr. Z.

Z and Guidry were at their Chicago location. It was a dumpy, insect-infested warehouse, but it had been a haven for them for some time. The news of Rodriguez and Reznick had forced them to make a rapid evacuation. They knew they had been discovered. Boxes littered the office space. Guidry was filling them with redacted documents and other belongings, and Mr. Z was destroying others. Z answered the phone on the first ring.

"Z, this is Albright. We have trouble."

"No shit? You're so fucking stupid. I should have killed you when I had the chance. Where are you?" Mr. Z screamed his anger.

"I don't know…somewhere far south, near the Mexican border. I need money."

"We're scattering. You're on your own," Z said firmly.

Albright breathed deeply, trying to find courage. Even over the phone, Z terrified him. "You need me. I know the formula. Hell, I designed the entire formula." He was frantic.

Z mockingly laughed. "I have your fuckin' formula. Things are on hold until we figure out who's wiping out the brothers."

"Brothers? You mean the stupids who allowed themselves to be found and murdered? I'm smarter than all of you. Get me some money, or I quit."

Again, Z laughed, but his anger was clearly understood. "You quit? Quit what? There's nothing to quit, dickhead. We don't need you or want you anymore. You're trouble, and we don't need any more of that. Get lost, if you know what's good for you." He slammed the phone on the desk.

"Z, are you there?" Albright yelled.

But Mr. Z had ended the call.

Albright beat his fist into the car seat. He had no one left, and his options were running thinner by the minute.

Guidry and Mr. Z knew that their time was coming to an end. Albright had been valuable at one time, but he had become a huge liability. Factor-7 had to be put on hold. Z swore he would not be defeated. Too much time, effort, and strategic planning had gone into the plan. Mr. Z still had his moles in the CIA. He had been warned that the State Department had been sniffing around too much, and they might have found something. The Collegium had to go underground. They had their hiding places, but there was still unfinished business. Some of the viruses were housed in an underground bunker near Dugway. They were safe for the moment. The brotherhood in that area would take care of that depository. But the Houston operation was getting too hot; Z and Guidry had to close that down.

Albright still had the disgusting odor of blood and bodily secretions in his nostrils. His shoes had dried from his attempt to clean them in the cattle water tank, but bloodstains remained. If police for any reason stopped him, even if for some traffic violation, he would look and certainly smell suspicious. He stank, was dirty, and...the blood was a dead giveaway that something vile had happened. He had to get clean, and he had to get more clothes. Z had been his last hope for help. But Z and Guidry had abandoned him. The FBI, and whoever else, were looking for him. Where could he get money, and quickly? Where else could he find someone carrying cash but a place that Dr. John Albright knew well—a hospital? Nothing was beneath him at this point. Survival was his only concern.

It had been nearly twenty hours since he had found Simon's butchered body. He had not eaten, and he had not slept. He had been in the rental car all night and most of that day. Maybe he had driven in circles, or maybe he had parked somewhere. He couldn't remember anything but running from the motel room and washing the blood off at the windmill. Even so, he now had clarity of his situation. He didn't even know the little town's name, but they had a hospital. He parked close to the doctor's rear entrance and waited for his opportunity.

Several nurses filed out, some alone and some accompanied by what appeared to be doctors and male nurses. It was now dark. The only light was in the far side of the parking lot. *They must not have much crime here*, he thought as he refined his first plan. Then he saw his opportunity. A small-built elderly man in a long white coat emerged alone from the hospital door. He was enthralled by something in a patient's chart and was not paying any attention to his surroundings. Albright stepped from his car, took a very deep breath, and approached the older man. He greeted him cordially and then grabbed the man by the neck, pulling him to the ground.

"I don't want to hurt you. But I'm desperate. Give me your wallet!" Albright demanded.

The man reached into his pants pocket and withdrew a black wallet. "Here, take it…don't hurt me!"

Albright grabbed it and ran as fast as possible back to his car. He sped from the parking lot into the darkness of the side road. He merged onto the highway and continued down the road. Fumbling while driving, he dumped out all that the wallet held. There on the seat were four one-hundred-dollar bills and some smaller currency, but it held a cache of credit cards. If he were to try to use the credit cards, he would have to do so quickly.

There was a rugged barbeque café with a sign that said Western Wear. He parked and briskly walked inside. Although he was not his usual meticulously dressed self, he still had on his gold Piaget watch and diamond ring, and that would give them the impression he could buy with the card. At least he convinced himself of that as he handed the cashier the jeans, boots, a cap and three shirts.

"Do you want cash back, Doctor?" inquired the young man behind the counter.

"What?" Albright asked nervously.

"There, on the machine. It's asking you if you want cash back on your transaction."

"How much can I get?"

The young man looked into his register. "Well, a big bill, I think."

Albright pressed the one hundred dollars cash back button. He stuffed the money into his pocket and grabbed the bag from the young man.

"Thanks for your business. Come back soon," shouted the clerk.

Albright ran from the store. Next on his list was to fill the compact car with gas. About three miles down the road, he saw a Walmart sign. That would be perfect for the items he needed. He successfully filled the gasoline tank, using one of the stolen credit cards. He needed some food and special supplies for his next daunting task. He also knew that the credit cards must continue to work inside the store, or he was royally screwed. He picked up some bottled water, a large jug of orange juice, some beef jerky, two pints of milk, 70 percent alcohol, peroxide, Band-Aids, and gauze. Then he slid two six-packs of beer under the cart with a Styrofoam cooler and ice. Grabbing several large bags of chips and the best brand of Ziplock bags, Albright paused and reviewed his supplies. He picked up another box of half-gallon-size freezer bags and held them in his hand for a moment contemplating the horrid role the bags would play in his escape game. He then went for what he considered the most disgusting item on the list, but it was imperative to his task. He picked up two packages of calf's liver from the meat department. Albright shuddered as he threw them into the basket.

Again, the machine displayed an option for cash back. He knew his chance to get money was then and probably not again. He pushed the button for one hundred dollars. The cashier handed him the money and his receipt.

His hands were shaking, and he had broken into a sweat. So far, the first plan had worked. He didn't have the luxury of excess time. Somebody was killing off the Collegium, and with the most gruesome of methods. The FBI and probably Texas Rangers were searching for him. He knew he was in the worst position imaginable. His thoughts were confused and jumbled. John Albright was raised privileged. He had attended the finest prep schools and universities. He had run with the highest of society, and he'd thought he was close to receiving the Nobel Prize for Medicine. His designer virus was beyond brilliant, he thought, but his delivery systems, the bacteriophages, were nothing short of genius, and he knew it. The mere fact that they could be suspended in the atmosphere and still be viable was beyond genius. It was savant, he thought. Once the Factor-7 plan had been implemented, he intended to announce that he had found a vaccine against it. He laughed out loud. Genius! *I create the germ…and the ingenious delivery system…and then I have the cure for my own creation.* He knew his vaccine would work, but it would only be effective if the Factor-7 was contained to small areas. He knew its mortality rate, but he was sure if the virus was used as intended and confined to the small intended areas, he would have time to warn the US or any country of the Collegium and the plague they unleased. He then would be the great hero. He had no loyalty to the Collegium. He had no loyalty to any government or country. He knew he would be the most sought-after scientist in the world and he would have gone where ever the money and prestige were the greatest. He screamed, "And it's all over. Everything is over!" His dreams were shattered. All his plans to become a hero were now gone. He never gave thought to the killing machine he had created or the deaths he would have been directly responsible for. He didn't care about that part of his involvement. All that was simply a means to an end…an end that promised him all he had ever wanted. "Damn them…damn them all," he shrieked.

His audible rant had cleared his cluttered mind. Just hearing himself was cathartic. But he was angry. He was insanely livid. He was not to be beaten any longer. He swore to an empty car that they would not find him. Earlier that day, he had considered committing suicide, but he was too much of a narcissist and too arrogant to take his own life. He always believed himself the most important player of the group. But as clarity of the present situation filtered out his brain fog, he realized that they already had the weapon and thus no longer had use for him. He no longer had purpose, and therefore he was disposable.

CHAPTER TWENTY-ONE

Sam turned on one of the national news networks as he lifted his head from the pillow. The morning sun was streaming through the shutters, and it adorned Rainee's face with golden rays of light. She looked angelic, Sam thought. She had finally gotten some sleep. He touched her hair with the thought of rolling over and making morning love to her. Then the news anchor announced they had received a special bulletin.

Rainee stretched. "What now?" she asked sleepily.

The reporter read the bulletin. "The Associated Press has just reported that a man was found decapitated in a bathroom at a motel in Pasadena, Texas. Local police on the scene have confirmed. He is being identified as an Israeli man and a member of the elite Mossad, Israel's intelligence organization. His name is being withheld until notification of the next of kin. They further stated that the FBI has determined that it was an act of terror because of the kind of sword that was left at the scene. It was a type used by the caliphates. The US president and United Kingdom prime minister have condemned the recent multiple killings and the terrorist organizations they believe are responsible. No further details, at this time, as to the type of sword recovered. Our sources, however, are saying that it appeared to be like a Middle Eastern pulwar or shamshir sword." A curved sword with a red-handled grip was shown on the screen. "The FBI has determined that it was probably a terror attack by an ISIS sympathizer, but no one has claimed responsibility at the time of the newscast. They are searching for an unnamed man who had checked into the motel with the deceased. Investigations are ongoing."

Rainee gasped. "I thought when Gustavo said he would have their heads that he was speaking figuratively. I mean, I thought it was like, heads will roll, or…" She paused and held tightly to Sam.

The disgust Sam felt was evident on his face. "They're looking for John. He must have gotten away."

"Or they took him."

"Yeah. Either way, it was no fuckin' Middle Eastern terrorist. That Mexican must be laughing his ass off between the puffs on his Cuban cigar."

CHAPTER TWENTY-TWO

Sam flipped through the pages of a plastic surgery manual. "We can do this," he whispered. Sam had prided himself on closing a wound or a surgery with precision. He had rebuilt noses and reconstructed body parts in the trauma units where he had spent half his life. He could give Gustavo a new face. He knew Rainee's skilled hands as a neurologist would be of great benefit when attaching severed nerves. But what about their nerves? Gustavo had sworn their safety if they gave him a new face, but what if he died? Or what if they messed up? They would surely die by the hands of Jorge or any number of El Espino's thugs.

Sam set the book on the side table and rubbed his eyes. He looked intently at Rainee napping next to him on the sofa, her head in his lap. So much dread, but she made it all OK. Sam stroked her face. "I wonder if there's any further information on Reznick or Albright." Sam turned on the evening news. "Wake up, sleepyhead."

"I'm not asleep," she replied. "I couldn't sleep after hearing the reports this morning. I mean, how grisly, Simon Reznick's death?"

The Houston reporter for KRPA was standing in front of the motel. The midmorning report stated the investigation was continuing. They named Simon Reznick and mentioned the attack at Ma'ale Adumim in the West Bank that killed his wife and maimed his daughter. A picture of his daughter was shown. She was in her wheelchair, apparently crying.

Rainee sighed. "She is so innocent. She never knew her father was a potential mass murderer. How can they exploit her like this?"

The newswoman continued. "The FBI is now stating that the man who accompanied Mr. Reznick is a person of interest." They flashed a recent photo of Dr. John Albright. "A nationwide search is underway to find this man. Authorities state that he is not under arrest, but they want to know what he knows about the hideous murder of the prominent Israeli patriot." The FBI was still referring to the murder as an act of terrorism.

"Prominent killer...patriot genocidal maniac...terrorism, my ass. Reznick will go down as a hero. What a fucking farce. Can't those morons get anything right?" screeched Sam. "Another fuckin' cover-up... pardon my language."

"Yeah, Sam. Get ready. They'll never report the facts. The truth won't ever come out. And it probably shouldn't. But we can help with our knowledge and get the information to the authorities. Isn't there someone we should talk to? I mean, under these new circumstances? Maybe tell them we saw Albright? We know so much."

"Rainee, we've been through this. I get what you're saying, sweetie, but we can't let anyone know that we know anything at all. If we go to FBI or police, we're hindering Gustavo, which ultimately means he has no need for us. As much as I detest all this, we have no choice but to allow him to continue his eliminations. He warned us. Anyway, if we involve someone…say Phil, my friend in Congress, who's to say we aren't putting him and his family in danger?"

"Yeah, but it just doesn't seem right."

"Darlin', there is nothing right, righteous, legal, or ethical that can come from this. Be prepared for anything."

Tears formed and streamed down her cheeks. "I'm so tired of the killing, the lies, and the horrors. I want it all to be over."

"Maybe someday." But Sam doubted that day would ever come.

Sam needed to go to the hospital, and Rainee was ready for a short nap. He kissed her goodbye and drove the fifteen minutes to St. Peter's. His first stop would be his office, to respond to any urgent messages.

He unlocked the door and walked into the dimly lighted office. From the door, Sam realized that his desk was in disarray. The few patient files and other papers on his desk were rearranged, but nothing seemed missing. "Damn janitors," he said aloud. Then he glanced at the wall to the right of his desk. There had been pictures of him with Dr. Roberts at a golf tournament and a couple of him and other physicians fishing off the coast of Belize. Both framed photos were gone. Only the wall hangers remained. Sam was infuriated and a bit concerned. Who would want the pictures? Had someone from the Collegium come to his office? Maybe they were looking for something. Maybe more than Albright and Reznick knew about where he and Rainee had been and what they had discovered while in Mexico. El Espino was already reaping his vengeance, but he would be of no help to Sam and Rainee now. And Sam wasn't about to contact him or accept one of his goons as a security guard, even if it was offered. One, Sam hated El Espino and everything he stood for. Two, if Sam was found to have contact with such a criminal, then he was destined for prison. So Sam's choice was to lie low and figure out who had burglarized his office and why. He had no one to turn to for protection. He couldn't even report it to Security.

Sam touched the pistol stuck in the waist of his jeans. He slammed his office door harder than intended and walked briskly down the hallway. If it had been the Collegium, they would have covered their tracks. After all, these were no half-ass criminals. They were experts in espionage. But why would they want his photos?

Then a thought slapped him. His heart sank. They wanted a photo of Sam so that whoever was looking for him would positively be able to identify him. He leaned against the cold steel door to the East Wing of the trauma center. Suddenly he felt a soft touch and heard a familiar voice.

"Well, Sam. I've missed you." She took a good look at him. "Are you OK?"

"Yeah, Sandra." He gave her a big hug. "I'm just tired."

"Well, when are you coming back?" she asked.

"Not sure even that I am. That's our secret, OK?"

"Sam, I'm stunned. Why?"

"Well, there's a lady now in my life, and we may start another adventure."

Sandra's eyes grew sad. "Oh, Sam, be sure of your decisions. You are the best, and we need you. Remember the proverbial bus…it runs every hour."

"Well, I've stopped at her. Pretty amazing lady. Anyway, thanks for that, Sandra, but Trauma has left me traumatized." He smiled, but she knew he was serious.

"It's tough, and you've been doing this a very long time." She forced a half-hearted smile.

"Hey, have any burglaries been reported here at St Pete's?" Sam tried hard to conceal his nervousness.

Sandra shook her head. "None I've heard about. And I would have heard, you know."

"Yeah, you know things before they even happen." Sam smiled. "Sandra, love you, but I have to rush off. I will be in touch. Promise."

"You better!"

Just then, Sam's cell phone rang. It was Rainee.

"Guess what?" she asked.

"Geez, I hesitate to try to guess."

"You have a new Porsche. They just delivered her."

"Whoopee! My toy has arrived." Sam hugged Sandra and walked to the parking lot, all the time surveying everyone who passed with a critical eye.

Sam decided as he drove home that he would not tell Rainee about his office break-in. It would upset her, and he had no answers to offer as comfort.

That afternoon, Sam and Rainee took the new ride for a drive. They stopped in to see Ana Roberts. Sam had been concerned for her well-being long before Albright had dropped the bomb that she had told Simon about their trip to Mexico. Ana answered the door promptly. She looked tired and as if she had been crying for some time. Sam hugged her and introduced Rainee. She took them to the back gazebo and, true to her routine, asked Julia to prepare a light snack and cold sangria.

"I'm going to miss Julia," Ana said.

"Why?" Sam asked. "Where's she going?"

"It's not her, but me. I've decided to sell this house and move to British Columbia. Bill and I made many friends in Campbell River throughout those summers we lived on the island. A house near our old one has come on the market, and I've already made an offer."

Sam nodded but felt a stab in his heart. Although Bill's memory had been tarnished, he loved both of them. Ana was still like a mother to him.

CHAPTER TWENTY-TWO

"But you and Rainee will always be welcome. Remember salmon fishing?"

Sam smiled. "I do, and I remember salmon eating too."

The three talked about all things except Bill and Simon.

Ana moved her plate to the side. "OK, let's finally send the elephant in the room packing."

Sam raised his eyebrows.

"I'm tired of being alone. I've lost my entire family, and yes, I admit I had grown fond of Simon. Now he's gone, and he died in such a terrible way. I'm worried for John too."

Sam cut his eyes at Rainee, but she ignored it and retained a sympathetic expression for Ana's sake.

"My heart aches, and my mind is cluttered with unanswered questions. I have to make a new start." Ana touched Sam's hand and smiled at Rainee. "I'm glad to see y'all are too."

Sam told Rainee as they walked down the long sidewalk toward the Porsche and away from Ana Roberts's home, perhaps for the last time, that he was saddened, but he understood Ana's decision.

"What's this?" Sam pulled a yellow piece of paper from under his wipers. "Ah, shit, not again."

"What?" Rainee snatched the paper. "Sam, this is scary. What do you think it means? That you won't get away with this…you can't do this to me. Get away with what? And doing what to whom?" Rainee's voice got louder with each question.

"I don't have a clue, and it's getting too creepy. Same thing that was on the Porsche when it was vandalized. I can't imagine. Doesn't seem like something the Collegium would do, does it?"

"Maybe Albright. You say he's dramatic, so he might just be getting his kicks."

Sam shook his head. "John Albright can't be around. He's a wanted man, and he'd be insane to hang around Houston now and in broad daylight." He shook his head again. "Weird and very creepy."

Rainee was quiet for a while, and then she touched his shoulder. "Sam. Ana might have the right idea. There's nothing holding us here either, and let's face it, recently this hasn't been the happiest of places for you."

Sam pushed the accelerator on the new Carrera. The engine roared, and they sped forward. He took Rainee's hand. "No, there's not a damned thing holding us here. It's time for a change."

Suddenly the Bluetooth phone rang. Sam glanced at the caller ID on the dashboard. He looked at Rainee. They both recognized the Mexico country code.

"It's El Espino," Rainee said.

"I hope you have been studying." The Mexican's voice was stern.

Sam threw back his head in frustration. "Yes, we're working on it," he replied.

"Is the lady doctor with you?"

"Yes, she's here in the car."

Rainee spoke up. "Yes, I'm here, and we're reviewing surgical techniques."

"Excellent. Muy bueno. I am keeping my promise too. Right now, my men are cleaning up the mess in Germany. If you know what I mean. So…" He coughed loudly. "I have set the date for your return. It will be in three months. I am on a diet, so my body will be as handsome as my face." He cackled. "I will let you know exactly very soon. I will tell you where you will be picked up." The call ended.

Sam and Rainee had no time to ask questions or reply, but they knew that El Espino made all the decisions. They had no choice but to do precisely as they were told.

After driving around to burn off anger and frustration, Rainee suggested they pick up a pizza and head home. The sun was still overhead, and Sam thought a bit of fishing might calm his raw nerves and soothe his senses.

Ascending the stairway to the upper deck, Sam noticed something sticking out from under the black vinyl door mat. He moved nearer to it. Rainee followed him closely. He bent down to get a better look but then recoiled quickly. The pizza flew from his hands.

"Damn, a rattler!" Sam shouted. "Stay back!"

"Is it alive?" Rainee screamed.

Sam got a shovel from the corner of the deck and slammed it down on the snake. He then nudged the creature's head. It didn't move. He pushed the mat over and nudged it again. It was dead. He scooped it up and flung it over the railing and into the bay below. "It was dead all along. Someone has been busy trying to scare me or us."

"And succeeding, I'd say." The color had faded from her face.

Sam opened the door to the house. Somehow it was unlocked. He gave a weary look toward Rainee. "They've been in here." Sam pulled his gun from inside his jeans and looked around. Another yellow piece of paper lay on the floor inside. "You think he has a bite! You ain't seen nothing yet if you keep doing what you're doing" was all it said.

"It's them, Sam. They know about us!" Rainee began to cry.

Sam pulled her to him and hugged her tightly. "I'll take care of you." But as with previous promises he had made to protect her, he knew he had no way to guarantee her safety.

CHAPTER TWENTY-THREE

A single guard was sitting in the makeshift guardhouse, smoking a cigarette, when Mr. Z and Guidry pulled up to the gate. Z flashed a badge, and the guard opened the wire gate to the unnamed compound near NASA.

The guard waved them in. He picked up his cell phone and entered a quick one-word text.

A light flashed in the distance, as if summoning the two men to drive in its direction.

"Must be a brother," Z stated.

As they approached the flashlight beam, floodlights filled the dark with blinding illumination.

"What the hell?" shouted Z.

A number of men in dark clothing ran to the large freight van and began to pull Guidry, then Z from the inside. They shouted something in Spanish just before taking a machete to Guidry's throat. Two men pushed Z to the back of the vehicle. His cane fell to the ground. Then he fell into the dirt.

"Open it," shouted one of the men.

Three more men roughly grabbed Mr. Z and lifted him to his feet. They chattered to each other, as if repeating instructions.

Z unlocked the double doors to the van. "Who are you? Leave me alone!"

Suddenly, the floodlights shut off.

Z heard a laugh coming from the front of the van, but it was too dark to see anyone. "I'm telling you; you're messing with the wrong people if you want to rob me. You won't get away with this!" Z screamed.

As soon as the words left his lips, he felt a rope go over his head and tighten around his neck. Someone kicked both of his ankles, and he fell again into the dirt face-first. He heard more men running his way, speaking Spanish.

The group carried Z through an open door and down a dark ramp that led to the underground bunker. Another group of men started unloading large metal boxes from the truck.

As they descended the ramp, the air became cooler, and the low hum of machinery could be heard. Then the lights turned on.

Z surveyed the men around him. There must have been at least six who were dressed in black clothing from head to foot. But there was now another man standing right in front of him. He was dressed in a suit and tie, and he held the end of the rope that wrapped around Mr. Z's neck. Gathering his courage, Z bellowed, "Who are you, the head dick?" gazing straight at the well-dressed man. "You the head goon?"

"Strong talk for a man with a noose around his neck," the man replied. He motioned to the group.

Suddenly, Z felt a hard blow to the back of his head. Blood ran down his neck, soaking his shirt. He fell to his knees. The blow had dazed him but had not rendered him unconscious. The Mexicans had no intention of knocking him out. He had a duty still to do.

"What is this?" slurred Z as another Mexican man pushed him from his knees to the floor.

Another slammed the butt of a machete into Z's ribs. He howled in pain. "What are you doing? Why me? Please, I'll give you anything you want. Please don't kill me."

The well-dressed man stepped closer. "I am Jorge Villa Lobos. Mr. Villa Lobos to you. I am here to deliver a message. You do not fuck with El Espino."

"El Espino? I don't know any fuckin' El Espino," Z shouted.

"Oh, but you know his money, and you fucked with him. You did not do what you said. None of your"—Jorge paused and then huffed out the next word—"brotherhood did what they promised, in exchange for his money. And you were a leader, so you are going to die."

Z began to whimper like a child. "I didn't have anything to do with that."

Jorge nodded to the man standing closest to Z. He kicked Z in his side, then delivered a blow to his gut.

Another wild scream of pain echoed throughout the bunker, but they were underground and far from any outside ears. And the representatives of El Espino cared nothing about his agony.

Refrigeration units lined each side of the bunker. A clipboard hung on the front of each. Stainless steel desks with glass vials, microscopes, and computers surrounded a large metal box in the middle of the bunker. It had a strange rounded top with double locks on each side. In every corner of the large area were explosive devices. The brotherhood had installed them for the purpose that Guidry and Z had come to perform. It was to destroy evidence when and if they were ever uncovered and the project was at risk of discovery. It would be the last thing done and the most undesirable final action that Z's wing of the Collegium would take.

Jorge set his hand on the large metal machine in the middle of the bunker. "What's in that box?" he asked.

Z strained to speak. "It's a large centrifuge. It holds deadly viruses. So, you see, you're in danger here. Any minute my men will come, and it will be over for you. Let me go, and I'll forget all about you."

Jorge took a step back almost showing fear, but then he laughed. "Such a fool I am not. Such an imbecile you are, if you think you can scare me."

"What are you going to do?" Z moaned. "What are you going to do with me?"

Jorge said nothing. He dragged Z by the neck to each of the metal boxes that had been brought from the van. "What do you have in these?"

Z lay on the cold floor, moaning and gasping for breath. "Documents. All names and places are expunged. Nothing for your concern."

"Open them," Jorge ordered.

Z crawled to his knees and unlocked the lids.

The men began to pull file folders and other papers from them. One man followed Jorge's instructions to pour gasoline on top of the pile.

Jorge walked around the room. He ran his hand over the explosive devices. He then shouted angrily, "Now set the damned timers. Set them for ten minutes from right now, and enjoy those minutes. They will be your last." He tugged the rope as if pulling a dog on a leash.

Z struggled to move. He feebly crawled to each of the four large boxes filled with dynamite. His blood smeared the concrete floor like a snail leaving its slime as he pulled himself from one device to the next. As instructed, he nervously turned dials on all the clock timers. Colored wires ran from the clocks into the metal boxes. When he was finished, he calmly lay on the floor by the last bomb. He spoke in a low, resigned voice. "You're the goons that murdered my brothers, aren't you?"

Jorge lit a cigarette. He walked over to Mr. Z, who was pathetically trying to sit up. He held it over the pile of gasoline-soaked papers. Jorge laughed and blew smoke in Z's face. "No more questions."

Jorge examined Z's work and appeared satisfied that the timers were set correctly. "You better not try to double-cross me, asshole! You're going to die, but if you double-cross me, it will be by cutting off body parts, one by one. The first will be your dick!"

"I won't. Please let me go." Blood was running down his cheek, and his nose had started to bleed.

Jorge took a step back from the boxes. "You were going to kill many. You used El Espino's money to make a terrible biological weapon, and you and the others gave nothing back to your benefactor. That is a real no-no, as you say here in your country." Jorge nodded, and the men began to gather nearer to him. "So your weapons are here? The bioweapon is here." Jorge laughed. "All that work." He laughed louder. "And blooee!" His voice mimicked a bomb explosion that echoed though the building.

"I'll get his money. Let me go, and I'll get the money," Z pleaded.

Jorge shouted to his men, "*Andale*, hombres," trying to rush them to finish their duties. He looked harshly at Z. "It is too late." He turned his back and began to walk toward the door.

Each of Jorge's men threw a match into the pile of documents. Flames flew into the air and the smell of gasoline mixed with smoke filled the bunker.

Z lay on the ground soaked in his own blood. "Please," he whispered. "Please, what will you do to me?" Z shouted.

Jorge pointed at the machete. One of the men handed him the large sword. He ran the blade under Z's neck without breaking the skin. "I could make this fast for you, but El Espino said that the weapon you made was painful and slower than a blade to kill. So..." He cocked his head to one side. "You are such a brave man to want to kill thousands of people you do not even know. But here you whine for mercy. You have no mercy, and you will not be shown mercy."

One of his men took the handle of the sword and slammed it down on Z's shins. The crushing sound of bone was mixed with a burst of howling screams.

"Please, I beg you. Whatever you want. What are you doing?"

"You will not walk away from this." He laid the machete on the floor next to Z. "Use it on yourself if you wish." He turned his back to Z with a nod of finality. He motioned to his men.

"What are you doing?" Z's voice trailed off, as if he had accepted his fate. "What are you doing?"

"Watching your suicide."

The group of Mexican men and Jorge left the bunker. The large metal door made a squealing sound when it scrapped the concrete floor.

Z heard the door lock from the outside. He buried his head in his bloody hands.

The men loaded into a large SUV. Jorge poured gasoline on the rest of the items in the back of Guidry and Z's van and set them on fire. Then he walked to Guidry's lifeless body. He wiped another machete in Guidry's blood. He flung the bloody machete into the dirt, sinking the blade into the ground beside Guidry's virtually detached head. "*Listo.* It is finished." He walked slowly to the waiting vehicle and took one last look toward the bunker. He got into the front seat and locked the door. The driver started the ignition. Jorge faced straight ahead as they drove toward the guard booth. They stopped and picked up the man from the booth, then sped from the compound onto the back road.

The SUV shook as the bunker exploded. Pieces of metal blew into the sky. Then, three more explosions rocked the vehicle. Jorge never looked back.

CHAPTER TWENTY-FOUR

Dr. John Albright turned off the highway and onto a two-lane farm-to-market road. He was stunned that he was already in the King Ranch and that far south. He had not known where he was for hours, and he had no idea of time. He stopped at the first dirt road he saw. As much as he despised what he had to do, Albright scuffed his new boots on the dirt and rocks. He rubbed grass and dirt on his new jeans and then grabbed a handful of soil to fill his fingernails. He scoffed at his appearance when he placed the John Deere cap on his head.

As he imagined, there was a farm-and-ranch store on the outskirts of town. He pulled into the lot and parked his rental car behind a horse trailer. He went inside.

"Afternoon, pard'ner," said the well-worn man behind the counter. "What can I do for ya today?"

Trying to keep with the country boy mode, Albright said he needed to do some vaccinating. "Got six heifers needin' it."

"Sure thing," replied the old man as he led Albright to the veterinarian section. "Everything ya need should be right over yonder.

Holler if ya need help. There's a tote over there. Just put your things in that basket."

Albright nodded. "Will do." He surveyed the equipment. He grabbed four very large syringes and four individually packed needles. He winced when he saw the gauge of the needles. But he had to have them. He threw a bag of clear plastic tubing in the basket with the rest of the items. "What am I forgetting?" he whispered to himself. "Duct tape." Satisfied with the items, he briskly walked to the front of the store and the counter.

"Did ya get what ya need?" asked the old man, who didn't give Albright the chance to answer. "Ain't seen ya around here ba'fore."

Albright pulled out the cash and laid it on the counter. "Just moving some cows through and forgot the stuff I needed to stick them before auction."

The man picked up the cash he needed. "Yep." He pushed the rest back toward Albright. "Yea-up you have a nice day now."

Albright looked inquisitively at the clerk as he just pushed money around on the counter. "Hey, thanks, man." He paused at the large cooler. "Oh, here…" He handed the man two additional dollars. "I need a bag of ice." He waved goodbye. "Oh shit, what a piece of crap," he mumbled as he left the store. He continued to mumble under his breath as he got in the car and started out of the parking lot. "I, Dr. John Albright, renowned scientist, am reduced to this crap. Those hicks have no idea who I am. I'm so much better than this." He huffed. "Sam Hawkins will pay."

In the distance he saw a motel sign. He drove to the back of the buildings and parked inconspicuously between two tractor-trailer rigs. The big rigs would hide his car from three angles. He looked around. It was surrounded by mesquite trees, shacks, and large barrels of trash. Dogs ran loose, and he could hear barking all around. It was a disgusting area of whatever town he was in. He didn't care as long as he could fulfill his task and not be recognized. He walked to the office situated on the side of the building.

"I need a room for the night," he said.

"No bags and staying all night?" asked the grinning toothless man.

Albright could barely contain his disgust. *What business is it of his if I have bags or not?*

"Yeah, all night. I'll pay now. I'll be leaving early."

"Yeah, sure you will…real early." The man stuck his tongue to the side of his cheek and moved it up and down in an erotic suggestion. He then cackled, and tobacco spit slung from his mouth. "Nobody stays here all night. If you get my drift. Be thirty bucks, probably what you're gonna pay the señorita tonight."

Albright stared disgustedly at the man. *Is this* Deliverance? He almost gagged. "What the hell?" he sneered. He pulled out thirty dollars and threw it at the haggard man and grabbed the key. "I'll be gone in the morning from this hellhole."

He heard the man make a sucking noise as he left the tiny office.

Albright gathered his things from the car and put large pieces of duct tape over the license plate. He locked the motel room door and moved the only chair in front of it. He sat on the bed. The roomed smelled of body odor, old beer, and cigarette smoke. The walls had strange stains and peeling paint. "Hellhole!" He assembled his purchases from the farm-and-ranch store and broke open a beer.

CHAPTER TWENTY-FIVE

Sam poured two glasses of red wine and set Rainee's next to her at the kitchen counter. "Aren't you tired of studying?"

She closed the laptop and took a sip of the wine. "Kinda like going back to med school, but a lot easier." She giggled and then caught herself realizing that there was nothing funny about why she had her head buried in the study of rhinoplasty.

"Come sit with me." Sam motioned to her while patting the sofa cushion. "I called an old classmate of mine. He practices in Houston. He's a pretty good plastics man…makes a ton of money. He's mainly in breasts and rears, 'cause that's the consistent money. But he said we could sit in on one of his face-lifts. He'll be doing one on Friday, and he'll redo her nose, cheeks, and chin."

"That's what we need to see."

"And he does it all under conscious sedation. He puts a drip in, and she'll be out, but no anesthesiologist needed."

"That's what we need too." Rainee stretched her neck. "Jorge would have us killed if his jefe died under anesthesia. El Espino might have us killed anyway. I mean, we really do know too much."

Sam bit his lip. "I don't think he will, unless things go south. And we're going to be too prepared for that. He won't die. I think he's a man of his word."

Rainee jumped to her feet, choking on the wine. "Sam, have you lost your mind? Who do you think you're talking about? He's a cold-blooded murderer! He's a butcher! He sells narcotics to children. He's the devil incarnate."

"Don't get pissed off." Sam gathered his thoughts. "I agree with you on all of that. He's one bad hombre. But he has done everything he said he was going to do, and we are still safe."

"Because he needs us. He has killed…no…*massacred* the Collegium. I really don't know how you can be so sure that he will let us go after the surgery."

"Well, you tell me our options." Sam stared at Rainee.

"We could leave tonight for Europe and get lost there."

"He'd find us. Maybe not right away, but he sniffed out the Collegium in five countries, and they're all eliminated. If we cross him, he'll surely do the same to us. I've given this a lot of thought. I believe he trusts us to do what he has asked and to keep quiet about ever knowing about him. In return, he got rid of the key players in the Collegium. He kept us from having to go to someone with Bill's journals, yes…but we didn't know who to trust. Maybe he has kept us from being killed, and we never had to put ourselves in the middle of that or an investigation." Sam shrugged. "I dunno, but maybe."

Rainee sat down from her pacing the room as Sam talked. "Maybe."

"Think about it. When we got back from Mexico, the Collegium must have known we had found and read Bill's documents. Albright knew we did. Simon Reznik apparently knew. Or they surmised we did. Whatever...anyway, John was trying to save his ass when he confronted us last week. He was probably sent to retrieve the journals on the threat of his own death. He was so nervous that day and so ill equipped to intimidate us that he was as effective as a kitten trying to catch a crow. He was running. That group of maniacs knew they were exposed." Sam paused. "Get my point?"

"Not entirely." She shook her head. "No. I think you're rationalizing."

"Bluntly, if El Espino had not taken the journals and ultimately terminated the big guys of the Collegium, we would have been their targets. Those planning the Factor-7 weapon would have killed both of us. Once we were gone—and they surely would have taken us out— they would have gone ahead with their plan. Millions would have died, and perhaps World War III would have broken out. So which devil do you think we should have played with?"

"OK, I get it. But we could go to the FBI or CIA with what we know. They can protect us!" She was almost shouting.

"Like they protected our last two presidents?"

Rainee sighed. "I'm so tired." She started to cry.

"I hate this, and I hate it more that you're involved." Sam put his arms around her and held her closely. "We're doing the only thing we can do. I hate it. I despise all of them. But I can't come up with any logical or safe way out of this. We have to go to Mexico, and we have to do what we promised. El Espino will be looking for us in three months. That's the sad and only truth." He turned on the news.

The press was reporting an explosion at a compound near NASA. Police and federal agents had barricaded the area. Information was sketchy, but they were calling it a murder/suicide. The fire was extinguished, but they were not entering the building, stating that there were hazardous materials.

"Yeah, bacteriophage with deadly viruses," Rainee cried.

"Rainee, don't expect anything other than this. The CIA, FBI, or the feds, whoever they are, might know about this. It won't be reported for the obvious reasons. I guess Dugway and the areas around Wright will be next. We know the consequences if the international press gets hold of the truth. The feds will cover this completely, and they are doing that right now."

Rainee covered her eyes, crying. "Sam, they blew up a Factor-7 repository! Viruses could have been released into the air! I guess we will know soon enough if this thing lives suspended in the atmosphere. A deadly cloud of viruses!"

CHAPTER TWENTY-SIX

John Albright awoke at 1:20 a.m. in the shabby motel room. He opened the seal on the orange juice and then opened the jerky and the milk. He took the rubber tubing from the plastic bag. He opened the syringes and placed a new needle on each, then laid them on the bedside table. He opened the large zippered storage bags and several pint-size bags and set them on the table beside the rest of the paraphernalia. He cut the tubing and placed it into the syringe. It was smaller than the opening of the plastic 50cc syringe. He wrapped duct tape around the end until it was a tight fit. Then he removed the newly constructed tubing from the syringe and set it aside. He breathed deeply as he wiped down everything, including his arm. He took more of the rubber tubing and tied it tightly onto his upper left arm. Pain shot down his arm from the unhealed graze of Sam's bullet. The veins in the bend of his arm pushed upward. He inserted the large cattle needle into the largest protruding vein. The extra-large 18-gauge needle hurt so intensely that he let out a loud moan. Catching his breath, he made a fist. Blood began to flow into the syringe. Before the syringe was filled, he removed the end of the syringe and replaced it with the plastic tubing. He opened and closed his fist. Blood ran through the syringe and into the tube, then flowed freely into the plastic bag. He watched as it filled, calculating the amount until he thought he had withdrawn nearly one pint of blood. The first bag was full. He placed it on top of the ice. He took a large gulp of orange juice. Blood dripped from his arm onto the dirty motel carpet. Following the same procedure, he repeated the blood withdrawal. As if following the rules of Lamaze, he took several deep quick breaths. When the second bag was full, he untied the tubing from his upper arm, released his fist, and withdrew the needle. His head was spinning, and his ears were ringing, as if he would faint, but Albright managed to put the second bag of blood into the cooler and seal the lid. He fell back onto the bed. He knew he had taken too much blood at one time, but he also knew his time was limited. Surely the Texas Rangers or US Marshalls were closing in on him, and the butchers, his unknown enemy that had murdered Simon Reznik, could beat down the door at any moment. He forced down a large glass of orange juice before he fell asleep.

The sound of a tractor-trailer rig starting its engines startled Albright from his deep sleep. He glanced at his watch. It was 4:15 a.m. He opened the cooler to get the milk. The sight of his own blood in the bags made his stomach churn. He felt weak and nauseous. He knew what he had to do, but it had been too soon. His body might not take the loss of blood so quickly, and if he passed out, everything he had done up to that point would have been futile, a waste of all the anxiety and pain he had endured. He drank the milk but was still unable to reconcile his thoughts to continue his self-inflected bloodletting. *How could it all be worth this?* he asked himself. He huffed out a deep guttural moan. All the plans, all the preparation, and all his dreams had been vanquished. He was tired and he was weary, but Dr. John Albright suddenly had full clarity of his situation. He had lost everything. He could either surrender to his enemies and face a certain gruesome death or give up to the authorities and go to prison or the death chamber. His crimes were against humanity, and his precious Factor-7 had indeed been used in Liberia and Sierra Leone, among other places. He was a criminal, and he would be charged with the worst crimes against humanity.

But John Albright didn't see things that way. His work was of a higher order than most other scientists. He was Dr. John Albright! He was the best of the best! There was no moral ground required for his genius. He was above the code with which others had to abide.

He sat up straight on the bedside and collected the new needles and bags. After all, he thought, he had been a part of a plan to rid mankind of the evils of terrorism, the threat of nuclear obliteration from unhinged dictators, and the scourge of what Simon Reznick called the spread of insidious Muslim ideologies on the world. He held out his bare left arm. Between the bullet and the needles, he was black and blue. The bruises were massive. All the pain and bruises didn't matter. Albright had one choice. Nothing else was even an option.

He tied the tourniquet and injected the needle for the second time. The pain was now excruciating. His eyes rolled back, and he saw flashes of light. He sat very still, taking slow and methodical breaths. Shortly, the faintness passed enough for him to start withdrawing his blood. He rested his left arm on a rolled towel, which also held the needle in his vein, thus allowing him to use his right hand to put a piece of jerky in his mouth or take the occasional sip of water. After an hour, he had successfully filled the third and the final fourth plastic bags. Although weak and dazed, he had completed the dreadful task.

He unwrapped the tubing from his upper arm and removed the needle, and the blood flow stopped. He wrapped gauze around his arm. He checked the seals of the plastic bags before placing them in the cooler. There were four full bags of his blood. He estimated he had taken just over four and one-half pints of blood. He couldn't take any more. He was surely acutely anemic from the quick loss of blood. Only his excellent physical strength, endurance, and determination had kept him alive so far, and that would keep him alive now. He closed his eyes for a few minutes, trying hard to not lose consciousness. When he roused, he forced himself to eat some of the raw liver. Gagging with each bite, he washed it down with water and orange juice.

Albright fell again onto the dirty pillow. The stench of dirty hair and body odor no longer mattered. He had to rest, if for no more than a few hours.

———————

Three hours later. Weak and sick, he put the stolen cards and wallet into the cooler. He gathered the needles, tubing, and syringes and placed them also in the cooler. The sun broke through the dirty motel windows. He gathered the rest of his belongings and left.

He drank the rest of the juice and milk as he drove toward Laredo. Two and a half hours later, he saw the sign for the Laredo International Airport. He entered the remote parking. He found a space on the far end, away from all other cars. He parked.

Albright leaned his head back onto the seat. He had to be precise in all his maneuvers from now on. The situation had gone from very serious to extremely critical. He had to gather his strength. It was the final hours, and his very existence depended on a clear head.

He pulled out his border-crossing card. It was as good as a passport for Canada and Mexico. He still had four hundred dollars. He stuffed the money into his pocket. He took off his ring and watch, put them in a plastic bag, and stuffed the bag into his pants. He wiped his brow of sweat with a wet towel he had taken from the motel.

The days had run together. He stared into the distance for longer than he realized. His options were exhausted. His very life depended upon what he was going to do next and how well he did it. He set the cooler outside the driver's door. He put his duffel and belongings on the floorboard of the passenger side of the car. He threw his credit cards and driver's license into the passenger seat. He only kept his passport border-crossing card and what little cash he had left. He stood outside the car and took several deep breaths. His task had to be done in a perfectly accurate and absolutely convincing way. He pulled the first bag of blood from the cooler. He poured it on the passenger-side floorboard and over his belongings. He wiped his hands in the blood and put bloody handprints on the windshield and the driver's side window as if there had been a struggle. He took another bag of blood and slung it over the interior of the car. Blood dripped from the windows and the headliner. He then took the final two bags of blood and poured them on the driver's seat, floorboard, and the dash. He took a shirt and swiped it in the blood. He dragged it across the driver's side entrance and down to the parking lot asphalt outside the car door. He bit off three nails and threw them into the car along with several strands of his hair. He washed his hands in the melted water in the cooler and wiped his hands and face with the towel. He grabbed the cooler and put the bloody shirt, towel, baggies, and duct tape inside. He then ran, carrying the cooler, to the terminal. He hailed the first taxi he saw and crawled into the back seat.

"The International Bridge," he said.

They sped off.

Albright took out the duct tape and wrapped the cooler closed. Moments later, he saw a shopping center. "Hey buddy, stop. I need to do something."

The taxi driver obliged and pulled into the center. Albright was gone for several minutes while the driver waited. There was a dumpster in front of one of the major department stores. Albright threw the cooler into it and rushed back to the taxi.

"OK, to the bridge," he said.

The driver seemed to have not paid any attention to what Albright had done. He pressed the gas and they sped onto the highway.

Moments later, the frenzied doctor shouted at the driver to stop. They were a few blocks from Albright's intended destination. The International Bridge was directly in front of them.

Albright paid the driver and exited the taxi. He pulled his cap low on his forehead and tucked his head near his chest as he passed the many cameras on the United States side of the bridge. Then he merged with the crowds to the center of the bridge. He was in Mexico. He paused momentarily, looking at the Rio Grande below and then back to the United States. "I'll be back," he whispered.

Workers and women with bags and crying babies were loading a bus when he entered Nuevo Laredo. The smell of diesel exhaust filled the air, and it nauseated him. He would smell a lot of that from this point forward, he thought. He showed the bus driver his border card and told him he would pay him double fare if he would let him on the overcrowded bus. Albright handed him $120 and walked onto the bus.

CHAPTER TWENTY-SEVEN

One month later Sam answered his cell on the first ring so as not to wake Rainee. He whispered, "Hawkins."

"Hey, Sam, am I calling too early?"

Sam got out of bed and walked briskly from the bedroom. "Well, it is five fifteen, Kelton, you motherfucker!" He laughed.

"Early bird gets the best cart. Sorry, I've got a foursome at six thirty in Houston. I need to talk to you."

"Sounds serious."

"Don't worry, I didn't find the clap in your blood."

"Oh, shit. I was ready to do my happy dance."

"Well, you won't when I tell you what I have to say. But first...did you have a date with Brenda Newman?"

"Oh shit. Yeah. She's not pregnant, 'cause..." Sam paused.

"Yeah, just a blow job probably. Her MO. Apparently, she gets her cookies blowing doctors. Sick bitch. I know of four guys at the hospital she's gotten her claws into. We are all mad as hell."

"Claws? What's going on?"

"Well, you know the hospital is full of a bunch of gossiping magpies, but in this case, it might be beneficial. I heard your Porsche was vandalized and your office broken into. Is that right?"

"Yeah, among other things."

"Ever see *Fatal Attraction?*" Dr. Thomas asked in a half joking manner.

"Horrid thought. Don't tell me. You think Brenda did those things?"

"She nearly broke up Elizabeth and me. I strayed one night when we were fighting. No excuse, but Brenda started threatening me and telling me that if I didn't leave my wife, bad things were going to happen. She would leave notes on my office door. No envelope, just open sheets of paper. Anyone who came first in the morning would see them. They were very descriptive of things we were supposed to have done and what she planned to do. Although I knew positively that it was Brenda, she never signed them, so it was kinda hard to prove it was her…at first. Plus, having cheated on Elizabeth and with my practice in mind, I didn't want a scandal, so I didn't go to the authorities. It was a nightmare. I had to convince my entire office staff that she was just some crazy woman, but the wife? Well, that was more difficult."

"Oh geez, Kelton," Sam groaned.

"Yeah. She started doing the same, putting letters and notes on my car and then on the front door of my house. I was a nervous wreck. Confronting her only made things worse. She called Elizabeth one afternoon and told her that she and I had been having an affair! There was no affair. Mind you, I went to her house, and we had sex one time. I didn't stay there afterward, and it was just that one time. In her screwed-up mind, she somehow thought or fantasized that we were a couple. She's fucking insane! Finally, after about a month of that crap, I told her to meet me in St. Pete's parking lot. I really verbally laid into her. I felt like slugging her, and had she not been a female, I would have beaten the holy crap out of her. I did grab her shoulders when she lunged at me. I was trying to stop her from hitting me. She ran off crying, but that night she threw a brick through our front window with a picture of her and me in the parking lot earlier that day. I had hold of her shoulders, but the photo looked like an embrace. I don't know who took it, but Elizabeth was ready to leave me."

"Sounds like a horror story. I'm pissed. I loved that Porsche, and well...I don't take kindly to people breaking into my office or house. And the rattlesnake—that was over the top. At least she hasn't contacted Rainee."

"Rattlesnake? That's very threatening."

"It was dead, but still." Sam shuddered, recalling the moment he first saw the viper.

"Well, give her time, and she'll be in Rainee's face. She really has no fear, and she'll try to ruin your life if we don't stop her. Sam, she worked in the administration office! She had access to all our...your information. She had all private numbers, house addresses, Social Security numbers, pension plan info, and the like. She's probably trailing you too. She's a real whack job."

"So, what do we do?" Sam asked with nervousness in his voice. "You think she's dangerous?"

"I think she's looney toons and will do just about anything. We're going to GPD tomorrow. It's going to be a bit embarrassing. We all ended up paying her off. However, blackmail is a crime. Ellis Jenkins paid the most. He almost lost his practice over her. That was his condo that she lives in. But we have to tell the cops and see what they can do to stop her. She might return to one of us or someone new as soon as she's convinced you will never saddle her horse."

"She could suck a golf ball through a garden hose, and I won't even water that horse. I don't want Rainee to know. It was before her, but she doesn't need this drama."

"Yeah, Elizabeth and I are slowly returning to normal, but I have to keep my nose very clean."

"As well you should, Kelton," Sam said.

"Right. OK, meet me at GPD at two thirty tomorrow afternoon. Bring photos of your car and anything else you might have as evidence. We've got to get her locked up or something." He exhaled loudly. "I want to meet this lady of yours. Later, Sam." Dr. Thomas hung up the phone.

Sam sat stunned. Every muscle in his body was tense, and his body was soaked in sweat. "That fuckin' bitch!"

Sam was uncommonly quiet when Rainee joined him nearly three hours later. He had sat at the kitchen bar the entire time contemplating his predicament. First it was Lauren to screw up his life, and now a one-night stand was about to do the same.

"Something wrong?" she asked.

"Nothing I can't handle." He kissed her cheek. "Let's take a ride and get some breakfast in Kemah."

"OK, but I can cook up something here," she said as she sleepily walked to the coffee pot.

"I need to get out and drive Penelope."

"So she has a name?" Rainee laughed.

"I dunno. Just came up with that. Penny is short for Penelope. I paid a pretty penny for her. Well, better than Peggy or Prudence, and certainly beats Pandora." Sam forced a smile.

"What's eating at you?" Rainee asked.

"Oh, I can't keep anything from you. I'll tell you at breakfast. Run, throw on some clothes. Get a headband or scarf. I'm putting down the top."

———————

The bay glistened in the early-morning sunlight. The fall air was cool and refreshing. Sam drove a little faster than Rainee wished, but this time, she would say nothing.

There was the normal weekday crowd at the open-air restaurant. Sam chose a table overlooking the water, and a waiter promptly brought a chalkboard showing the daily fare.

"Benedict's serves only eggs Benedict." Sam read the sign out loud. "Do you want eggs Benedict with fried oysters and shrimp, crawfish, salmon, lobster, or a crab cake?" he asked.

"What? No huevos rancheros?" She giggled.

"Not today, but soon," Sam said, still holding on to his thoughts of the morning phone call.

"Since you seem crabby today, I'll have the crab cake."

Sam looked hard into her eyes. Then he smiled. "You read me so well. And I love that about you." He took a sip of water and ordered two crab cake eggs Benedicts.

Rainee cocked her head. "OK, what's going on in your alleged brain?"

"Alleged?" Sam laughed. "It all happened before I knew you. I was asked to dinner by a hospital employee. I wasn't even divorced yet, but I told her I would come to her house for a homemade meal. The evening was not what I had in mind and turned out rather risqué."

"How so?" Rainee took his hand and smiled lovingly. "Leave out nothing."

Sam smiled at her friskiness, but he soon became somber. He proceeded to tell her what details he could without making it into a pornographic conversation. He then told her about the subsequent phone call from Kelton Thomas.

"I'm angry and ashamed," Sam said as the food arrived. It was hard for him to look Rainee in the eye. He ordered a bottle of champagne from the waiter and then slowly turned to her. "Are you angry or disappointed at how I handled that?"

Rainee took a deep breath. "You got a blow job, and you probably needed it about that time in your life. Just see that something like that never happens again. Only I can touch that part of you."

Sam smiled. A weight the size of the *Titanic's* anchor had been lifted off of him. Rainee continually amazed him, and he knew his love for her was never going to fade but grow stronger with each day.

———————

Rainee insisted on accompanying Sam to the Galveston Police Department. They arrived at the same time as Dr. Kelton Thomas.

"So nice to finally meet you, Dr. Arienzo," Dr. Thomas said after Sam introduced her. "Jenkins and the other two are coming at three o'clock, so we can go on in."

She smiled cordially. "Under better circumstances would have suited me, but I am happy to meet you as well."

The three walked into the station, where two detectives were waiting. They were escorted to a small room with two metal tables and several folding chairs. One of the detectives pulled out the chair for Rainee, and the other motioned for the other doctors to sit down.

"I'm Martinez, and he's Detective Ayers. I'm going to record your statements," said the older detective. "Do you object?"

Sam and Kelton both nodded in agreement.

He turned on the recorder. "You are aware and consent to being recorded. Is that correct?"

They nodded again.

"Please answer with a yes or a no."

"Yes," they replied in unison.

"Please state your name." The detective pointed to Sam.

"Samuel Paul Hawkins."

"And your profession?"

"I am a medical doctor…a surgeon and emergency physician by specialty, and presently head of emergency and trauma at St. Peter's Memorial Hospital. I am on a temporary leave, however. It is a personal issue and has nothing to do with why I am here."

The younger detective then asked about the incidents that they were there to report.

Sam detailed the day that his Porsche had been vandalized, the insurance adjuster's estimate of over $75,000 in damage, the break-in and burglary of his office, the note on his car outside Ana Roberts's house, and the rattlesnake and note at his home. Sam handed him pictures of the beaten sports car and the yellow handwritten notes.

He then was asked to describe his relationship with the woman both men were accusing.

Rainee excused herself, and then Sam gave his detailed account. The detectives never changed their expressions as Sam discussed Brenda Newman's aggressive sexual behavior and assertive demeanor. Sam explained how the evening abruptly ended and how Ms. Newman's anger exploded.

"Is there anything you wish to add?" asked the older detective.

Sam paused. "Only that I'm not the only person affected here. Her terrorizing actions, such as the rattlesnake, put great fear into my girlfriend."

The detectives made note of Sam's comments and then took Dr. Thomas's statement. When they were finished, they assured both doctors that Brenda Newman would be questioned, and if they found just evidence, they would report it to the district attorney. She would most likely be charged with multiple felony crimes.

Sam hugged Rainee when he found her sitting outside on a cement bench. "That was not fun."

"No, but necessary. She has to be stopped." Rainee took Sam's hand and led him to the parked Porsche. "Let's go home."

CHAPTER TWENTY-EIGHT

One week later Sam and Rainee returned to the small villages that El Espino had designated. They followed his orders to set up health care for the residents. It had to be done precisely if they were to stay alive. They had to do all the bidding of the devil, El Espino. But he never showed his face. His men, on the other hand, were always conspicuously present.

Sam and Rainee were contacting charitable medical organizations. Maybe the doctors who gave their time to underprivileged and underdeveloped countries would help them set up more of the medical facilities that Gustavo wanted. He was surely going to ask about the progress soon. They were able to secure a few registered nurses and one nurse practitioner who would travel to Mexico to issue vaccinations and do minor physicals. Two newly graduated doctors agreed to join them before they got their resident matches. It would be an on-again, off-again three-month stint. They had not decided their specialty and had time for a humanitarian cause. Gustavo would pay them well, but the money was of the dirtiest kind. They all would be housed and fed in grand order. The young doctors would never know, and Sam tried constantly to put the source of Gustavo's charitable funds from his mind. He found himself often conflicted. El Espino was a cold-blooded killer. As Rainee always pointed out, he was a drug lord who took advantage of the addicted, the poor, and the young. Sure, some of his cocaine ended up on the tables of the rich and famous, but they were their own worst enemies, and what they did was up to them. The others, the majority of his buyers, were not those who could help themselves. The opioid crisis was everywhere. Crackheads were increasing in huge numbers, and there was no end in sight. Meth was ruining lives of the young who couldn't afford the cheapest of Gustavo's other drugs. Drug addicts were unable to put food on the table when the money all went to their habits—El Espino's gold mine.

It sickened Sam, yet here was El Espino, saving the lives of his own people. Sam had saved and lost hundreds of overdosed patients. How could he justify Gustavo's plans? He and Rainee were a part of the operation that Gustavo had built from others' death, agony, and pain. There was no satisfaction in dwelling on how they had ended up being under Gustavo's thumb. They were there, and the drug lord had full control over their every move. Their efforts, however, were not without some rewards. They found it challenging, yet rewarding, during the brief moments when they forgot how and why they had gotten where they were. Gustavo had set up minimally supplied clinics, but each was adequate to care for children who had never seen a doctor. The drug kingpin was getting recognition from his people. He was like a god to them. He would build schools soon, so as to execute his plan to make the next generation of indigenous Mexicans more self-sufficient and stop the scourge of poverty and ignorance.

Sam knew it was a lofty and perhaps slightly noble plan, and he couldn't help having some empathy for the criminal and murderer. He had become who he was out of ignorance of any other way to make a living, and it had been sheer self-survival. But then, no doubt, it was unmitigated greed that had driven him to the highest position in any cartel. He was the kingpin…the jefe…the boss. Sam and Rainee were doing what they had to do for him for their own survival. Sam thought of Bill Roberts. He had done what he felt was right for liberty and freedom, but in the end, he was no better than a common killer. Everybody does what they have to do, when they have to do it. Sam and Rainee were doing what they had to do, like it or not. Moral compasses don't always point in the same direction when one is desperate.

Rainee, on the other hand, had no time or love lost for the man. She wanted him dead, and before they had to go back to his safe haven and remake his face. But both knew that was unlikely.

They had not yet begun looking for businesses that would legitimize El Espino. And the winery had proven to be almost impossible to find. But they had made some progress meeting his demands. Sam hoped it would be sufficient for the present time.

So, after two weeks in the mountains of Mexico, they returned to Texas and continued to refine their skills by studying and observing Sam's plastic surgeon friend perform his magic. So the surgeon would not question why they were being tutored in plastics, Sam concocted a story. It was that he and Rainee were going to do a trip to Mexico and Central America with other international doctors to repair and reconstruct injuries and help children with malformities. The scheduled date was nearing, and their options were nil. They had a little over a month before they would be summoned to return to change El Espino into a different man. But that difference could only be on the outside. He was who he was, and a new face would never change that.

CHAPTER TWENTY-NINE

A week had passed since Sam and Rainee's return, and the killings had stopped. The news had ceased reporting anything about Simon Reznick, Guidry, and Mr. Z. It had become apparent that the FBI and the State Department had hushed everything up, and what happened to those men was old news. El Espino had eliminated the main people of the Collegium, just as he had vowed.

Sam had temporarily put Brenda Newman aside for other pressing business, but he knew it was constantly in the back of Rainee's mind. It was time to know what was going to happen. He called Kelton Thomas.

"Hey, Kelton. What's the word? I've been out of the country." Sam held his breath for the answer.

"I called Detective Martinez yesterday, as a matter of fact. I was getting a bit anxious without word. I was going to call you tonight. He faxed me the police report about an hour ago. Seems they found all sorts of incriminating stuff at her condo...your pictures with her face glued where someone else's face once was; photos of my house, wife, and kids; stuff that ties her to blackmailing Jenkins and other crimes.

He said there were stacks of yellow legal pads and notes crumpled in the trash. They could see through their specialized forensics where she wrote notes.

"And another thing. This is weird. She has a brother. He's mentally challenged, with about a twelve-year-old's mentality. He confessed to doing all the dirty work. He had taken the picture of me with her in the hospital parking lot, and he had killed the snake that was put at your house. Although he was an accomplice to her deeds, Martinez said that he will most likely not be charged because he does not seem to know right from wrong. The state has taken over, and he will go to some institution. But Brenda has been arrested and is being held under house arrest with leg monitors. Trial is set for after the first of the year. She's out of our lives."

"Until we have to testify," Sam said.

"Yeah, until then. Elizabeth and the kids are standing by me right now, but who knows once it's dragged back through the courtroom and the lesions are reopened? My lawyer is requesting a closed court so the media doesn't get hold of this and we docs get crucified by the press."

"It will be raw and painful. Maybe try to keep your family out of court too. See about them just taking our depositions."

"Certainly, no kids; but I'd never keep Elizabeth out, even a deposition."

Sam made a low moan. "Yeah, I get it. I'm sure I won't keep Rainee out either." He then thought of her and how she seemed to be pulling back from him. *If she is still around*, he thought.

"See you next week?" Kelton asked.

"What's next week?"

"The hospital golf tournament. It's at Memorial County Club. You're playing, right?"

Sam sighed. "Ah, man, I had completely forgotten about that. We'll see. I'll let you know."

"Better do so soon. Tomorrow is the deadline to get a foursome. You can be on my team with the two low-life duffers from Radiology."

Sam laughed. "I'll tell them what you think of their game." It would be fun, but he had other issues to confront, and they were too many and too secret to enumerate to Dr. Thomas.

Rainee had made her plans clear. After they finished what they had to do in Mexico, she would return to Italy. Sam had not been invited during any of the conversations. He had quit his position at the hospital, and there was no reason why he couldn't go with her...but only if she wanted that. They had a passionate relationship, and Sam knew he loved her. She said she loved him too. But she had been strangely distant since their return. Sam had to approach the subject. There needed clarity about their future together. But he knew that clarity and future were in direct contradiction to their reality. How could they plan a future when it was so unstable and so very unsure?

The conversation they had on the plane returning to the States haunted Sam. Rainee had suggested that they were together by fate, and maybe it was not real. She said that she feared that they had clung to each other because of Bill Roberts. He had thrown them together, as a team, to find, read, and act upon his journals. They had followed though as best they could, and they had attached themselves to each other out of pure fear and a need for comfort when there was nothing comforting or safe in their lives. She reminded him that he was newly divorced, and he had been treated very badly by Lauren. Rainee suggested that he was looking for anything to hang his future on. Between his divorce, the Factor-7, and the horrors of Mexico, it was not beyond the realm of possibility that she might be right. He shook his head. No! He was truly in love with her. He wanted to discuss it but was afraid of her response.

Was he ready to marry her? It had not been even six months since they met. And those months were filled with every imaginable fear. All the mental anguish they had endured and all they had witnessed had perhaps permanently changed them both. But they had endured it all together. He couldn't let her go. There could be so much more. There could be a lifetime of happiness ahead of them. But right then, that dark heavy cloud of El Espino loomed ominously over their heads.

He called for her to come out on the deck. She brought two glasses of wine and sat beside him. The evening had always been their favorite time. It couldn't end…not before it had really started.

Sam took her hand. "I've been thinking about what you said on the plane. I think we do have a future together. I know I want that. Maybe we wouldn't have gotten together if it hadn't been for what Bill threw us into, but although I have hated all we have seen and experienced… and what is yet to come…I am thankful to him for forcing us together. It was providence again for me. I love you, and it's not because we needed each other during this conflict. I needed you before I met you. I have needed someone like you all my life. The fates brought us together. I'm not about to let you go now."

Rainee looked at him and then gazed out to the bay. Her pause was long. "I hear what you're saying. I love you too, and I want that future you speak of. I just don't know if now is the time to make any long-term plans."

"If not now, then when? When is the right time for that commitment?" Sam asked. "I told you a long time ago, it doesn't take me long to look at a horseshoe. You didn't know that country saying then…

but you remember it now. I know you do. I knew I loved you from the beginning. You took my heart the first day I saw you. You were exasperating, but you were and are everything I ever wanted or needed. Stay with me."

Rainee took a sip of wine. "I'll give you this right now. If we make it out alive after the surgery on El Espino and we can see some peace in our lives, we will talk about that commitment. Sam, I'm here with you now. You are with me, and neither of us is going anywhere right now. Let's just be content as it is. When we can see into the future without the fears consuming us, as they still do, then we will know what to do." She leaned over and kissed him.

Sam held her closely. "Fair enough. But I'm not letting you go. Remember, never let the *now* ruin the *future*."

———

TWO WEEKS LATER

Sam's cell phone rang. He looked at the time. It was 7:00 a.m. He answered it, although there was no caller ID.

"Hello, Hawkins?" asked the man.

"Yes. Who is this?"

"This is Don Huitt. I need to speak with you."

"If it's about me coming back to the hospital, the answer is no."

"No, it is not about the hospital. I need to see you and Dr. Arienzo. I trust she is with you?"

"OK, what do you need?" Sam asked, not confirming that Rainee was there.

"In person. I'm coming to your house. I'll be there in an hour." Huitt ended the call.

Sam sat up in bed. "Well, that son of a bitch!"

"What's going on?" Rainee asked.

"Don Huitt is coming here in an hour. He didn't give me time to say shit."

Rainee got out of bed and put on a robe. "Well, I better get coffee started."

In exactly one hour, Huitt knocked on the door.

Sam looked out of the window. There were two men with him. He recognized them as the men who were in his office the day they had words. "Auditors, huh?" he said. He opened the door.

Rainee invited them inside and introduced herself.

Huitt unbuttoned his suit coat and pulled a black case from the inside pocket. The other two followed him, doing the same thing. He opened the case. A large gold-colored badge flashed in the sunlight. "I'm not the hospital administrator, Dr. Hawkins. I am the director of the FBI for this district, and these are my associates, Special Agent Williams and Special Agent Mathis. We are here on official FBI business."

Sam and Rainee were speechless. They both stood expressionless for a few moments.

Sam finally found words. "FBI? But…I don't understand."

Huitt began talking. "You see, I've been undercover. I was put into the hospital to watch the surroundings three days after Dr. William Roberts died there. Simon Reznick and Dr. John Albright were there when he died. They had been on our radar. So we knew something was going on in the area. Then you were witness to something. We know that."

"How did you know that?" Sam asked, raising an eyebrow.

"Well, actually not for a few days, but we knew fairly soon that you knew something. So we set up shop in the hospital, as well as other key locations. Please allow me to continue, and you'll understand more. You see, after Dr. Roberts died in your Trauma Department, the CIA, among others, beefed up their probe into the Collegium."

CHAPTER TWENTY-NINE

Sam flinched at his declaration that they knew the Collegium.

"The FBI began our domestic investigation. I ran that federal operation. Houston and surroundings became our focus. I'm director of the Houston field office. My expertise is in intelligence. Our State Department, FBI, CIA, and Justice Department knew about the Collegium, but all information was sketchy. The international community, including MI6, the French DGSE, and the German BND Intelligence Services were watching key figures. Interpol and the OCPW knew about it as well. All agencies involved were very careful to not make it a system-wide investigation. As I said, what we knew was hard to prove, and we had to keep it very quiet because of the potential hostile consequences. If any adversarial governments or splinter radical factions got wind of what these people were doing, any leak would be extremely problematic. So everything—all investigations—were covert. The Collegium was very good at secrecy. Well, half of them were CIA, Mossad, or MI6 trained, so of course, they were good at what they did. They stayed steps ahead of us for years. They had people working with them or at least sympathizing with them from all over the world. They took the name *Keepers* from an ancient society that I am not sure really exists, but they had sympathizers from conspiracy theory factions because of what they called themselves. The first inkling that the Texas area was a hot zone was from information obtained from Steven Roberts. Then Dr. Roberts's death. We knew that the area was holding a den of vipers that communicated with the rest of the reptiles."

Sam's eyes widened. "Bill Roberts's brother, Steven? He was killed in Washington."

"Precisely. As he was leaving a remote rendezvous with our agents and the Brits' operatives. Apparently, he had been tailed for some time, and after that meeting, the Collegium took him out. You see, Dr.

Roberts's brother, Steven Roberts, was playing both ends from the middle. He was telling us about the Collegium and telling the Collegium about us. We're still not sure why he was working with both of us, unless he had been threatened to let them know when we were getting close so they could block us. He had high-level security clearance, so he was valuable to them. Until he wasn't. We had a good idea of his involvement but had to let the plan play out. We had to know who was involved in the labyrinthine organization, but it had to stay covert. They were like a giant multiheaded octopus. They had heads and tentacles all over. We didn't know who to trust."

"Well, we identify with that," Rainee said.

"Well, honestly, we didn't know if we could trust you, Sam."

"What? You didn't think I was involved?"

"At first, we didn't know. But soon, we knew you were just privy to info," Huitt said. "But we couldn't go to you with what we were doing. And to be honest—"

Sam angrily snapped, "Oh, yes, please...let's be honest!"

"I had to see what you really knew," Huitt said.

"That's insane," Sam bellowed.

Rainee stood from her chair. "You mean you let us go into the depths of hell, and you could have stopped it?"

"Dr. Arienzo, please. We didn't know much, nor did we really know the involvement of either of you. We had word that something odd took place when Dr. Roberts died, and he said the word *Collegium*. It was an anonymous caller, but we knew who she was, and we trusted her information."

"Someone from the Trauma Room that morning, huh?" Sam asked indignantly.

Huitt did not reply. "We knew neither of you was directly involved at that point. But we had to follow that lead. You had good information, and we needed it. But because of the sensitivity of the investigation and the possible catastrophe that any leak could create, we had to keep our interest in the matter secret, even to you. If the truth had ever been revealed, it would have been devastating. We had to go deep—even the president could not know, because of the threat it would impose upon the United States and her allies. We are just now piecing it together. Now we're in a better position, and I'm here to let you know where it all stands…at least as much as I am allowed to say…and I believe you have information that will be helpful to us."

Sam interrupted. "Excuse me for saying so, but someone really screwed up. Two presidents have been killed, so I don't see how that was keeping the threat out of the White House."

Huitt breathed deeply. "We can only confirm that President Winger was murdered. And that was probably because Steven and Bill Roberts were contacting him, and he had some idea that there was a nefarious plot happening. Furthermore, he didn't handle the information the way some in the Judicial Branch and the State Department thought that it should be handled, so…I'll leave it right there. That's an ongoing investigation. I am not at liberty…I can say no more." He took a deep breath and exhaled it slowly. "Trust that the president knows enough now, as does Congress and the Senate. The leaders at all levels of government are aware of the threat and what could still exist."

Sam stood up. "Well, if the Congress and Senate know, that means it will leak, you fool. Hey, wait a minute. The president? Hoosier was VP, and he was the one who threatened Bill Roberts…he and Poole. At least that's what was in Bill's journal."

Rainee nodded. "Yes, Dr. Roberts said that in his letters, but I can't recall his exact words. But it was not Winger he said was killed. Winger died after Bill. It was Walther."

Huitt listened but again said nothing.

"Your timeline's fucked up, Huitt," Sam said.

The two men with him were scribbling down Sam's and Rainee's words.

"I know the timeline," he said indignantly. "The president does not necessarily have to know all of the intelligence we have so he has absolution from it and does not have to lie to the American people. Our work is not over. Not by a very long shot. The folks in Washington who are privy to some of this, like the judicial committee, are able to keep information from any staffers or potential whistle blowers. It's always closed door. If there was a leak, it would be taken care of. We always shut them up." Huitt looked intently at Sam and Rainee. "I have not told you this yet, but now is as good a time as ever. You both are strongly advised to never speak a word about any of this to anyone. The only reason I'm here or have told you what I have is because you were privy to what Dr. Roberts's documented. You might know more than we." He stretched his neck. "You would, furthermore, be advised—strongly advised—to not repeat what you just said about President Hoosier and Attorney General Poole. It is for your safety as well as theirs."

Sam grinned facetiously. "That's sounds peculiarly like a threat."

Huitt nodded. "No threat, Dr. Hawkins. It's the law."

Outraged, Sam shook his head and heaved a long breath. "You should have told me all this the day I was in your office—Williamson's office—at the hospital. I would have steered away and been quiet too. Instead, we were your pawns, so to speak." He pointed to Rainee. "She could have been killed. We both could have been. And you are the one who hacked into my computer or you had it done."

Huitt remained calm. "I know your frustration, but if you had known who I was, you would not have followed the clues that I know you received from Dr. Roberts the morning that he died. No, I did not hack your computer. I don't know anything about that. You have my word. We needed you to get the information, but we didn't go to your computer for it. Personally, I didn't think you were that stupid to put information on a computer that anyone at the hospital could access. We needed your knowledge. We couldn't get that without drawing attention to the investigation. Among that information is, of course, the journals. We needed his documentation. We didn't know where Roberts hid it. We surmised one of you had that information. We knew something was happening when you teamed up. Our agents were in the middle of our investigation of the Collegium group. If you had made a mistake and they found out about us, it would have blown the operation. We couldn't take that chance. I know now, after what you have seen and read, that you realize the international threat that disclosure would have caused. So, we need those journals now."

"Sacrificial lambs. You would have sacrificed us if it would have furthered your investigation or was beneficial." Sam shook his head. "Well, whatever. Just thanks a lot for nothing." He paused and gathered his thoughts. "I'm sure we do have information, but only from Dr. Roberts. We read his journals, but..." Sam paused and looked at Rainee. "They were stolen in Mexico."

"Stolen?" Huitt barked angrily. "You're lying. Do I need a search warrant?"

"We're telling you the truth. I swear. We don't know who the thugs were, but we no longer have the journals," Rainee said. "They took jewelry and money too. Then they dumped us on some dark road."

Sam glanced at Rainee as if to say, "Good thinking!"

"Well, I'm very disappointed." Don Huitt stared at Sam and Rainee incredulously. "We needed everything in those journals. Well, I trust that you can confirm a few things," Huitt said, showing annoyance that he couldn't get what he had obviously come to retrieve. He began to ask Sam and Rainee questions.

Sam confirmed that Simon Reznick, Guidry, and Z, among others, were all mentioned, and he gave as much detail as he could recall. He provided information on how the virus was to kill and how it was to be delivered. He wanted to tell Huitt that they knew that the murders of the members of the Collegium had not been by terrorists or murder/suicide or any of the other lies that had been reported, but he wasn't going to show his hand until he knew what cards Huitt was going to play and maybe not even then. The conversation continued for over two hours while Sam and Rainee took turns recalling details of what Bill had revealed in his journals. But they took care to not mention Gustavo Galvan. El Espino would surely eliminate them if they exposed him.

Huitt seemed satisfied with the information. He retained the opportunity to talk to them again and even hinted that one of his superiors might order a search of Sam's property. As he stood, preparing to leave, he said, "The head of the snake has been cut off. We feel confident that the Collegium has dismantled their plans...at least for now." He smiled. "We'll take it from here."

Sam huffed, showing his doubt. "Good luck."

Rainee touched his arm. Her eyes told him to shut up.

He knew the look but couldn't hold his tongue. He had witnessed what the Houston director of the FBI had not. Sam and Rainee had been warned of things that Huitt had possibly not even considered. Sam told Huitt that Dr. Roberts had made many entries in his notes that the Collegium was international, and they had holes all over the world in which to hide. Huitt had acknowledged, but quickly dismissed, Sam's advice.

"One more thing that might set your minds at rest. We found Dr. John Albright's rent car at the Laredo International Airport. We can confirm he's dead." Huitt turned to his two associates who nodded in agreement.

"John Albright is dead? How?" Sam asked, trying to not show his skepticism.

"There was no body, but we have a probable DNA match. He was apparently brutally murdered inside the car and his body dragged away. There was too much of his blood at the scene, so it's highly unlikely he could have lived through such an attack. We got hair and nail samples that matched. His belongings, including driver's license and credit cards were in the car. It was an atrocious attack. He won't be bothering you again."

Sam looked at Rainee. "Well, that's good news."

Huitt remained emotion free and laid his card on the table. "Use the cell number. Day or night, if you remember something."

The following morning, Sam was awake when Rainee rolled over to him.

She gave him a loving nudge. He seemed deeply in thought. "What's on your mind?" she whispered.

"I dreamed all night. I was back in the Trauma Room, and Bill was on the gurney. I kept hearing the words he said. I saw his face so clearly. It was unnerving."

"It was a bad dream. Probably because of Don Huitt yesterday. You had to relive it all."

"Yeah, but I kept hearing Bill say 'All right.' That was the last thing I heard him say that morning."

"Well, again, a bad dream."

"A bad dream, but I think I now know what he said. He didn't say 'All right.' He said 'Albright.' I saw him say it last night in my dream. His face was in anguish. If he thought things were all right, maybe all right for him to die, why so much fear and anguish? No! He told me, 'Albright.' I'm sure of it now. He was warning me about John Albright!"

Rainee sat up and kissed Sam's forehead. "No more worries. John Albright's dead, and all his horrific deeds died with him."

Sam kissed her back. "Don't I wish?"

"Why do you say that? It's over, at least, for us. The head of the snake's been cut off, using Huitt's terminology." She rolled her eyes. "All we have to tend to is El Espino, the snake killer, and that's huge." She groaned, thinking about what they would encounter in Mexico. "Don't fret over Albright. He's gone. Let Huitt and all the others tend to the Factor-7."

Sam nodded and hugged Rainee. "Well, it's clear that Huitt slipped up and verified that both presidents had been assassinated. He tried to cover it, but the cat was already out of the bag."

Rainee agreed. "But it's over for us. Let them handle it."

He wasn't convinced about anything, but he kept quiet so as to not distress her with his remaining fears.

It was almost noon by the time Sam retrieved the Sunday newspaper. Hidden on the back pages was a short story. Nine people in Friendswood, a small community near NASA, had died over the weekend from an unidentified virus. They were all members of the same family. They listed their names. They all had the last name of Al Kaman. The official story was that they had contracted the unknown virus while traveling to the Middle East for Ramadan celebrations. He told Rainee about the article.

"That's what they will claim to avoid mass hysteria. Did you expect anything else?" She frowned. "Nine innocent souls who just happened to have the right DNA are dead from the cloud of germs that floated into the sky after the explosion. Just more fallout…more gone, and their deaths will not be avenged. There will be no justice for them. Only one cover-up after another." Rainee buried her head in her hands. "It sickens me."

Sam's phone rang. It was Huitt.

"I realize that you know a lot and probably more than you told me, but I am advised to tell you again that this entire ordeal is top secret.

You are required by law, and for your own safety, to never speak of this to anyone, at any time. We are handling the threat, and you and Dr. Arienzo are relieved of any involvement." Huitt was firm and to the point. "I trust you understand the gravity of this."

Sam didn't answer for a moment, weighing his thoughts. "Yes, we get it. I told you that. But don't you know, with as many people you said that are working, ah…covertly"—Sam huffed at the thought—"that there will be leaks? There always are."

"And we will handle that as we always do," Huitt replied resolutely.

"You'll say it's some whacko conspiracy theory. You'll make some far-fetched statement to the mainstream media that the story was made up by some foreign government or fringe group. You'll cover it up. Or maybe you just kill them to shut them up! Is that what you guys do?"

"All I'm telling you is that you are ordered to secrecy. It is national security, Dr. Hawkins."

"Why are you telling me again? We get that. We've known that for months. We've known that probably before you," Sam shouted.

"See that you do." The call ended.

Sam looked at Rainee. "That was Huitt. He all but threatened us if we leak anything that we know or we suspect. He must have higher-ups on his ass for something to feel the need to call us today."

Rainee poured another cup of coffee. "He was rather candid at times yesterday. It's the nine deaths. He knows we know. One cover-up after another. But we will be the last people to leak."

Sam mumbled, "One lie always leads to another lie."

CHAPTER THIRTY

The jet was sitting on the tarmac when Sam and Rainee arrived. The well-starched pants waited at the terminal door. He took their bags and led them to the waiting plane. A young woman welcomed them on board. It was déjà vu as they sat in the same seats they had on the flight five months earlier. Sam ordered two Bloody Marys and huevos rancheros with extra hot sauce. Rainee only ordered food. She knew she would drink one of Sam's cocktails.

El Espino had arranged for the jet. Upon landing in San Miguel de Allende, he had instructed them to take a taxi to the center of town. He had arranged their hotel room as well. The next morning, his men would transport them to the unknown destination. Everything had been arranged, and nothing was to be changed or further discussed.

"We welcome you on board this morning. We will be landing in San Miguel de Allende in three hours. Please enjoy the flight."

Rainee leaned back her seat. "Enjoy," she hissed.

Neither Sam nor Rainee could relax. They knew what they were up against. But they had done their homework and knew if all went right, Gustavo Galvan would soon have a new face and a new identity. Ever since Dr. Bill Roberts's death, they had been on the run in some form or another. It had taken drastic tolls on their minds and bodies. They were perhaps seventy-two hours away from their freedom.

When they reached the public square, El Jardin, in the center of San Miguel de Allende, the Christmas decorations amazed Sam and Rainee.

The center of town and the square were in full Christmas mode. There were red-and-green banners flying from all the high points of the Parroquia. The old cathedral bells were playing Christmas music that the local people knew but which Sam and Rainee had never heard. Nevertheless, they thought it was stunningly beautiful. There were dancers in bright costumes and Santa Claus men walking around passing out candy to the children. Their costumes had seen better days, but their laughter and joy filled the air with Christmas spirit.

Their room was still being cleaned, so they found a table in the al fresco café at the hotel. The wait staff were adorned with Santa hats, and the bartender was dressed as an elf, right down to his green turned-up pointed-toe shoes. There was celebration everywhere, but none of it annoyed Sam and Rainee. Even the children running by and throwing confetti on the tables made them smile.

They had become engrossed in the festivities and had, for a brief time, forgotten why they were there. But when a man walked by and laid a white envelope on their table, the reality of their visit resurfaced like a bad dream.

Sam opened the envelope and read it to Rainee. "There will be a black Suburban in front of your hotel at exactly six thirty a.m.

tomorrow. Everything is ready for your arrival. Please be there on time. You will be El Espino's guest for at least the next four days." It was signed Jorge Villa Lobos. Sam put the note in his pocket. "Ugh. Four days in that makeshift mansion."

Rainee smiled. "Did you expect anything other than that?"

Sam shook his head. "No. Just have to complain a bit."

"You know, Jorge never told us his last name. Villa Lobos—place or house of the wolves." She shivered as if she had a chill.

"The Big Bad Wolf, I'd say," he replied.

The alarm on Sam's phone buzzed them awake at 5:00 a.m. Coffee and pastries were to be delivered to the room at 5:15. Sam took his shower first, as he was in and out, and she took a while to get ready in the mornings. Each knew the other's routine now, and it never needed to be discussed. It was simply understood. They stepped onto the outside sidewalk at exactly 6:25 a.m. The Suburban must have been waiting for them down the street, because it pulled up at the same time.

There was only the driver inside. He got out and walked around the car. He opened the back-seat door and motioned with his hand for them to enter. They did, and he closed the door behind them. Nervously, they buckled their seat belts. They were willingly going with him this time, but the past was still on their minds, and the horrors they had endured were still raw. The driver pulled out onto the empty street. He went about a block on the other side of the square and then into a long drive-way that led to the back of an abandoned restaurant. Out of the darkness walked a man in a black suit. He got in the front seat. It was Jorge.

"Good morning, Doctors," he said with a rare smile. "Thank you for being so prompt and for coming as you were asked. El Jefe has sent his regards and is eager see you." He turned around and smiled again. "I trust you had a nice evening. The town is ready for the blessed birth." He made the sign of the cross and then kissed his fingers.

Rainee whispered in Sam's ear. "Who is this man?"

Jorge overheard and laughed kindly. "I am a nice man, unless I am otherwise."

Sam smiled at Rainee and rolled his eyes. "Unless otherwise," he said. "I like that, Jorge. I'm not, unless I am." The three laughed together, but it was without the sentiment of genuine frivolity.

Jorge looked at the driver and said something quietly in Spanish.

The driver handed him two black blindfolds.

"Please put these over your eyes. You are safe, but our destination is known by no one, and we will keep it that way." He handed them to Sam. "Please now, do as I ask." His voice was calm and kind. His demeanor perplexed Sam and Rainee. He was a different man than they had seen just a few months before. But it was a welcome change. "We will have lunch ready for you when you arrive. El Jefe will not be joining you, as he said your instructions were very clear. Nothing to eat or drink."

Rainee said, "Or smoke."

"That I cannot guarantee," Jorge said softly.

Sam winced and whispered, "Can't guarantee much from El Jefe... the big boss man."

There was little conversation while they traveled. Although unable to see anything the first time and nothing now, Sam remembered some of the sharp turns and the sensation of going up a mountain. His ears would sometimes pop, indicating the change in altitude. But what he remembered best was the turn onto the dusty road. He recalled that the first time, the smell of dirt had filled the interior, and the ride had become profoundly rougher. Moments later, he knew they were at their destination. He felt around for Rainee's hand. "I think we're here."

She simply moaned affirmatively.

The SUV stopped. The front door opened, and Jorge had apparently stepped out. Indistinguishable voices of men outside were all Sam and Rainee heard. Sam figured they waited an unbearable fifteen minutes before Jorge returned.

When he finally opened the doors of the back seat, he kindly said that they could remove their blindfolds. "Please follow me."

Although the intense fear they had previously experienced had likely skewed his memory, there were a few points of the previous trip that Sam recalled. But there was one thing that was seared into his memory and probably would be for eternity. It was the Danger sign that he remembered the most. His palms began to sweat as he relived the terror of that day when he had seen Rainee disappear into the darkness.

Jorge motioned for them to follow him.

Sam gathered himself and made sure Rainee was emotionally capable of following the man in charge, and then they began walking. Rainee seemed impervious to the surroundings, but Sam knew she was remembering the same horrors. Her nonexpression and stoic gait were nothing more than a ruse, and Sam knew it. He pulled her close. His felt her taut body and her heart beating in her chest.

They entered the darkness, then passed into the light. Jorge led them down the well-polished halls that were the caverns once used to extract silver. Now they were in the underground mansion and refuge of El Espino. Sam recalled the décor and the sculptures as they descended deeper into the old mine.

This time, Jorge took them both into a finely appointed room. There was a large marble dining table and twelve gilded chairs. There was a crystal chandelier above it, which illuminated the silver serving dishes and chargers, set for two. A man in a white coat and chef's hat stood in the corner.

"Your lunch will be in here. Please enjoy." Jorge pointed to the table and then motioned graciously for them to sit down.

They obliged.

The door closed, and they heard a lock click. They were still prisoners, although this time, they were being treated almost as royalty. The chef nodded. He set a silver terrine on the tray that lay in the middle of the table. He asked in fairly competent English if they wished to have his lobster bisque.

Rainee nodded at the chef. Then she looked at Sam. "I bet El Espino flew them in for us."

"Maybe from Cozumel," Sam said.

"I'd like to go there someday."

Sam shook his head. "Resorts are probably OK, but you still have the cartel problem."

"El Espino wants to change that." Rainee took a few sips of the soup.

"It may a bigger problem than even he can fix. Remember, you can't set buzzard eggs and hatch canaries. Mexico's semi-socialist government has not cared for their people in hundreds of years. The rich stay very wealthy and the poor are poor and can't get out of that poverty trap. Even education is limited. This government's intentional lack of necessities and education keeps their people suppressed. There has been a growth in middle class but still—it's like Espino said, his people are trapped. Without education or access to a good job and money— all they can do is what their parents, grandparents and so on did—stay impoverished or leave the country. The US can't take all of them. Some turn to crime, as we well know." Sam looked around the room and raised an eyebrow. "As long as the cartels can make their big money, Columbia and other Central American countries supply them, the government of Mexico and the US don't stop them and the demand remains high for their services, there will, most certainly, not be any canaries."

"Don't forget *los soboros*," Rainee said. "Without bribes, they couldn't stay in business in any country."

"We called it mordida. That's slang, but that's the sum of it." Sam shook his head. "Yeah, it's a bad deal. Money talks for sure."

Soon the chef brought two small whole fish. The fish were the ugliest Rainee had ever seen. The mouths were open, showing sharp teeth that looked horribly intimidating. It reminded her of the alien in the same movie as its name, or perhaps a gremlin, but certainly not something of this earth that she wished to eat. The sides of the creature were scored, exposing white meat. The chef laid small pieces on their plates. He continued to detach the meat from the many bones until the wretched skeleton of some fish from hell appeared. Once completed, he opened a silver bowl that had been warming over canned heat and served tiny potatoes and various colored squash. He bowed and walked away.

"What the hell is that?" Rainee touched the fish.

"Humm. I've never eaten it, but I think it's piranha. I think they're abundant in Columbia. Supposed to be good."

"Well, I don't know about this," she replied with a disgusted expression. "Probably came in with one of his cocaine shipments."

Sam mimicked her distressed face. "Wouldn't say that too loudly… eyes and ears are everywhere. Anyway"—Sam picked up the now-naked fish bones—"it's all in the presentation."

———

Soon Jorge returned. He led them into a small white room that had obviously been prepared specifically for the surgery. New air filtration units had been installed, and it was a very cool sixty-two degrees Fahrenheit. The room was sterile. The furnishings and medical equipment were apparently new.

Jorge told them that he would be right outside if he was needed.

Sam and Rainee started to inventory the items. They found everything they had requested. Rainee set out three sealed bags of glucose and then hung one on the IV pole. A rolling table was put on each side of the adjustable bed, which also had wheels. Sam would work on one side and Rainee the other. There were sterile sheets and pads, a blood pressure monitor, a machine that made oxygen from ambient air, an electrocardiograph, and a heart monitor. El Espino had also bought a defibrillator at Sam's request—just in case. Ideally, the two doctors would have an equipped crash cart, which would contain everything needed in the event of an emergency. But Sam was a MacGyver when it came to improvisation in an emergency. After all, he had spent twenty-six years treating emergencies, twenty of those at a level-one trauma medical facility. He surveyed the supplies and equipment. It would suffice, even in an urgent situation.

Rainee opened boxes of sterile surgical gloves, shoe covers, and masks for each of them. The various-size scalpels and scissors were new and were in a sterilization unit. Everything was high quality and medical grade. But of course, money was no object for the Mexican drug lord.

El Espino had gotten the correct sizes of numerous syringes and hypodermic needles.

Sam reached into his bag and retrieved the items that they had brought from the United States. He wasn't sure that the implants that they needed or had seen used in the surgeries they had observed would be available, or of the quality they needed. Sam and Rainee had discussed the antibiotics and were convinced it wiser to bring that also. In the event of an emergency, they brought atropine and epinephrine.

Rainee set all the supplies in their proper positions and connected the intravenous lines to the bags.

Sam took out two bags containing liquid antibiotics.

Rainee filled six syringes with lidocaine and laid them on a sterile pad. However unlikely, the local anesthetic was in case he felt pain during the surgery. But they had a special cocktail planned.

Sam filled two syringes with Versed, the drug they would use to put El Espino to sleep but not render him unconscious. He added fentanyl to the intravenous line for pain. El Espino would not feel any pain or remember anything if he did. He would breathe on his own throughout the entire procedure. Sam covered the syringes with a sterile cloth.

Rainee laid out two white cups and placed a 20 mg Valium tablet in each. She poured a small amount of water into another cup.

They were ready for the patient.

The large man they had once feared as much as the Collegium and its viral weapon was now lying on the surgical table and completely at their mercies. But Jorge and a small army of men sat right outside the door. They were ready to do whatever, if the need arose, to ensure the safety of El Espino.

Rainee handed their patient the white cup with one of the Valiums inside. She gave him the water, instructing him to drink only as much as he needed to swallow the pill. He lay back on the bed as the two surgeons inserted the IV into his left arm. The fluids began to flow properly. Rainee put the blood pressure cuff on his right arm so it could be monitored throughout the likely two-hour surgery.

Thirty minutes later, El Espino had not relaxed as much as Sam would have liked. He gave him another Valium, knowing that the heavyset man would well tolerate the larger dose.

Rainee listened to his chest and abdomen. The sounds were what she wanted. They put a tube into his nose for supplemental oxygen.

Sam placed a mouth guard into El Espino's mouth. Then he nodded at Rainee. The patient was asleep, and it was time to inject the Versed.

Rainee pushed the needle into the IV, and the fluids with the sedative flooded into him.

Sam held his stethoscope on his heart while the drug took him into a deeper sleep. Sam nodded again. "OK, he's ready. Let's do this."

Rainee made a thin incision at the hairline just above his right ear. Sam did the same on his left side. They ran the incision to his forehead, where they met in the center. Each stretched back the skin, getting the tautness they wanted. Once they were satisfied that the skin was tight and the desired lift of his brow line was achieved, they snipped off the excess skin and placed staples in the hairline.

Sam cleaned the incision and wrapped gauze around his upper forehead.

Rainee then made a very thin cut on each of his upper eyelids. Again, the excess skin was removed, and she put surgical glue on the thin cut.

Sam made a long, thin incision under each eye. Carefully, he removed a narrow bag of fat. That incision again was closed with surgical glue. "OK, already ten years younger." Sam grinned as he picked up a new blade.

"OK, Sam, nice work on the forehead and the blepharoplasty," Rainee said, playfully complimenting her fellow surgeon and lover. "Now for the big changes in his appearance. Just making him look ten years younger won't do." She smiled at Sam.

"Onward through the fog, my dear." Sam suggested they start from the top and work down. They would implant the cheeks first. Sam removed the mouth guard and filled the areas between El Espino's gums and teeth with rolled gauze. He then cut the inside top of his lip just under the nose. The incision ran from the corner of his mouth on the inside to the opposite corner. Sam made an opening to the cheek area. The implants were pushed into place through the opening from inside the mouth to his cheek. First the right implant was done, and then the left. Sam stood back to look at his work. "Not bad. Your turn."

Rainee was going to place the jaw implants next. This would alter the shape of his face and should make a substantial difference in his appearance and profile. She studied her angles, feeling his jawline and neck. Suddenly her expression changed. "Sam, come around here, please."

Sam walked around the back of the bed to where Rainee was standing. He saw her feeling Espino's neck just below his ear.

"Feel that," she whispered.

Sam repeated what Rainee had just done. He looked at her and shook his head.

"It's a tumor...hard...wrapped around the carotid, right?" she asked.

"Yeah, and what I can feel on the outside is about twenty centimeters long. Not good."

"Malignancy, most likely," she whispered again. "It's hard and it's big. It doesn't feel like a fatty tumor. Now that I'm looking, I can see it protruding on his neck. I never saw it before, but we weren't looking for it either."

"No, it's not a fatty for sure and it's not a node...a no-node." Sam winced and bit his lip. "Cubans got him." It was not time to try to be funny, but he couldn't contain himself.

Rainee shook her head. Neither had any love lost for the criminal, but it seemed wrong to make jokes when he was apparently very ill.

"All right, you think we should tell him and advise him on what he should do?" Sam asked.

"No. Are you nuts? We can't. You know why. And you know the possible outcome if we did. We can't be that foolish."

Sam acknowledged what she had said. "Yeah, he'd both blame us and then kill us, or he'd make us stay and treat him, which would almost be as bad as death."

Rainee nodded. "Let's get this over with." She reached for her scalpel. She made a small tunnel to the jaw line, using the incision Sam had made through the upper lip. Each jaw implant was placed. She then made an incision inside the lower lip and inserted the chin appliance.

Sam sewed the upper and lower interior lips with dissolving sutures. "Hope he has a case of straws."

"Sam, you're having too much fun," she said.

"No, just trying to keep my sanity in this insane environment."

The last thing was his nose, and that would be the most tedious. Sam glanced at the clock on the wall. They had had him under the Versed for an hour and fifteen minutes. He pushed another few ccs into his vein.

The nose that they planned would be very different from El Espino's natural one, but more aesthetically pleasing. Rainee had suggested a Roman nose. El Espino had statues of Roman gods and busts of Caesar all around his underground hideaway. The new nose would be thinner, yet longer. It would change his entire face but fit correctly with the other implants. He should be well pleased with that look.

When the surgery was finished, they wrapped his entire head and neck with gauze. Only a small slit was left for him to see and to drink liquids through a straw.

Sam set up the last bag of antibiotics and started them to flow into Espino. "He'll be asleep for a while longer. Just rest until he wakes up."

In about forty-five minutes, the drug lord began to rouse. He moaned a few shallow sounds, going in and out of sleep. Sam and Rainee talked to him until he was awake enough to open his eyes.

Rainee bent down, close to his face. "It's over. You did very well."

He grunted. "Am I as handsome as Brad Pitt?"

Rainee took his hand. "More."

He attempted a laugh, but the pain was too intense.

"We're going to give you something for pain. Jorge will take you to your room. We will be near and check on you throughout the night," Sam said authoritatively.

El Espino tried to nod but only could move a small bit. He wiggled his fingers as if to say that he was ready to go.

Jorge and two men wheeled the bed into the hallway. Sam and Rainee walked behind the bed. El Espino snored, and one of the men laughed. Jorge scolded him. He immediately resumed his serious demeanor, obviously afraid of El Espino's right-hand man.

The large room was dark and cool. The bed was turned down to reveal the GEG monogram on the sheets and pillowcases. There were two women dressed in white waiting for them. A man dressed in a long black robe sat in the corner of the room by a lighted candle. He did not look up when the group entered the room.

The two men lifted El Jefe, as Jorge called him, onto the bed. The women pulled the sheets and the down comforter to his chest.

He was sleeping quietly. Sam and Rainee stayed for another hour monitoring his breathing, heart rate, and blood pressure.

The man, who was obviously a priest, was now in a chair on the right side of the bed. He held a rosary and silently prayed. At one point, he looked at Sam and Rainee.

Rainee spoke to the priest in Spanish. She assured him that El Espino would be fine.

The priest nodded and said, in Spanish, that El Jefe was the benefactor for many of his parishioners, and they were all praying for him.

Rainee said, "He says that Gustavo helps many people, and they are praying for him."

Sam slightly smiled. "So am I."

Rainee knew he was being flippant but was speaking with some seriousness. If El Espino died under their watch, it was certain they would be next.

———————

The evening came, although there was no change in the lighting in the old mine. It was impossible to tell day from night except with a clock or wristwatch.

Jorge returned. "I will show you to your room. You will eat there, and I will come for you again later to check on El Jefe."

Sam nodded, and they followed Jorge down a long hallway. He turned left into a short passage. It was well-honed-out rock, as was the rest of the hideaway. He unlocked a door, which opened to a very large room. It was as large as most one-bedroom apartments. There was a small well-equipped kitchen, a living room with an electric burning fireplace, a large TV, a stereo system, and a gaming table. A bar with glass shelves holding any and every type of top-shelf liquor was set against the wall. Brandy decanters were placed on the bar, as was chilled champagne. There were three bottles of white Bordeaux chilling in ice and three bottles of cabernet next to them. There was a tray of various cheeses and fresh vegetables on the bar, next to an iced bowl of very black caviar. Chopped boiled eggs, capers, and finely diced red onions surrounded it. French baguette pieces were in a silver basket.

Jorge showed them the bedroom. Their bags were on a bench near the bathroom. "There are no cameras in this room. If you need anything, push that button, and someone will be here." He pointed to a speaker and button by the entry door.

Sam nodded. "We need to check on El Espino in three hours or if needed."

Jorge acknowledged and left the room.

They heard the door lock again from the outside. Rainee collapsed onto a leather sofa as Sam fixed plates of the goodies supplied by their warden.

The chef who had served them lunch delivered dinner. He loitered in the corner as they ate.

After the dinner had been completed, he wheeled the table from the room. Again, the door locked as he exited.

"We won't go hungry," Sam said.

"I hope it's not feeding the proverbial fatted calf," Rainee said. "I still don't trust any of them."

"And well you shouldn't," Sam said. He poured a cognac. "Want one?"

She held her fingers about two inches apart. "A little."

They knew they had to check on El Espino in a few hours, so the evening dragged on. They were tired and weary of the entire situation. But they were his guests and his prisoners.

"I've been thinking," Sam said. "How do you feel about not going right back to Houston?"

Rainee looked at him with pure skepticism. "Oh, shit. What?"

"It's not bad, so relax. What if we just flew straight to British Columbia from here? I can get Jorge...well maybe...to arrange for us to go straight to Vancouver."

"And why would we do that? It's rainy and cold and dark there this time of year." Rainee was annoyed at the thought.

"Just thinking."

Rainee smiled and touched his hand. "That's dangerous. Anytime you're '*just thinking*', I get worried."

Sam smirked. "No, really. Ana's there, and she should be moved in by now. Just thinking we should see her."

"All right. In the spring, if we make that commitment we discussed." Rainee stared at Sam.

"I think now. And I think we should make that commitment. That discussion about us not staying together is just plain stupid. I've made my commitment to you, and I'll keep it forever."

"What are you not telling me?" She playfully put a stranglehold on his neck.

"I'm telling you that I love you and want the rest of my life with you." Sam took her hand. "I mean that."

Rainee looked into his eyes. She took a cleansing breath. "Well, our journey's been rough, and the future is uncertain, but I won't let the now ruin the future. I love you too, and I will spend my life with you. Hell, a team like ours shouldn't be separated. We're damn good together." She smiled.

Sam gave her a long hug, holding her as tightly as he could. "I will never let you down or let you go," he whispered.

Rainee pulled away, smiling. "So what about this trip to Canada? What's eating at you?"

"I can't do anything without you figuring me out," Sam said.

Rainee looked at him without saying anything. Her eyes widened, as if telling him that she needed an answer.

"All right. I think Ana was the informant to the FBI." Sam took a deep cleansing breath. "It had to be her."

"Why? You said she didn't know anything." Rainee shook her head. "Oh, come on. I doubt it. That little lady knew nothing."

"Well, after Huitt's visit, I figure it's either Sandra or Ana. Sandra would have no reason to talk to the FBI, and Ana was the only one who knew most of what I knew before we went to Mexico. And she told Simon we went. It just makes sense."

Rainee sat quietly for a few moments, thinking of what Sam had told her. "So you think she'll tell you if you go there? And if she *was* the one, what will that accomplish?"

"I don't think she's involved. But knowing the truth and the rest of the story, so to speak, will bring some closure for me. I need to see a finish. I need to know what she knows and how she knows it. Has she deceived me all those days after Bill's death? I asked her over and over, and she denied knowing anything. If she lied to me, I want to know why. I don't know. It sounds crazy when I verbalize it. But yes, it's eating at me, for sure."

Rainee gazed off, considering her reply. "I get that. But what will you do if she tells you that she knew?"

"Well, she did know a lot. I told her a lot, actually."

"You want to be sure she didn't betray you. You thought of her as a second mother. That betrayal hurts. I get it. OK, if you think it's something that will set your mind at rest, let's go. But Sam, it's not going to change one thing." Rainee poured another cognac. She held the glass to the light, peering into it as if it were a crystal ball. "This liquor won't change anything either. We're still locked up."

Sam and Rainee checked Espino three times that night. Neither slept. They knew that the most critical hours were the first twenty-four. Although rather invasive multiple surgeries were done, it was standard practice for a patient to go home to recover. El Espino was no ordinary patient. Every moment, Sam and Rainee knew that his recovery, and his contentment with the results, was their passport to freedom. If that didn't happen, it would be their death sentence.

They passed the days, as he healed, locked in their luxurious cell. They wanted for nothing except their freedom. They watched movies, read magazines, and ate. A lot of the time was spent with Rainee beating Sam at poker. But mostly they thought.

Rainee thought of what she would do when it was over and they could start over with the normality of their lives.

Sam, on the other hand, couldn't materialize the thought of ever being free of the curse, Factor-7. They were locked in an old silver mine with some of the world's most wanted. And the Factor-7 had, indirectly, put them there. He thought of Ana and how she was possibly the informant. Perhaps she had found something, or maybe she just put the dots together and began to see the bigger picture, a portrait of her husband, the man who would have been a mass murderer.

The original four days that they were to stay with El Espino had turned into seven. He had not healed as quickly as they had hoped, and he had requested they stay until all the bandages and nose packing could be removed. He had begun to be able to chew soft foods and had requested a cigar. Although he did not know about his tumor, under the circumstances and the degree of seriousness with it, Dr. Hawkins and Dr. Arienzo could not refuse him his Cubans.

The morning of the seventh day, Sam and Rainee took off all his bandages. Sam slowly pulled the gauze packing from inside his newly shaped nose. Rainee handed him a mirror for the first time.

El Espino stood from his chair. He stared for a long time into the mirror at his new reflection. He had some remaining bruising and swelling, but the new face was easy for him to see. "Doctors, I am pleased," he said with a loud, enthusiastic voice. "Yes, this is good. Si, es muy bueno." He threw his arms into the air. "Bravo! Well done!"

Jorge was in the room and smiled agreeably, and then he nodded at Sam and Rainee. "Yes, it is good, and he is pleased. Please come with me."

El Espino attempted a smile, but his face was still too swollen and tight to exhibit much more than a small upward motion of the sides of his newly enhanced lips. He lifted his hand and waved a cordial good-bye. "I will see you one more time today," he said.

They followed Jorge back to the large dining room where they had eaten the day of the surgery. The same chef stood in the corner of the room. Jorge motioned for him to serve. He opened a domed tray.

"Chef heard you say that you liked huevos rancheros, so he has made them for you today," Jorge said.

Sam nodded agreeably. "Yes, thank you."

Rainee however, was not so enthused. She asked for him to pour her a glass of orange juice and coffee with cream.

Jorge motioned again to the chef, who lifted a silver dome from the second tray on the table. "Perhaps you prefer eggs Benedict."

Rainee smiled. "Yes, thank you. I would." She whispered to Sam, as Jorge left the room, "If I never see or hear huevos rancheros again… it will be too soon."

Sam smiled. "Oh, beans."

———————

Jorge returned about an hour later.

Sam and Rainee were finishing their coffee, and she picked at a pastry. They stood when he entered the room.

"We want to know if you are ready to leave," Jorge said.

"Yes, yes," Rainee spouted, a little more enthusiastically than she had planned.

"We have a driver to take you to the airport in Mexico City. You will fly on a commercial jet back to Houston. Or you can wait to take the private jet tomorrow. It is not available until then."

Sam spoke quickly. "No, commercial is fine. Thank you."

Jorge led them back to their quarters and advised them that he would return in an hour.

Sam and Rainee gathered their belongings, except for all the medical items they had brought. They placed those on the kitchen counter, rather glad to be rid of the need for them.

As promised, Jorge returned precisely in an hour. He led them back to El Espino.

The large man was now sitting at a vanity, admiring his new features. "Please come in," he said. "I am very happy with my new face. I will tell you that I am also changing my name. I am now Leondro de Estrellas." He tried to smile. "Do you like my name?"

Rainee smiled back. "Leon of the Stars, in English. Yes, very nice name."

The Mexican man nodded. "Yes, it is a very fitting name for a man who is changed. A star of hope, perhaps. A star of light for my people."

Sam swallowed hard. The prose that El Jefe had recited almost nauseated him. The drug lord was no Messiah. But Sam gathered himself and forced a compliment.

Espino stood and walked closely to Sam and Rainee. He reached out his hand and softly took Rainee's arm. "I thank you very much." He took Sam's arm. "Thank you for everything. You have done much to help with the changes in my life. I am now able to see my family without threat. You have changed my life."

He motioned for Jorge to get something.

Jorge reached below the bed and retrieved a large black leather suitcase and a gold-colored box. He laid the case on the bed and handed the box to his patron, his boss.

Leondro de Estrellas, as it would now be, lowered his head to the doctors. "I have much gratitude. I hope I am your friend. Please..." He opened the box and pulled out two suede pouches. He handed one to each of the doctors. "Please open my gift to you."

They each pulled open the string and pulled out matching gold-and-diamond crosses. Each cross hung from a beautifully braided gold chain.

Rainee was first to speak. "Oh, sir, these are quite beautiful, but there is no need."

Sam agreed with her and started to give his back.

"I ask that you take my gift, with my blessings that God follow you through your life." He was suddenly acting very spiritual, and his words were as sincere as they had ever heard from him.

But Sam was cynical when it came to Leondro. He had brutally murdered the members of the Collegium because they had double-crossed him. He said he had changed, but his drug operations were not shut down. No matter what he said, he was still evil. He could change his name, but evil is evil no matter what it's called.

"In that case, we accept your generous gift. And we wish the same for you," Rainee replied, kindly touching his hand.

Leondro motioned to Jorge to open the case on the bed.

As the case opened, he said, "I also want to give you this. I am a very rich man. I have more than I need. Please accept my gift." He pointed to the open case.

Sam tried to hold back his gasp but was unsuccessful. "Señor, there must be over a million American dollars in there."

Rainee took Sam's hand. She cut her eyes, telling him to not reject the gift.

Leondro grinned and then chuckled under his breath. "There are almost a million and one-half in the case. No more would fit." He chuckled. "It is a gift and payment to you. I want to stay your friend. Please come back and see me in one year." He told Jorge in Spanish to show them to the waiting car. "We will not keep you any longer. Have a safe travel home." He closed the door to his bedroom as they exited.

———————

Jorge placed their belongings in the back of the Suburban. He set the black suitcase between them in the back seat. He then handed them the blindfolds. "I am sorry, but you must put these on again. It is for your safety. What you do not know will not hurt you," Jorge stated firmly. "Thank you, and we hope to see you again."

Over my dead body. Sam squeezed Rainee's hand as he handed her one of the blindfolds.

Jorge watched from outside of the driver's side window as Sam and Rainee put on the blindfolds. He then knocked on the hood and the driver started the engine.

When they had been traveling for more than an hour, the driver told them, in broken English, that they could remove their blindfolds.

They both did.

Rainee looked at the black suitcase that had been placed on the floorboard of the back seat. "We are *not* taking that blood money."

Sam lifted the heavy case full of money. "It's a lot of dough, but I doubt we could get back into the US with it anyway. I'm not sure why he thought we could. Maybe he was still under the impression we were flying on the private jet. But now, even on a private jet, customs will inspect it. Then we would be detained as criminals transporting money. That'd be hard to explain. Anyway," Sam said, "I agree. I don't want to handle this ill-gotten-gains moola."

"You sound like a thug."

"OK, so we've gotta lotta bread here," he said, trying to mimic a gangster accent.

"Come on, silly. What're you thinking?" she asked, annoyed at his frivolity. "We can't just leave it here. Then El Espino...I mean Leondro...will know we didn't accept his gift. Not smart."

"I'm working on that. Enjoy the scenery. I'll tell you in a bit." Sam leaned his head back on the headrest and closed his eyes.

Still annoyed, Rainee sat quietly until they got to the outskirts of the Mexican capital. "Sam, we're near Mexico City."

Sam yawned and looked out of the window. Then he looked at his watch. "We have four hours until we need to be at the airport. When we get farther into town, I'm going to ask the driver to stop at a restaurant or something."

Rainee widened her eyes, knowing Sam was up to something, but she would play along. "I'm a bit hungry, I guess."

Sam touched her hand. "Better still. Not a restaurant. I'll feed you soon—promise." He smiled and winked. "Ask him, in Spanish, how far we are from the University at Puebla. Tell him we're interested in their medical school."

"Are you thinking about giving the money to the med school?" she asked under her breath.

"Hell no. How would we explain that?" he whispered. "But I bet we can get a taxi there."

She followed Sam's request.

The driver told her that it was a short ride there and that he would wait. Sam instructed Rainee to find some way to convince him that it was all right to leave them there and that they would be able to get a taxi to the airport.

Reluctantly, the driver agreed, and once near the campus, he pulled over.

They watched until the Suburban was out of sight. Then Sam looked for a taxi. It took several minutes, but Sam was able to flag down a small green compact car.

The taxi driver asked, in Spanish, where they wanted to go.

Rainee looked at Sam. "OK, now you must tell me where you want to go, because the driver needs to know."

"Tell him the largest garbage dump in Mexico City."

Rainee frowned. "You're going to throw the money away in the garbage dump?"

"Not quite. You'll see. Just trust me."

Rainee shook her head. Sam was becoming more annoying by the minute. She told the driver, who looked at both of them as if they were crazy.

The driver moved into traffic, mumbling something in Spanish, but Rainee understood him to say, "Stupid Americans."

———————

The stench of the massive quantity of trash had overpowered the smell of Mexico City's pollution. The driver parked several yards from a pile of garbage. Sam told him, in adequate but not great Spanish, to wait for them.

The driver looked at Sam and Rainee as they exited the car. He really did think he had two nut cases, but he was only interested in getting paid for the trip.

Sam held the black suitcase in his right hand and held Rainee's hand in the left. They walked behind a mound of garbage. The atrocious odor was sickening. But despite the hideousness of a garbage dump, there were young children digging in the rotten waste. Women with babies wrapped in rags sat on the edges of the mounds, trying to breastfeed. They could hear crying, and the air reeked of trash and human excrement. It was a sort of hell, which neither of them had ever imagined.

"People really do live here—even now," Rainee said, almost crying aloud. Tears flowed down her cheek. "This is unimaginable," she sobbed.

Sam moved closer to a small crowd that had gathered. He opened the suitcase and began to lift out bundles of cash. He threw it in every direction. By the time the case was empty, there must have been at least five hundred nearly naked and hungry peasants surrounding him.

Some were singing, and others were on their knees thanking Jesus and the Virgin Mary for the money raining from heaven and for the American man who had delivered their miracle.

Sam hugged a small barefoot child before turning back to Rainee.

She was sobbing and ran toward Sam. "I should have never doubted you. I love you, Sam Hawkins. I love you."

CHAPTER THIRTY-ONE

Rainee's eyes were bloodshot from crying and fatigue. Sam pulled her head onto his shoulder. She was asleep before the plane lifted off the runway.

Sam just gazed out of the window. He needed to see Ana. It haunted him, and he needed answers. He needed closure to what Don Huitt had told him. If it had been Ana, why had she not told Sam what she knew or that she had contacted the Houston FBI office? Was she afraid, or was she hiding something? Could the sweet, long-winded Ana have really been putting him off? And if so, why?

Rainee had said she would go to Canada, but that had been days ago. Too many things had happened since that agreement. They were both exhausted and relieved. Was Sam going to put Rainee through more or just drop the whole thing? He closed his eyes. Soon he was also asleep.

They collected their luggage in Houston. Sam asked Rainee to sit with him for a few moments.

She hoped that Sam had forgotten or given up the idea of going to Canada, but that would have been too good to be true.

As suspected, Sam asked her if she was still up to going to see Ana Roberts.

What could Rainee say, other than she was agreeable to the idea? After all, she had agreed previously, and Sam would have done the same for her. If it indeed brought closure for Sam, then it would also be beneficial to her.

"There's a flight to Vancouver at seven forty p.m. We should see if there are seats." Sam pushed the cart of luggage to the reservation counter.

"I don't have clothes for cold weather," Rainee said.

"We'll get whatever we need there. We don't need much. Where Ana lives is south of the fashion border. Jeans and a sweatshirt will be just fine." Sam watched her roll her eyes. He knew jeans were fine with her, but a sweatshirt? It just wasn't her style. He smiled to himself. *Anything on or off her is beautiful.*

Rainee was afraid to ask about his personal inside joke. Sam had a way of amusing himself, and sometimes it was just private. She liked that about him. He would find humor or make his own when things got tough. It had helped them both through the worst of predicaments.

The flights to Vancouver were full, but there were two seats left to Seattle. That was the next best thing, Sam thought. They reserved the last two first-class seats.

Rainee felt unusually tattered from the entire ordeal of the day. She could still smell the garbage in her nostrils and couldn't wait to wash her face and hands. She excused herself.

Sam watched her as she walked to the ladies' room. She didn't need a thing. She was perfect, according to him.

They took the second row of seats at 7:15 p.m. The flight attendant served a cocktail before the other people boarded.

Rainee pulled out her headphones from her carry-on and laid them in her lap. She fiddled with her playlist until she found the sound that suited her. She got her lip moisturizer out and a small pack of tissues. All her little necessities sat next to her, arranged in her specific desired order.

Sam stared at her as she made her little nest for the flight.

Rainee caught a glimpse of him. "What?"

"Just admiring the view," he replied.

She impishly smiled while giving him a little push. "Go away."

"Never, my dear. Never."

It was cold and raining when they landed in Seattle. The taxi took them to the hotel that Sam had reserved while they were waiting at the Houston airport. It was on the water and close to where they would catch the high-speed catamaran the next morning. The colored lights of the many houseboats glistened in the bay.

"Seattle is beautiful, even when it's raining," Sam said. "Maybe someday we will come and enjoy the city."

"Perhaps." Rainee yawned. "Right now, I can only think about settling down for a long winter's nap."

"'Twas the night before Canada, and…sorry, can't find something funny to rhyme," Sam said.

"Too late for funnies anyway. Come on, shower with me." She motioned for him with her index finger.

Sam smiled impishly. "And Christmas is over. It's New Year's Eve tomorrow," Sam said. He pulled her to him and started to slowly undress her. As each piece of clothing fell to the floor, he removed another until she stood naked in front of him. "Happy New Year!"

———————

The catamaran slipped across the water at high speed. They docked at 12:45 p.m. in Nanaimo, on Vancouver Island. Sam rented a car, and he and Rainee drove slowly up the coastline to Willows Point. There was nothing in the small village but a gas station and a Chinese restaurant. He pointed out the lane where Bill and Ana had once spent their summers. He assumed her new home was also on that same little tree-lined road.

But first, they needed to go into Campbell River, the closest town and the only place to get a hotel room. Sam suggested a beautiful historic lodge across from April Sound. It had great restaurants and beautiful views when the dark clouds weren't floating on the ground.

"Don't you think we should call Ana?" Rainee asked.

Sam thought for a few moments. "I'm debating. One side of me says that we should, and then the other thinks we might just surprise her."

"Surprising her is very rude."

Sam slowed the car to turn into Painter's Lodge. "Yeah, but she might not want to see us when she figures out why we're here. I mean, any way you cut it, Ana lied to me. I know that now."

"You may be right, but maybe she had a good reason," Rainee said.

"Maybe, and maybe not." Sam parked, and they went into the old but elegant fishing lodge.

As they climbed the stairs to their room, Sam told Rainee that he was not going to call Ana. They would find her home and stop by unannounced. He knew Rainee disapproved, but something told him that it would be better that way.

———————————

There was a man standing in his front yard, so Sam stopped to ask if he knew where Ana Roberts lived. The elderly couple was only renting, so they were unable to help him with locating her. But the second stop was Ana's old friend. She directed them three houses down from hers… just around the bend. Sam parked in the sloping driveway. He recognized Ana's car in the open garage.

"Well, let's see what she has to say," Sam said softly.

Ana had heard the car doors and was peeking through the cracked front door when Sam and Rainee stepped onto her porch.

"Surprise!" Sam shouted.

Ana started fingering her hair. "I'm such a mess; you should have called. I'm so embarrassed."

Rainee said, "I told him that, but he insisted on surprising you."

"Well, he did *that*. Come in." She turned away from them and did not hug Sam, as was her normal greeting.

Sam couldn't read Ana. She was disheveled. Her normal soft face was strained, and he didn't know if she was distressed over the surprise, or if she was angry that they were there at all. She had been moving in, but nothing seemed to have been put up. The kitchen had stacks of dishes, appearing that she had started putting things away but simply had stopped. The rest of the house looked the same.

"Excuse the mess. I'm just tired of unpacking. Well, I can't believe you two are here. So, what's the occasion?" Ana asked.

Sam smiled. "We were just in the neighborhood, and I thought I'd borrow a cup of sugar."

"Oh, Sam, always the joker. No, really. What brings you so far and without notice? You are so transparent, Sam. Spill it." Ana stood and walked to the window. "Or do I already know?"

Sam walked to her. He put his hand on her shoulder. "All right, Ana. I had hoped to not just poop out what I wanted to talk to you about, but you, as always, know when I'm searching for something."

She stared at him. "OK, let's have it." Her eyes narrowed, and she seemed resolute, almost indifferent to Sam.

"Ana," Sam stammered, "I'll get right to the meat of things. Were you the informant to the FBI about the brotherhood, the Collegium?"

Rainee remained perfectly still, as if she expected a bomb to go off. "Yes," Ana said coldly. She made no immediate explanation.

"But Ana, you told me that you knew nothing about what Bill told me on his deathbed. I followed up with you at your house, trying to make heads or tails of his vague references. You said nothing. You told me nothing. In fact, you said you didn't have a clue about anything that I was talking about. Clearly that was not true."

"No, Sam, that was not true."

"Well, don't you think I have a right to know why you, of all people, would keep that from me? Rainee and I have been through hell. Maybe had you said something…anything…we would not have spent over six months running, hiding, and being afraid for our lives, so we might discover what Bill meant by his cryptic deathbed messages. I took that obligation from my dear friend seriously. And we were almost killed. And you say that you knew all about it?"

"Not all," Ana said. "It's not that important anymore. Ya'll are fine now, right?"

"No. We're both scarred and traumatized from what we have endured. And you did know a lot, enough to go to the FBI. We were in over our heads all these months. How could you do that to me?"

CHAPTER THIRTY-ONE

"Calm down a bit, Sam," Rainee said. "Maybe if you calm down, Ana can explain."

Sam shook his head. He had fretted over meeting with Ana for a long while. He had played out every scenario imaginable. But to know Ana had known most of everything about Bill's involvement was more than he could take calmly.

Ana looked expressionless at Rainee, then toward Sam, but their eyes did not meet. She walked to the kitchen. "I'll make some coffee."

Sam looked around. "I'd rather have a strong drink. I think I'm going to need it." He saw a bottle of bourbon on the shelf. He poured three fingers into a glass.

"I have ice," Ana said calmly.

"I'm good just like this. Talk to me." Sam sat abruptly on the sofa.

"I don't know where to start," Ana said timidly. It was the first sign of any emotion since they had entered her house.

"The beginning might be the best start." Sam's eyes flashed anger.

Ana stretched her neck and stared at the ceiling for a long moment. She then exhaled as the words left her lips. "Bill came home a few years back from a trip to Washington. He told me many things about an organization called the Keepers Brotherhood or sometimes called the Collegium. He told me of their plan and the progress they had made toward development of a biological weapon. He said that they wanted him to join the group. We talked most of the night. We cried together about James. He would not have been killed had he not been fighting the very enemy that the brotherhood intended to wipe out. Bill didn't know if he wanted to become involved. I pushed him into it. I was the catalyst that pushed him into that group of maniacs. I wanted revenge for James. Cold-blooded humanity-hating men and women who preferred death to life murdered him. How do you conventionally rid the world of that? They welcome death, so they can be martyred. Sanctions, talks, a few bombings here and there. President after president, prime minister after prime minister, French, German, Russian—it didn't matter. None had made a dent to stop and eliminate for all time ISIS, the Taliban, Al-Qaeda—none of them. The brotherhood would wipe them out forever. More splinter factions of the new caliphates were being created every moment of every day. Those people seethed hate for us. And I for them. Nothing short of the Collegium was going to end their reign of terror." Ana took a breath but showed no remorse for what she had just admitted.

Sam rubbed his eyes but only said, "Go on."

"They would soon be everywhere if they were not stopped. They kill our Americans with trucks and vans when they can't get bombs. They cut off heads and ruin ancient sites, beautiful artwork and try to burn down history. They kill innocent concertgoers, office workers, and children. They find softheaded sympathizers and recruit them to kill young boys like my James. In my enraged brain, I saw no way to eliminate this pandemic on humanity. Bill was skeptical, but he also felt as strongly as I. We hated them for what they did to James. I hated them with every fiber of my body. I hate them now. I'm sorry that I was weak and pushed Bill into the lion's den, but at the time, I wanted to see every Muslim who might have even thought twice of becoming a radical dead! And if the Collegium had a bioweapon, soon they would as well. Then their terror would be biological and deadlier than their bombs. Bill thought it better if he and his friends did that first. You see, it's only time until that's the new weapon of choice for those radicals, and the only countries that won't use it are the ones that keep playing the nice game. You can't play nice with radical extremists. You think the radical Islamic terrorists and countries that hate us won't jump at that—China, North Korea, perhaps Russia? Maybe they already have...secrets...lies...cover-ups. We aren't told the truth.

Don't you know the elitists think we, the people, are too stupid for the truth? They make up the truth and then the media picks it up, gives it another spin, and then you get a pack of lies thrown at you. We don't know what's going on in the world. Soon, there will be no rules. We have to strike first and with deadly aim, because the government and our allies won't."

"Ana, you're taking it far too radically yourself. We know about terrorism and hostile nations, but I can't see how you justified the so-called brotherhood. Two evils do not make one bit of right. All of this is so unlike you." Sam took a drink from his glass. "And I knew you were hurting, but never, never could I have imagined you would help such a demonic cause as Operation Nemesis and Factor-7." He huffed. "And if you think the game is to strike with bioweapons first before they do, you are opening up the end of civilization as we know it. That would only give permission to the world to follow suit. You better hold on to your butt then…life would be over."

Ana frowned. "I don't care about living anymore. I'm not the person that I once was. They took my kindness, my gentle heart, and my soul from me when James was murdered."

"James was killed by a terrorist bomb, but he was also there fighting to defend our liberties and preserve our freedom," Sam said. "It was war, and it was brutal. But he wanted to defend liberty. He knew the risks and was a fine man to fight for what he believed."

"Don't be a fool, Sam. There was and never will be any just cause or any cause at all to fight for over there. Every act done was and is terrorism. They might call it a war that James fought, but it was pure and unmitigated radical Islamic terrorism. Pure and simple. That's the demon's name!"

Sam couldn't contain his frustration and disgust. "And you mourned James by potentially putting us into the hands of murderers." Sam bit his tongue. Ana could never know about El Espino or the promise and deal he had made with Rainee and Sam. The coalition between them and the Mexican drug lord executioner would stay a secret for the rest of their lives.

"You didn't die, did you?" she screamed. "But, yes, I am responsible for Bill's death. He had gotten in over his head. He was ill, and he needed medical care for his cancer. I was so full of hate that I pushed him to the end. He was tired of the secrets and the hate-filled conversations. He was scared. He would rather die than continue the lies. I swear I didn't know he was going to kill himself. But as I look back, there were signs."

Sam shook his head again. He could barely look Ana in the eyes. "Did you see the hideous death that Bill endured? Your husband, whom you said you catapulted into this insidious plan, died the most gruesome and vile death. And I know he died to get the truth out. Truth that wasn't in you. And your husband started his journal with an apology to you. You called the FBI, but you called them too late for Bill, and you called them too late for all those who were in the crosshairs of the Collegium's test locations. There was and would be tremendous collateral damage. Innocent people would have died while all you sickos were thinking about nothing but getting rid of terrorists."

"Sam, you say innocents died, and more would have died. That's right. I feel little remorse for the wages of war, and that's exactly what's happening. OK, it's war. It's war, so they can wipe out anyone who doesn't agree with their cause. Oh, call it terrorism, call it insurgence, call it religion, caliphate...civil war...but it's war, and my innocent son, Simon's innocent wife, and on and on, were killed by terrorists. There were innocents killed at Hiroshima, and the war ended. So it was justified then, and I justify it now."

Sam glanced at Rainee. The scowl on his face had turned to ultimate revulsion. "You're deranged, Ana. You say they, the terrorists, would wipe out anyone who does not agree with them. Isn't that exactly what the Collegium was planning too?"

Ana wouldn't look at Sam. She stared at the floor and whispered, "I didn't know Bill wrote an apology to me. Yes, Sam, I did all that, just like you say." Her voice trailed off as she seemed to reminisce about better times. "But Bill loved me and would have gone to his grave, and did, doing all he could to keep me safe." She suddenly stood as if a lightning bolt hit her from behind. She raised her voice again to a near scream. "Yes, I did go to the FBI, but first, I tried to cover everything that might implicate Bill with the brotherhood. I would do anything for him too, you see. I saw that you were searching for information. The truth is that I used you. I used you!" She lowered her voice and turned directly toward Sam and Rainee. "Truly, I thought that if you found something, I could either destroy it or…I even thought at one time, maybe I could tell you the truth, and you would destroy it. But I decided to do it myself. I have destroyed all that I could find. I put a flash drive with the truth in Bill's grave. I threw it into the dirt with one of Bill's roses. Then they covered it up. It will be forever gone."

Sam's eyes cut to Rainee. He wanted to run or throw something. Ana was who Bill had trusted with the flash drive. He bit his tongue to not lash out at her and reveal that he and Rainee had read what Bill had written. "Certainly, you used me! Truth? It could hit you in the ass, and you wouldn't know how to deal with the truth. Or perhaps you don't know truth from fiction anymore. You're a very sick woman." Sam took a deep breath. His body vibrated with anger, and he felt sick at his stomach from the deep hurt of her long and hateful lies and deception. "But oh, yes, please tell the truth, Ana…tell me the truth for once in your miserable existence," Sam said sarcastically.

"Didn't you think it odd that Bill was taken to St. Peter's in the first place?" Ana spouted. Her voice was cold and cynical.

"Yes. Bill could have been taken to any number of closer hospitals," he said.

Ana walked to a cardboard box that sat on a table near the kitchen. She pulled out a manila folder. "Here." She slapped the folder onto the table in front of Sam.

Sam picked it up and cautiously opened it, as if some monster was going to jump out. He took out a white folded piece of paper and held it between his thumb and finger for longer than normal. Exhaling a long breath, Sam read it silently, then gazed off into the distance before handing it to Rainee. He felt deep emotion build in his chest, and his nostrils and throat burned.

"Bill instructed you to take him to me," he whispered. "It was totally Bill's idea. He *did* want me to know. He needed help. The pain and deep grief that poor man must have endured to get to that point." Sam hung his head. "And you, Ana, started it all. You are responsible for killing your own husband. And I have felt so sorry for you all these months. You wicked woman!"

Rainee lovingly touched Sam's leg. "It says, 'Take me to Sam.'" Rainee shook her head and frowned. "But why were Reznick and Albright with you?"

Ana turned her back on Sam and Rainee. She stared out the window. "I called them. I wasn't prepared to face Bill dying over what I had made him do, and I wasn't any more prepared for being an accomplice to what he had done."

Sam groaned. "What a joke. You weren't prepared?" He scoffed. "Well, it puzzled me that they were there at St. Peter's. I should have realized then that you three maniacs were up to something," Sam angrily shouted. "So why didn't you just let him die on the bathroom floor? If you were so afraid of being implicated with the Collegium's evil; wouldn't that have been easier for you? Maybe easier to live with yourself?"

Ana interrupted. "If Bill had died at home, there would have been police and others there to investigate. His body would have gone to the county for an autopsy right away, and…well…I called Simon, and he and Albright told me to follow Bill's instructions. They said that Bill would go quickly, and no one would know why he had died. Simon assured me that St. Peter's was our best option. Bill's medical records, including his cancer diagnosis, were there. Simon promised me the virus was swift and undetectable. So I had the ambulance take him to you. John and Simon were there for my protection."

Sam sneered. "Your protection? You're as evil as they, and you kept me around as your little poker chip. You played me. You hoped I'd not report Bill's death as anything other than what the fake autopsy report-ed. Well, in a way, you were right. All this makes me sick. You, Reznick, and Albright. What a fuckin' murderous trio."

"I had to keep Simon and John around. Don't you see? Simon came with the territory, and Bill recruited Albright. When Bill died, the three of us decided to get rid of Bill's remains quickly, so any trace of the virus or anything that led to the brotherhood or their plans could not be discovered. The secret had to be concealed, or terrible things would happen."

"So, the hasty cremation. And you actually dug a grave for his ash-es, rather than blowing them in the wind or any of the other typical ways to honor him." Rainee exclaimed. "Well, you should know, Ana, that Don Huitt, the FBI director of the Houston Regional Office, said that John Albright is dead along with Reznick and the others. The heads of those vicious serpents have been cut off, and I'm not just speaking figuratively either. You know that. And the ones left, if any, will be running for cover. The brotherhood"—she sighed—"is out of business, at least for now."

Ana sat motionless, emotionless. "Yeah, perhaps the brotherhood is gone. But the terrorists are like Hydra." She cocked her head to one side and widened her eyes. "All their heads will never be severed. Terror will just grow until they get what they want. And I'm afraid that the world is just sitting back and going to give it to them. My wrath is alive—one terrorist head to me would be like Salome's gift on a silver platter." Ana stared at Rainee. "We are all fools in our own right. I didn't see then what I know now. The plan that Bill and I sanctioned as good turned out much worse. It never came to fruition, and the terrorists were not eliminated, but good people died. I'm not referring to the Collegium's test locations either." She put her face in her hands. Her words came out muffled and breathy. "Horrible things happened. Bill died for nothing. It was all for nothing." She paused and looked straight at Sam and Rainee. "And the Collegium must have killed the presidents. And Winger might have been the only president to ever do anything about terrorism."

"Do you know that for a fact?" Rainee asked.

Sam sat quietly. He had heard too much already.

"No," Ana whispered. "Do you?"

Rainee shook her head. "No, but I suspect."

Ana scoffed. "Suspicions do nothing." She poured herself a drink. "I had lost everything. James, Bill, Steven, you, myself. I lost my dream of eradicating them from the earth like a pack of vermin. Bill wanted out, and death was his way. I thought of that, but I'm a coward. So I called the FBI, and I told them almost everything that I've told you. But I didn't tell them that I had been the one to catapult Bill into it. See, I'm a miserable coward."

Sam stood up and faced Ana. "You should be in prison. No, that would be too good for you." He turned his back to her. "You could have won an Academy Award for your acting. You fooled me." Sam wheeled around on his feet and lashed out his fury. "All the tears, all the 'I love you, Sam,' all the 'You're like a son to me, Sam,' all the lies! I've heard enough! Well, happy fuckin' New Year. This does it for me!" He pulled Rainee to her feet and started toward the door. "I guess you got immunity for your stoic confession."

"Not exactly. I'm here, but the international authorities keep in touch. I'm still talking to them." She touched his shoulder. "I'm sorry, Sam."

"Ana, you are evil, and I'm sick to death of all this and you." Sam kicked the front door.

Ana shouted, "Don't you know that I had no choice?"

Sam turned to her for the last time. He glared angrily into her eyes, evidence of his loathing for all he had heard and, sadly, for Ana as well. "We always have choices. You just made the wrong ones."

———————

Sam and Rainee did not speak all the way to the lodge. Sam was livid, devastated, and hurt beyond words. Rainee knew his pain, and she allowed him the time to process. When they arrived at the lodge, Sam walked directly to the bar. Rainee followed. He pulled out two barstools and helped her onto one.

"What do you want?" he asked.

Rainee pulled him close. "I want you to do whatever will ease your pain. I'm here, and I love you."

Sam hugged her. A tear ran down his cheek. Rainee was all he had left. He had loved Bill and discovered he was weak, weak enough to give up everything for a terribly misguided cause. He had loved Ana and realized she was full of hate. Bill was dead. Ana was dead to him.

Rainee ordered a martini, dirty. She looked at the appetizer side of the menu and ordered fried calamari and halibut nuggets, in hopes that Sam would eat.

Sam ordered a double Canadian whiskey on the rocks. Making conversation was difficult. He was consumed with emotions, but after a few minutes and a several sips of his drink, Sam said, "It's gone full circle now. Babe, maybe we're free."

Rainee touched his hand. "We are. We can't take back the last few months or even smooth it over. What happened, happened. But one good thing came out of it."

Sam looked at her adoringly. "You."

"No, Sam. Us."

The New Year rang in exactly as Sam and Rainee wanted. There were no parties or fireworks. They made love and watched TV and the ball drop at midnight in Times Square. They held each other closely and knew that the other was content. The New Year held hope. They had been through too much to endure any more. But it was over. It was hard for either to imagine being free, because it had been so dreadfully long. But they were finally safe and free; and they loved it. And they loved each other. Sam had never been happier, and Rainee admitted that she never knew what it was like to have a perfect man.

Sam laughed. "Far from perfect, but maybe incredibly handsome, sexy, hardworking, and faithful, among other extraordinary traits."

Rainee knew he was joking, but ironically, she actually believed all those things. She added, "And the love of my life."

There was no need to stay in Canada any longer. Sam had gotten his information, although it was not what he had hoped. He wouldn't tell Huitt about seeing Ana or her confession. She would have to live with herself now. She had already lost everything. That would be her punishment.

The weather was as foul as his memories of the previous day. It was January 1, a new year, and perhaps a new start.

CHAPTER THIRTY-TWO

The flight back to Houston provided hours for Rainee and Sam to talk. He had been considering their future. She wanted to go back to Italy. He had no desire to return to St. Peter's or any other trauma center. He was trained in other disciplines and had options. Rainee did as well. She had mentioned her lack of interest in starting a practice, although she could practice medicine in the United States and Italy. He abhorred the thought of working for a large corporation, and she found no pleasure in working at a research hospital. His thoughts kept running back to the indigent people they had served in the new clinics they set up for the man now called Leondro. He couldn't get the children at the garbage dump out of his mind's eye. The vivid memory of so many sick, hungry, and homeless continually haunted him. Although he knew there was no way to fix them all, maybe there was a way to make a difference. The thought suited his psyche. They had experienced so much but had come out on the other side relatively unscathed. Maybe a few weeks of helping those who were unable to help themselves would do their minds good.

He mustered up the courage to make his suggestion. She might think he was crazy, and he admitted to himself that it would not be too far from the truth, but it was worth a try. "We are set, pretty well, for money," he started.

Rainee looked at him strangely. "Yes, we both have enough, at least for some time. Why are you saying that?"

"I know we've talked about future plans. I think we should go to Italy in the spring and stay a few months. I know you want to do that, and I'd love to see your home. But regarding using our medical abilities…" He paused. "Well, I was thinking, maybe joining up with Missions of Medicine, at least before the end of the year. Maybe next summer."

She smiled and threw back her head.

"Oh, you hate the idea," Sam muttered.

She leaned over and hugged him. "No, I like the idea. It's perfect! Anyway, corrects the lie you told so we could learn to remake *Leondro's* face. I'll never get used to using that name he conjured up for himself."

"Then that's the plan." Sam sighed his relief.

"Yes, sir, that's the plan, Sam."

Recalling the first time she had said that, they both laughed.

But even though Sam and Rainee agreed, they knew that Missions of Medicine was a dangerous endeavor. It was made up of a group of fine medical personnel who were willing to go where other medical groups would not. But the group had superior credentials in saving lives where the suffering was doubled, tripled, or quadrupled with other dangers.

———

The two went back to Sam's bay house for the month of January. They occupied their time closing up the house and securing the outside in case of a big storm or an early hurricane. They packed and tied up loose business. On February 5, they boarded the flight to Naples, Italy.

––––––––––

Rainee had left her Fiat at a friend's house while she was in the United States. Georgina picked them up at the Naples International Airport. Rainee translated as Georgina rattled off in Italian about all the things that Rainee had missed. Rainee told her about Sam, his work, his house, and a bit about the beauty of San Miguel de Allende. But when the question of how they met arose, she was at a loss. All she could say was "mutual acquaintances." When they got to Georgina's house, they found the Fiat wouldn't start, so the conversation continued at warp speed until the battery took the charge.

Sam fell asleep while the girls chattered on like a couple of magpies.

Rainee would drive. She knew the narrow and winding roads to Castellammare, a small community just north of Sorrento. It would be about a forty-five-minute drive from Aeroporto Capodichino, the Naples airport, to the apartment she had in an old seventeenth-century castle. The driveway to the apartment was built at a frightening downgrade. Sam held his breath until she turned onto a level surface and into her one-car garage. The apartment had been her father's, and although it was a rental, they kept a very long-term lease. When Sam saw the view and the inside of the apartment, he understood why. From the deck, one could see Capri to the left. The Sea of Naples and the rugged coastline was like a photo out of a *National Geographic* magazine. Directly in front, at a distance, was Mount Vesuvius. It could only be seen on very clear days, but it was a stunning view that afternoon.

"We must go to Pompeii," Rainee said. "You know that's the volcano that destroyed them."

CHAPTER THIRTY-TWO

Sam nodded. "Seems too beautiful to have changed history."

"Wait until tomorrow. We'll drive to Positano. You'll love the Amalfi coastline. But I warn you, the road from Naples to here is like the German Autobahn. The road to Positano is very narrow and very high above the Tyrrhenian Sea—and beware; it's very winding. And we Italians drive like Mario Andretti."

Sam sighed. "I can't wait."

"Remember the truck ride to Charlie's and the wild ride in San Miguel?" She laughed. "It's payback time!"

The month was filled with touring the coastline and all the beautiful fishing towns. They ate everything that was available and drank limoncello until Sam started to have nightmares about it.

Sam had been there before, but Rainee showed him things that the normal tourist never saw. They played bocce ball with some old men on the very small side of the road to Positano.

He tasted fresh olives and nearly threw up. Rainee had warned him, but he insisted he had to try. They watched farmwomen make mozzarella from buffalo milk, and they walked the beaches until dark.

March arrived, and Capri was opening up after a winter's hiatus. Rainee called the Lancia. The boat took them across the bay to Capri. Since they had suitcases, Rainee suggested not riding the funicular up to the town, but rather taking a taxi. Sam was all for not carrying bags any farther than necessary. They spent the next few weeks strolling along the ancient streets where Roman emperors once walked. They swam in the crystal-clear waters and kissed in the Blue Grotto. Rainee got Sam to ride the gondola up the mountain to Anacapri, but they took a taxi back. He was not getting on it again. They had a laugh about his fear of open heights. Rainee nicknamed him, just for the day, Finocchio, slang for "sissy" in Italian. When he asked what it meant, she told him it meant the vegetable fennel, and she wasn't lying. The word had two meanings. Sam would never know.

Rainee dropped Sam off in Sorrento on Saturday after their return to the mainland. She was going to get her hair and nails done. He assured her that he could well occupy his time.

He took a chair in a small sidewalk café and ordered a slice of chocolate cake and a coffee. He perused a local shopping guide magazine. Then, a few blocks down the street, Sam found what he wanted. He rang the buzzer at the store, and a finely dressed woman opened it. She welcomed him in Italian but soon realized that he did not speak her language. She began to speak excellent English, and Sam told her his mission. An hour and three glasses of local wine later, he bought what he had come to get, and he was pleased.

That night, Sam took Rainee to a restaurant that cantilevered the cliffs and overlooked the water. He ordered a pitcher of red local wine and asked the waiter to chill a bottle of his finest champagne. He hoped the champagne would be in order. He prayed the night he planned would not become a disaster. He had not talked to Rainee about his intentions, and the subject had never really been discussed.

Sam fidgeted nervously and played with his food and his napkin throughout dinner. He seemed far away half the time and engaged in the conversation the other half. He was a mess.

Rainee watched him, wondering what he had up his sleeve. She always could read him, and this time was no different. She knew he was up to something, but she just didn't quite know what.

After dinner, he ordered the waiter's suggestion, a dark-chocolate soufflé. He said it would be good with the champagne.

So, the stage was set, and his plan had been made. He was flying by the seat of his pants when he got down on one knee. The entire restaurant turned toward the couple. Sam felt like a fool but wanted the occasion to be the memory of her lifetime. But if she rejected him, it would be a memory from hell for him.

He loved her, and he would take the leap.

"Rainee Francesca Arienzo, I love you. I will always love you." He pulled a small velveteen box from his jeans pocket, revealing a vintage three-carat emerald-cut diamond with baguette accents set in platinum. "Will you marry me?"

The hush in the restaurant was deafening while Sam waited what felt like an eternity for her reply. He could hear his heart beating in his chest. He felt like a schoolboy.

She looked at the ring and then at Sam. She was expressionless. Her eyes began to water, which only made them sparkle brighter under the string lights of the restaurant. A tear came to her eye. She smiled, took the ring and clutched Sam's hand, and he slid the ring on her perfect-size finger. "I thought you'd never ask! Of course, I will marry you."

The restaurant broke out into some Italian song, led by the waiters. The restaurant brought more house wine in large ceramic pitchers to serve the small audience. The owner of the establishment made a toast in Italian and took pictures for his "wall of fame." The liquor and wine flowed continuously. Everyone danced and celebrated into the early-morning hours. Rainee had to walk around and show her ring to all the locals, who congratulated them.

It was almost 3:00 a.m. Sam and Rainee had not been up that late since they met. Neither was used to partying at such a wild pace, but they had no regrets. Sam hailed a taxi. Both of them knew that neither was capable of driving. Rainee was passed out by the time the driver parked at the Castellammare apartment. Any other time, Sam could have carried her, but he was having enough trouble just walking. He gently roused her.

"Hey, Sleeping Beauty. We're home."

How they got into the house and to bed remained a mystery to both of them.

———————

Sam rolled over to touch her and watched her admire the ring on her hand for a moment before speaking. "Good morning, sunshine." He looked at the clock and huffed. "I mean afternoon." It was 1:30 p.m.

Rainee crawled on top of him, initiating sex, but promptly fell to his chest. "Oh, my aching head!"

Sam curled his leg over her and wrapped both of his arms around her naked body. He held her there for some time, hearing her breathe and stoking her back and buttocks. They were in love, and it was good.

CHAPTER THIRTY-THREE

The two months in Italy had flown by. April was upon them, and they had less than a month before embarking on their next adventure together. They had set the date for their wedding. It would be December 24 of that year, and it would be where Rainee had said she wanted to spend Christmas. They would celebrate the holiday and their new life together in San Miguel de Allende. Rainee had contacted a bishop in Guanajuato to allow them to marry at the Parroquia de Miguel del Archangel. He would officiate. The memories of the Mexican town were somewhat tarnished from the trauma they had endured. However, both wanted to go back to the beauty and somehow establish new memories where they had indeed first fallen in love.

The doctors with Missions of Medicine had suggested they were needed to accompany a group to Mali. Both would concentrate their work in Bamako, the capital. Terrorism was an issue, but the group felt safer in the larger city, and with its huge population, the work would be daunting. Sam and Rainee knew full well the difficulties they would endure in that country. The poverty level was among the highest in the world. The hygiene was nil, and the sanitation was equally dreadful. Only 63 percent or less of the people had safe drinking water. Consequently, Rainee knew that cholera would be high on the list of her priorities. Arthropod-borne diseases, such as malaria, were rampant. Tuberculosis was killing thousands. So, her infectious-disease training would certainly get a workout. The simplest tasks, such as immunizations, to the hardest tasks, such as caring for a baby with HIV/AIDS, were things they had to anticipate.

Sam would concentrate on surgeries. There would be resetting bones that had healed incorrectly, restricting a person from working. He would do cesarean section births and tend to the babies in an attempt to reduce the high infant mortality rate. Cleft palates and child deformities were high on his list of things to address. There would be no shortage of gall bladders and even tonsil surgeries. His work would run the gamut from the simplest to the most delicate and complex.

They would work in a hospital or a tent set up at the hospital for two weeks. Then the group was to go to a field hospital where the inhabitants in the area had no way to get medical care or travel for it.

The population was made up of mostly people under the age of sixty-five, and almost half were younger than twelve. Sam hoped he would be working much of his time on children. It had been a child hugging him in a garbage dump in Mexico that led him to this decision, which he and Rainee would soon see come to fruition. But he still asked himself regularly why he would jump back into the fire. "Must be a glutton for punishment," he said.

They had many fears, and they were conflicted for their own safety. But the more they heard and the more they visited with the other doctors, the more they knew it was their destiny to go.

"Strange irony," Sam said the morning before they were to leave. "Ninety percent of the population is Muslim." He knew he was not responsible for what he and Rainee had endured with the Collegium and El Espino. But the hate and the wickedness had cut a hole into his soul. The medical trip to Mali was a poor attempt for Sam to find redemption for sins other than his own.

The fear of an outbreak of the Factor-7 or contact with its creators had consumed Sam and Rainee for nearly a year. Sometimes Rainee wondered how she could be stepping right back into the darkness of fear and disease. However, that was her passion, and knowing that she would be helping people of the Islamic faith seemed fitting to her also. The everyday people shouldn't be made to suffer for the sins of a very few who don't share the true value of their faith. They were poor, malnourished people with children they loved. A child might not see its first birthday. The ravaged surviving children knew that the inevitable death was, unfortunately, as common and expected as the gnawing hunger in their small bellies.

Rainee and Sam met the others of the United States team of doctors in Atlanta. They watched while the crew loaded medical equipment and cases of supplies onto the chartered 727 commercial aircraft. They would fly to London to refuel and pick up some other physicians and then fly all night before they landed in Bamako. There were three armed security guards on board, and they would protect the team while in Mali.

The lead physician spoke as the group took off. There was no alcohol on board, and they were advised to sleep as much as possible. Once they landed, they would hit the ground running. The mercy mission would be a grueling fifteen days. It was his fourth trip with several of the others. He admitted the threats and stress were real, and the accommodations were not always the best. But without question, the rewards were great.

Every one of the doctors and nurses already knew, in detail, what they were to encounter. There had been months of preparation. They had received inoculations of every sort to ward off the many infectious diseases. But even so, that risk remained great. Some pathogens spreading around the world still lacked a viable vaccine. There would be possible attacks by radicals. They were subject to kidnapping and confiscation of their supplies. It was not that these medical personnel were extremely brave or even thrill-seekers; they were the best of their kind, and they were willing to take the huge risk for humanity.

Sam looked at Rainee after the introductions were made. "Another irony," he noted. "We knew the Collegium, who were set on killing the very ones whom these men and women are willing to risk life and limb to heal."

Rainee agreed but added, "We owe this to someone; I just don't know who that is yet."

Sam took her hand. "We paid our dues, but this helps. Just remember this, babe: you can't fix the whole world."

"It's time someone tried." She frowned. The vicious circle of Factor-7 and the Collegium…the damn brotherhood, or any number of their demonic monikers…the terror of El Espino, then the truth about Ana, had left an indelible mark on them. It was the kind of memory that no amount of time could erase. The trip to Mali was their attempt to make something good in what had been a world of evil.

Sam and Rainee were among the newest to the team. There were, maybe, three others who would be experiencing the struggles for the first time. There were doctors and nurses from multiple countries. They spoke different languages and wore different clothes, but they all had one common mission.

Although unsettled about the trip, with emotions running rampant, Rainee began to set up her nest. Sam smiled at her predictable routine.

She put on her headphones and closed her eyes.

Sam leaned back for the long trip. He couldn't sleep. He relived the surgery to make a new identity for a man who was as wicked as the Keepers Brotherhood. They had played a dance with a Mexican man who was a brutal murderer, with crimes so revolting that there was no adequate name for them. They had had no choice but to do what they had, reluctantly, done. He thought of Ana's last words: "I had no choice." Maybe in her pathetic, sick mind, she had had no other options. Sam knew that he and Rainee had also had no opportunity to do things differently, but somehow they had survived and somehow had come out on the other side, perhaps better than when they went into it. Hate is a vile and virile enemy of the soul. Fear is almost as lethal. Both will rob and devour your soul, freedom, and judgment. Sam would not let that happen. He thought about Lauren and hoped she was doing well. Indeed, Sam had changed. The past heartbreaks, emptiness, horrors, and sadness had changed him. He gazed over at Rainee. She was his reward, and suddenly he realized that all the pain was worth that single payoff. He whispered something his grandmother had recited when times got bad or trouble loomed. Until that moment, it had never meant so much. "I have refined you, but not as silver. I have tried you in the furnace of affliction."

The lights abruptly came on in the large aircraft. The captain announced their approach into Bamako, Mali. One of the flight attendants was walking down the aisle passing out coffee, teas, and protein bars.

The night had been long, and neither Sam nor Rainee had been able to sleep but a few hours. The gigantic yellow-orange African sun peeked through broken clouds as Sam sipped on strong black coffee. Rainee dipped her green tea bag over and over into the hot water. The time had come. Even the minutest detail had been covered by the leaders of the medical teams, but seeing their first sunrise in Mali was both frightening and exciting.

They would be taken directly to the hospital upon landing. Food and drink would be served while they heard the orientation from one of the resident doctors. Then their work would begin.

And so, it did. Within two hours, the lines of future patients exceeded anyone's expectations. The different nationalities of the medical teams were in separate sections of the compound or the hospital, so the languages each group spoke would never be misunderstood and no orders would be incorrectly performed. Translators would be there to assist with the Mali people. Tents filled with medical personnel from the many countries littered the grounds that surrounded the only hospital. The days went into nights, and the mornings came early.

Rainee would often walk through the tent city. She visited with some of the other medical teams, as she was multilingual and among the most experienced with infectious diseases. But it was difficult to remember or differentiate whom she talked to, because everyone wore a white mask.

Every morning there would be no less than five hundred men, women, and children waiting in a line for medical care. The Mali federal police tried to control the crowds, turning away as many as they allowed into the area. The stench of sickness filled the nostrils of every doctor. While waiting in line, people died from cholera and the other diseases that were proliferating from the filth and lack of clean water. The dysentery and vomiting were everywhere. The children suffering from malnutrition were too many to count. Their weak and frail bodies begged for help. It was a hell zone.

At the end of their seemingly endless days, Rainee and Sam were as tired as they had ever been.

Sam was used to eighteen-hour or longer shifts at St. Peter's Trauma Department, but comparing the two, he saw no resemblance. He had never seen such widespread sickness. He had never taken the time, he thought, to realize the suffering. How could he? He knew that no one could fathom such despair unless they witnessed it firsthand. They were dealing with what would normally be called an epidemic. But this was a multiple-disease epidemic brought on by extreme poverty and ignorance. It was a result of the so-called governments that had lined their own pockets at the expense of their people. Sam thought the scenes that were unfolding in Mali would be the same or worse if the Factor-7 virus was ever used. And the worst part of that scenario, he thought, was that no one would know how to treat it. There was no limit to death from having too little of the barest of life's necessities. And there was certainly no limit to death from greed and hate. So once again, those unbearable realities were boldly staring Sam in the face. And he despised it. He despised all of it.

Sam would find Rainee scrubbing herself in the middle of the night in a poor attempt to cleanse herself of the misery. All he could do was hold her as she wept for the people.

She wished she had never learned French, because what the little children said to her wreaked havoc on her soul. "I can't do this anymore," she said on the sixth night, but when the first light of day shone through the window, she was out and doing her duty.

As the final day came in Bamako, the lines and the workday were no shorter than the first day they arrived. They had helped thousands, but there were many more who never reached the end of the line. The field hospital would be next, and they now realized they really did not know what to expect.

It was a day's trip by mobile caravan to a region near Kayes, in Western Mali. They would be only about sixty miles from the Senegal border. It was flat and arid. The region was more desolate, hot, and dry. The people were multiple times more desperate than those in the city. And the accommodations for the doctors would be much worse. There had recently been deadly clashes between Malians and jihadists. The medical groups had assembled and decided ahead of time that the risk was worth taking and that all precautions would be put in place.

Traveling to the remote area was treacherous. One caravan transported thirty of the doctors and nurses. Sam and Rainee were among them. Others were carried by small planes and some by another guarded caravan. Rainee watched as a single-engine plane landed on the unpaved runway. It was a frightening landing, but they were all safe.

The plan was the same. The 120 doctors and nurses would work tirelessly until the final day—the day when that particular piece of hell would be over too.

On the second day, they were notified that terrorist alerts and gangs of thieves had prevented the second caravan from reaching the site. They had turned around and were safely on their way out of the country. The United States government and the German government alerted Sam and Rainee's team of the threats and advised they exit the country of Mali immediately. Two chartered large jet planes would carry doctors to London, where they would board a commercial flight back to their respective countries.

No one wanted to stay, but no one wanted to leave so many sick people either. Fatefully, again, they had no choice.

The big planes roared onto the makeshift dirt runway. Dust consumed every breath. Security guards who had traveled with the group were rushing the doctors and medical personal onto one of the 727 jets as other people were loading medical equipment and medicine onto the second jet. Since there was no actual airport, no security searches or customs declarations happened. But it had become bedlam and mass confusion. Then one of the small planes left, leaving several people stranded yards away from Sam and Rainee. They began to run to the waiting jet.

Sam grabbed Rainee's arm. "Get in line. They must know something's going on."

Rainee held on to Sam, but they were at the end of the line with four other doctors and two nurses.

Suddenly, there was a stifling and blinding cloud of dust. A truck with wooden panels around its bed sped into the controlled area, knocking down any and all barricades that were to protect the medical personnel.

Sam saw men, children, and women with babies crowded in the truck. They were stacked like cattle or firewood. Rainee heard loud shouting in French.

"They're telling us to get down—men with guns," she screamed.

The security guards were at the bottom of the stairs. "Get on the plane...go...go...go," they yelled.

The line was long, and the people on board did not realize the urgency. Sam and Rainee and five souls were left on the stairs. The guards had not made it that far.

As quickly as the truck had pulled into the compound and the shouts came from the innocents in the back bed, automatic gun fire exploded from the bottom wood planks. People who had been screaming were falling dead in the truck, and some managed to jump to the ground, where they were executed like wild animals. Bullets ricocheted against the metal sides of the aircraft.

Sam pushed Rainee inside and fell on top of her. She landed hard but was cushioned somewhat by her medical bag. They both lay just inside the plane's door. Gunfire echoed, and the awful sound of screams and moaning consumed the dirty air. The others on the stairs took bullets. Sam grabbed the arms of two and pulled them inside as the plane lunged forward. The flight attendant jumped over Sam and pushed the button to close the rear door. Sam saw the others in line were already dead, and one nurse had tumbled down the stairs and under the plane. She landed face-first, but soon Sam could see no more, but the sound of gunfire was all around them.

In moments they were airborne. Sam closed his eyes. But he could no longer concentrate upon the horror they had left behind. There were two wounded medical personnel on the floor in front of him. He grabbed their identification and handed it to the flight attendant.

"She's Dr. Lelji, and the man is Dr. Heinrich," she said.

Rainee managed to get to her feet. She immediately began to place cloths and apply pressure across the abdomen of the wounded male doctor. He was mumbling something in German, and although she spoke that language, she was unable to understand.

Sam and several other physicians were attending the female doctor.

The floor was covered in red blood, but the blood and fluids from the male doctor were greenish black.

Rainee touched Sam's arm. "Sam, look at this."

Sam took a breath and pursed his lips in a profound frown. "Give him as much morphine as needed or as possible."

Rainee looked straight into Sam's eyes. "The bullet penetrated his liver."

Sam nodded and began to slowly shake his head. "It'll only be minutes. Get rid of his pain," he said resolutely.

Rainee filled several syringes with morphine and Demerol pain killer and injected two into the dying man.

Sam had stopped the bleeding of Dr. Lelji, but she was still in shock and had bled profusely. "I need a blood donor. O negative...

now." Sam held his hand on the largest wound, which had penetrated her thigh and greater saphenous vein and exited through her left hip.

The plane was bouncing as if it were a ball on a basketball court. Lightning flashed, and the plane dropped several hundred feet. The turbulence was like nothing Sam had experienced. In addition, he was trying to save a life and give peace to a dying man. But that was what Sam did. He knew serious trauma injuries, and he was at the top of his game even in the most unconventional environments.

Rainee held a stethoscope on the German doctor, but he had died. Nothing would have saved him. She looked up at Sam and shook her head.

They pushed his body to the side, and the flight attendant laid a blanket across his face. Her tears streamed down her face, and the fear she experienced was undeniable. But the young woman did as she was told, and Sam gave her a tender nudge of encouragement.

Rainee crawled closer to Sam. "*I'm* null type RH Negative...O negative." She had tubes and two syringes pulled from her bag.

"No," Sam pleaded. "Not you."

"I'm here, and I carry the universal donor blood type. She'll die without my blood."

"There are others on this plane. And I might need you."

"And she is dying, and not a person has come forward. I think she needs my blood more than you need my hands to help. And we might need more than just my blood...so take my damned blood!"

Sam shook his head.

"Take my blood, dammit. Sam. Take my blood," Rainee screamed over the sound of the roaring engines.

Sam held her stare. She was serious, and she could save the woman. "OK."

Rainee took the large needle and handed it to Sam. He inserted it into the badly injured doctor and then another into Rainee. He connected rubber tubing, and blood ran from Rainee's open vein directly into the woman. When Sam felt that two pints had been transfused, he removed the needles from Rainee and from the doctor.

Rainee took several deep breaths. Two pints had weakened her. She leaned against the front-row seats; her legs extended forward.

Sam continued tightly wrapping gauze and heavy bandages around the woman's injuries. Stopping the blood loss and the transfusion was priority, and it had been successful. They would remove bullet fragments in London. She would have major issues with the shattered hip, but she was alive. He glanced at Rainee, who had become very pale and was nodding her head as if she was about to fall asleep. Sam listened to her heart and breathing. He then shouted, "Get me orange juice or a Coke with sugar...please!" Sam ordered the flight attendant.

Rainee had drifted off to sleep. Her body was limp and slumped to one side. The mixture of stress, the shortage of nourishing food over the past two weeks, and lack of sleep, tripled by the loss of blood, had put her into a deep sleep.

Two doctors came to sit with the injured doctor.

Sam tended to Rainee. He carried her to an empty row of seats. There were several empty rows around them, so she should have peace and quiet to rest. She needed both. He slowly got her to drink eight ounces of orange juice. She slept for a few hours, but Sam never took his eyes from her.

The injured doctor had regained consciousness and was also taking a few liquids. They moved her to a seat, and several doctors were monitoring her.

Sam continued to watch Rainee as she slept. Occasionally he took her pulse, and it was good. She was just tired and finally getting some much-needed rest. Her body was rejuvenating itself with the juice and the sleep.

Hours passed. They had gone through storms, in more ways than one, and the plane was flying smoothly though the pitch-dark sky. The lights were off inside the plane. Most of the people onboard had finally gotten to sleep as well. It was quiet except for the hum of the jet engines.

Sam squeezed Rainee's hand. She softly squeezed back. He laid his head next to hers and inhaled the fragrance of her hair. Even after everything, she still had the fragrance that Sam had learned to love. Suddenly a man sat in the aisle seat next to him.

"Dr. Hawkins?" the man asked, exhibiting a strong Chinese accent.

"Yes?" Sam turned to the man. "What may I do for you?"

"You've already done too much," he replied in a whisper.

"Pardon me?" Sam looked closer at the man. "I'm a trauma surgeon, and I did what anyone would do."

"Oh no, you have done much more." The man forcibly took hold of Sam's arm.

Sam grabbed the man's hand and pulled away. "I'm not fond of being constrained, sir."

"You are now my prisoner, as is she."

"What the hell are you talking about?"

"Have you ever heard of the Keepers? Or maybe you know it as the Collegium?" The man smirked and cleared his throat.

"No. Who the hell are you?" Sam tried to whisper, but his voice rose in volume with each word.

"I'm the crap your nightmares are made from, as you wretched Americans say." The man took a second hold on Sam's arm. "Do not speak," he commanded.

Sam stared at him but said nothing.

Rainee heard the confrontation. She remained with her head down and pretended to be asleep. She slowly reached into her right-hand pocket and felt the three remaining syringes she had previously filled for the dying doctor. She did not move.

"You think the Mossad, the CIA, the MI6, the KGB, and all the others can outwit us?" He laughed. "You are a fool. I outwitted even the Collegium." He laughed under his breath.

"What do you want?" Sam asked.

"I get. I do not want. But you are in my way. You know too much, and you know what I need to know." He laughed again. "You think I care about what you and those idiots of the Collegium refer to as radical Islamic terrorism? I don't. Those fools will never get on our Chinese soil. But I'm not the Chinese government. It has gotten too friendly with the West and your president. We will not be compromised. Our philosophy, our communist ideology, will never be compromised by your capitalistic so-called democracy. We will wipe you out. We have help from North Korea, and we will wipe you off the earth. North Korea will never surrender." He laughed. "You fool. We are playing you. The germ that your so-called Keepers Brotherhood developed just gave us a silent way to rid ourselves of you. No nukes…just a silent killer developed by your American scientists and others in the world. Ironic, isn't it? Ha ha…you're fucked, as you say. My country will thank me someday. But fear not. We are patriots, as you say, and we will destroy you."

Sam recoiled. He was at a loss for words. "You cannot beat the United States or the idea of our Constitution." He had to keep the Chinese man talking, so he babbled as he tried to figure out how to get rid of him. He couldn't awaken the others. There would be too many questions, and it would explode into mass hysteria both on the plane and off. "All men are created equal…except maybe you."

Rainee moved her hand below the armrest and slowly touched Sam's leg. He touched her trembling hand with his right hand. She laid the three syringes filled with Demerol into his hand. It was enough to put a horse to sleep.

"So, you are part of the Keepers Brotherhood?" Sam snarled.

"Ha, never. I am Chinese. I am communist, comrade. We will take out you and your American capitalism and the West that is following your lead. I just used the Collegium. I know you read the journals the old fool wrote, and you read the formula for the germ that will now wipe out all of you. I want that virus!"

"I read journals, yeah. But there was no formula."

"Liar!" He threw his elbow into Sam's ribs.

Sam groaned. "You fuckin' bastard. One scream, and I will have a planeload of help to take you out."

"I have a bomb in my attaché case behind you. All I need to do it push the lock code, and all of us will be blown up. And I am willing to die for my country. I was going to get you back in the desert. The wild animals would have eaten your guts." He laughed. "But that damned truck messed up the plan. Don't make me do it. If you cooperate and give me the formula and the basis for the last sequence of the DNA of the virus, we will kill you and the woman quickly when we get to London. Otherwise, you and a plane full of people will not be alive in an hour. If that happens…well, it's all your fault. It is death to you two doctors, or if you prefer, death to all on this plane."

"I don't have any idea what you're talking about. You're barking up the wrong bonsai tree, you prick." Sam adjusted his hand so he had a good reach to the Chinese man's neck. "So what is your name?"

"Perhaps you have heard of me. I am Wong," he indignantly replied. "China, my country, has many labs. We can produce many viruses, and we do. But the Factor-7 is special, and I want it!"

Apparently, the Chinese man, whom Bill Roberts said he never trusted, had been following their steps for some time and considered the mission as an opportunity to get close to Sam and Rainee. It was apparent that people would go to the ends of the earth for Factor-7, and this man had. And so far, he had succeeded. Rainee had mentioned that she was unnerved every time she passed the Chinese tents. There had been a man who seemed to follow her, or at the least who carefully watched her. Perhaps Wong was lying about a bomb. But he couldn't take that chance. Sam leaned forward and twisted his body. Wong had to lean forward also, since he had hold of Sam's left arm. A bit of confusion set in for a split second.

"Hey, you crazy son of a bitch. I don't know you or your name, and I don't know anything about a virus." Sam pushed the needle caps off the syringes with his thumbnail.

Wong made an unusual but lucky move for Sam. He shook his head in sarcastic defiance and leaned his forehead against the back of the seat in front of him. "You have five minutes to reconsider."

Sam suddenly pulled away from the man and threw a hard blow to his face with the back of his fisted left hand. "You don't!" He surprised the man with another strong jolt with his fist and then grabbed Wong, threw him abruptly forward, and stuck three syringes into the side of his neck. He pushed all the Demerol into the artery.

Wong glared at Sam and then took a gasping breath. His head fell forward. He was asleep or unconscious.

Rainee sat up and grabbed Sam. "Sam, what are we going to do?"

No one on the plane had apparently heard or paid any attention to the scuffle. Sam took several deep breaths. "He's out and will be for a while. Let me think. We can't tell anyone; you already know that," he whispered. "Make up two or more needles if you have any Demerol left. If not, use whatever sedative you have."

CHAPTER THIRTY-THREE

"There's a bomb behind us, Sam!" she whispered.

Sam nodded. "Pray he was telling the truth about how it would detonate."

Rainee followed his instructions and made three syringes. She laid them on the edge of the seat next to Sam.

Sam got his carry-on bag and placed it in the seat behind him where the Chinese man had put his attaché. The entire row was empty, so he took out his coat and shaving bag and filled each seat with an item, in hopes no one would choose to sit there later. He looked around. Everyone appeared to be sound asleep. He pulled a pillow and blanket from the overhead bin. Sam reclined the seat, covered the man, and secured the pillow under his head. He felt his neck for a pulse. "Slow but beating. If anyone asks, he's asleep."

"No one will ask. What about the attaché?"

"Leave it where it is. If he's not lying and had any sense at all, he would have secured the case so only his touch would set it off. The turbulence we went through was horrendous, and it didn't set it off. We've been flying for a while, so honestly, I doubt it's on a timer. No one is that dumb. He wanted something—the Factor-7 formula. He didn't want to die by his bomb. Hell, we don't even know if there is a bomb."

"Are you willing to gamble that?" Rainee asked, almost in tears.

"Everyone's sleeping. No one will mess with the case. We can't have mass hysteria with a hundred and twenty-four people on board. When we are off this plane, I'll let someone know. It shouldn't be much longer until we get to London," Sam said, trying once again to reassure Rainee that all would be fine. But he was just as worried as she.

She nodded and sighed. "How can this just keep happening? Call Huitt when we land. He will notify the international community and take him into custody."

The quiet was broken by the overhead speakers. "We are forty minutes out from London. Under the consideration of the recent tragic events, Heathrow is not available for us, so we will be landing at Stanstead Airport. There will be the press, police, and government officials asking questions about what has happened. We have been on the radio with multiple authorities, including emergency medical personnel. Tell your story to the investigators. Transportation will also be waiting for you once you have satisfied Interpol and other investigative authorities. We bid you well. The flight crew thanks all of you for the immeasurable service you have shown. After clearance, Dr. Heinrich's body will be flown to Germany to his family. This has been a tragic and nearly unbearable trip. Doctors and nurses such as you are why medicine will remain the most valued profession on this planet. You are true heroes. This flight crew thanks you."

Sam looked at his watch. "It's seven p.m. in London. Wong didn't anticipate the attack back there. As tragic as that was, maybe that one thing has saved our lives. He had planned to take us down in Mali, but then the attack. It must have messed up his plans pretty badly. His thugs won't know the change in our destination, and if they happen to know we are no longer landing at Heathrow, they certainly won't try anything with the world watching and the grounds surely blanketed with police and intelligence agencies. Not sure how he put a bomb together back there. Like you say…maybe there really isn't one."

"He had been walking back and forth down the aisle. I noticed him early on but just thought he was going to the rear lavatory. He had time to construct a weapon. He may have had it the whole time in Africa. I'm not going to say he has an explosive or not, Sam."

"Well, we'll know soon enough." Sam cleared his throat. *Or maybe not, if the damn thing detonates,* he thought. "It will be dark when we land."

Rainee stared out of the window. "Dark is good."

The plane landed with a hard thump. The flaps and brakes squealed, and all the passengers were thrown forward in their seats. But this time felt rougher than normal. Tensions were high and showed on all the doctors' and nurses' faces. However, Sam and Rainee were more concerned about the attaché. But as seconds ticked by, nothing happened.

The captain had said it well. The trip had ended most tragically. It was still so evident. Blood soaked the floor and carpets, and many of the medical personnel on board were covered in blood, either their own or someone else's. Sam and Rainee were no exception. Rainee's jeans were saturated in dried dark-brown blood, and the stench was nearly unbearable. Sam was bathed in blood, and even his hair had remnants of either the German doctor's blood or that of the doctor who survived. The flight attendant still had mascara stains on her cheeks and blood on her legs. But no one cared about anyone else's appearance. They only wanted to get home and be safe.

When the doors were opened and the attendant announced that everyone could unfasten their seat belts and exit the plane, the silence was unnerving. It was as if everyone on board was holding their breath.

Sam leaned forward against the back of the seat in front of him. He lifted the end of the blanket and pushed the additional two syringes into the right thigh of the sleeping Hui Wong.

"Just in case he rouses while we're getting off," Sam whispered. "Don't mention him to anyone here. I'll text Huitt, and he can handle it. Give me the other empty syringes."

"We're sitting next to him," Rainee said with a shaky voice.

"We know nothing, and that's our story, and we're sticking to it." Sam took the needles and syringes from Rainee. There was a Coke can stuck in the seat back pocket across from Wong, Sam, and Rainee. He dropped the needles and syringes inside the can and stuffed the can into one of the vomit bags. He twisted the top, sealing it and probably sealing his secret. He stepped on the bag and smashed the can flat. *No cleaning crew will get stuck now with Wong's used needle.* Surely, no one would open vomit bags and check the contents. But Sam and Rainee didn't need more investigations, and no innocent cleaning crew needed to be exposed to a used needle. Luckily, no one paid any attention to what he had been doing. They were watching the medical teams remove the body of the dead German doctor and the injured doctor from the plane.

But Rainee was watching his every move. "What will you do with them?"

The passengers began to file out. Sam and Rainee were midplane. Sam watched the faces as fellow physicians prepared to exit. No one even attempted to say goodbye. Getting off that plane was their only thought.

"Let a few from behind us go first," Sam said quietly. "I need time to think what to do with this stuff and the attaché."

Suddenly an Oriental man stopped at their row. He shook Wong, trying to awaken him. He said something loudly in Chinese. He glared angrily at Sam.

Sam quickly spoke loud enough so everyone around could hear, "I saw him take something earlier. He's out." Sam and Rainee stood and gathered their personal items.

The Chinese man continued to angrily stare at Sam but then started walking down the aisle to the exit.

Sam touched Rainee's arm. "Let's go. Step over him. Keep looking forward and moving ahead."

As they neared the door to exit the plane, Sam heard the Chinese doctor who had tried to awaken Wong beckon for the flight attendant.

She stepped from her place in the galley to the first row of seats, where the livid Chinese man was standing. Her attention was now no longer on the galley or the other passengers. Sam eyed the galley and saw his opportunity. He dropped the vomit bag into the trash bin. Sam stepped into the open cockpit. "Captain, please do not ask me any questions, but you must get off this plane, and now. Get your crew. There might be a bomb on board. Aisle forty-six. I cannot explain this even if I had the time. Just do what I tell you." He and Rainee picked up their pace down the stairs and onto the tarmac. They were surrounded by uniformed and nonuniformed personnel. Medical teams were going from passenger to passenger and asking if any needed assistance.

Sam and Rainee blended into the crowd but moved quickly away from the plane and the potential bomb. Sam pulled her to his side and put his arm around her waist. "Stay calm."

Reporters and cameras were being restrained behind barrier tape, and armed police lined the barricade. The reporters were shouting questions. "Can you tell us what happened? Do you know who the attackers were? Were they terrorists?"

Sam ran his hand across Rainee's back. "Were they terrorists?" Sam shouted back. "What a stupid question! No, they were duck hunting, you assholes!"

"Sam, please," Rainee scolded.

"I'm so sick and tired of this crap. And those media and sensation hunters make me sick! You'd think they would know how to ask an intelligent question."

"The world wants to know," she replied calmly.

Sam shook his head, still disgusted with the media circus. "I guess. But they can wait."

Rainee turned around to see another stretcher being carried down the stairs. "I think they have Wong."

Sam turned and nodded. He took his cell phone from his coat pocket. He retrieved Huitt's card from his wallet. He texted him. Sam typed: *Big trouble in Mali. Bigger on plane. Hui Wong/ Collegium on plane. Does not share mission. Rogue Chinese and helping N. Korea. Threatened us. Says bomb in attaché, floor aisle 46. He is being carried off plane, asleep. Don't ask but have Interpol arrest him immediately. I informed captain of potential bomb. Highly Dangerous.*

Sam kissed Rainee's cheek. "It's done."

Rainee stood stone faced. "I doubt it. Worms can crawl into very small holes."

Suddenly, two men in suits approached Sam and Rainee. Their badges shone brightly even in the foggy light.

The taller and older man spoke first. "May we ask you some questions?"

Sam took a deep breath. "Sure. But who are you?"

"We are Scotland Yard," the man replied, touching his badge.

"You need your MI6; this is of international importance."

"Doctors, I assume you are physicians. We are just gathering information."

Sam and Rainee nodded.

"We just want to hear from you both. Tell us what you remember, please."

Sam began to talk. "We were warned to 'bug out,' as they say. But it was too late, actually." He looked to his right and saw the captain and all the crew off the plane. He released a sigh of relief. "An older-model panel truck moved into the compound. It was loaded with civilians, but the terrorists were on the bottom. The civilians were shouting. Dr. Arienzo speaks French and understood them to be warning us. That too was of no help and too late. The terrorists began shooting the civilians and at all of us." Sam took a step away from Rainee's side. "We were almost killed. Those behind us were shot or killed. I think several were left there…dead on the ground." He nodded toward Rainee. "Dr. Arienzo and I tended to both Dr. Heinrich and Dr. Lelji. They were the worst injured. Dr. Arienzo transfused her blood into Dr. Lelji and saved her life with her own blood."

The older detective smiled. "Very brave, madam."

Rainee shrugged. "We attempt to save lives."

"Did you hear any shouting or announcements from the shooters? Like who they were, or why they were shooting at doctors?" asked the young detective, who had a distinctive Cockney accent.

"No, we were too busy trying to get everyone on board the plane." Sam coughed.

"You both are kind to tell us your story. It's about what we are getting from everyone, just different angles of observation. Thank you. Please give your names and contact information to the lady in the front. Authorities might need additional time to speak with you, but you are not detained. You may return to your homes."

Sam and Rainee forced a smile.

Sam glanced back at the plane. Through the darkness and heavy fog, he saw a shadow of a man running from behind a tire. Then he saw the briefcase. Sam grabbed Rainee and pushed her onto the ground. He fell on top of her, covering her body with his. He shouted, "That man has a bomb…that man has a bomb!"

Suddenly, there was a huge explosion. The reverberation could be felt throughout their bodies.

"Oh shit, cover your head and eyes!" Sam shrieked. He glanced around, and everyone else was also lying face down, either for protection or from the explosion. The smoke billowed into the sky, and shards of glass and metal were flying everywhere. Then he saw the Chinese man who had asked the flight attendant about Wong. He was on his feet and beginning to run. "Catch that man. He set off that bomb," Sam screamed.

The police heard Sam and began to chase the Chinese man. They tackled him within seconds.

Sam pulled Rainee to her feet and started to walk swiftly toward the exit that the Scotland Yard officers had previously indicated was their way out. There was chaos all around. People were screaming and running, and police and firefighters were confused and dazed from the explosion. But Sam knew what had happened, and he had the clarity of mind to get out of there and not look back. Huitt would contact the proper international police. Sam and Rainee would certainly be interrogated, but that would have to wait.

A cabbie was available, and Sam and Rainee slid into the back seat.

"Take us to the nearest small town with the most remote inn. Step on it, please," Sam ordered.

The cab driver nodded and began to slowly maneuver through the chaos of traffic and cameras. "I can take you to Essex. There are a couple of quaint inns there."

Rainee laid her head on Sam's shoulder and took a long breath. "You know there will be others. El Espino couldn't rat out all of them. If Wong found us across the other side of the world, more will certainly be able to do the same."

He dialed Don Huitt. "Huitt, Sam Hawkins here. You get my text?"

"Yes, a short while ago. Are you and the doctor all right?" Huitt's voice crackled with the poor reception.

"I suppose. We're not hurt. I'm going to be quick. You undoubtedly know details about the attack in Africa on the doctors. Dr. Arienzo and I were there and witnessed it all. I have given our statements to the authorities at the London airport where we just landed. I did not tell them this, however. Hui Wong was there. He was on the plane. He must have tracked us all the way across the world. He accosted me on the plane. Said he had a bomb. He wanted the letters from Bill Roberts and the Factor-7 virus recipe, if you will. Of course, we did not and do not have that. His Chinese associate detonated the bomb that was in Wong's attaché left on the plane." Sam paused.

"Go on," Huitt said rather indifferently.

"Well, anyway. I think they got Wong, and maybe the other guy. We had to neutralize Wong with Demerol, or we all could have died. But if Wong is still around, then there are others. This has gone on long enough. You need to know this…"

Rainee glanced at Sam. "What are you going to tell him?" Her eyes widened in either fear or anticipation or both.

"What he needs to know." Sam touched her knee and halfway smiled as if suddenly resigned to a duty that was most dreaded. "We saw Ana Roberts a while back in Canada. She admitted to me that she had been the informant. So don't try to lie to me about that. What you do not know is that Dr. Roberts gave her a flash drive of his original letters. Rainee and I read the copy. It was stolen from us, but there is a flash drive, and it has the names of most everyone of interest in the Collegium. It has the Factor-7 compounds and where all the bacterio-phages and vaccines are stored."

"And she has that?" Huitt asked, showing far more interest than before.

"No, she threw it into Bill's grave along with a rose. It's buried in the ground in Bill Roberts's grave!"

"Hum, I see."

"I tell you this because I'm sick to death with all of it. It's some-thing, every time Rainee and I turn around. Do your damn job, man! Get them all, Huitt! Track them all down and destroy this madness."

Sam ended the call. "I hope he does this without any repercussions toward you and me, because I just gave away our last ace."

Rainee put her arm around him as they walked into the inn.

Sam groaned. "Tonight, please, let's just rest, and my mind will be clearer tomorrow."

She kissed his dirty cheek. "By the way, bonsais are Japanese."

CHAPTER THIRTY-FOUR

Sam sorted through the stack of mail that the housekeeper had collected during their absence. Midway through, he found a registered letter addressed to him from the City of Campbell River, British Columbia, Canada. It was from the city coroner's office. It simply stated that the body of deceased Ana Lucille Roberts was being held for thirty days, pending collection or instructions of next of kin. Sam was listed as the next of kin. He called Rainee into the room.

"Ana has died." He handed her the letter. He showed no emotion.

"Sam, we have to make arrangements. Is there a number to call?" Rainee flipped through the official documents. "Yes, here."

Sam picked up his cell phone and called.

A man answered the phone. "Coroner's office, city morgue."

"Yes, my name is Dr. Samuel Hawkins. I have a letter from your office regarding a Mrs. Ana Lucille Roberts. She is a United States citizen." He paused. "I've been out of the country. It's dated seven days ago."

The man was off the phone for some time. All Sam heard was crackling on the line. Finally, another man answered. "Buckingham here."

Sam repeated what he had told the first man. He added, "It says she named me as next of kin, but—"

The voice on the other end interrupted. "Are you going to arrange for the body to be shipped somewhere?"

Sam thought for a moment. "Is there a mortuary there in your town that can do a cremation?"

Buckingham said "Well, yes," as if insulted that Sam would think the town was perhaps too small to have such a business.

"May I please have that number? I will arrange for them to get the body."

"All right. Please give me the case number on the form you were sent, ay." Buckingham said. "You'll need to sign that form and fax it to me at the number on the form. Then we can release her body." He gave Sam the phone number for Hallett's Mortuary. "It's near where she died. Almost in Willow's Point."

Sam took a cleansing breath. "Can you tell me how she died?"

"Well, since you're next of kin. She must have been fishing in her little boat. Body was found on the beach in front of her house. The boat was found capsized 'bout half a kilometer north of there. Musta been an accident. But why that woman would go out in those waters alone…well, some people…"

Sam sighed. "Yeah, some people."

———————

Federal Express delivered Ana's remains to Sam. Inside a plain corrugated box was a plastic bag filled with coarse gray ashes. A white card read, "With our condolences, the family at Hallett's Mortuary and Funeral Home."

Sam considered pouring the ashes in a trash dumpster, but, of course, he could not do such a thing. He and Rainee took them to the cemetery and had them buried without any service. Ana's ashes were in a Talavera-colored urn that matched Bill's and buried in a separate grave between her son and husband.

Rainee asked Sam if he wanted to linger there for a while.

Sam snapped, "No, I'm done." He took a step away. "Bill and James are buried, Ana is buried, and the flash drive is buried."

Rainee had not taken offense to a sharp answer, knowing full well that Sam had not come to terms with Ana's deceit. Perhaps he never would. She had not offered an apology, only her excuses. So perhaps he never should. Rainee thought if the Collegium and Factor-7 had not been stopped or at least halted for a time, Ana would have been as guilty as all the others. Yes, perhaps both of them should never forget. Keeping a bad memory might not always be harmful, she thought. It will keep you on your toes.

A lawyer for Ana called Sam the following day. He had received a copy of the will in the mail, but it had been sent before Ana's death. There was a letter enclosed from her also. Sam was her sole beneficiary.

Sam didn't know how he felt about the newfound windfall of cash, real estate, and valuable coins and jewelry. There were stocks, bonds, mutual funds, and certificates of deposit. All belonged to him. If the Houston lawyer had received the instructions prior to her death, it obviously was not an accident. She had either committed suicide or died in some other unthinkable manner that she had anticipated. Ana's torment was over. Unfortunately, Sam thought, his might never be.

"Seems every time I think all the horrors of our past are over, another shoe drops." He put his head against Rainee's hair, taking a deep breath of her scent. "You make it OK."

She put her arms around him. "Maybe it's over now."

CHAPTER THIRTY-FIVE

The next few months were spent in relative peace. Sam and Rainee craved solitude, but it was disrupted somewhat while Sam figured out Ana's estate and what they would do with it. Sam had consulted Rainee, and they donated large sums to multiple charities. They set up wings in hospitals and made some money available for low-income students who wanted to go into medicine. The loan was dependent upon the future physician spending at least one year serving with Doctors without Borders. If they did so, the money would be forgiven, and they would never have a debt. They felt good about the decision to give a small house to Julia, Ana's former housekeeper. Rainee suggested that some of the money go to no-kill animal shelters. There was much more to do, but Sam and Rainee had the time.

Sam had always been charitable, but since he and Rainee had gone through the depths of hell and come out on the other side, he wanted to do much more. Ana's money and property would enable them to do better than she or Bill had ever done. After their involvement with the devil, it just seemed right.

Three months had passed since Sam and Rainee had returned from Mali. Things with Ana's estate were settling down, and Sam had become more serene and settled into the new reality.

Don Huitt had not contacted them in two months. His last communication indicated that the Collegium had all been terminated or were hiding in their worldwide holes. Hui Wong and his accomplice were in jail in London, awaiting trial at the Hague. But he added that China was making a stink and that they would most likely be extradited back there. A consensus among the FBI and CIA was that the US and other countries' leaders thought it best to just let him go back to China. The man knew too much, and *that* knowledge, if revealed in a high court, could set off global alarms that their unconditional secrecy had squelched. The fallout of his revelations could be devastating. He could be more dangerous during a trial than he would be back on Chinese soil. So, Wong was either going to go back as a hero, or the Chinese might take harsher action than the World Court. That was anybody's guess. But apparently and rightfully so there was little concern over his well-being. The multiple repositories had been uncovered in most of the countries, and the produced bioweapons had been destroyed. Huitt had been released from his position and seemed happy to no longer be a part of the Federal Bureau of Investigation. He never expounded upon why he had been fired but said that he had handled the whole Collegium thing the best he could. He was going to concentrate on family and happier times. He assured Sam that the threat had suffered a substantial loss and was virtually eradicated from US soil. The CIA would be in charge from that point forward.

Sam felt safe and finally free. He remembered the bottle of 2008 Domaine De Chevalier. "Let's open this and have a toast. Bill and Ana gave it to me for a birthday a few years back. Costs a fortune." He handed a glass to Rainee.

They touched the rims of the glasses and toasted their future. Each took a sip. The fine red wine had turned to vinegar.

Rainee looked at Sam and squinted her eyes. "Do not even think it. I don't believe in omens."

CHAPTER THIRTY-SIX

ONE MONTH LATER

The early-morning sun was blinding, even through the black sunglasses. Don Huitt sat in the back seat of the dark navy-blue sedan. The driver and one male occupant looked straight ahead. The three men entered the gates to the cemetery. The driver flashed his Central Intelligence Agency badge at the gate attendant and handed him the judge's court order. The attendant was aware they would be coming and opened the gate to allow them entry. The cemetery was closed to all public for the day, but one of the agents got out of the car and stood guard to further ensure that they would not be interrupted. The CIA agents drove to the back of the cemetery and parked. All of them walked slowly toward the men sitting in yellow backhoes. Three more men in coveralls stood by the trees that Ana had planted at the graves of her son and husband. One man sat on the bench.

"OK, let's get started," said Lou Howard, the agent in charge. He glanced at Don Huitt. "So you're going to the airport from here?"

Huitt nodded.

"Good. Your job is done. I'll return your issue to the agency. We thank you for the information and the location of the flash drive."

Huitt handed his government-issued sidearm to the man. "I'm done. It's all yours."

The backhoes roared as they started up, and the shovels began to cut through the sod. The agents stood around watching the machinery and chatting as they dug up Dr. Bill Roberts's grave and searched the soil around the concrete container that held the Talavera urn filled with his ashes.

"You said she threw a rose into the grave, and the flash drive was tied to it?" Howard asked.

Huitt nodded. "That's what I was told. It was an intentional move on her part."

"Then we'll find it. Must be a ribbon there. It hasn't been long enough for a ribbon to deteriorate." He paused and looked at Huitt. His eyes narrowed, and a solemn expression came upon his face. "Pretty risky item to have lying around for the next hundred years. It won't be there for long. We'll find it. It would be a bad mark on our country's image if someone in the future found that thing. Whatever is on it will be gone. We make our history." He laughed and gazed into the distance. "Like I heard a long time ago…it's not history unless it's put on paper—or in this case, on a flash drive."

Another one of the agents walked toward Huitt. "This was your case from the beginning?"

"From the beginning that I knew about it." He smiled at his ambiguous answer. "Don't know who else has been on it. I was sent when the action moved to Houston."

"So you must know a lot," Howard stated.

"I guess you can say that," Huitt replied, raising an eyebrow.

"Who else knows the details of the Collegium?" the agent asked.

"Guess you'd have to talk to our director or yours." Huitt took a step back.

"This crap has to be kept top secret," stated another man who sat on the bench.

Huitt nodded. "Yes, it does."

The backhoes dumped three buckets of dirt onto the grass above Bill Roberts's headstone. Men in coveralls began to sift through the soil.

"So why were you terminated from your position?" Howard asked.

"I don't know," Huitt said. "They just told me it was time to retire."

"What happened to the Chinese man? Wong. Why isn't he in US custody instead of going to China? CIA could have taken care of his ass. He was in your area and a known member of the Collegium. We knew about him at the agency! He's a free man. You should have picked him up a long time ago, I'd say."

"He slipped by us when he was in the United States," Huitt said.

"Well, so did Dr. John Albright, and he was in your territory for months," Howard said.

Don Huitt shook his head. "Albright is dead. You know that story."

"Well, I've heard stuff." The director walked over to his associate and then turned back to Huitt. "Ever mention Housier in any conversations?"

"No."

"What about Winger or Walther?"

"No."

Howard walked to the grave and peered into the hole. "Make it wider. Dirt needs to be extracted alongside the concrete container." He turned back to Huitt. "So you never mentioned anything about assassinations? Or that you thought Walther and Winger might have been murdered?"

"Of course not," Huitt answered indignantly. But in fact, he had mentioned it to Sam and Rainee. He had confused the timeline of the two presidents' deaths, but in doing so had virtually confirmed both Walther and Winger had been assassinated.

"Hey, over here," called one of the men who was sifting the dirt. "I think I have it."

Howard took the blue plastic case from his agent's hand. He opened the case. The flash drive was there and intact. "Perfect."

"Good job, guys," yelled the agent sitting on the bench.

Lou Howard swaggered over to Don Huitt and another agent who had moved in closer to the graveside. "Well, what if I told you that a little bird told me you had said too much?"

Huitt's eyes widened. "I'd say they're a liar!"

"Hummm...calling your own men liars? Or perhaps you should know the term *top secret*? Maybe you should choose your agents better when you want to be Chatty Cathy and when you're on such a highly classified case."

Huitt stood stoically but said no more.

"This was obviously too big for you. Maybe you've gotten soft or senile. You don't remember what you said? Well, in any case the FBI should have backed out a long time ago."

"I'm a damn good agent. Been with the bureau for thirty years!"

"You didn't rid us of the Italian doctor and her boyfriend. We had to hack into his computer to see what he knew. You didn't even do that." Howard huffed under his breath. "Didn't find shit that I didn't already know!"

"Who? You talking about Hawkins? He's a good man. They've been through hell, and a lot of this has been because they did a good job of keeping quiet. I'd not know about the flash drive had it not been for them." Huitt's voice was shaky, and his normal ruddy complexion had begun to glow.

"You know what top secret, classified means. Anyone in the government that talks like you did should be prosecuted to the full extent of the law. That *is* the law. You told classified information that could jeopardize our national security. But a trial also means a breach in security as the story would come out. Can't have that," Howard said coldly.

The man who had not talked at all during the excavation walked from the tree where he had been leaning. He was a solemn man with bloodshot eyes and a twitch in one. He took a long draw off his cigarette and then threw it into the open grave. His voice was raspy as the smoke seeped from between his clinched teeth. "Sounds like the doctors know too much. They better know the consequences of talking." He stepped next to Howard. "And you know everything. You're a civilian now."

Howard took a step backward, allowing the man to get closer to Don Huitt. "Huitt, you fucked up. The Collegium, the virus, the presidents' deaths, and anything else remotely related to this incident should have been sealed. You should have made arrests. You know what top secret means, man!" Howard shook his head and narrowed his eyes. "As they say…loose lips sink ships. The bureau doesn't give a shit about you." He tightly pursed his lips and shook his head. His nostrils flared. "You fucked up!"

As Lou Howard's words left his lips, the other man pulled a gun from inside his coat. A silencer was attached to the end. He fired the almost-silent bullet into Huitt's forehead.

Howard turned to the men. He waved to the three agents on the other side of the grave. "Put his body in the hole."

They pushed the still-warm body into the deeply dug hole. It fell between the concrete container and the side of the excavation. Don Huitt now shared a grave with Bill Roberts.

The men on the backhoes began to fill the grave as Howard and his men walked to their parked sedans.

"No history here," Howard said as he got into the passenger side of the car. "Bad things happen to people who talk. Yep, I am a plethora of clichés." He half chuckled as if he amused himself. "As they say, 'Dead men don't talk.'" He took out his handkerchief and wiped his forehead. "Damn, I always hate it when I have to do that."

CHAPTER THIRTY-SEVEN

The winter winds and rain were setting in. Thanksgiving Day was special for Sam and Rainee. She cooked her first turkey, and Sam made his grandmother's cornbread dressing. He admitted it was not up to snuff, but his memory could have been jaded by the fond memories of days long gone. It was time to start new traditions and new memories. He and Rainee had a wedding planned in less than a month. Sam reserved the private jet, and Rainee was shopping for her perfect but not over-the-top dress. It was a happy time. It was the best time of his life. The bad memories were fading, although they would never be completely gone. They were making plans for the rest of their lives. They laughed freely and felt unencumbered by any threat. It was perfect!

_____

On December 2, their freedom and peace crashed around them once again. Jorge Villa Lobos called.

"El Jefe requests your presence," he said without hesitation. "It is his desire that you come to his home in Mexico."

Sam shook his head. "No, impossible. We can't."

"It is not optional." Jorge paused. "El Jefe requests your company. The driver will pick you up in Mexico. Your flight is arranged for noon tomorrow. I'll text your boarding passes." He hung up the phone.

Sam stared motionless at Rainee. "The asshole said we are required to go see El Espino. Damn that wine."

Rainee didn't react to Sam's quip about the omen. She started to cry, and the color faded from her face. She stared at Sam, "I thought it was over. What if he wants more surgery? Or maybe he's scarred? Did Jorge say if he is angry?"

Sam held her as she sobbed. "He said nothing except that we have to go. We don't have a choice. He owns us and always will. His people will hunt us down if we don't go. Maybe it's no big deal. If he has good intentions now and we don't go, they won't be good when they find us. You know we can't refuse his invitation."

Rainee reluctantly agreed. "I don't want to marry in San Miguel. I can't bear the thought of him ruining our day. He all but ruined our lives along with all the other evil beings that crawl around on their bellies."

"He won't ruin our day. We'll marry, even if it's not on December twenty-fourth or in Mexico. Maybe in Italy."

Rainee forced a smile. It was not the best scenario, but perhaps the second best.

———

They boarded the 737 Jet at Bush International at 12:20 p.m. for Mexico City. It all was prearranged. Sam smiled. Even in the direst of circumstances, Rainee laid out her nest. It was predetermined, and it pleased him each time she did her routine.

The first-class flight attendant served their martinis and gave them the menu for the two-and-a-half-hour flight. When he delivered the meals, they just picked at their food. Sam ordered two more martinis, and Rainee, typically, drank one of them. Their trepidation was overwhelming. The last time El Espino had summoned them, they knew the reason. This was a mystery, and neither of them could come to grips with the drug lord's possible intentions. It could be his face no longer pleased him. And that could create a serious threat for them. Or perhaps he had some other mission for them, which neither of them wanted or was willing to engage in. Few scenarios were acceptable to them, but they had no options.

A man in white greeted them at the baggage claim. He guided them to the waiting brand-new Range Rover. Jorge sat in the front seat.

"Thank you for coming. El Jefe will be pleased you are here."

Sam asked, "Why *are* we here?"

"He has asked for you. You will see him soon." Jorge motioned for the driver to leave the airport.

The ride was relatively short. There were no blindfolds and no harsh words from Jorge.

Shortly, the Rover turned into a driveway. The gates automatically opened to show the massive home that sat behind them. There were noticeable armed men surrounding it.

Sam glanced at Rainee. His eyes showed his apprehension.

Jorge opened the back door. Sam crawled out first, then Rainee. Armed men came and patted down both Sam and Rainee. Sam was livid that they had touched her, but his anger was of no value. They were going to take all precautions. Men flanked them as they were led to the front door of the magnificent Mexican hacienda. The gate at the front door opened upon their arrival. A woman greeted them. She led them into a large room. Bottles of tequila and wine were arranged on a table. The mixed fragrance of fresh flowers and food cooking permeated the air. They were instructed to take a seat.

Within five minutes three young men entered the room. A beautiful young woman followed them. None seemed to be older than twenty-five. They sat across the table from Sam and Rainee.

One of the young men spoke. "I am the oldest son. My name is the same as my father's. I am, however, called Tavo. My brothers are Manuel and Santiago," he pointed to the brother to his left, but he's called Chico. My sister is Angelica." He paused and looked at his siblings. "My mother is dead." He continued. "My Father, Gustavo... Leondro...has asked for you. I welcome you to our home."

Sam glared at them. "Why are we here?"

The young woman began to speak. "Our father is very ill. He has trust in you and hopes you can help him. Will you see him?"

Sam looked at Rainee. He wanted to scream, "Hell no!" But what choice did they have?

She nodded. "Yes."

They were led to an upstairs bedroom where the Mexican drug lord lay. He was thin and pale. His breathing was labored, and his voice was unrecognizable. He forced a smile when he saw Rainee and Sam. "Please help me," he moaned.

Sam put his ear to his chest. He then began to feel the obstruction in his neck. It had multiplied in size and was clearly visible with the naked eye. "Has he had any treatment for this tumor?" he asked.

"He went to the hospital here in Mexico City, but they would not treat him. They said he should go home and..." The daughter collected her thoughts. "They said they could not do anything for him."

"Has he had a CT or PET scan to know how the cancer has spread?" Rainee asked.

El Espino forced a reply. "Cancer?"

Rainee took his hand. "Yes Señor, I am sure it is cancer." She pressed on his abdomen and glanced up at Sam. "Hard upper right quadrant."

Sam leaned into the man. "I agree it's a cancerous tumor. I think we must tell you that in our opinion, it has spread."

His daughter handed a paper to Rainee. "It's in Spanish."

"I can read it. He did have a scan. We can't do anything. It has spread to many parts of his body, but the lungs, esophagus, and liver are his greatest threats now. And he apparently has been having strokes. CT report shows some bleeding in the frontal cortex."

The man now called Leondro tried to sit up, but his lack of strength caused him to fall back to the bed. He whispered, "I am ready to die if you tell me there is nothing you can do. I trust you."

Rainee was still holding his hand. "Sir, I wish there was, but we are not God, and he is your hope now. I am obligated to tell you the truth."

Sam glared at her, screaming with his eyes that she was too blunt.

But the Mexican man nodded and whispered with a weakened voice, "I like your honesty."

"We will get you medicine for pain, and we will watch over you, but sir, you must understand that we cannot make you well."

Sam glared her again. *What is she doing?*

"Señor, we will be with you until the end." Rainee squeezed El Espino's hand. "Your family who loves you is also here."

He stared at Rainee and tried to speak but was no longer capable of the effort. In a few minutes, he fell asleep. Sam, Rainee, and his children sat by his side.

Sam and Rainee explained to his children that he was in the end days. He had a malignant tumor that most likely had spread to many of his vital organs. He had a yellow tinge to his skin and eyes, and that undoubtedly meant his liver was badly affected and not functioning properly. They had no equipment, but Sam told them that he and Rainee needed nothing to see the reality of their father's future. And the earlier CT scan had confirmed it. They had seen too many advanced cancer cases to misdiagnose this classic one. They sent Jorge for various medications that would keep him comfortable.

On the third day, he died peacefully in his medically induced sleep.

Jorge joined Sam, Rainee, and the family in the large dining room. It was over. El Espino, El Jefe, Gustavo Galvan, or Leondro de Estrellas was gone.

His sons moved to another side of the room. They were in deep conversation. How would they go on? Grief and concern were written all over their faces. The daughter simply sat with other ladies and cried.

Suddenly Jorge jumped up. Men with drawn guns flocked to the dining room. "I am now El Jefe. I will be called El Lobo, and I run the most powerful cartel in the entire world. He has given me the control. I am in control!"

The children stood in anger. "Never!" screamed the oldest son. "He would have chosen me."

Jorge pulled a gun from his shoulder holster. He fired it into the ceiling. "Your father did not want his sons in this business. You may stay in this house, but you are finished. My gunshot is my warning to all that go against me."

Sam and Rainee felt fear grip their very being. El Espino's death was something that really did not sadden them, but the truth that his empire would not be eliminated was real and terrifying. There would never be an end to his drug trafficking until there was no demand for it, and that was not in the foreseeable future. Furthermore, Jorge had no need for them.

Jorge looked straight at Sam and then to Rainee. "If you wish to live, you will come now. We are through here. It is mine, and I will control it at my will."

Sam grabbed Rainee. "We gotta get out of here." They ran to the front door. Two armed men rushed them to the driveway.

"You come with me," shouted Jorge as he forcibly threw Sam and Rainee in the back of the Range Rover. "I am cordial to you, but this is the last time. Go home, forget what you know, and forget me."

Sam stared at Jorge. "Gladly."

As they pulled from the mansion, the sound of celebratory and defensive gunfire rang through the mansion and its grounds. The sides were clashing already. The sons were trying to take back control of what they felt was their destiny. The loyal men of the Galvan family started shooting at El Lobo's army. Some men would ultimately side with the family, and some had already made their choice to go with Jorge Villa Lobos. But in reality, the only ones who would survive would be the latter. Jorge would make sure only his loyal supporters would be allowed to live.

Arriving at the Mexico City airport, Jorge's men literally pushed them out of the vehicle.

"Go and forget," the driver wailed.

"You can count on it," Sam shouted back.

There wasn't an available flight for six hours. Sam and Rainee found seats at the restaurant and bar, near where they would later board the flight. Sam ordered two drinks while they tried to relax from yet another horrendous experience. El Espino was dead, but another ruthless man had taken his place. It would be a bloodbath war between El Espino's loyalists and family, and those who sided with Jorge. Sam and Rainee were out of it. It was a war, but it was not their war. Sam's money was definitely on Jorge. Sam promised Rainee that they would no longer be involved. They would marry in Italy or the United States. Mexico was beautiful, but the cartels and Jorge were toxic and deadly, and it was not a place to begin a new life.

Sam guzzled his drink. It didn't relieve his stress. Nothing would take away what he and Rainee had seen, heard, and experienced.

Two hours later, they were still waiting for their flight. Rainee was a little drunk, and Sam was tired and maybe a bit tipsy too.

Rainee excused herself to the ladies' room. As she stood by her stool, she glanced at the man sitting by the window. "Sam, look at that man over there. He looks like…" She stopped. "Well, he looks familiar, but I'm drunk."

Sam glanced to where she indicated. The man held a newspaper concealing his face. Sam touched her arm. "No fear. It's nothing. Never seen that beach bum before."

Rainee sighed. "I don't know. Looked like…hell…I don't know. Can't be anyway." She brushed it off as nothing as she left the bar.

The public-address system started calling Sam and Rainee's flight. Sam paid the bartender and wheeled himself around on his barstool. The man at the window began to advance toward Sam. He wore a white Mexican guayabera shirt, white pants, a straw hat, and beach sandals. His gray hair was pulled into a ponytail, and he had a scruffy white beard and mustache. He sported gold-rimmed glasses, making him appear like someone straight out of Margaritaville. Sam moved his eyes from the passing man. Suddenly he felt a push on his arm. The man momentarily stood still, staring at Sam. His blue eyes burned into Sam's brain, and his too-white-to-be-real teeth smiled a familiar sinister grin. Their eyes locked for a much-too-long moment. The man held his right hand over his left upper arm. His hand and long, slender fingers were formed to imitate a gun. As he slowly walked past Sam, he pushed his thumb to his forefinger, as if firing a pistol. The man then picked up his pace and left the restaurant.

Sam gasped. He ran into the corridor. The man was nowhere to be seen. He had simply vaporized into the crowd. Sam wasn't sure if, perhaps, the man was an illusion. After all, he and Rainee had been drinking for three hours. The encounter had been quick, but it was also profoundly unnerving.

Rainee walked up to Sam. He was leaning against the wall. The color had drained from his face. "Sam, are you all right? You look like you've seen a—"

"Don't say it, please," Sam said softly. "They're calling our flight. I'm fine. Just hot in there." He pointed to the bar and restaurant.

Rainee sat on the aisle and began her routine. She put on her headphones. Sam sat in the window seat and stared out. When he closed his eyes, he could vividly see the face of the man in the bar. His heart beat rapidly. Beads of sweat formed on his forehead. He tried to slow his breathing, but it just wouldn't cooperate. Rainee saw Sam's distress. She took his hand and whispered into his ear, "Espino's dead, Huitt says the Collegium is gone, Ana's gone. They're all gone. We have nothing left to fear. It's over, Sam. It's finally over."

Sam focused on the ground as it grew farther and farther away. The face of man in the bar seemed to manifest on every passing cloud. He took a deep cleansing breath. It was not necessarily John Albright that Sam feared. It was what he represented. And he represented the foulest of humankind. It was an abomination. It was an atrocity of which there was no equal. It was a tenacity to successfully deliver his personal wickedness for no other reason but to further himself. Somehow, John Albright had survived. If so, there were others. There would be many others. It would only be a matter of time before the scourge of vermin revealed themselves, and then what would become of him and Rainee? *And so it begins again*, he thought. Factor-7 might be only one factor in a long, insane mathematical equation whose total would equal death and annihilation. Life is all about choices, but sometimes a person is out of options. Sam whispered to himself, "This will never be over."

CHAPTER THIRTY-EIGHT

Another autumn had come and gone. Sam and Rainee had not been bothered by any of the adversaries for almost a year. It had been a glorious year. They had made their plans to go to Italy in the spring and marry. Again, Rainee was making her lists and looking for venues and the perfect dress. Sam was looking at opening a small clinic for emergencies and had interviewed a number of new emergency doctors. He had once thought he could leave medicine, but as things settled down, he and Rainee both knew that they were happiest when they were saving lives.

One cold and wet morning, Sam's cell phone rang. He did not know the number, but since it was a local area code, he answered. "Hawkins."

"Dr. Sam Hawkins?" The voice on the other end was difficult to understand at first. But soon Sam realized he was speaking to someone with a strong Scottish accent. "I am looking for Dr. Samuel Hawkins."

"This is he," Sam said, bewildered as to what the man might want.

"I need to see you, Dr. Hawkins. I can come to your home."

"No. What are you selling?"

"Nothing, Doctor. I am not selling. I have something to give you and something to tell you that is of utmost importance."

"Then tell me."

"Not on the phone. I can meet you anywhere you wish. But it is best if it has some private place to talk."

"Do I know you?" Sam asked.

"No, sir, we have never met. But I feel sure you know of me and my associates."

"How's that?" Sam looked at Rainee. "Says we know of him and his associates."

Rainee's eyes widened. "I don't like this."

"Doctor, we should really speak in private and face to face," insisted the Scottish man.

Sam exhaled an exasperated breath. "I'm going to Houston in a while. I'll meet you at a small restaurant off Highway 45. Exit like you're going to League City. It's called Charlie's. This better be good," he said. He was curious and alarmed, but he was not going to let something from his past get the best of him ever again.

Sam put his pistol in the back waistband of his jeans and threw on his Stetson and a leather bomber-style jacket. He rushed Rainee into a heavy coat.

"Sam, you look nervous," Rainee said.

"Not really, but let's face it. The past year has been almost too good to be true."

Rainee shook her head. "I don't think we should go." She glanced at the date on her watch. "Damn, it's Friday the thirteenth."

Sam rolled his eyes and smiled. "You're not superstitious." He kissed her cheek. "The man said he would come to our house. So if we don't go see him, well…let's just say I do not want another John Albright incident." He patted the gun and glanced at Rainee.

She frowned. "Not again. Please, God, not again."

———————————

Sam and Rainee sat down at the first picnic table with an umbrella to shelter them from the light rain. They ordered two coffees.

"What do you really think?" Rainee asked. The color had faded from her face.

"I don't know what to expect," Sam said. "But this is a fairly public place. Cops eat here. I can't see any huge confrontation happening here." He gave her a hug. "Relax. It's probably nothing. Maybe we won the Publisher's Clearing House. He said he had something to give me."

Rainee growled, "Sam."

Soon a small car pulled into the parking lot. Two men got out. One man was older, with a well-manicured mustache and goatee. The other man looked to be about forty or forty-five. They walked toward Sam and Rainee.

"Doctors Hawkins and Arienzo, I presume?"

"Hawkins, and this is Dr. Arienzo," replied Sam.

The man smiled. It was a gentle grin, and his eyes were peaceful and kind. "My name is Colin Aonghus, and this is my young friend, Arnulf Bode."

"What can we do for you?" Sam asked.

"It is not that we want anything from you. You see, Doctors, we have heard of what you have been going through, and we want to thank you. We know it was difficult."

"OK, how do you know about us?" Sam asked.

"I will tell you. We know a great number of things," said Colin Aonghus. "I live in Scotland, and my friend is from Germany. There are many who know what you did to save all of us from evil. I have been designated by them to give you this." He handed Sam a small black leather bag. Inside was a disc. It weighed about as much as a silver dollar and appeared to be made of pure gold. One side had the Eye of Providence etched into the gold. Sam flipped it over to see several Roman numerals and a design he thought was King Solomon's Seal of Wisdom.

Sam looked at it for a moment and then handed it to Rainee. "What is this?" Rainee asked.

"It is your safety net forever. May God watch over you and may wisdom guide your steps," replied Arnulf Bode.

"I beg your pardon?" Sam asked.

"You and Dr. Arienzo may need help in the future. It took us a while to track you down, but we have known about you and what you did for some time now. You did not have to take on the task, but you chose goodness over wickedness. You sought the truth at your own peril. That is a noble undertaking. You saw evil, and you conquered it with decency and morality. We are in every country, and we know everything. We must know everything, because it is our destiny. We are good, honest people, and we have taken an oath to care for those who love peace and liberty. If you need help, you simply call the number, which is coded as Roman numerals. Someone from whatever country you are in will quickly be at your aid."

Sam stared at the older man.

"I understand your confusion, but you may need us someday, and we will be there."

"And who do you mean when you say *we*?"

"Dr. Hawkins, Dr. Arienzo, we are the Keepers."

The End

A SPECIAL NOTE FROM J. D. MAY

I want to thank you for choosing to read Factor-7. I hope you loved it as much as I loved writing it. If you did, I'd be very grateful if you could write a review on Goodreads and share your feedback on social media, tagging one of my handles. I'd love to hear what you think, and it makes a huge difference helping new readers to discover my book.

I greatly enjoy hearing from my readers—you can get in touch with me by my website, email, Facebook page, Twitter and Instagram. And watch for the upcoming sequel to Factor-7.

My heartfelt thanks,

J.D. May

www.authorJDMay.com
Email: authorjdmay@gmail.com
f @authorjdmay
𝕏 @authorjdmay
◎ @jdmaywrites

ABOUT THE AUTHOR

J.D. May is a third generation Texan from the Lower Rio Grande Valley. She loves her band of house cats as well as the large tribe of fat, happy TNR'd feral cats that came with her rural property in a small citrus-growing community. Palm tree-lined roads, natural waterways, and roaming wild animals including alligators, deer, wild hogs, and birds of every color make Bayview a perfect place for a writer and painter. She also loves the beach, rock and roll, Tex-Mex food, cooking, Shiner Bock beer, and she believes wine is a legitimate food group. She shows her paintings at The Laguna Madre Art Gallery in Port Isabel, Texas.

J.D. May attended Sam Houston State University, San Miguel de Allende Instituto, and Rice University where she studied drama, art, creative writing and Spanish. J.D. May worked in advertising for most of her career. She is married to a former award-winning surfer and has a daughter and soon to have a brand-new granddaughter.

9 781641 118651